Praise for
Kristin Hannah and
DISTANT SHORES

"For any woman who has ever put her dreams on hold to tend to hearth and home, *Distant Shores* is a must-read.... Kristin Hannah has created believable characters in Elizabeth and Jack; people who might temporarily lose their way but never lose sight of what really counts."

—EILEEN GOUDGE
Author of *Stranger in Paradise* and *Taste of Honey*

"Hannah is superb at delving into her main characters' psyches and delineating nuances of feeling."

—*The Washington Post Book World*

"An effective and affecting chronicle of the ways in which human beings make wrong personal choices for the sake of the wrong things."

—*Statesman Journal*

"[Hannah] writes of love with compassion and conviction."

—LUANNE RICE

"In addition to a satisfying story, there is much good writing here. I enjoyed *Distant Shores* and I imagine millions of other women will too."

—Bookreporter.com

"This insightful look into the dynamics of marriage will resonate with readers, and mark Hannah as a strong voice in women's fiction."

—*Booklist*

DISTANT
SHORES

By Kristin Hannah

KRISTIN HANNAH

DISTANT SHORES

A NOVEL

BALLANTINE BOOKS TRADE PAPERBACKS

NEW YORK

2011 Random House Trade Paperback Edition

Published in the United States by Ballantine Books Trade Paperbacks, an imprint of The Random House Publishing Group, a division of Random House, Inc., New York.

BALLANTINE BOOKS TRADE PAPERBACKS and colophon are trademarks
of Random House, Inc.
RANDOM HOUSE READER'S CIRCLE & Design is a registered trademark
of Random House, Inc.

Originally published in hardcover in the United States by Ballantine Books, an imprint of The Random House Publishing Group, a division of Random House, Inc., in 2002.

Library of Congress Cataloging-in-Publication Data
Hannah, Kristin.
Distant shores / Kristin Hannah.
p.   cm.
ISBN 978-0-345-46937-3
I. Title.

PS3558.A4763 D47 2002
813'.54—dc21
2002066612

Printed in the United States of America

www.randomhousereaderscircle.com

2 4 6 8 9 7 5 3 1

Book design by C. Linda Dingler

For Benjamin and Tucker.
As always.

Autumn

There is a tide in the affairs of men,
Which, taken at the flood, leads on to fortune;
Omitted, all the voyage of their life
Is bound in shallows and in miseries.
On such a full sea are we now afloat,
And we must take the current where it serves,
Or lose our ventures.

—Shakespeare, *Julius Caesar*, Act IV, Scene III

ONE

Seattle, Washington

$\mathcal{I}$T ALL STARTED WITH A SECOND MARTINI.

"Come on," Meghann said, "have another drink."

"No way." Elizabeth didn't handle alcohol well; God knew that had been proven conclusively back in 1976 when she'd been at the University of Washington.

"You can't refuse to drink at my forty-second birthday party. Remember how drunk I got last spring when you turned forty-five?"

What a debacle *that* had been.

Meghann sensed hesitation, and like any good attorney, she pounced on it. "I'll have Johnny pick us up."

"Are you sure Johnny's old enough to drive?"

"Now, that hurts. *All* of my boyfriends have their driver's licenses."

"And I thought you had no standards."

"I keep them as low as possible." Meghann raised her hand and flagged down the waitress, who hurried over. "We'll take two more martinis. And bring us a plate of nachos—heavy on the refried beans."

Elizabeth couldn't help smiling. "This is going to be ugly."

The waitress returned, set two elegant glasses down on the table, and picked up the empties.

"Here's to me," Meghann said, clinking her glass against Elizabeth's.

For the next hour, their conversation drifted down old roads and around old times. They'd been friends for more than twenty years. In the two decades since college, their lives had gone in opposite directions—Elizabeth had put all her energies into wife-and-motherhood; Meghann had become a first-rate divorce attorney—but their friendship had never wavered. For years, as Elizabeth and her family had moved from town to town, they'd kept in touch via e-mail and phone calls. Now, finally, they lived close enough to see each other on special occasions. It was one of the things Elizabeth loved most about living in Oregon.

By the time the third round was delivered, Meghann was laughing uproariously about the sound the cash register made.

"D'ya see tha hunk o' burning love in the corner over there?" Meg glanced slyly at a college-age boy sitting by the window. "He looks lonely."

"And look—no braces. He probably got them taken off last week. He's just your type."

Meghann dug through the nachos, looking for one with a lot of cheese on it. "Not everyone is lucky enough to have married their college sweetheart, kiddo. Besides, I don't have a type anymore. I did once. Now I'll stick with what makes *me* happy."

Happy. The word hit Elizabeth hard.

"I wonder if a big ole wet one from a birthday girl—Birdie? What's the matter?"

Elizabeth pushed the martini away and crossed her arms. It had become her favorite stance lately. Sometimes, she found herself standing in a room alone, with her arms bound so tightly around her own chest that she couldn't draw an even breath. It was as if she were trying to trap something inside of her that wanted out.

"Birdie?"

"It's nothing, really."

Meghann lowered her voice. "Look. I know something's wrong, Birdie. I'm your friend. I love you. Talk to me."

This was why Elizabeth didn't drink. In such a weakened state, her unhappiness swelled to unmanageable proportions, and the cap she kept on her emotions wouldn't stay put. She looked across the table at her best friend, and knew she had to say something. She simply couldn't hold it all inside anymore.

Her marriage was failing. Thinking it was hard; saying it was almost unthinkable.

They loved each other, she and Jack, but it was a feeling wrought mostly of habit. The passion had been gone for a long time. More and more often, it felt as if they were out of step, dancing to different pieces of music. He wanted sex in the morning; she wanted it at night. They compromised by going months without making love, and when they did finally reach out, their passion was as tired as their need.

Still, they were the envy of their friends. Everyone pointed to them and said, *Look, a marriage that lasts*. She and Jack were like the final exhibit in a museum that had been emptying for years.

She couldn't possibly say all of that. Words had too much power. They had to be handled with fireproof gloves or they'd burn you to the bone. "I'm not very happy lately; that's all."

"What is it you want?"

"It'll sound stupid."

"I'm half drunk. Nothing will sound stupid."

Elizabeth wished she could smile at that, but her heart was beating so hard she felt light-headed. "I want . . . who I used to be."

"Oh, honey." Meghann sighed heavily. "I don't suppose you've talked to Jack about this."

"Every time we get close to talking about something that matters, I panic and say nothing's wrong. Afterward, I want to hit myself in the head with a ball peen hammer."

"I had no idea you were this unhappy."

"That's the worst part of it. I'm not *un*happy, either." She slumped forward. Her elbows made the table rattle. "I'm just empty."

"You're forty-five years old and your kids are gone and your marriage has gone stale and you want to start over. My practice is full of women like you."

"Oh, good. I'm not only unhappy and overweight, I'm a cliché, too."

"A cliché is just something that's commonly true. Do you want to leave him?"

Elizabeth looked down at her hands, at the diamond ring she'd worn for twenty-four years. She wondered if she could even get it off. "I dream about leaving him. Living alone."

"And in those dreams, you're happy and independent and free. When you wake up, you're lonely and lost again."

"Yes."

Meghann leaned toward her. "Look, Birdie, women come into my office every day, saying they're not happy. I write down the words that will tear their families apart and break a lot of hearts. And you know what? Most of them end up wishing they'd tried harder, loved better. They end up trading their homes, their savings, their lifestyle, for a nine-to-five job and a stack of bills, while hubby-dearest waits ten seconds, then marries the salad-bar girl at Hooters. So, here's a million dollars worth of advice from your best friend and divorce attorney: If you're empty, it's not Jack's fault, or even his problem, and leaving him won't solve it. It's your job to make Elizabeth Shore happy."

"I don't know how to do that anymore."

"Oh, for Christ's sake, Birdie, let's be martini-honest here. You used to be a lot of things—talented, independent, artistic, intellectual. In college, we all thought you'd end up being the next Georgia O'Keeffe. Now you organize every city fund-raiser and decorate your house. I got a law degree in less time than it takes you to choose a fabric for the sofa."

"That's not fai—"

"I'm a lawyer. Fair doesn't interest me." Her voice softened. "I also know that Jack's job has been hard on you. I know how much you wanted a place where you could put down roots."

"You *don't* know," Elizabeth said. "We've lived in more than a dozen houses since we got married, in almost half that many cities. You've lived in Seattle forever. You don't know what it's like to always be the stranger in town, the new wife with no friends or résumé of your own. Hell, you started college at sixteen and still managed to fit in. I know I've let my house become an obsession, but it's because I *belong* in Echo Beach, Meg. Finally. For the first time since I was a child, I have a home. Not a house, not a condo, not a place to rent for a year or two. A home." She realized she was practically yelling. Embarrassed, she lowered her voice. "I feel safe there. You can't understand that because you've never been afraid."

Meghann seemed to consider that. Then she said, "Okay, forget the house. How about this: I can't remember the last time I saw you paint."

Elizabeth drew back. This was something she definitely didn't want to talk about. "I painted the kitchen last week."

"Very funny." Meghann fell quiet, waiting for a response.

"There wasn't time after the kids were born."

Meghann's expression was loving, but steady. "There is now."

A subtle reminder that the girls were at college now, that Elizabeth's reason for being had moved on. Only a woman with no children would think it was so easy to begin again. Meg didn't know what it was like to devote twenty years of your life to children and then watch them walk away. On shows like *Oprah*, the experts said it left a hole in your life. They underestimated.

It was a crater. Where once there had been flowers and trees and life, now nothing but rock remained.

Still, she had to admit that the same thought had occurred to her. She'd even tried to sketch a few times, but it was a terrible thing to reach for a talent too late and come up empty-handed. No wonder she'd poured all of her creativity into her beloved house. "It takes passion to paint. Or maybe just youth."

"Tell that to Grandma Moses." Meghann reached into her handbag and pulled out a small notepad with a pen stuck in the spiral column. She flipped the pad open and wrote something down, then ripped off the piece of paper and handed it to Elizabeth.

The note said: WOMEN'S PASSION SUPPORT GROUP. THURSDAY, 7:00/ ASTORIA COMMUNITY COLLEGE.

"I've been waiting almost a year for the right time to recommend this to you."

"It sounds like a meeting of porn stars. What do they talk about? How to keep your lipstick on during a blow job?"

"Funny. Maybe you should try stand-up. And God knows a blow job has saved more than one marriage."

"Meg, I—"

"Listen to me, Birdie. I have a lot of clients in Grays County, and I send them to this meeting. It's a group of women—mostly newly divorced—who get together to talk. They've all given up too much of themselves, and they're trying to find a way back."

Elizabeth stared down at the note. She knew that Meg was waiting for her to say something, but she couldn't seem to find her voice. It was one thing to get drunk and complain about her unhappiness to a best friend; it was quite another to walk into a room full of strange women and declare that she had no passion in her life.

She hoped her smile didn't look as brittle as it felt. "Thanks, Meg." Still smiling, she flagged down the waitress and ordered another martini.

The bedside clock dropped one blocky, red number after another into the darkness. At 6:30—a full thirty minutes early—Jack reached over and disabled the alarm.

He lay there, staring at the slats of light sneaking through the louvered blinds. The bedroom was striped in bands of black and white; the horizons of darkness made everything look strangely unfamiliar. He could make out the barest hint of rain falling outside. Another gray, overcast day. Normal early December weather on the Oregon coast.

Elizabeth was asleep beside him, her silvery blond hair fanned across the white pillowcase. He could hear the soft, even strains of her breathing, the occasional muffled snore that meant she would probably wake up with a cold. She'd probably caught a bug last week when she'd gone to Seattle.

In the earlier days of their marriage, they had always slept nestled together, but somewhere along the way, they'd started needing space between them. Lately, she'd begun sleeping along the mattress's very edge.

But today, things were going to get better. Finally, at forty-six, he was going to get another chance. A Seattle production company was starting a weekly sports program that would cover the highlights of northwest sports; it had been picked up by the NBC affiliate. If he got the anchor job, he'd have to commute three days a week, but with the extra money, that wouldn't be such a hardship. It was a hell of a step up from the pissant local coverage he'd been doing.

(Not where he *should* be, of course, not where he belonged, but sometimes one mistake could ruin a man.)

He'd be *someone* again.

For the last fifteen years, he'd worked his ass off, making progress in steps too small to be seen by the human eye. In a series of shitty little towns, he'd paid for his mistakes. Today, finally, he had a decent opportunity, a chance to get back into the game. There was no way in hell he was going to drop the ball.

He got out of bed and immediately winced in pain. This damp climate played hell with his knees. Grimacing, he limped toward the bathroom. As usual, he had to walk over fabric samples and paint chips and open magazines. Birdie had been "redoing" their bedroom for months now, planning every move as if she were the defensive coordinator in a Super Bowl game. It was the same story in the dining room. Stuff heaped in every corner, waiting for that rarest of moments: his wife actually making a decision.

He had already showered and shaved when Elizabeth stumbled into the room, tightening the thick cotton belt on her bathrobe.

"Morning," she said with a yawn. "God, I feel like crap. I think I'm getting a cold. You're up early."

He felt a flash of disappointment that she'd forgotten. "Today's the day, Birdie. I'm driving up to Seattle for that interview."

A tiny frown tugged at her brow; then she obviously remembered. "Oh, yeah. I'm sure you'll get the job."

In the old days, Birdie would have pumped up his ego, assured him that it would all work out in the end, that he was destined for greatness. But she'd grown tired in the past few years; they both had. And he'd failed to land so many jobs over the years, no wonder she'd stopped believing in him.

He'd tried like hell to pretend he was happy here in Oregon, that all he wanted out of life was to be the noon sports anchor, covering mostly high-school sports in a midsized market. But Birdie knew he merely tolerated living in this nothing town on the edge of a barely-there city. He even hated being a mid-level celebrity. All it served to do was remind him of who he used to be.

She gave him a perfunctory smile. "More money will be great, especially with the girls in college."

"You can say that again."

Then she looked up at him. "Will the job make everything better, Jack?"

Her question sucked the air from his lungs. God, he was tired of this discussion. Her endless quest for the answer to *what's wrong with our lives* was exhausting. Years ago, he'd tried to tell her that all her happiness shouldn't depend on him. He'd watched as she'd given up more and more of herself. He couldn't stop it, or didn't stop it, but somehow it had become all his fault. He was sick to death of it. "Not today, Elizabeth."

She gave him the sudden, hurt look that he'd come to expect. "Of course. I know it's a big day for you."

"For *us*," he said, getting angry now.

Her smile was too bright to be real. "I picked a place for us to celebrate your new job."

The sudden change in subject was their way of smoothing over the rough spots in their marriage. He could have stayed angry, forced a discussion, but what was the point? Birdie didn't fight back and there was nothing new to say. "Where?"

"There's a bear camp in Alaska. A place where you fly in and stay in tents and watch the grizzly bears in their natural environment. I saw an interview with the owner—Laurence John—on the Travel Channel."

He unwrapped the towel from his waist and slung it haphazardly across the edge of the bathtub. Naked, he turned and headed into the walk-in closet, where he grabbed a pair of underwear, stepped into them, and turned to her. "I thought you were going to say dinner at the Heathman and dancing in the Crystal Ballroom."

She moved hesitantly toward him. He noticed that she was twisting her wedding ring—a nervous habit from way back. "I thought maybe if we could get away . . . have an adventure . . ."

He knew what she was thinking, and it wouldn't work. A new location was no more than a different stage upon which to act out the same old scenes, say the same old lines. Still, he touched her face gently, hoping his cynicism didn't show. There was nothing he hated more than hurting her, although she'd grown so fragile in the past few years that protecting her emotions was an impossible task. "The bear camp sounds great. Do we get to share a sleeping bag?"

She smiled. "That can be arranged."

He pulled her against him, holding her close. "Maybe we could celebrate right here in our own bed when I get home."

"I could wear that Victoria's Secret thing you got me."

"I won't be able to concentrate all day." He kissed her. It was long and sweet, a kiss full of promise. The kind of kiss he'd almost forgotten. For a split second, he remembered how it used to be between them, back in the days when sex was unbelievably good. When spending the day in bed seemed like a perfect idea.

As he pulled back from her, he looked down into her beautiful, smiling face. Once, not all that long ago, they'd loved each other unconditionally. He missed those days, those emotions.

Maybe.

Maybe everything really could change for them today.

Two

TRAFFIC IN SEATTLE WAS STOP-AND-GO. JACK COULDN'T BELIEVE the number of cars on the freeway. The city was a study in gray, shrouded in mist, buttressed by concrete. Even Lake Union was rainy-day dull today. Every few minutes came the honk of a horn and the screech of rubber on wet pavement.

He loved the hustle and bustle of it all. The energy. It was the first time he'd been in a city-on-the-go in a while. The tech industry had given Seattle a hipness, an edge that it never used to have.

He drove across the floating bridge. He hadn't been here in years, probably not since his college days at the University of Washington. The changes were amazing.

In the seventies, Bellevue had begun life as a bedroom community for commuters who wanted a rural lifestyle. Families settled in clumps, buying matching tri-level homes in cul-de-sacs with names like RainShadow Glen and Marvista Estates. Thick black asphalt had been rolled in four-lane strips from east to west and north to south. Before the streets had even dried, the strip malls popped up. Flat-topped, white-sided shoebox buildings that huddled beneath the neon glare of their own signage. For years, the suburb grew unchecked; by the late eighties, it looked like southern California.

Then the Internet exploded. Microsoft and Immunex moved into this sprawl of tract homes and suddenly a city was needed. A place that the growing number of hip, young millionaires could call home. The changes came as fast as the money did. Strip malls gave way to beautiful, themed shopping centers. Trendy restaurants offered alfresco dining on concrete, under umbrellaed tables. Barnes and Noble built a flagship superstore in the old bowling alley.

At the corner of Main Street and 106th stood an imposing and ornate building, a sleek combination of concrete and glass with a trendy rococo facade at the entrance. It was a perfect representation of the "new" Bellevue—expensive, brash, and trendy, with just enough atrium space to display its northwest roots.

Jack parked on the street out front. He sat in the quiet car for a minute, gathering his confidence, then he headed into the building. On the seventeenth floor, he quickly adjusted his silk tie—more out of habit than any real fashion sense—and stepped into the expansive brass and glass reception area.

He thought, You're Jumpin' Jack Flash. They'd be lucky to get you; then walked up to the desk.

The receptionist smiled brightly. "May I help you?"

"Jackson Shore to see Mark Wilkerson."

"One moment, please." She picked up the phone and announced him. After she hung up, she said, "Have a seat. Someone will be with you shortly."

He sat down on the sleek red leather sofa in the waiting room. A few moments later, a woman walked toward him. She was tall and thin—nice body. The gold jewelry at her throat glittered in the overhead fluorescent lighting. She offered her hand. "It's a pleasure to meet you, Mr. Shore. I'm Lori Hansen. My dad always said that you were the best quarterback the NFL ever had. Well, you and Joe, of course."

"Thank you."

"This way, please."

Jack followed her down a wide, marble-floored corridor. There were people everywhere, clustered in pods around the copiers and doorways. A few smiled at him as he passed; more ignored him.

Finally, they reached their destination—a closed door. She knocked softly and opened it.

Jack closed his eyes for a split second and visualized success— *Jumpin' Jack Flash*—then smiled confidently.

The man behind the desk was older than Jack had expected— maybe seventy or more. "Jackson," he said, rising, extending his hand.

They shook hands.

"Have a seat," Mark said, indicating the chair in front of his huge, mahogany desk.

Jack sat down.

Mark did not. He stood on the other side of the desk, seeming to take up an inordinate amount of space. In a black Armani suit, Wilkerson was an industry prototype for authority and power, both of which he'd been wielding so long his hands were probably calloused. His was the largest independent production company in the northwest.

Finally, he sat down. "I've seen your tapes. You're good. I was surprised at how good, actually."

"Thank you."

"It's been, what, fifteen years since you played for the Jets?"

"Yeah. I blew out my knee. As I'm sure you know, I led my team to back-to-back Super Bowl wins."

"And you're a Heisman winner. Yes," Mark said, "your past triumphs are quite impressive."

Was there the slightest emphasis on *past*, or had Jack imagined that? "Thank you. I've paid my dues in local broadcasting, as you can see from my résumé. Ratings in Portland have gone up considerably in the two years I've been at the station." He bent down and reached for his briefcase. "I've taken the liberty of outlining some ideas for your show. I think it can be dynamite."

"What about the drugs?"

Just like that, he knew it was over. "That was a long time ago." He hoped he didn't sound defeated. "When I was in the hospital, I got hooked on painkillers. The networks gave me a big chance— *Monday Night Football*—and I blew it. I was young and stupid. But it won't happen again. I've been clean for years. Ask my previous employers. They'll stand up for my work ethic."

"We're not a huge company, Jack. We can't afford the kind of scandals and disappointments that are standard operating procedure at the networks. The truth is you're damaged goods. I don't see how I can risk my success on you."

Jack wished he could be the man he'd once been. That man would have said, *Cram your shit-ass little TV program up your wrinkly white ass.* Instead, he said, "I can do a good job for you. Give me a chance." Each word tasted black and bitter on his tongue, but a man with a mortgage, a dwindling stock portfolio, and two daughters in college had no choice.

"I'm sorry," Mark said, though he didn't look it.

"Why did you bother to interview me?"

"My son remembers you from the UW. He thought a face-to-face meeting would change my mind about you." He almost smiled. "But my son has substance abuse issues of his own. Of course he'd believe in giving a man a second chance. I don't."

Jack picked up his briefcase. He used to think that losing football was rock bottom, the damp basement of his existence. It had been what sent him reaching for a bottle of pills in the first place.

But he'd been wrong.

Nothing was worse than the slow, continual erosion of his self-esteem. Times like this wore a man down.

Finally, he stood up. It took all his strength to smile and say, "Well, thank you for seeing me."

Although you didn't, you officious prick, you didn't see me at all.

Then he left the office.

ELIZABETH SAT IN THE DINING ROOM, with fabrics and paint chips and glossy magazine pages strewn across her lap, but she couldn't concentrate on the task at hand.

Maybe tonight, she kept thinking.

For years, she'd listened to daytime television talk shows. The shrinks agreed that passion could be rekindled, that a love lost along the busy highway of raising a family could be regenerated.

She hoped it was true, because she and Jack were in trouble. After twenty-four years of marriage, they'd forgotten how to love each other; now, only the barest strand of their bond remained.

Their marriage was like an old blanket that had been fraying for years. If repairs weren't made—and quickly—they'd each be left holding a handful of colored thread. She couldn't keep pretending that things would get better on their own.

She had to *make* it happen. That was another thing the shrinks agreed on: You had to act to get results.

Tonight, she'd give them a new beginning.

She kept that goal in mind all day as she went about her chores. Finally, she came home and made his favorite dinner: coq au vin.

The tantalizing aroma of chicken and wine and spices filled the house. It took her almost an hour to get a fire going in the living room hearth (flammable materials were Jack's job, always, like taking out the trash and paying the bills). When she finished, she lit the cinnamon-scented candles that were her favorite. Then she dimmed the lights. By candlelight, the yellow walls seemed to be as soft as melted butter. On either side of the pale blue and yellow toile sofa, two dark mahogany end tables glimmered with streaks of red and gold.

The whole house looked like a movie set. Seduction Central.

When everything was perfect, she raced into her bathroom and showered, shaved her legs twice, and smoothed almond-scented lotion all over her body.

At last, she went to her lingerie drawer and burrowed through the serviceable Jockey For Her underwear and Calvin Klein cotton bras until she found the lacy white silk camisole and tap pants Jack had bought her for Valentine's Day a few years ago. Maybe more than a few. She'd never worn them.

Then, she'd dismissed them as a gift for him. Now she saw the romance in it. How long had it been since he'd wanted to see her in sexy clothes?

She frowned.

It looked awfully small.

And her ass was awfully big.

"Don't do this to yourself," she said, starting to put it back.

Then she caught sight of herself in the mirror. A forty-five-year-old woman stared back at her, wrinkles and all. Once, people had told her that she looked like Michelle Pfeiffer. Of course, that had been ten years and twenty pounds ago.

She looked down at the lingerie in her hands. Size ten. A size too small. Not so much, really . . .

If only she could surgically remove the memory of once being a size six.

Very slowly, she slipped the camisole over her head. There was only the slightest pull of fabric across the breasts.

Maybe it was even sexy.

Besides, it was dark in the house. Hopefully, she'd get naked quickly.

Not that that was a particularly comforting thought.

She stepped gingerly into the lace-trimmed tap pants and breathed a sigh of relief. Tight, but wearable.

She looked into the mirror.

Almost pretty.

Maybe it *could* happen. Maybe a few little changes in habit could turn it all around . . .

She went to her closet, found the vibrant blue silk robe that had been another long-ago gift and slipped into it. The fabric caressed her smooth, perfumed skin, and suddenly she *felt* sexy.

She applied her makeup with exquisite care, adding a little Cleopatra-tilt of eyeliner and a shining layer of lip gloss.

By the time she'd taken all those years off her face, it was six-thirty, and she realized that Jack was late.

She poured herself a glass of wine and went into the living room to wait. By the time she'd drunk a second glass, she was worried. A quick phone call to his cell phone didn't help; no one answered.

It was a long drive from here to Seattle—at least three and a half hours. But if he'd gotten a late start, he would have called . . .

By eight, dinner was ruined. The chicken had fallen off the bone, and the onions had cooked down to nothing. There wasn't enough sauce left to taste.

"Perfect."

Then she heard his key in the front door.

Her first reaction was a flash of anger. *You're late* were the words that filled her mouth, but she took a deep, calming breath and released the air slowly, evenly. So what if he should have called.

For this one night, she wanted to be his mistress, not his wife. She poured him a glass of wine, and headed toward the door.

He stood in the doorway, staring at her.

And she knew.

"Hey, honey," he said without smiling. "Sorry I'm late." He didn't comment on anything—not the fire, the candles, her outfit.

She moved toward him, feeling suddenly self-conscious in her silk robe.

"I didn't get the job."

"What happened?" she asked softly, knowing what the answer would be.

"Wilkerson didn't want to gamble on a guy who used to do drugs." Jack gave her a smile so sad it broke her heart. "Some things don't ever go away, I guess."

She could see how badly he was hurting, but when she reached for him, he pulled away. He walked into the living room and stared into the fire.

"Remember when you blew out your knee?" she said, following him. "We closed all the curtains in your hospital room, and I climbed into bed with you, and—"

"That was a long time ago, Birdie."

She stared at him, feeling lost. He was less than an arm's length away, but it might as well have been miles. Twenty-four years of marriage and here they stood. Both of them unsure; neither able to offer the other a steadying hand. In crisis, they'd become strangers. She didn't know what else to say, or even if she should speak at all. In the end, she took the safe route, and yet, as she spoke, it felt as if her bones were cracking. "Here. Have a glass of wine."

He took the glass she offered and sat down, then opened his briefcase and pulled out a stack of papers. Without looking up, he said, "Can you turn on the lights? I can't see a damned thing here."

"Sure." She turned away from him quickly, before he could see how much he'd hurt her. Then she tightened the wrap of her ridiculous robe and headed toward the kitchen. "I'll get you something to eat."

"I love you, Birdie," he said to her back.

"Yeah," she answered softly, walking away from him. "I love you, too."

THREE

THE NEXT MORNING, ELIZABETH SAT ON A STOOL AT THE kitchen counter, with her hands curled tightly around a mug of chamomile tea.

"Coffee?" Jack asked, pouring himself a cup.

"No, thanks. I'm trying to cut down on caffeine."

"Again?"

"Yeah, again." She set her cup down on the granite countertop. Her fingertip traced the rough, striated ceramic surface of the mug, the slightly bent handle. This cup was one of her many relics, a memento from her pottery period. She often thought that when she died, an anthropologist would be able to visualize who she was from the trail of her hobbies. Pottery. Stained glass. Hooked fabric rugs. Jewelry made from antique silver spoons. Macramé. Photography. Photo and memory albums. And then there were the endless classes she'd taken at local community colleges. Shakespearean literature, art history, political science. Once she'd lost her ability to paint, she'd gone in search of a substitute, something that would light a fire of creativity inside her. Nothing had ever taken hold.

Jack rinsed out the coffeepot and placed it gently back in place. He looked tired, and no wonder. He'd tossed and turned all night long.

"Why don't you stay home today?" she said. "We could go out to lunch. Maybe take a walk on the beach. Or go Christmas shopping in town. The stores are all decorated."

"It's too cold."

She didn't know what else to say. Once, it wouldn't have mattered if it were raining or snowing. Being together was the point. Now, even the weather came between them.

He moved in beside her, touched her shoulder and said softly, "I'm sorry."

The shame in his eyes almost undid her. It took her back in time. For a second, all she could see in the man standing beside her was the boy she'd fallen in love with all those years ago. "You'll get another chance, Jack."

"I love you, Birdie."

This time, she knew he meant it. "I love you, too."

"So, why isn't it enough?"

Elizabeth wanted to look away. "What do you mean?"

"Come on, Birdie, this is the discussion you always want to have, isn't it? The perpetual, burning question: What's wrong with us? Well, now *I'm* asking it. Why isn't what we still have enough?"

"I want it to be."

"It shouldn't be this hard," he said in a voice so soft she had to strain to hear it.

What she said next mattered; she knew that. They so rarely dared to approach the truth of their unhappiness. But she couldn't imagine being honest, saying *I'm afraid we don't love each other anymore*. "I know," was all she could manage.

Jack's shoulders sagged; his mouth settled into a frown. "You exhaust me, Elizabeth." He drew back from her. "You moan and whine about how unhappy you are, but when I finally try to discuss it, you clam up."

"I didn't say I was unhappy." She wished instantly that she hadn't said that, that she'd been truthful. But it was so . . . big . . . what they were circling now, and it frightened her.

"Of course not. You never actually *say* anything."

"Why should I? You never listen anyway."

They stared at each other, neither one certain of where to go from there. Woven into the silence was the fear that one of them would finally admit the truth.

"Okay, then," Jack said finally. "I'm off to work. Maybe today I'll score that big story."

With that, they merged back onto the comfortable highway of their lives. Jack might have briefly hit his turn signal, but in the end, no lane-changing was allowed.

JACK STOOD IN FRONT OF THE STADIUM, freezing his nuts off. A chilling breeze whipped through the parking lot, kicking up leaves and bits of fallen debris.

"There you have it," he said, giving the camera one of his patented PR smiles. "The two teams competing for this year's State Boys B-8 football championships. They might be small in size and number, but they more than make up for it in spirit and determination. From downtown Portland, this is Jackson Shore with your midday sports update."

The minute the camera light blinked off, he tossed the microphone to his cameraman. "Shit, it's cold out here," he said, buttoning up his coat. With a quick wave good-bye, he walked back to the station. He could have waited for a ride, but the techies were taking forever breaking down their equipment.

Once inside the station's warmth, he got a double tall mocha latte and headed into his office; then he sat down at his cheap metal desk and tried to think of something to do. Nothing came to mind. He got up and went to the window. Outside, the day was as gray as pipe metal. A drizzling rain fell in strands almost invisible to the naked eye. Stoplights threw beams of red and green light onto the wet pavement.

He could always go down to the college and see what was up with the Ducks, but their basketball team didn't look promising.

Maybe something was going on with the Trail Blazers . . .

There was a knock at his door. "Come in," he said, not daring yet to turn around. He knew he'd have to look "up" for whoever had just walked in, but in an end this dead, sometimes it took a few seconds' worth of effort to draw up that PR smile.

"Mr. Shore?"

Finally, he turned. It was Sally something-or-other, one of the station's new production assistants. She was young and beautiful and ambitious. He'd recognized that ambition the first time he'd seen her. Looking at her now, seeing the passionate fire in her gaze, made him even more tired. "What can I do for you?"

"I wanted to thank you for Tuesday night."

Jack thought for a minute. "Oh, yeah. The Bridgeport Pub." A bunch of the producers and videographers had gone out after work. At the last minute, Jack had invited Sally.

She smiled up at him, and he was caught for a minute, mesmerized by her dark eyes. "It was really nice of you to invite me along."

"I thought it'd be good for you to hang out with the producers a little. It's a tough business to break into."

She took a step closer. "I'd like to return the favor."

"Okay."

"Drew Grayland."

He didn't know what he'd been expecting, but that sure as hell wasn't it. "The Panther center?"

"My little sister was at a party with him on Saturday night. She said he was drinking straight shots and doing all kinds of drugs, and that he took a girl into his room. When the girl came out, she was crying and her clothes were all ripped up. Later that night, a drunk driver hit a dog up on Cascade Street. The rumor is that Drew was driving and the campus police are covering it up. Thursday is the big UCLA game, you know."

Jack hadn't had a tip like this in . . . ever. "This could be big." He allowed himself to imagine it for just a second—a national story, big-time exposure, his face on every television in America. And Henry, the lead sportscaster, was out of town. A vacation in the Australian outback, no less.

"Can I be your assistant on it?" Sally asked.

"Of course. We'll need to see if that woman filed any charges against him. We can't run with campus gossip."

Sally flipped open a small notepad and started taking notes.

"I'll talk to the news director. You get to work on questions and leads. We'll start with the campus police. Let's meet in the lobby in . . ." He looked at his watch. It was twelve-forty-five. "Thirty minutes, okay?"

"Perfect."

"And, Sally, thanks."

"What goes around comes around, Jack."

When she grinned up at him, he felt a flash of the old confidence.

BY THE TIME ELIZABETH GOT HOME, she was dog tired. The library meeting had run overtime, her book group had taken almost an hour to get started, and the carpenter she'd interviewed was too damned expensive to do her any good.

Exhausted, she tossed her purse on the kitchen table and went back outside. On the porch, she settled into the rocking chair. The even, creaking motion of the chair—back and forth, back and forth—soothed her ragged nerves.

The endless bronze ocean stretched out before her. The thick green lawn, still damp from an afternoon downpour, glittered in the fading sunlight. A pair of ancient Douglas firs, their boughs sagging tiredly downward, bracketed the view perfectly.

A fleeting *if only* passed through her mind; she immediately discarded it. Her painting days were long behind her. But if they hadn't been, if she hadn't let that once-hot passion grow cold, this was what she would paint.

Close by, a bird cawed loudly. A plump crow, berating her, no doubt, for daring to invade its space.

But this was *her* place, her solace. From each of the three hundred bulbs she'd planted in the garden, to the picket fence she'd built and painted white, to every stick of furniture inside the house. Each square inch of this property reflected her dreams. No matter how unhappy or stressed-out she felt, she could come out to this quiet porch and stare at the ocean and feel at peace.

She watched the golden sun sink slowly into the darkening sea, then got to her feet and went back inside.

It was time to start dinner.

She had just walked through the front door when the phone rang. She answered it. "Hello?"

"Hey, kiddo, are you done saving the Oregon coast for the day?"

Elizabeth smiled in spite of her exhaustion. "Hey, Meg. It's good to hear from you." She collapsed into a Wedgwood-blue-and-yellow-striped chair and put her feet up on the matching ottoman. "What's going on?"

"Today's Thursday. I wanted to remind you about that meeting."

The passionless women.

Elizabeth's smile faded. "Yeah," she said, "I remembered," although of course she hadn't.

"You're going?"

Yeah, right. Walk into a room full of strangers and admit that she had no passion? "No, actually, I'm not. It's not my thing."

"And what exactly is your thing?"

That stung. "You're using your lawyer voice."

"What are you going to do tonight, alphabetize your spice drawer? Believe me, Birdie, you're going to wake up one day and be sixty years old, and you won't remember the last time you were happy."

Elizabeth had no answer to that. The same ugly scenario had occurred to her. Often. "If I went—and I'm not capitulating, mind you—but if I went, what would it be like?"

"A bunch of girlfriends getting together. They'll probably talk about how it feels to be lost in the middle of life."

That didn't sound so bad; she'd imagined an Inquisition. Perhaps with torture aids. "Would I have to talk?"

"No, Marcel Marceau, you could sit there like a rock."

"You really think it would help me?"

"Let's put it this way, if you don't go this week, I'll make next week such a piece of hell that by next Thursday you'll be begging to go."

Elizabeth couldn't help smiling. Years ago, when Meghann had suffered through her terrible, heartbreaking divorce, Elizabeth had treated her in exactly the same way. Tough love. Sometimes a friend had to strong-arm you; that was all there was to it. "Okay, I'll go."

"Promise?"

"Bite me."

"For the hearing impaired, I ask again, you promise?"

This could go on all day. "I promise. Now, don't you have some deadbeat dad to harass?"

"No, actually, but I have a date. He's Italian. Giuliano."

"You finally ran out of Americans, huh?"

They talked for another twenty minutes about Meghann's lack of a love life, then hung up. Elizabeth poured herself a glass of wine and took a pair of chicken breasts out of the freezer. As they defrosted in the microwave, she checked the answering machine. There was a message from her younger daughter, Jamie, and one from Jack. He was tracking down a big story and wouldn't be home until late tonight.

"There you have it, sports fans," she said aloud. It was yet another of her crazy-older-woman traits; she talked to herself. "I'm going to the meeting."

She took a shower, then went into her walk-in closet. She stared at her neatly organized clothes. So much of what she bought was bright and colorful: hand-painted scarves, hand-knit sweaters, batik silk-screen prints. She loved art in all its forms. Since her teen years, she'd been complimented on her fashion sense. But none of that helped her now. The last thing she wanted to do was stand out in the crowd.

Look, there. A woman with no passion.

After several false starts, she chose chocolate brown wool pants and a cream-colored cashmere turtleneck. She decided against a belt. It had been years since any of her good ones fit, anyway. She applied her makeup, then pulled her straight blond hair (in need of a dye job, she noticed) back into a french braid. She removed the dangly hammered-silver-and-turquoise earrings she usually wore and put in a pair of pearl studs, then studied herself in the mirror.

"Perfect." She looked as bland as a wren.

At six, she left Jack a note on the kitchen counter, just in case he got home before she did. It was a wasted gesture, of course. With his homing skills, she'd be through menopause by the time he found it.

Twenty-five minutes later, she pulled into the parking lot.

The community college had been built in the late seventies and looked like it. Textured concrete walls supported a flat orange metal roof. Winter-bare trees lined the pathways and gave the campus a strangely sorrowful mien. Haggard, worn holiday decorations—grayed snowmen and faded menorahs—hung from the streetlamps, rustled in the slight breeze.

Elizabeth clutched her handbag tightly under her arm and

kept going. As she moved down the interior hallways, she was glad she'd worn her loafers. Her footsteps were muted, barely noticeable. No one would hear a thing if she decided to turn back.

Finally, she came to room 106. Unfortunately, there was no window in the door, no way to peek inside and find a reason to change her mind.

Cautiously, she opened the door. Without allowing herself another pause, she walked inside.

It was a small classroom, ordinary. A green chalkboard showed the eraser-swiped remnants of a math equation. In the middle of the room sat a semicircle of folding metal chairs; some of them were empty; others held nervous-looking women. Off to the left, a white-clothed table held a coffeemaker and a tray of baked goods.

"Don't be shy. Come on in."

Startled, Elizabeth spun around and found herself nose-to-nose with a stunningly beautiful woman wearing a scarlet suit. A name tag on her lapel read: SARAH TAYLOR.

"I'm Sarah," the woman said, smiling brightly. "Welcome to the meeting."

Elizabeth couldn't manage a smile. "I'm Elizabeth."

Sarah touched her shoulder, gave her a reassuring squeeze. "Everyone's nervous at first." She turned to the other women. "Charlotte, why don't you welcome our newest member?"

Elizabeth panicked. She wasn't really a member, was she?

Charlotte—a large woman wearing black velour sweats and green rubber gardening clogs—was already moving toward her. "Hey," Charlotte said simply. "Welcome to the group. Come on in." She took hold of Elizabeth's elbow and guided her toward the circle of chairs.

Elizabeth sat down.

Beside her was a tiny, bright-eyed young woman dressed in a denim jumpsuit and scuffed cowboy boots. "I'm Joey," she said, smiling brightly. "My husband left me to join a rock band. He plays the harmonica. Can you believe it?" She laughed. "They call themselves Dog Boys. I call 'em Dog Shits, but not in front of the kids."

Elizabeth nodded stiffly. Joey kept talking, smiling all the while. All around the circle, women chatted with one another about ordinary things. Kids' school schedules, loser ex-husbands, dead-end jobs, and child-support checks. The voices blended into a steady, blurring drone. More women drifted into the room, took seats in the semicircle. Some joined in the conversation. Others, like Elizabeth, sat quietly.

Finally, Sarah closed the door and took a seat in the middle of the group. "Welcome, ladies. It's nice to see so many new faces tonight. This is the Women's Passion Support Group." She smiled. "Don't worry, we're not as erotic as that sounds."

Laughter followed that remark, some of it nervous.

"Our objective here is to help each other. Simple Simon. We have something in common, and that something is a sense of loss. We've reached a certain age and discovered that we've misplaced a vital part of ourselves. For lack of a better word, I call the missing element passion. Our goal is simply to share our feelings with women who understand. Together we can be strong. To begin, let's go around the circle and share one dream each." She turned to the woman seated beside her. "You've been here before, Mina. Why don't you begin?"

Mina, a plump, red-haired older woman dressed in a flowery, polyester housedress, seemed entirely at ease. "I started coming to these meetings about six months ago, when my husband— Bill—was diagnosed with Alzheimer's." She shook her head, made a tsking sound. "It's a horrible thing, losing someone you love by inches. . . . Anyway, I promised my daughter that I'd come to the meetings. I couldn't imagine finding passion, but now, I'm taking driving lessons. It doesn't sound like much to you young gals, but it's given me a new freedom. Next week I'll be going in for my final test. Hopefully I'll drive here on my own next time."

The group applauded, and Mina giggled.

When the room quieted, the next woman began to speak. "My name is Fran. My husband ran off with his secretary. His *male* secretary. The only passion I have lately seems to center around buying a handgun. Unfortunately, I can't decide which one of us to shoot." She smiled nervously. "That was a joke."

Sarah leaned forward. "What do you love doing, Fran?"

"I loved being a wife." She paused, shrugged. "My friends act like I have a terminal disease. This is the first time I've left the house in weeks. My divorce attorney recommended it, but I don't see how you can help."

"We can all relate to that," Joey said. There was a murmur of assent.

"Think about it, Fran," Sarah said. "What would you do if you knew you couldn't fail? Answer fast. One word. Don't censor yourself."

"Sing." Fran looked surprised by her answer. "I used to sing."

"I belong to a women's choir," Mina said. "We sing at local nursing homes and hospitals. We're always looking for new members."

"Oh, I didn't mean to imply that I was a good singer."

Mina chuckled. "We sing to people who wear hearing aids. Really, join us. We have a lot of fun."

Fran looked uncertain. "I'll think about it."

Several women started talking at once. Many of them, it seemed, had reached for unexpected things, too. Flying, skydiving, marathon running. The consensus was that anything could be a start.

"*That's* what we're all about," Sarah said. "Finding your passion isn't just about careers and money. It's about finding your authentic self. The one you've buried beneath other people's needs. Fran, you might be amazed at how much difference a little thing like joining a choir can make." She nodded to the woman beside Fran.

The woman moved her fingers nervously, rubbed her hands together. She was tall and thin, dressed all in black; maybe forty years old. She'd bleached her hair the color of straw; her roots were jet black. "I'm Kim. When my shit-head husband left me for a woman with *braces*, I started drinking. Believe me, it became a passion. I've been sober now for three months, but I'm thirsty all the time. I have no idea how to replace booze. My mom heard about this group on television and made me promise to come, so here I am."

"What do you do in your spare time?" Sarah asked.

Kim tugged on one of her long, silver earrings. "All I have is spare time. He left me plenty of money. I dyed my hair and got a tattoo—it says, '*Fuck Don.*' Those are positive steps forward, don't you think?" She wasn't smiling. In fact, behind all that black eyeliner, her eyes were pools of pain.

"Maybe you could get a job," someone said. "Earn your own money."

"Believe me," Kim snapped, "I *earned* that money. Besides, what could I do? I left college to get married and raise my daughter, who is now sixteen and thinks I'm dumber than a lug wrench. Volunteer work and husband ego-boosting hasn't qualified me for a whole hell of a lot. I can't see getting dressed in DKNY every day and saying, 'Would you like fries with that?'"

"There must be something that interests you."

Kim sat back. Her fingers played a pianolike rhythm on her black pants. "Nope, nothing. Sorry." She looked up. "Does revenge count?"

The group fell silent. Sarah said, "Maybe if you just listen tonight, you'll stop being so afraid."

"I'm not afraid." Kim reached into her purse and pulled out a pack of Virginia Slims. When she realized what she'd done, she crammed them back into her bag.

Sarah leaned forward. "You're in a desert right now, dying of thirst, but you're afraid to reach for water. Just don't give up,

Kim. Sooner or later, you'll get to a point where it's more frightening to do nothing than to do something, and then you'll reach out."

Kim gave Sarah a look of barely veiled contempt. "Can I find that crocheted on a pillow somewhere? Really. Maybe at a Losers 'R' Us outlet store?"

Sarah let the silence continue for a moment, then nodded at the woman beside Kim, who immediately started talking. After her, another spoke, then another and another.

Elizabeth realized suddenly that it was her turn.

Everyone looked at her.

Sit here like a rock, huh, Meg? She'd look like an idiot if she passed. She took a deep breath. "I'm Elizabeth. I'm an ordinary housewife with two grown daughters. Stephanie is almost twenty-one; Jamie is nineteen. I haven't been divorced or widowed or dumped on. Everything that's wrong with my life is my own fault."

"Blame isn't what we're looking for," Sarah said. "We're interested in what you want from life. Your dreams, Elizabeth."

Elizabeth knew that if she didn't answer, her turn would last forever. "I used to paint." Surprisingly, it hurt to say the words out loud.

"I work at an art supply store. Picture Perfect on Chadwick," one of the women said. "Come down this Saturday, and I'll help you find everything you need."

Elizabeth had plenty of supplies. Paints and brushes were the least of what an artist needed, and no support network could convince her otherwise. "There's no point, really."

"Don't be afraid," Sarah said. "Buy the paints and see what happens."

"You're lucky," Joey said, her voice wistful. "You actually have a passion. I've been coming to the meetings for months and I still have no clue."

"I wish *I* could paint," added another woman.

Elizabeth looked at the faces around her. They believed this was helping her. In fact, it was making her feel worse.

"Sure. I could do that," she said just to end her turn. "It'd probably be fun to paint again."

She thought the women were going to start break-dancing.

Except for Kim, who sat there, dressed in her mournful black, staring at Elizabeth through knowing eyes.

FOUR

FOR THE NEXT WEEK, JACK AND SALLY SPENT EIGHTEEN-HOUR days following the story. They got to the office early—Jack left home long before the sun had risen—and stayed late. Twice, he'd even slept on the couch in his office.

They'd interviewed dozens of people, tracked down countless leads, and tried to bullshit their way past closed doors.

Innuendo, anecdote, gossip—these they had found in abundance. By all accounts, Drew was a sleazy, not-too-bright young man who had an exceedingly high opinion of himself, an almost total disregard for other people's feelings, and an unshakable belief that society's rules didn't apply to him. In other words, he was a real pain in the ass.

He was also Oregon's brightest collegiate athlete, the best state basketball player in two decades. Speculation was high that he could lead the down-on-their-luck Panthers to their first ever NCAA championship season.

It was hardly surprising that no one in Panther athletics would talk to them—not even to issue a *no comment*. The basketball coach had been unavailable all week. And no one seemed to have seen the incident with the girl except Sally's sister. In short, they had no proof. No one liked Drew Grayland, it was clear, but no one would say anything on the record.

After another fruitless day, Jack and Sally went to a local steakhouse for dinner. They sat in a back booth where it was dimly lit and quiet.

"What now?" Sally asked.

Jack looked up from the notes spread out across the table. He was surprised to find that the place was almost empty. When they'd come in for dinner, every table had been full. "I think it's time for another drink." He raised a hand, flagged down the waitress.

She hurried over, pulled a pencil out from above her ear. "What can I get for you, Mr. Shore?"

Jack smiled tiredly, wishing—for once—that he hadn't been recognized. He felt like getting drunk. "Dewar's on the rocks."

"Margarita rocks, no salt," Sally said.

The waitress returned a few moments later with the drinks.

Jack sipped his, staring down at the notes again. He'd been staring at them for an hour, trying to glean something he'd missed. Someone to whom he hadn't spoken. But there was no one. He couldn't figure out where in the hell to go from here. All he knew for sure was that he'd failed. Again. This time, he'd taken bright-eyed Sally down with him. "Henry will be back from Australia tomorrow. Maybe you should take the story to him."

"We'll nail this story, Jack. You and me."

Her confidence never seemed to waver. Throughout all the dead ends and *no comments*, she'd kept believing in Jack. He couldn't remember the last time someone had had such faith in him.

He looked at her. Even now, when things were going so badly, her black eyes shone with optimism. And why not? She was twenty-six years old. Life was just beginning for her; it would be years before she learned the tarry taste of disappointment.

At her age, he'd been the same way. After three stellar years at the UW, and that amazing Heisman win, he'd been a first-round draft pick—to a loser team who needed him desperately. Behind an ineffective line, he'd had to run his ass off just to stay alive, but he'd worked hard and played his heart out. Three years later, the Jets picked him up.

That had been the first of his Golden Years.

In the fourth game of his first New York season, the starting quarterback had gotten hurt, and Jack's moment had come. He threw three touchdown passes in that game. By the end of that season, no one remembered the name of the quarterback he'd replaced. *Jumpin' Jack Flash* had been born. Crowds chanted his name; cameras flashed wherever he went. He led his team to back-to-back Super Bowl wins. It was the stuff of which legends were made. For years, he'd been a superstar. A hero.

Then he'd been hit.

Game over. Career ended.

"Jack?" Sally's voice pulled him back into the smoky bar. For a second there, he'd been gone. "What happened to you?"

He sighed. *Here it comes.*

"When I was a little girl—"

Oh, good.

"My dad and I used to watch football together. You were his favorite player. He pointed out every move you made, analyzed every pass you threw. I was eleven when he died—cancer—and when I remember those days, I always think of football. Every day after school, I sat beside his hospital bed. On the weekends we watched the games together. I think it was better than talking." She looked at him. It took her a second to smile. "He always said you were the best quarterback to play the game, and now you're in Portland, Oregon, on the lowest rated newscast in town. What happened?"

It was what they all asked, sooner or later. *How did you lose it all?* He always gave the same answer. "You know I blew out my knee."

She leaned forward, gazed at him earnestly. "There's more to it, isn't there?"

It felt dangerous suddenly, this moment; a slow, conscious skate toward the edge of intimacy. He knew better, of course. Every man his age did, but he'd been lonely for a long, long time, and just now that burden seemed heavier than before. "It started in the hospital."

Amazingly, he told her all of it, how he'd gotten addicted to his pain medications and blown his shot on *Monday Night Football.*

It came back to him like a handful of broken glass, all sharp edges and reflected light. He knew that if he held it too tightly, his hand would bleed, but he couldn't stop himself.

He'd tried so hard to pretend that losing football didn't matter, but the game had been his life. Without it, his days and nights had unfurled like scenes in a silent black-and-white movie. He'd anesthetized himself with pills and booze. His excesses had become legendary. He went from golden boy to party animal. There were huge chunks of time he couldn't even remember.

But he remembered The Accident. It had been late, or early, depending on your perspective, on a cold and snowy night. He shouldn't have been driving, not after a long night spent drinking at the Village Vanguard. But hindsight was twenty-twenty. What he remembered most was the screeching scream of tires and the smell of burning rubber.

"I didn't hurt anyone," he said softly, but that wasn't the point. "My agent kept it out of the papers, but my career was over anyway. After a stint in rehab, the only job I could get was for a local station in Albuquerque. It's been a long, slow climb back."

He looked at Sally and knew that something had changed between them. For the first time, she was seeing beyond Jackson Shore, Football Legend, to the man he was inside.

He tried to look away. Couldn't.

She touched his arm. "This story is going to make both of our careers."

Her touch was like an electrical spark.

He forced himself to look down at the papers spread out between them. He tried to read. Words drifted up to him, meaningless and unconnected. Then he noticed something. "The campus is closing today for winter break."

"I know."

He had to do *something*. Anything was better than sitting here, suddenly aching for a woman he couldn't have. "What do you say we go back, drive around? The administrators and staff will be gone. Maybe someone will talk when the wardens aren't around."

"It's worth a shot."

Jack paid the bill; then they left.

Back on campus, they tried all their usual places, looked for all their previous sources. They made themselves impossible to ignore, easy to find.

Nothing.

Finally, they pulled into the parking lot and sat in the car beneath a bright streetlamp. A silvery rain beaded the windshield.

"I guess that's that," he said at last, reaching for the keys. A glance at the dash clock revealed that it was one in the morning. In a few hours, he'd have to show up for work again.

A knock at the window shocked the hell out of both of them.

Jack rolled down the window. There, sidled close to the door, was a uniformed campus police officer, a man they'd tried to interview earlier. Sally immediately reached for a notepad and flipped to a blank sheet.

"You're lookin' for the dirt on Drew Grayland?" the officer whispered.

"Yeah. We heard he got picked up for drunk driving last Saturday night."

"Nothin' new in that. These athletes get away with murder. I'm sick of it. I've got daughters, you know?"

"Can you confirm that Drew was arrested on Saturday night?"

The officer laughed. "Arrested? I doubt it."

"What's your name?"

"Mark Lundberg."

"Can we quote you on the record?"

The officer shook his head. "I got two kids to feed. I can't take on this fight. But I can't stand by and do nothin' anymore. Here." He slipped a manila envelope through the open window.

Jack glanced down at the envelope. There were no markings on it of any kind. When he looked back outside, Lundberg was gone.

Jack opened the envelope and withdrew the papers, scanning them. "Oh, my God . . ."

"What is it?" Sally asked, her voice spiking up in anticipation.

"Incident reports. Four women have accused Drew of date rape."

"And he's never been arrested?"

He turned to look at her. "Never."

ELIZABETH CHECKED HER TO DO LIST FOR THE FINAL TIME.

> Mail packages
> Pick up dry cleaning
> Stop mail
> Stop milk delivery
> Change batteries in smoke detectors
> Confirm seats

Everything was done. By this time tomorrow, she'd be at her dad's house, with her daughters and family around her, celebrating an old-fashioned Christmas.

After one last obsessive-compulsive pass through the house, she grabbed her purse and headed for the car.

But as she stepped out onto the porch, light spilled down from

the quilted gray sky in flashlight-bright beams. It was what the locals called a "sunbreak." Her yard looked magical in this light, like
a long-forgotten corner of some enchanted forest.

She stared at the cement pavers that ran like Gretel's white
rocks to the edge of the property. They seemed to invite her to
come forward.

Instead, she went to her car.

She made it to Portland in good time. For once, it wasn't raining, and the downtown streets were quiet. She supposed it was
a sad reflection of the times. In years past—especially in the
dot.com years—these streets had been crowded with holiday
shoppers. Last year she'd had to wait almost an hour in the Meier
and Frank wrapping area; this year, there'd been no line at all.

At the station, she parked in the visitor's section of the underground lot and went upstairs to the lobby.

"Hi, Eleanor," she said to the nose-ringed receptionist. "Happy
holidays."

"Hey, Miz Shore. I don't celebrate Christmas—too commer-
cialized—but thanks anyway. Same to you."

Elizabeth restrained a smile. She had never been that passionate and questioning, even in her youth. While some of her
sorority sisters had spent long nights in the B&O Espresso on
Capitol Hill, arguing about the political upheaval in Iran, she'd
quietly immersed herself in painting.

In retrospect, she wished she'd rebelled a little more. A nose-
ring-wearing, tattooed past would probably have done a woman
like her a world of good.

She went upstairs and found Jack's office empty. Glancing
worriedly at her watch, she hurried down to the studio, checked
in, and slipped into the darkened room. There were fewer people
in here than usual—probably a skeleton crew because of the
holidays.

Jack was behind the big desk on set. In full makeup, with the
lights bright on his face, he looked movie-star handsome. As

usual. It was unfair, she thought suddenly, that he'd held on to his youth while hers seemed to be sliding south.

". . . In this exclusive report," he was saying, "Channel 6 has uncovered a number of sexual misconduct allegations made against Panther center, Drew Grayland. In the past two years, four different women have made rape or sexual misconduct reports against Mr. Grayland. Campus officials did not turn these reports over to the Portland police, according to Police Chief Stephen Landis. Olympic University athletic director, Bill Seagel, had no comment today when apprised of the allegations, except to say that to his knowledge no criminal charges had been filed against Grayland. Coach Rivers confirmed that his star center will start against UCLA next week. This story is one we are continuing to follow; we'll bring you live updates as information becomes available."

Jack smiled at the female anchor beside him. They spoke for a second or two, then Jack took off his microphone and stood up. As he crossed the room, he noticed Elizabeth and grinned broadly. He grabbed her hand and led her back to his office, laughing as he kicked the door shut behind them.

"Can you believe it, Birdie? I did it." He laughed. "This is the story I've been working on for the past week. With any luck, the networks will pick it up." He swept her into his arms and lifted her off her feet.

She laughed along with him. No one did success like her husband. It had always been that way. In the good times, Jack was a rushing torrent of water that swept you away.

He loosened his hold, and she slid back down to the floor.

They stared at each other; their smiles slowly faded. After a long, awkward moment, she said, "Are you ready to go?" She glanced down at her watch. "Our plane leaves in two hours."

Jack frowned. "We leave tomorrow."

Son of a bitch. He'd done it again.

She was proud of her control when she said simply, "No. We leave today. December twenty-second."

"Shit."

"Your bags are in the car, don't worry. I packed everything. All you have to do is drive us to the airport."

The door to his office smacked open. A young woman in a gray knit dress and knee-length boots ran into the room. "You're not going to believe this," she said, rushing forward. She got halfway across the room before she realized that Jack wasn't alone. She stopped, smiled pleasantly at Elizabeth. "I'm sorry to interrupt. But this is big news. I'm Sally."

Elizabeth's smile was cinched tight. She was too angry with her husband to be sociable. "Hello, Sally. I believe we met at the station's Labor Day picnic."

"Oh . . . yeah."

Clearly, I made an impression.

"I'm sorry to interrupt, Jack, but I knew you'd want to see this." She handed Jack a sheet of paper. "Three more women filed complaints against Grayland."

"Have they arrested him?"

"Not yet. Coach Rivers said—and I quote: 'In this great land of ours, a man is innocent until proven guilty.' "

"In other words, Drew plays until they shut the prison door on him."

"Exactly. But here's the really great news: I just took a call from one of the girls. She'll talk to you. On camera."

"Meet me in the lobby in thirty minutes. We'll come up with a game plan."

"You got it." With a hurried nod to Elizabeth, Sally left the room. The door banged shut behind her.

Elizabeth looked at her husband. "Let me guess. You're not coming with me."

He took her in his arms. "Come on, baby," he murmured against her ear, "you know how much I need this. Like air."

And your needs are always important, aren't they, Jack?

It pissed her off that she couldn't say it aloud. At what age would she finally learn to speak her mind?

"I'll make it up to you," he promised. "And I'll be at your dad's before Christmas Eve."

His voice was as soft as silk, seductive. She knew he had no doubt at all that he'd get his way. Her acquiescence on all things was expected, a support beam of their sagging marriage.

They were close enough to kiss, but she couldn't imagine any more distance between them. "Mean it, Jackson," she said.

"I do."

The two words reminded her of all their years together. She wondered if he'd chosen them specifically. "Okay, honey. I'll go on ahead."

He kissed her hard and let her go. She stumbled backward, off-balance.

"I love you, Birdie."

She wanted to answer, but couldn't. He didn't seem to notice anyway. His mind had already followed young Sally out the door.

Later, as she walked through the station's empty parking lot, she wondered—and not for the first time—how often could a woman bend before she broke?

ELIZABETH HATED TO FLY ALONE. It made her feel like a stick of licorice in a bowl of rice. Noticeable and wrong.

She didn't say a single word except "thank you" on either of the flights, just kept her nose buried in a romance novel.

At the rental-car agency in Nashville, she chose a sensible midsized white Ford Taurus and filled out the paperwork. Amazingly, she'd never done this before. She'd always stood silently by while Jack did all the writing. Her job had been to keep the documents in a safe place until they turned the car back in.

When everything was finished, she got into the car and drove south.

Each mile driven calmed her nerves.

She was back in her beloved Tennessee, the only place in the world beside Echo Beach that felt like home.

At the Springdale exit, she hit her turn signal and eased the rental car off the freeway.

First, she noticed the changes. Springdale had definitely grown up in the three years since her last visit. The main part of town had migrated east, as if all those glorious old buildings were carriers of some communicable disease. They stood clustered together, a brick-and-mortar enclave huddled around what had once been the only stoplight in town.

Now a four-lane road ran through Springdale, with long, strip malls on either side. A Wal-Mart sat kitty-corner from a Target; foes locked in a discount dogfight in a blue-collar town. There were golden arches and neon Winn-Dixie signs and even a Blockbuster Video store. Everything was decorated red and green for Christmas. Countless signs advertised holiday sales.

But there, tucked on the corner of First and Main, between a sprawling new Kroger and a Cracker Barrel restaurant, was the tavern her daddy had loved. More than once, Elizabeth had dragged him home from there. . . .

Why, darlin', he'd always say in that roaring voice of his, with laughter just below the surface, *it can't be time for supper yet?*

A mile out of town, the road thinned down to two lanes again, and she was back in the place where she'd grown up. On either side of the quiet road, empty tobacco fields stretched to the horizon, broken only by occasional groves of bare trees. A few homesteads presided over it all, the houses hidden from view by carefully planted evergreens. The only signs of progress were dozens of manufactured houses and the billboards that looked down on them. Up ahead, there was a four-way stop. On one of the corners was a tall pole; a rusted orange tractor sat atop it on a metal plate. It had been the landmark entrance to Sojourner Road for as long as anyone could recall.

Elizabeth turned onto the long gravel road that bordered her father's land.

To the right, everything belonged to Edward Rhodes. Acres

and acres of tilled red earth. Soon, the crops would be planted. By July, the corn would be as tall as a man and go on forever. By October, the leaves would be brownish gold and thin as paper, and when the early winter winds came, the rustling stalks would sound like a hive of bees. That was the cycle of the land, the measure of time. Everything in her daddy's world had been tacked to seasons. Things came and went and lived and died according to sunlight.

At last, she came to the driveway. A huge, scrollwork metal arch curved above the road. Swinging gently in the breeze was the copper sign, long since aged to blue-green, that read: SWEETWATER.

Elizabeth eased back on the gas. The car slowed as she drove down the driveway. On either side of her, bare, brown tree limbs reached beseechingly toward the winter-gray sky.

She was home.

The Federal style brick house stood proudly on a manicured yard. Clipped evergreen hedges outlined the perimeter, the perfectly shaped line broken here and there by ancient walnut trees. One of those trees still held the tire swing that had been young Elizabeth's favorite place to play on a sunny summer's day. Beneath it, the ghost of a long-unused footpath remained.

Elizabeth parked in front of the carriage house turned garage and shut down the engine. When she stepped outside, she smelled chimney smoke and wet earth and mulch. She pulled her garment bag out of the car and headed up to the front door, where she rang the bell.

There were a few moments of silence, then the shuffling of feet and a muffled voice.

Daddy opened the door. He wore a blue-checked flannel shirt and a pair of crumpled khaki pants. His white, flyaway hair was Albert Einstein wild, and his smile was big enough to break a girl's heart.

"Sugar beet," he said in that gravelly voice of his. His molasses-thick drawl stretched the words into taffy, *Sugah beeat*. "We didn't expect ya'll for another hour or so. Come on, now, don't stand there a-starin'. Give your old man a hug."

She launched forward. His big arms curled around her, made her feel small again, young. He smelled of her childhood, of pipe smoke and expensive aftershave and peppermint gum.

When she drew back, he touched her face. It had always amazed her that a hand so big could be so gentle. "We missed you something awful." He glanced back down the hallway. "Hurry up, Mother, our little girl is home."

There was an immediate response. Elizabeth heard the gatling gun sound of high heels on marble flooring. Then she smelled flowers—gardenias. Her stepmother's "signature" scent.

Anita came running around the corner, wearing cherry red silk evening pants, stiletto black heels, and an absurdly low cut gold spandex top. Her long, platinum blond hair had been coiled and teased until it sat on top of her head like a dunce cap. When she saw Elizabeth, she let out a little screech and barreled forward like Bette Midler on speed. "Why, Birdie, we didn't expect ya'all so soon." She started forward, as if she were going to hug Elizabeth, but at the last minute, she came to a bumpy stop and sidled up to Daddy. "It's good to have y' home, Birdie. It's been too long."

"Yes, it has."

"Well . . ." Anita's painted smile came and went. One of those awkward pauses fell, the kind that always punctuated Anita and Elizabeth's conversations. "I better check my cider. Daddy, you show our Birdie up to her room."

Elizabeth tried to keep her smile in place. Of all her stepmother's irritating habits (and they were legion), calling her husband "Daddy" was top of the heap.

He grabbed Elizabeth's garment bag and led her upstairs to her old bedroom. It was exactly as it had always been. Pale, lemony walls, honey-oak floors, a big white French Provincial four-poster bed that Daddy had gone all the way to Memphis for, and a white bookcase and desk. Someone—Anita, probably—had lit a candle in here; the room smelled of evergreen. There was still a framed, autographed picture of Davy Jones on the wall by the bureau. It said: *To Liz, love always, Davy.*

Elizabeth had found it at a garage sale out near Russellville one Saturday afternoon. For three years—between seventh and ninth grades—it had been her prized possession. After a while, she'd practically forgotten that it hadn't been signed for her personally.

"So, where's golden boy?" Daddy asked as he hung up her garment bag.

"He broke a big story and needed another day to wrap it up. He'll be here tomorrow."

"Too bad he couldn't fly down with you." He said it slowly, as if he meant to say more, or maybe less.

She couldn't look at him. "Yes."

Her father knew something was wrong between her and Jack. Of course he knew; he'd always seen through her. But he wouldn't push. If there was one thing a Southern family knew how to keep, it was a secret. "Your mother made us some hot cider," he said at last. "Let's go sit on the porch a spell."

"She's not my mother." The response was automatic. The moment she said it, she wished she hadn't. "I'm sorry," she said, gesturing helplessly with her hands.

There were other things she could say, excuses and explanations she'd tried on like ill-fitting sweaters over the years, but in the end, they amounted to empty words, and she and her father knew it. Elizabeth and Anita had never gotten along. Simple as that. It was years too late to change it . . . or to pretend otherwise.

Daddy heaved a big-chested sigh of disappointment, then said, "Walk your old man outside. Tell me about your excitin' life in that heathen Yankee rain forest."

As they'd done a thousand times before, they walked arm-in-arm down the wide, curving mahogany staircase, crossed the black-and-white marble-floored entry, and headed for the kitchen, where the cinnamony scent of hot apple cider beckoned.

Elizabeth steeled herself for another round of stiff, awkwardly polite conversation with her stepmother, but to her relief, the kitchen was empty. Two mugs sat on the pale wooden butcher block. A silver sugar bowl was between them.

"She always remembers your sweet tooth," Daddy said.

Elizabeth nodded. "Go on outside; I'll bring our cider out."

As soon as he started for the door, she poured two cups of cider and carried them outside.

The back porch wasn't really a porch at all; rather, it was a portico-covered square of stone-tiled space. Winter-dead wisteria and jasmine twined the white pillars in veins as thick and gnarled as an old man's arm. Overhead, it hung in sagging, ropy skeins that bowed the massive white beams downward. Now, in the midst of winter, it gave the area a vaguely sinister look, but come spring, when the green shoots exploded along those seemingly dead brown limbs, that same wisteria would turn this back porch into a fragrant bower. Beyond, huddled in darkness, was her mother's garden.

Several black wrought-iron chairs hugged the back of the house. Each one faced the sprawling yard. Elizabeth handed Daddy his cider, then sat down in the chair next to his. The chairs creaked back and forth on runners that had been old ten years ago.

"I'm glad you could make it home this year."

Something about the way he said it bothered her. She looked at him sharply. "Is everything all right? Are you healthy?"

He laughed heartily. "Now, sugar beet, don't try to make me old before my time. I'm fine. Hell, your moth—Anita and I are plannin' to kayak in Costa Rica this spring. There's a place called Cloud Mountain—or some damn thing—that speaks right to m' heart. Next year we're gonna climb up to Machu Picchu. I'm just glad you could make it down here, is all. I miss seein' you and my granddaughters."

"I believe you forgot to mention Jack," she observed dryly.

"Like you keep forgettin' to mention Anita. Hell's bells, honey, I reckon we're too old to be fabricatin' feelings. But as long as you're happy with golden boy, I'm happy with him." He paused, glanced sideways at her. "You *are* happy, aren't you?"

She laughed, but even to her own ears, it was a brittle sound, like glass hitting a tile floor. "Things are great. The house is finally coming together. You'll have to come see us this year. Maybe for the Fourth of July. That's a beautiful month on the coast."

"I've been hearin' about your beautiful coast for two solid years now, but every danged time you call me it's rainin'. And that includes the summer months."

This time Elizabeth's laugh was real. She leaned back in her chair, stared out at the yard that had once seemed so big. The shadowy stalks in Mama's garden glinted in the moonlight. She could hear the snarling rush of the creek down below, almost a river this time of year. Come summer though, it'd be a lazy ribbon of water where dragonflies came to mate.

She remembered another time in this backyard, back when she'd been a little girl. It had been after her mother's funeral. The moment she'd realized that Mama was really gone. Forever.

She'd been sitting in the grass, a kindergartner catching fireflies in a mason jar, listening to the distant buzz of adult conversation. It had been spring—April—and the night air smelled of the honeysuckle and jasmine her mama loved. When everyone had gone home, her father had finally come to her and squatted down. *You want to sleep in my room tonight, sugar beet?*

That was what he'd said to her. Nothing about Mama or grief or the endless sadness that was to come. Just one simple sentence that was the end of one life and the beginning of another.

She remembered how wrecked he'd looked, and how it had frightened her. She'd known loss from the moment they'd told her that Mama had *gone to Heaven*, but it was then, from Daddy, that she'd learned about fear.

As she stared ahead, watching the silvery ghost of a little girl looking at yellow-bright lights in a glass jar, she said, "The moon looked just like this that night."

"What night?"

"Mama's funeral," she said softly, hearing her father's sharply indrawn breath when she mentioned the taboo subject. "I sat out in the backyard all day. I think everyone in the county came out to give me a hug and a kiss."

Daddy planted his big, splayed hands on his pants and pushed to a stand. In the pale blue moonlight, he looked thinner than usual. "I think I'll call it a night." He leaned down, pushed the hair from her eyes in a gesture as familiar as her own reflection, and kissed her forehead. " 'Night, Birdie."

She shouldn't have mentioned Mama. It had always been the surest way to get rid of her father. He was at the screen door by the time she found the courage to say softly, "You never talk about her."

He stopped. The door screeched open. She thought she heard him sigh. "No, I don't."

She knew the end of a conversation when she heard it. The finality in his voice was unmistakable. As usual, she gave in gracefully, knowing how much it hurt him to remember Mama. "Good night, Daddy. Tell Anita I'll see her in the morning."

"Some wounds run deep, Birdie." When he spoke, his voice was as soft as she'd ever heard it. "You'd best remember that."

Then the door banged shut, and she was alone.

FIVE

THE GIRL WHO HAD COME FORWARD—ANDREA KINNEAR—LIVED with two roommates in a small 1930s brick Tudor near the university. A messy brown yard led up to a porch that was littered with empty planter boxes and mismatched chairs. The only holiday decoration was a colorful snowman stuck to the front window. A stack of empty Rainier beer cans formed a pyramid beside the door.

Jack paused at the gate. "Wait here," he said to Kirk, his cameraman, and Sally. "Let me introduce myself first."

Then he faced the house. He'd never done anything like this before, an on-camera interview with the victim of a violent crime, and he was nervous.

Alleged victim.

That was the kind of distinction that mattered in the news biz. Pros like Dan Rather and Bob Costas probably didn't even have to remind themselves of it.

Jack was out of his league here, no doubt about it. But he'd go down in flames before he'd let this story out of his hands. As the old saying went, another reporter would have to pry the notes from Jack's cold, dead fingers.

He walked down the cracked, moss-furred concrete pavers and climbed onto the splintered porch. Sally and Kirk followed him at a respectful distance.

He knocked at the door.

A few moments passed, so many that he started to worry that Andrea had changed her mind. He glanced back at Sally, who shrugged.

Then the door opened. A small, pale young woman with carrot-red hair stood in the opening. She wore a cotton twill skirt, white blouse, and navy blazer.

"Hello, Mr. Shore." She cleared her throat, then added, "I'm Andrea."

"It's nice to meet you, Andrea. Please, call me Jack. And this is my associate, Sally Maloney."

Sally stepped forward. "Hello, Andrea. We spoke on the phone."

"It's nice to meet you."

Andrea stepped back into the house. "Come in."

Jack motioned to the cameraman, who immediately started toward the house.

Andrea led them to a small living room that was crowded with garage-sale furniture. Papers and coffee mugs covered every table. She turned to Jack. "Where would you like me to sit?"

Kirk answered, "How about that chair by the window?"

Andrea sat down, though her body remained stiffly upright, her hands clasped tightly together.

Jack sat down opposite her, on a faded denim ottoman. While the camera was being set up, he looked through his notes for the thousandth time; then he put them aside. "I'm just going to ask you some very straightforward questions, okay? I won't ambush you or anything like that." He frowned. She looked . . . fragile suddenly. "Are you sure you're okay with this?"

Great reporter, Jack. Way to go for the kill.

"It's just . . . humiliating."

Sally moved in close, touched Jack's shoulder, then drew back. It was the signal; they were rolling film now. Jack knew he could stop, introduce her for the camera and officially begin the interview, but he didn't want to interrupt what he'd already started. Instead, he leaned toward her and said, "You have nothing to be ashamed of, Andrea."

She tried to smile. It was heartbreaking to see. "How about stupidity? I didn't even get to know him. I saw him across the room and knew who he was—everyone knew him. I was a cheerleader in high school—Corvallis—and I used to watch him play. He always seemed so . . . perfect. I knew girls came up to him all the time, and I wasn't pretty enough or cool enough, but that night I'd had a few drinks and I was brave. I thought: *maybe*, you know? So, I went up to him and started a conversation. At first, he was so nice. He really looked at me, like I was someone who mattered. When he went over to the keg for a beer, he brought me back one, and when other girls came up to him, he blew them off and stayed with me. The way he smiled at me . . . touched me when he talked . . . it made me feel so special." Her voice cracked. She fingered the gold cross that hung from a delicate chain around her throat.

Jack thought: *You are special, and you shouldn't need a boy to prove it.* It was what he hoped someone would have said to his own daughters.

She let go of the cross, let her hand fall to her lap. Her gaze followed. "After a while, the party started breaking up. Drew—"

"Grayland?"

"Yes. He was telling me a funny story about last week's practice, and when I looked around, I saw that only a few people were still in the room. There was a couple standing by the television, making out. Another few guys were at the keg. Drew leaned over and kissed me. It was so . . . gentlemanly. When he asked me to come up to his room, I said yes." As the admission leaked out, she paled. Her lower lip trembled; she bit down on it. "I shouldn't have done that."

This time Jack couldn't help himself. She was so damned young. "You're nineteen, Andrea. Don't judge yourself too harshly. Trusting someone isn't a crime."

Her gaze found his. It was surprisingly steady. "What he did to me was a crime, though."

"What . . . did he do?" He winced at his own hesitation, hoping they could edit it out.

"At first we were just lying on the bed, kissing, but he started getting aggressive. He held me down so I couldn't move, and his kisses . . . I couldn't breathe. I started pushing him away, but that made him laugh. He grabbed me, hard. I started yelling at him, screaming for him to get off me."

Jack could see how hard she was trying not to cry.

"He hit me once in the face. No one's ever hit me before. It isn't like the movies. It hurt so much I couldn't even cry. And then he was ripping my clothes off, yanking my underwear down. I heard them rip. Then . . . then . . ." When she looked up, her eyes were glazed with tears. "He raped me."

Jack pulled out a handkerchief and handed it to her.

"Thank you," she whispered, wiping her eyes. It was a moment before she went on. "I don't even remember leaving the house. My roommate took me to the emergency room, but we had to wait forever. I finally gave up and went home."

"You didn't see a doctor that night?"

"No. What was the point? I watch lots of lawyer shows on television. I knew people would say I asked for it. I went to his room and followed him onto the bed."

Jack realized that his hands had balled into fists. He softened his voice; it seemed grotesque suddenly, asking these intimate questions for a bit on the six o'clock news. "Did you tell anyone beside your roommate? Your parents, maybe?"

She made a little sound, maybe a sob. "I couldn't. I guess I'll have to tell them tonight. But I went to the campus police the next day. I knew they wouldn't do anything, but I wanted to make sure they knew what he'd done to me."

"What happened?"

"An officer listened to my story, then excused himself and left the room. About fifteen minutes later Bill Seagel came in. He's the Panther athletic director. He laid it all out for me. How I had no proof, no doctor's report, no witnesses. How I could have walked into a wall to get my black eye, and how I'd been drinking. He told me nothing would happen to Drew if I came forward, but my college years would be ruined. So I shut up about it."

"Why did you come forward now?"

"I saw your report on the news." She looked up again. "I wasn't the only one, and they knew that. Those *assholes* knew it. I didn't want him to be able to hurt anyone else."

"So you went to the Portland police."

"It probably won't do any good, you know. I waited too long and did everything wrong. But I feel better. At least I'm not afraid anymore, and I'm not just lying there, taking it. Do you think I did the right thing?"

Jack knew he shouldn't answer. This interview wouldn't be much good if he ruined his credibility by showing that he cared.

But she was sitting there, staring at him through eyes that were heartbreakingly sad. And she was so damned young.

"I have a daughter who is just your age. My Jamie. I pray every day that she is safe at college. But if anything . . . bad ever happened to her, I'd hope she could be as brave as you've been today. You did the right thing."

Was that his voice, all soft and throaty? They'd have to redub his answer for sure. He sounded like he was going to cry, for God's sake.

"Thank you for that."

"Thank you for the interview."

After that, an awkwardness drifted between them. He noticed

suddenly how close he was to her. Their on-air intimacy cracked apart, broke as quickly as it had formed. After that, everything felt uncomfortable. Jack didn't know what to say and Sally remained silent as they all went their separate ways. Kirk was the first to leave, then Jack and Sally said good-bye to Andrea and walked back to their car.

Jack didn't realize until much later, when he and Sally were driving toward the station, how shaken he was. How pissed off. "God *damn* Drew Grayland," he said, thumping his palm against the steering wheel for emphasis.

"How are we supposed to stay detached on something like this? I kept thinking about my little sister. She's a freshman, you know. I warned her about strangers, but what do you say about friends?"

"Hell, don't ask me. I was about as detached as her own father. My career is going to do a swan dive when this airs."

"Anyone who could sit with that girl and not be moved has no right to ask her those questions. She deserved your emotion."

There didn't seem to be much to say after that. He and Sally grabbed a hamburger with fries at the local drive-through restaurant window and ate their dinner on the road. Afterward, they spent the next four hours in the editing room. The poor holiday-crew editor finally threw his hands in the air. "That's it, Jacko. Either it's done or throw the sucker away. I'm goin' home."

Jack glanced at the clock. It was ten P.M. Too late to stop by the news director's house. *Damn.* He'd have to do it first thing in the morning; unfortunately, he was scheduled to fly out at seven A.M.

There was no way he could make that flight.

Elizabeth would kill him.

THE NASHVILLE AIRPORT was quieter than normal for the holidays. Another sad sign of the uncertain times. Since September 11, every potential trip was considered carefully, weighed in importance. More and more people had chosen to stay home.

Elizabeth had arrived almost an hour early, and now she had to bide her time. She browsed through the newsstands and flipped through a magazine that promised her a "YOUNGER, FIRMER STOMACH IN TEN MINUTES A DAY—"

(Yeah, right.)

—and bought the newest Stephen King novel.

Finally, she went to the gate and took a seat in front of the dirty picture window that overlooked the runways.

She tapped her foot nervously on the floor. When she realized what she was doing, she forced herself to sit still.

It was embarrassing. A grown woman this excited to see her children. They'd probably have to lock her up or tie her down by the time she had grandkids.

She had never been one of those women who took her children for granted.

Stephanie had been twelve years old, a seventh grader with budding breasts and gangly legs and braces when Elizabeth had first realized: *Time is running out.* She'd watched her almost teenage daughter flirt with a boy for the first time, and Elizabeth had had to sit down. That was how unsteady it made her. In a split second, on a blistering cold winter morning, she'd glimpsed the fragile impermanence of her family and she'd never been the same since. After that, she'd videotaped every semiprecious moment, so persistently that her family groaned in unison every time she said *hold it!* They knew it meant she was going for the camera.

She heard an announcement come over the speaker and she looked up.

The plane had pulled up to the Jetway ramp.

She stood up but didn't move forward. The girls hated it when she crowded to the front of the line. She'd learned that back in the old ski bus days. Once she'd even—God forbid—dared to walk into the school to meet them.

We're not babies, Mom—Jamie had said impatiently.

Of course, Jamie said almost everything impatiently. Her

younger daughter had been in a hurry from the moment she was born. She'd started walking at nine months, had been talking at two years, and she hadn't slowed down since. She ate life with unapologetic enthusiasm and took as many helpings as she wanted.

"Mom!"

Stephanie emerged from the crowd of passengers. As usual, she was the picture of decorum—pressed khaki pants, white turtleneck, black blazer. Her chestnut-brown hair was pulled off her face and held in place by a black velvet headband. Her makeup was lightly, but perfectly, applied. Even as a child, Stephanie had had an invisible, unshakable grace. Nothing was beyond her grasp. Everything she did, she did well.

Elizabeth ran forward, hugged her daughter fiercely.

"What?" Stephanie said, laughing as she drew back. "No camera to record the auspicious event of our deplaning?"

"Very funny." Elizabeth's throat felt embarrassingly tight. She hoped it didn't ruin her voice. "Where's your sister?"

"There was a seating mix-up. We got separated."

Jamie was the last person off the plane. She stood out from the crowd like some gothic scarecrow. First there was her height, almost six feet, and her hair color—cornsilk blond that fell in a wavy line to her waist. And then there was her outfit. Skintight black leather pants, black shirt that must have sported a dozen silver zippers, and black combat boots. The mascara around her blue eyes was thick as soot.

She pushed through the crowd like a linebacker. "God almighty," she said instead of hello. "That was the worst flight of my life. The child next to me should be institutionalized."

Nothing was ever in between to Jamie; it was either the best or the worst.

She kissed Elizabeth's cheek. "Hi, Mom. You look tired. Where's Dad?"

Elizabeth laughed. "Thanks, honey. Your dad had to stay behind for a day. Some big story."

"Gee, what a shock." Jamie barely paused for a breath and started talking again. "Could they *put* more seats in that plane? I mean, really. When the guy in front of me leaned back, my tray dropped down and almost snapped my jaw off. And you have to be Calista Flockhart to get out of your seat."

Jamie was still talking when they pulled up to the house.

Daddy and Anita must have heard the car drive up (they'd probably been standing at the window for the last thirty minutes, waiting impatiently); they were already on the porch, holding hands, grinning.

Jamie bounded out of the car, hair flying, arms outstretched. She launched into her grandfather's open arms.

Elizabeth and Stephanie gathered the bags together and followed her.

"Stephie," Anita said, teary-eyed, taking her granddaughter in her arms.

After a quick round of *hello-we-missed-you-how-was-your-flight?* they all went inside.

The house smelled like Christmas; fresh-cut evergreen boughs draped the mantel and corkscrewed up the banisters; the cinnamony scent of newly baked pumpkin pies lingered in the air. On every table, vanilla-scented candles burned in cut crystal votive containers. There were artifacts of the girls' childhoods everywhere—clay Christmas trees that leaned like the Tower of Pisa, papier-mâché snowmen covered in glitter and acrylic paint, egg cartons cut into nativity sets.

They spent the rest of the day talking and playing cards, wrapping presents and shaking the packages already under the tree. By midafternoon, Stephanie and Anita had disappeared into the kitchen to make homemade dressing and a bake-ahead vegetable casserole.

Elizabeth stayed in the living room, playing poker for toothpicks with Jamie and Daddy.

"So, missy," Daddy said, puffing on his pipe as he studied his cards. "How're things at Georgetown?"

Jamie shrugged. "Hard."

That surprised Elizabeth. Jamie *never* admitted that anything was difficult, not this child who wanted to climb Everest and publish haiku and swim in the Olympics.

"Jamie?" she said, frowning. "What's wrong at school?"

"Don't lapse into melodrama, Mom. It's just a tough quarter, that's all."

"How's Eric?"

"That is *so* over. I dumped him two weeks ago."

"Oh." Elizabeth felt oddly adrift suddenly, unconnected. Once she'd known every nuance in her daughters' lives; now boyfriends appeared and disappeared without warning. In the other room, the phone rang and was answered. "Are you seeing anyone else?"

"Hell's bells, Birdie. Who gives a rat's hindquarters about boys? How's the swimming, that's what matters. Are we gonna get seats to see you at the next Olympics?"

Jamie had vowed to win Olympic Gold when she was eleven years old. The day she'd won her first race at the Ray Ember Memorial Pool.

"Of course," she answered, smiling brightly.

But there was something wrong with that smile, something off. Before Elizabeth could say anything, Anita walked into the room, heels clacking on the floor. She was holding the cordless phone to her ample breast.

"Birdie, honey, it's Jack."

Elizabeth knew instantly: bad news.

ELIZABETH HADN'T SLEPT WELL. All night, she'd tossed and turned on her side of the bed. Finally, at about five A.M., she gave up, got dressed, and went downstairs.

Jack hadn't been able to get away yesterday.

Of course he hadn't. Something *important* had come up. *The video, honey, it's first rate, but* blah, blah, blah. *I'll be there tomorrow night. I promise.*

Promises were a lot like impressions. The second one didn't count for much.

Elizabeth made herself a cup of tea and stood at the kitchen window, staring out at the falling snow. Then she wandered into the living room to make a fire.

There, sitting on the coffee table was a red cardboard ornament box.

Her father must have left it out for her last night.

She put down her tea and reached for the ornament that was on top. It was a lovely white angel, no bigger than her palm, made of shiny porcelain with silvery fabric wings. Her mother had given it to her on her fourth birthday; the last such present Elizabeth could recall.

Each year, she'd wrapped and unwrapped it with special care, and taken great pains to choose the perfect place for it on the tree. She hadn't taken it with her when she moved out because the angel belonged here, only here, in this house where her mama had lived.

"Hey, Mama," she said quietly, smiling down at the angel in her palm. Once, it had seemed so big. The most important part of the angel was the memory attached to it.

Can I hang up the angel now, Mommy? Can I?

Why, darlin' Birdie, you can do most anything. Here, let me lift you up . . .

She had so few memories of Mama; each one was valuable.

She hung the ornament from the second-highest branch, then plugged in the lights and stood back. The tree looked beautiful, sparkling with white lights and festooned with decades' worth of decoration. Everything from the pipe-cleaner star Jamie had made in kindergarten to the Lalique medallion Daddy had bought at an auction in Dallas. Golden bows adorned the branches.

Anita walked into the room. She wore a frothy pink negligee and Barbie-doll mules. "I had a heck of a hard time finding that box."

Elizabeth turned around. "You left this box out for me?"

"You picture your daddy rootin' around in the attic for a certain box of Christmas ornaments, do you?"

Elizabeth smiled in spite of herself. "I guess not."

Anita sat down on the sofa, curled her feet up underneath her. The puffy pink pom-poms on her slippers disappeared. "I'm sorry Jack couldn't get here yesterday."

Elizabeth turned back to the tree. She didn't want to talk about this. For all her pancake makeup and fiddle-dee-dee-don't-confuse-me airs, Anita sometimes saw things you'd rather she didn't. "He's busy with some big story."

"That's what you said."

There was something in the way she said it, a hesitation maybe, as if she didn't believe the excuse. "Yes, it is," Elizabeth answered curtly.

Anita sighed dramatically.

It was how they'd always communicated, in fits and starts. Ever since Daddy had brought his new wife home.

Elizabeth had been thirteen, a bad age anyway, and worse for her than most.

And Anita Bockner, the beautician from Lick Skillet, Alabama, was the last person she would have chosen to be her stepmother.

This is your new mama, Birdie, he'd announced one day, and that was that.

As if a mother were as replaceable as a battery.

Mama had never been mentioned again in this sprawling white house amid the tobacco and cornfields. No pictures of her graced the mantels or the tables, no stories of her life had ever been spun into a wrap that would warm her lonely daughter.

Anita had tried to mother Elizabeth, but she'd gone about it all wrong. They'd been oil and water from the beginning.

Elizabeth had hoped that time and distance would sand away the rough edges of their relationship, but that wasn't how it worked between them. They'd remained at odds for all these years. For Edward's sake, they'd learned at last to be polite. When things got too personal, one of them always changed the subject. It was Elizabeth's turn. "I hear you and Daddy are going to Costa Rica this spring."

"I'm a fool, that's for sure. I could choose a beach somewhere, with margaritas and pool boys, but *noooo*. I agree to visit a country that's famous for snakes and spiders."

"A lot of women dream of exotic vacations with husbands who love them."

"That's because most women can't remember why they fell in love with their husbands. Without that . . ." Anita let her voice trail off. "You have to work to remember the good things sometimes."

Elizabeth wasn't sure whether this conversation was idle chitchat or not. It didn't matter. Anita's comments were getting too close to the truth. It was bad enough that Elizabeth's marriage had gone stale. She wasn't about to add insult to injury by talking to her stepmother about it. "Did you notice the snow? The back-yard looks beautiful," she said, scouting through the obviously empty box, looking for a not-there ornament.

"Ah, the weather. Always a good topic for us. Yes, Birdie, I saw the snow. Edward thought we'd all go down to the pond tonight."

"I think—"

The doorbell interrupted her. She glanced back at Anita. "Are you expecting anyone?"

Anita shrugged. "Benny, maybe? Sometimes when he has a hot date, he does his deliveries at the crack of dawn."

"Who in the sweet bejesus is that?" came Daddy's voice from upstairs.

Elizabeth went to the front door, opened it.

Jack stood there, looking rumpled and tired. His hair was an adolescent mess. Tiny pink lines crisscrossed his cheeks like an old road map. His blue eyes were narrowed by puffy skin. "Hey, baby," he said, giving her a lopsided grin. "I woke up the news director at midnight and gave him the tape. Then I flew all night. Forgive me?"

Elizabeth smiled up at him. "Just when I think I'm going to trade you in for a newer model, you do something like this."

She let him pull her into his arms, and when he leaned down to kiss her, she kissed him back.

Six

THE FROZEN POND LOOKED LIKE A PANE OF MIRRORED GLASS tucked into a mound of cotton batting. At the silvery edge, a tractor was parked; its engine was running. Two bright headlights shone toward the ice. A boom box played Elvis's "Blue Christmas."

For as long as Elizabeth could recall, ice-skating on this pond had been a Christmas day tradition. In the attic, there were dozens of pairs of skates, some dating back a hundred years.

They always did it the same way: first, a lazy morning of gift opening, then a late afternoon holiday dinner of turkey with all the trimmings, then a pot of hot, mulled wine made in the huge fireplace in the living room. Once they'd transferred the wine to thermoses, they climbed onto the slat-sided, tractor-drawn wagon and rolled through the snow-blanketed pasture toward the wood whose Native American name had been long forgotten. Daddy always attached a string of bells to the back of the wagon.

This pond was magical. Here, when Elizabeth was four years old, her mother had taught her to skate. It was one of her favorite memories. One single day, barely more than an afternoon, but never forgotten. Her Mama had been underdressed and freezing; when she reached down for Elizabeth's hand, her touch had been icy cold. *You just hang on to Mama, darlin'. I won't let you fall.*

Elizabeth had often remembered that promise in the empty years that followed, especially when Anita moved into Sweetwater.

Now she sat on top of the picnic table, wrapped tightly in a multicolored woolen blanket. On the ground beside her, a bonfire crackled and snapped and sent gray ash into the slowly darkening sky.

Out on the ice, Jamie was teaching Jack to skate backward. His ungainly movements and uncharacteristic lack of coordination kept his daughters laughing. When he fell hard, Jamie rushed toward him, made sure he was okay, then immediately broke into a fit of the giggles.

Anita skated toward Jack and helped him up. They skated off together, Adonis and Dolly Parton on ice.

A minute later, Daddy skidded to a stop in front of Elizabeth. "You quit awful early," he said, huffing and puffing. White clouds of breath accompanied his every word.

"I was watching."

"You do too danged much o' that, sugar beet. Now, come on out here and skate with your old man."

She unwrapped the blanket and eased herself off the picnic table. Steady on the blades, she walked to the ice and put her gloved hand in his.

As they'd done a thousand times before, they glided across the ice. Moonlight glittered on the frosted surface. In the background, "Frosty the Snow Man" was playing. For a single, perfect moment, she was a little girl in pigtails again, skating in a puffy pink ski suit that was two sizes too big, while her mama and daddy stood watching from the shore. . . .

"You always were a good skater," Daddy said, sweeping left at the end of the pond. "You were good at a lot of things."

It depressed her, that observation, made her feel old. She thought of the conversation she'd had with Meg: *Let's be martini-honest, here, Birdie. You used to be a lot of things—talented, independent, artistic, intellectual. . . . We all thought you'd be the next Georgia O'Keeffe.*

"Life is short, Elizabeth Anne. When was the last time you traveled someplace exotic? Or scared yourself silly? Or took up some crazy thing, like hang gliding or skydiving?"

They'd had this discussion a dozen times in the past few years. It stung more each time. "I prefer to scare myself in ordinary ways, Daddy. Like letting my children cross the country for college. Why bungee jump when you can put a kindergartner on a school bus? Now, that's *real* terror." She laughed, as if it were a joke.

Daddy twisted Elizabeth around until she was skating backward in front of him. "I'm only gonna say this once, Birdie; then we can pretend I kept quiet if you want." He lowered his voice. "You're missin' out on your own life. It's passin' you by."

The words were a sucker punch that left her breathless. "How do you know that?"

"Just 'cause my glasses are thick as Coke bottles doesn't mean I can't still see my little girl's heart. I hear the way you talk to Jack . . . and the way you don't talk to him. I know an unhappy marriage when I see one."

"Come on, Daddy, you've been married two times, and wildly in love with both of your wives. You can't know about . . ." She shrugged, uncertain of how to proceed. "Whatever it is I'm going through."

"You think I never had my heart broken? Think again, missy. Your mama about killed me."

"Her death broke all our hearts, Daddy. That's not the same thing."

He started to say something, then stopped.

She sensed that he'd been about to reveal something. "Daddy?"

He smiled, and she knew it had flown past them, whatever opportunity had almost existed. As usual, he wouldn't say anything about Mama. "Show me one of those pretty turns Anita taught you." He spun her around and gave her a gentle push.

She pirouetted until she was dizzy. Then, breathing hard, she slowed down. In a lazy, swirling arc, she glided across the ice.

Jack came up beside her, half skating, half walking clumsily. His breath shot out in broken, cloudy white gusts. He grabbed her hand, squeezing hard. "Is this archaic southern ritual almost over? Any more quality traditional time and I'll probably fracture my hip."

Elizabeth couldn't help smiling. There were so few things Jack couldn't do well. Frankly, it was nice to be the accomplished one. "You could stand by the fire."

He glanced in that direction. Edward and Anita were there, cozying up to one another. "And talk to your father? No thanks. Last night he practically called me an alcoholic—while he was sucking down his fourth bourbon-and-soda."

"He doesn't understand what you do for a living, that's all."

"That's not true. He thinks I do nothing. He thought playing football was useless; *talking* about football is even worse."

Jack almost fell; Elizabeth steadied him. "It's what we think that matters."

"I can't wait for you to see the interview I did. What happened was . . . no, wait. Let me start at the beginning. About a week ago . . ."

You're missin' out on your own life.

She wanted to listen to her husband, but her mind kept drifting back to her father's words. It was just another of Jack's look-at-me stories, anyway. She'd heard enough of them to last a lifetime.

Life is short, her dad had said.

She knew it was true. Every motherless child knew that.

But just now, with her husband's voice droning on and on, she couldn't quite grasp hold of that.

Because there was something else, equally true. When you were forty-five years old and *missing out*, it felt as if life were very long indeed.

IN AN ORDINARY YEAR, the week after Christmas was quiet, even dull. A time for boxing up ornaments and taking down decorations, for eating leftover turkey sandwiches and watching old movies on television.

Elizabeth hadn't been back in Echo Beach more than twenty-four hours when she realized that this was not going to be an ordinary year. They'd been in the Nashville airport on December 27 when Jack received the first phone call. She hadn't thought much about it at the time, hadn't understood yet that their life had altered in the past week. While she'd been relaxing with her family in Tennessee, things in Oregon had undergone a subtle shift.

Jack was a hero again.

The Drew Grayland story had broken on the day after Christmas. The next day he'd been arrested, charged with rape. The story immediately went national. The *National Enquirer* ran it as a cover piece.

All across the country, people sat in bars, arguing over the case. What was date rape? When does *no* mean no? Can a woman "ask for it"? Do ordinary rules apply to extraordinary athletes? These questions and others were suddenly on the menus in diners all across America. Radio hosts asked their listeners for opinions; op-ed pieces popped up in newspapers from Portland, Oregon, to Portland, Maine.

From the second Jack and Elizabeth got home, the phone never stopped ringing. Everyone, it seemed, wanted to interview Jack. He'd become a story himself. After all these years in partial obscurity, he was famous again. Not like he'd been in the past, certainly, not a household name, but *somebody*.

It wasn't as if just anybody had broken the Drew Grayland story.

Oh, no. The story had been brought to America by a man who'd once been a god, then stumbled and lost his way. His reemergence into the heat of fame was a story all by itself. Aging, overweight, unhappy men from California to New York saw Jackson Shore's return and thought: *Maybe it could happen to me . . . maybe life could turn around in an instant.*

That was the baton Jack now held: *Never give up.* He'd become the poster boy for redemption.

This new life of his was evident in everything he did. He walked taller, smiled brighter, slept better.

Unfortunately, as he grew, Elizabeth seemed to diminish. She couldn't quite make herself be happy for him, and that shamed her.

She was his wife. Every woman knew the secret handshake that went along with the church ceremony. You had signed on to be a cheerleader whether you'd known it or not, whether you felt like it or not. Supposedly what was good for one of you was good for both.

How could she admit to being jealous of her husband's happiness and success? And if she dared to voice those poisonous thoughts to Jack, he'd be hurt and confused. He'd give her that frowning look—the one he always wore when she tried to talk about their relationship—and say, very matter-of-factly, *Well, Birdie, what is it you want to do?*

She had come to despise that question.

So, instead of telling Jack that she felt lost and more than a little abandoned by his sudden happiness, she ripped the hell out of the dining room.

It had been a perfectly functional, if boring, room before, tucked as it was between the kitchen and living room. Like many of the original cottages built along this part of the coast, the house had begun life as a summer getaway for a rich Portland family. Built for limited, high summer use, it had a big main floor with a

large kitchen and even larger living room, and two small bedrooms upstairs. Over the years, under a variety of owners, the
house had been expanded and remodeled and reshaped. By the
time Jack and Elizabeth had stumbled across it in 1999, the poor
place had become a jumbled mess.

All Jack had been able to see was the cost: a run-down house
with peeling paint and outdated plumbing fixtures . . . bedrooms
that were too small, windows that were too thin, a yard gone bad.
Not to mention the commute. Echo Beach was quite a drive from
Portland.

But Elizabeth had seen past all that, to a beautiful little cottage with a wraparound porch and view to die for. She fell in love
with the pouting lip of land that overlooked a secluded curl of
beach.

For the only time in their marriage, she put her foot down,
and Jack yielded.

She'd started work immediately. In the last two years, she'd
made a remarkable number of changes. By herself, she'd stripped
things down to the good, old-fashioned bones. She'd ripped up
yards of avocado-green shag carpeting and found a beautiful
honey-gold oak floor beneath, which she'd refinished. Then she'd
painstakingly removed the white paint from the river-rock fireplace and pulled up the plastic molding that ran along the base-
boards. She'd scraped fifty years' worth of paint off the kitchen
cabinets and replaced the countertops with exquisite granite tiles.

Because she worked alone, her progress was slow. Although
she'd finished (mostly) the kitchen and living room, she was still a
long way from done. Only last week, the dining room had seemed
to be a low priority, much less important than fixing up the master
suite. After all, the kids were rarely here anymore, and when they
did come home, they were off with friends for dinner. She and
Jack didn't entertain much; it was just too far away for most of his
colleagues to drive.

But last night had changed her outlook. She wasn't even
sure why.

She and Jack had been sitting in the living room, watching television. The phone had rung every fifteen minutes, and he answered every time, talking endlessly about himself and the story.

Elizabeth had heard the resurrection in his voice and it sparked a lot of memories. Few of them were good.

In the early years of their relationship, she'd loved football. Watching him play in college had been thrilling. For an overly protected southern girl who'd been raised to speak softly and only when spoken to, the high-octane world of football had amazed her. Every time Jack won, he brought a dusting of victory and fame home with him. They'd loved each other then, wildly, madly, deeply.

But time had changed that, had changed them. Somewhere along the way—she thought it was when they moved to New York—he'd become a Star, and stars acted differently than ordinary men. They stayed out all night, drinking with their teammates and slept all day, ignoring their wives and children. They slept with other women.

She and Jack had barely made it through those dark and terrible days. What had saved them, ironically, was the end of his fame. When he'd blown his knee out and gotten hooked on drugs, he'd needed Elizabeth again.

Last night, as she'd listened to him talk ad nauseam about himself, she'd glimpsed their future; it was a mirror image of the past.

And suddenly, she'd looked into the dining room and thought, *That wall needs a set of French doors.*

The next morning, after he left for work, she went to the hardware store, bought herself a paper dust mask and a sledgehammer, and got to work. Every time the phone rang, she smashed the sledgehammer into the crumbling wall.

Now, almost eight hours later, she stood back from her work. She was breathing hard, and her arms ached.

A huge, gaping hole showcased the wet, winter-dead garden

beyond. It was, by her precise calculations, exactly the right size for a standard set of French doors.

She scooped up lengths of thick blue plastic sheeting and stapled it across the opening. She'd have to order the doors tomorrow. Hopefully, it wouldn't take too long to get them in stock.

Whistling happily, she went into the kitchen and made dinner. It wasn't much tonight, just a chicken and rice casserole. Truthfully, her hands and arms hurt so badly she could barely open the oven door.

At almost seven o'clock, she heard Jack's car drive up. She couldn't wait to show him what she'd done. He always teased her about how long it took her to make a decision. Well, not today.

She hurried toward the living room.

He was smiling when he walked through the front door.

"Hi," she said, taking his briefcase and coat. "I want to show you—"

"You won't believe what happened to me today," he said. "I tried calling you, but you must have been out."

"I made a couple of trips to the hardware store."

"This was too cool to leave on the message machine. Come here." He looped an arm around her and led her to the sofa. They sat down. He stretched his legs out, planted his feet on the coffee table.

From this angle, she could see through the house to the dining room. A long strip of blue plastic showed. She tapped her foot nervously, waiting for him to notice.

"Guess who called me today?"

She was no good at this game, but it never stopped him from playing it. She glanced at the dining room again. "Just tell me, honey."

"Come on, three guesses."

"Julia Roberts. Muhammad Ali. President Bush."

He laughed. "Close. Larry King's executive producer."

"No kidding?"

"No kidding. He booked me for Tuesday. He bumped some political bigwig to get me scheduled. And it's not one of those via
satellite gigs. I'll be in the studio."

She sat back. "Wow." This was big. She felt a flash of the old
pride in him. "You're on your way now."

Your way. She'd chosen her words badly; they excluded her
somehow, left her behind.

"He's sending two first-class tickets. We'll have a great time.
There's a restaurant I've heard about—Birdie?"

She looked at the dining room, at the gaping hole in the wall.
There was no way she could get it finished in time to go with him,
and she sure as hell couldn't go out of town with the house like
that. There wasn't much crime on the coast, but you still couldn't
be crazy. She tried to think of someone she could call, but all of
her friends had kids and husbands. They couldn't just pick up and
move into this house for a weekend. She supposed she could close
the gap with sheets of plywood—*if* she could find them locally on
such short notice—but in truth, the thought of spending a few
days all alone was pure heaven.

"What is it, honey?"

She pointed toward the dining room. "I knocked out the wall
today."

Frowning, he stood up. As he crossed the room, she knew he
was seeing more and more of the plastic. In the archway that separated the two rooms, he stopped and looked back at her. "What in
the hell?"

"You know I wanted a bigger window there. It overlooks the
garden. Today, I decided on French doors instead."

"Today? You decided today? It takes you seven months to
choose a paint color for the kitchen and twenty-four minutes to
decide to smash out a wall?"

She lifted her hands helplessly, feeling more than a little stupid. "How was I supposed to know Larry King was going to call
you?"

Jack sighed heavily and stepped over the rubble on the floor. Without turning to look at her, he said, "You can't leave the house like this."

She picked her way through the two-by-fours and crumbled bits of Sheetrock on the floor, and came up behind him. Wrapping her arms around his waist, she pressed her cheek to his back. "I'm sorry, Jack."

He turned, took her in his arms. She could see how hard he was trying to be fair. "It's not your fault. I didn't mean to sound like an asshole. You did a lot of hard work here. I'm sure it'll be great."

Why was this always the way of things these days? Nothing came easily anymore, not even a romantic getaway. She ought to *want* to go on this trip with him. In the old days, she would have moved a mountain to make it possible. "It shouldn't be this hard," she said softly, realizing that he'd said the same thing to her only a few weeks before.

"Not tonight, Birdie," he said, drawing back. She knew what he meant. She didn't have the energy for another what's-wrong-with-us discussion, either.

She forced herself to smile. "Well. Let's go figure out what you're going to wear. I might need to get Mrs. Delaney out of bed for a rush dry-cleaning job."

He smiled back, and though it was tired, that smile, it was the effort that mattered. "I was thinking about that navy suit you bought me at the Nordstrom's anniversary sale this summer."

"With the yellow tie and shirt?"

"What do you think?"

What do you think? That was a well too deep to explore; better to keep on the surface of the water. "I think you'll look incredibly handsome."

"I love you, Birdie."

"I know," she said, wishing the emotion came as easily as the words. "I love you, too."

WINTER

Woman must come of age by herself . . .
She must find her true center alone.

—ANNE MORROW LINDBERGH, *GIFT FROM THE SEA*

SEVEN

ON THIS COLD, BLEAK WINTER'S DAY, NOT A GLIMMER OF SUN-light pushed through the heavy gray clouds.

Jack checked into the hotel and went up to his suite. There, he hung up his garment bag and immediately headed for the ornate cherry armoire in the sitting room. He chose a tiny bottle of Chivas Regal from the minibar and poured himself a drink.

The phone rang.

He knew it would be Birdie. She'd always had an uncanny ability to pinpoint the very second he'd arrive in his room. "Hello?"

"Mr. Shore?"

He sat down on the bed. The ice rattled in his glass. "This is Jack Shore."

"I'm Mindy Akin, one of the producers. A car will pick up you and Ms. Maloney tomorrow afternoon at three o'clock."

"Thank you."

You and Ms. Maloney. There was something ominous in that sentence. He wondered—and not for the first time—if it would have been better to come alone.

But Sally had earned this trip. And they'd sent two first-class tickets; it would have been stupid to waste one.

Besides, he wouldn't have invited Sally if Elizabeth had come. So, really, it was his wife's fault that Sally would be staying in a room right down the hall.

He had barely hung up the phone when it rang again.

This time it was Elizabeth. "Hey, honey. How was your flight?"

He leaned back into the stack of pillows and put his feet up on the bed. "You should see my suite, Birdie, you'd love it."

"A suite, huh? Pretty cool, Jack."

He frowned. Amazingly, even on this day of days, she managed to sound unimpressed, a little distant.

God, he was tired of this. Their relationship had become a sea of undercurrents and riptides with no shallow, placid water to be found. "Yeah, it's great."

"The dining room is really shaping up. I can't wait for you to see it."

The house again. Christ. You'd think it was a mansion in Bel Air instead of a redone summer cottage in the butt-crack of nowheresville. "That's great."

"How long will you be there?"

"Two nights. The interview is tomorrow. I'll be home late Wednesday."

"I'm jealous," she said.

She *should* be. She'd had every reason in the world to be here with him. If she'd really wanted to, she could have gotten one of her friends to watch the house.

His second line buzzed. "Just a second, honey. I'm getting another call." He put her on hold and answered line two. It was Sally, saying she'd meet him at the car in an hour. He felt a flash of guilt, as if he'd been caught doing something wrong. But that was crazy; it was simply dinner with a colleague.

"Great." He went back to line one. "Honey?" he said, "I've got to run. I've got dinner reservations."

"I'm proud of you, Jackson," she said softly.

That's what he'd been waiting for—her pride in him—and he hadn't even realized it. "I love you," he said, wanting to mean it with a ferocity that surprised him.

"I love you, too. I'll call you tomorrow after the interview."

"Perfect. Bye, honey."

He hung up the phone and went into the bathroom. By the time he'd taken a shower and dried his hair, he'd finished one drink and poured another. He dressed quickly in a pair of gray slacks and a black Calvin Klein sweater. Then he stood at the window, sipping his drink until it was time to leave.

At seven-thirty, he went downstairs. The limousine was waiting for him. The uniformed driver got out and opened the passenger door. "Good evening, Mr. Shore."

Jack got into the car and settled back into the plush, dark seat. It was only a moment before the door opened again and Sally joined him.

She was stunningly beautiful in a plain black dress with a round collar and barely-there sleeves. Her hair—how was it that he'd never noticed how blond it was, almost white—hung straight down the middle of her back. When she sat down beside him, he couldn't help noticing her legs . . . or the sexy, spike-heeled sandals that Elizabeth wouldn't have worn in the middle of summer, let alone in the middle of winter.

"You look beautiful." He'd meant to say "nice." He tried to loosen his collar. It felt too tight suddenly. "Is the heat on?" he asked the driver.

She leaned toward him. "Here, let me."

He smelled her perfume, and the sweet, citrusy fragrance of her shampoo.

She unbuttoned the top button of his sweater. "There. Now you look a little more hip."

He looked down at her. All he could see were red lips. "I'm too old to be hip," he said, trying to put some distance between them. Years were a natural boundary.

"Henry Kissinger is old. You're . . . experienced."

The shimmering heat of possibility suddenly swirled between them.

He looked at the driver. "Tagliacci Grill," he said. "We've got eight-o'clock reservations."

ELIZABETH WAS EXHAUSTED. She'd spent the last twelve hours working on the dining room. Amazingly, the local hardware store had had a perfectly lovely set of French doors on sale. Someone had ordered them and declined acceptance.

The doors were exactly what Elizabeth wanted, and she got them at a discounted price. The only downside was that she'd had to increase the size of the opening by six inches, then frame the damn thing and figure out how to mount the doors. The whole back-breaking process had taken her hours to do.

Now her shoulders ached and her fingers were cramped up like an old man's, but the new doors were in place. She set down her hammer and tool belt and made herself a cup of tea. Sipping it, she went out onto the porch.

A full moon hung overhead, huge and blue-white against a sil-very sky. From this small, jutting lip of land, the stars seemed near enough to touch. It made Elizabeth feel small and safe; no more important in the great scheme of things than a blade of grass, but no less important, either.

She walked down the porch stairs and stepped out onto the mushy grass of her front yard.

She was about to go back inside when a sound caught her attention.

At first she thought it was the wind, moaning through

the trees. But there was no wind. Turning slowly, she faced the ocean.

Far out to sea, moonlit waves radiated in broken rows away from the shoreline.

She heard it again. A plaintive, elegiac like sound that lingered long after the final note had run out. She knew what it was.

She crossed the front yard, ignoring the way her old work boots sank into the wet soil. She stopped at the edge of the cliff steps.

The rickety stairway snaked thirty feet straight down to a crescent of sand. Caution held her as firmly as any mother's touch. It was dark and the stairs could be slippery, dangerous.

Then she saw them.

Killer whales, at least a dozen of them.

Their fins rose tall and straight out of the water. Each one seemed to cut the moonlight in half.

She held on to the splintery railing and hurried down.

It sounded again, haunting and mournful. A vibrato, humming that wasn't of this world at all; it was a music borne of water, carried by the waves themselves. Out there, a whale breached up from the water and slammed down again; a second later, there was a great whooshing sound, and air and water sprayed up from one of the animal's blowholes.

Elizabeth was mesmerized.

After they were gone, the sea erased all evidence of them. Moonlight shone down on the water as it had before. It would have been easy to wonder if they'd ever been there at all, or if she'd dreamed it.

She wished Jack were here. She would have turned to him, then let him take her in his arms. But he was faraway, with—

Larry King.

"Oh, *shit*."

She'd forgotten to call him.

Forgotten. Worse yet, she hadn't even watched the show. What in the hell was wrong with her?

She ran up the stairs and back into the house.

Nervous excuses cycled through her mind as she dialed the number: *Sorry, honey, I was in a multicar accident. The Jaws of Life just set me free only minutes ago. I ran right to the phone booth.*

I ate something that disagreed with me and lapsed into a coma.

The hotel operator directed the call to Jack's room.

It rang. And rang.

"Get out of bed, Jack," she whispered desperately. She couldn't screw up this badly. She *had* to talk to him tonight. He deserved that at the very least.

The voice mail kicked in. She left a message and hung up. For the next three hours, she called every fifteen minutes, but he never answered.

There was no way Jack could sleep through all those rings. Not even if he'd gotten drunk after the interview.

She knew him too well. Jack *always* answered the phone.

So, where was he?

JACK STOLE THE SHOW.

A few minutes into the interview, Larry had asked him a straightforward question—something like "Are today's athletes good role models, Jack? Should they be?"

Jack had rehearsed his answer to that a dozen times. He'd known exactly what to say, but then, when he'd opened his mouth, he'd spoken from his heart instead.

"You know, Larry," he'd said, "I'm angry. We've taken nineteen-year-old kids and turned them into multimillion-dollar celebrities. We've absolved them of responsibility for everything except performing well in the arena. They drive drunk, we slap their wrist. They rape women, we say the women should have known better. They bite off their opponents' body parts, for God's sake, and a few years later, they're back in the ring, earning millions. When I was in the NFL, the world opened up for me. All I had to do was play well. I was unfaithful to my wife and unavailable to my kids. And you know what? No one blamed me for any of it. Everyone talked about the pressures of being a star quarterback. But life is tough for everyone. It took me fifteen hard years, but I finally learned that I was nothing special. I could throw a ball. Big deal. We have to quit letting our celebrities and our athletes live by their own standard. We need to become a nation of good sports again."

"There are a lot of people who are going to like that answer," Larry had said. "And more than a few who won't."

That was when Jack knew. He hadn't ruined his career by being honest; he'd made it. Bad-boy athletes and team owners would hate him. Fans and parents would love him.

And nothing caused a media sensation like controversy.

By tomorrow, sound bites from his impassioned speech would be replayed from one end of the country to another.

After the show, he'd gone straight to his hotel to call Birdie. There had been no answer. Then he called his daughters. There, too, no answer.

Disappointed, he'd wandered down to the lobby bar and ordered a drink. A double Dewar's on the rocks.

Now, an hour later, he was on his second round.

He drank it down, then stared at the empty glass. Weak light created myriad colors in the melting ice. He'd never been good at being alone, and it was worse at a moment like this. "You shouldn't be alone tonight."

Jack looked up. Sally stood beside him, wearing a clingy blue dress that was held in place by two impossibly skinny shoulder straps. A glittery dark butterfly clip anchored the hair away from her face. Her cleavage was milky white.

She smiled, and it took his breath away.

"Are you going to invite me to sit down?"

"Of course." His voice was thick and raspy. He cleared his throat. "I thought you were off to your aunt's house tonight."

She laughed and sidled into the booth. "A few hours in suburbia is plenty for me. One more anecdote about little Charlie's first tooth would have sent me screaming into a busy street. I mean it's a *tooth*, for God's sake. Everyone gets them. It's not like he wrote a piano concerto."

Jack felt her leg against his. The heat of her body felt so good. He tried to remember the last time Elizabeth had looked at him as if she truly desired him; that memory would form his armor. But he couldn't find it. Elizabeth hadn't reached for him in bed in years. It was easy now to forget how hot their sex used to be. Some fires just went out and left you icy cold.

The waitress came by. Jack looked at Sally. "Margarita on the rocks, no salt, right?"

"You remembered."

He downed his own drink and ordered another. He could practically *hear* the steel girders of his marriage vows weakening. It made a low, grinding noise that sounded like a man's despair.

"You were phenomenal today," she said when they were alone again.

"Thanks."

The waitress came, delivered the drinks and left. Somewhere, a jukebox started. "Time After Time" started to play.

"You'll be a star after tonight."

Her words struck that soft, needy core deep inside him. He felt suddenly as if *he* were the young one and she had all the experience. He couldn't help looking up.

"I know you're married," she whispered. "I don't want to ruin that. I just want to spend a night with you. One night, then we can forget it ever happened. No one ever has to know."

Jack tried to summon Elizabeth's face, but he couldn't remember what she looked like, and he hadn't touched her in so long he couldn't even pretend to recall how she felt. For the first time in forever, he felt wanted. His body ached to give in to desire. "I'd know," he managed to say.

She touched his face, forced him to look at her. "Just a kiss, then," she murmured.

He felt her breath against his mouth, hot and moist. He almost groaned.

"You can say it was a victory kiss."

Now she was even closer. He could smell her perfume and the sweet scent of her shampoo. Her lips brushed his.

"There's nothing wrong with a victory kiss," she said, and he could hear the new harshness in her voice. She wanted him as much as he wanted her. If he reached under the table now, and slid his hand under her dress and into her panties, she'd be wet for him already.

"No," he said softly, groaning at his own weakness. "I have to go." He stood up.

It took everything in him to walk away.

THE NEXT MORNING, Elizabeth was wakened by the phone. She rolled over and answered sleepily. "Hello?"

"Hey, Birdie, rise and shine. Did you watch the show?"

She sat up, pushed a hand through her tangled hair. "Hi, honey." She couldn't tell him she'd forgotten. It would hurt him too much. She tried to manufacture a reasonable excuse.

But he didn't seem to notice her awkward pause. "I did it, baby. You're married to a superstar."

"I've always been married to a star, Jack." She let out a breath. "I knew how good you'd be, Jack. I'm proud of you."

"I need to stay an extra day for some press opportunities. Do you mind?"

"Of course not."

"Great. I'll be home tomorrow, then. We'll celebrate by ourselves, okay?"

"Okay, honey. I love you."

"Love you. Bye."

Slowly, Elizabeth hung up the phone. She hadn't dared to ask him where he'd been last night.

Still, she couldn't help wondering whether he'd been with another woman. It had been years since she'd questioned his fidelity, but he'd stepped onto the old fame track again, and that was where the road had taken them before. Infidelity could be forgiven, but forgetting it was impossible.

Strangely, that wasn't what bothered her the most.

What bothered her was that she didn't really care.

EIGHT

JACK SAT AT HIS DESK, STARING DOWN AT THE NOTES SPREAD OUT in front of him, sipping a double tall mocha.

Over the last few days, the Drew Grayland story had spread like wildfire, and every bit of coverage mentioned Jack. The Larry King interview had pushed him back into the spotlight. He was hot again, but it wasn't enough. Broadcasting was a *what-have-you-done-for-me-lately?* world. Yesterday's news was just that.

He had what he'd wanted for years: a chance. People were watching him again. Now he needed a follow-up story to cement his reputation. Something that would make the networks sit up and take notice.

Last night, as he'd lain in bed, listening to Birdie talk about her new design for the bedroom, he trolled desperately for an idea. About three A.M., it had come to him.

It started with Alex Rodriguez. Seattle had turned on the famous outfielder like a pack of rabid dogs when he'd signed the contract with Texas. As if Alex should have turned down the biggest contract in baseball history.

People didn't understand how fleeting an athlete's professional life was. You were old at thirty, ancient at thirty-five, and that was if your body held up. But how could a body take that kind of punishment year after year and not give out too soon? You had to take the money when it was offered. Tomorrow, there might be no one offering. No current athlete could dare talk about such a thing— they were too rich to be believed. But an aging, once-golden athlete who'd lost his career was perfect.

He looked down at what he'd just written: *Through an athlete's eyes. What it's like to be a breakable god.*

It had the right mix of glamour, corruption, and heartbreak. And Jack knew the subject inside and out.

Suddenly his phone rang. He picked it up. "Jackson Shore."

A voice he hadn't heard in years said, "Hey, Spaghetti-arm, how're they hanging?"

"Warren." Jack leaned back in his chair. "Hell, Butterfingers, I haven't heard from you since the last time you got married and wanted me for your best man. Is that it—are you marrying another one?"

"No, no. Truth is, I had a little scare with my heart. A few nights hooked up to machines in the hospital will sure clear a man's head."

"Are you okay?"

"Better than ever. Turns out it was a friggin' panic attack. Can you believe that? Fourteen years of pro ball and nothing. A few years as a studio analyst and I'm stressed-out. The docs say I need to relax. So, I decided to give up the broadcasting gig. Too much travel and horseshit, but the guys at Fox don't want to let me bow out gracefully. They came up with this idea for a new one-hour show. It's called *Good Sports*. They're picturing a combination of *Real Sports* and *Oprah*, if you can believe that. We'll be looking at athletes in a whole new way, trying to understand the pressures and heartbreaks. And highlighting the role models out there."

"That sounds great. Maybe I could be a guest sometime, you know, talk about the Grayland thing."

"Actually, we want you as more than a guest. They were gonna call you today, but I begged for the chance to be the one. The bigwigs—and me, of course—think you'd be a natural to coanchor with me. I've been trying to get someone in New York to take a chance on you for years. After this Grayland thing, they're finally ready to listen. Think of it, Jacko, it'd be like the old days. We'd be a team again."

"Don't fuck with me, Warren. I'd give my left nut for that job."

"Keep your peanut-sized balls. Just be in New York tomorrow for an interview."

"You're serious?"

"Of course I'm serious. Have your secretary call Bill Campbell at Fox. He'll send you a ticket. Then give my secretary your itinerary. I'll pick you up at the airport."

"I'll get the first flight out. And thanks, Warren. I mean it."

"It's not a sure thing, Jacko. But I know we'll knock 'em dead. See ya tomorrow."

Jack hung up the phone and immediately called home. Elizabeth answered on the second ring.

"Hello?"

"Hey, honey, you won't believe—" He stopped. What if he didn't get the job? He'd disappointed his wife too often in the past. There was no point in building up her hopes for nothing. "I have to go to New York tomorrow. Can you pack me a suitcase?"

"New York? How come?"

He thought fast. "Some hotshot high school quarterback just signed a letter of intent with the Ducks. I gotta interview him."

"Oh, that's odd. How long will you be gone?"

"Two nights. Hey, let's go out for dinner tonight. How about the Stephanie Inn? It's romantic as hell out there."

There was a pause on the other end. "What's going on, Jack?"

"Nothing. We haven't gone out for dinner in too long; that's all," he answered. It was true. He couldn't remember the last time he'd called from the office and made a date with his own wife. But everything was going to be different from now on. He'd move Heaven and Earth to get this job; then he'd return home in triumph. Oh, she'd grumble about moving east, but in the end, she'd do the right thing. This job would finally—*finally*—offer them a second chance. "Everything's great."

And it was. For once, it was.

ELIZABETH STOOD BACK, her arms crossed tightly.

Jack was by the front door, garment bag in hand. Even at this predawn hour, he looked bright and eager, almost boyish.

For a moment, he was so handsome he took her breath away. Strangely, she remembered the first time he'd kissed her. A lifetime ago. They'd been lying on the grass in the Quad, supposedly studying. She hadn't seen the kiss coming, hadn't braced for it, and when his lips touched hers, she'd started inexplicably to cry. She'd known with that one kiss that her life had been upended . . . that she'd love Jackson Shore until the day she died.

It was probably even still true.

But was it enough?

She looked up at him, wondering if he could see the longing in her, if it shone through her eyes. Or if he'd seen that look so often and so long that it had simply become *Elizabeth*. "Maybe I could go with you," she said. It was what she should have said when he went on *Larry King Live*.

His smile faded as he dropped the garment bag and moved toward her. "Not this time, Birdie. I'll be running full speed. I wouldn't be able to spend any time with you."

She nodded, swallowed the lump in her throat. He used to invite her on every business trip, but she'd never wanted to leave her children. It was only later—too late—that she realized what her decision said about the marriage. It was her own fault she'd missed her chance.

"Next time, then. I hate New York, anyway."

He touched her face, gently forced her to lift her chin and meet his gaze.

She put her arms around him and held on tightly, afraid suddenly to let him go. "Be careful," she whispered.

He stepped back. "I'll call you from the Big Apple. I've got a room at the Carlyle. The phone number is on the fridge."

"Okay. Have a good trip. Good luck."

"Winners don't need luck."

She stood there, arms crossed, until long after he was gone.

Somewhere in the house a beam settled; wood creaked. In the living room, the mantel clock chimed five o'clock.

She tried not to think about the endless, narrow hallway of the day before her. It was early; she could go back to bed. But she wouldn't sleep.

She walked into the kitchen, opened her daily calendar, and began to plan her day. She was halfway through her To Do list when she realized it was Thursday.

Passionless women night.

Maybe she'd go. It wasn't as if she had anything better to do.

JACK LIKED EVERYTHING ABOUT FIRST CLASS: the impossibly short line at check-in, the roomy, comfortable gray seats, the clean white trays that held edible food, the drinks that never stopped coming.

Hot towels, sir? Can I get you a brandy for after dinner, Mr. Shore? Can I take your coat for you?

Service was something he'd forgotten existed in air travel until recently. Their family vacations over the last few years had consisted of four people crammed into the el-cheapo package.

He reached under the seat in front for his briefcase. Noticing the scratches and scuffs on the black leather, he wondered if he should have splurged on a new one. He knew what Birdie would say. *You don't get a second chance to make a first impression. Do it right the first time.*

Suddenly he wished he'd told her about the interview. She would have agonized over his clothes choices, matching the right tie with the right shirt. There would have been no question about the briefcase.

It was how she'd helped him prepare for Albuquerque so long ago. *You're a star,* she'd said fiercely, squeezing his shoulders, *and don't you forget it for a second. Channel 2 should fall on its knees at the chance to hire the great Jackson Shore.*

"A star," he murmured, realizing a second too late that he'd spoken aloud. He glanced around, but no one seemed to have noticed.

He could still remember how it felt; that was the hell of it, the thing that had haunted him. When you were on top, you glided rather than walked . . . doors magically opened for you long before you reached for the knob . . . and tables at the best restaurants were held for you. Most of all, he remembered how people looked at you.

"Mr. Shore? The captain has turned on the seat-belt sign. We're about to land."

He shoved his briefcase back under the seat in front of him, then smiled up at the flight attendant. "Thanks."

The plane touched down gently, shuddered a few times, and rolled easily toward the terminal. Within moments, the flight attendant reappeared, holding his garment bag. "Here you go, Mr. Shore. You didn't have a coat, did you?"

He flashed her a smile. "I forgot one. I haven't been back east in a while."

"How could anyone who played for the Jets forget a New York winter?"

She knew who he was. This wasn't ordinary first-class service; she was *flirting* with him.

"I'm from Minneapolis, myself. I've got a two-day layover here . . . at the Warwick Hotel."

Jack heard the shuffling, banging sounds of people deplaning. It all seemed very far away.

All he had to do was nod, say, *I'll be here for the night, too; what a coincidence*, and ask for her name. They could spend tonight in the dark corners of a smoky cocktail lounge, with their legs pressed excitingly close together, making small talk until the time was right to stop talking altogether . . .

For a moment he wanted it—wanted her—so much he felt light-headed. Then he thought about Frank Gifford and took a deep breath. His equilibrium returned. Those days were behind him.

He reached for his garment bag, took it from her. "Thanks. Have a great time in New York."

Her smile started to fall. She reinforced it quickly. "Have a good trip, Mr. Shore."

"You, too." He shouldered his bag and left the plane. At the gate, there was a crowd of people waiting for the next flight.

Warren stood out from the crowd like a two-hundred-year-old Douglas fir in a new-growth forest. He was tall and expensively dressed, but that wasn't what separated him from the others.

The crown of celebrity sat comfortably on Warren's head. He moved forward, grinning. The crowd parted to let him pass. They were pointing at him, whispering among themselves. Jack didn't think Warren even noticed.

"Warlord, how the hell are you?"

"Jumpin' Jack Flash," Warren said loudly enough that people turned to stare. Recognition found its way onto a few older faces. The kids with bleached hair and nose rings moved on, uninterested.

Warren pulled Jack into a bear hug, then clapped an arm around his shoulder and guided him away from the gate. "God, it's good to see you." He kept up a steady stream of we-haven't-seen-each-other-in-years-and-how-have-you-been-and-have-you-seen-the-old-gang conversation as they strode through the terminal, got into Warren's red Viper, and roared onto the expressway.

It was a gray winter's day. Clouds blanketed the expressway, sent a sputtering, drizzling sleet onto the windshield.

"Remember playing in this shit?" Warren said, honking his horn and swerving into the next lane to avoid hitting a Lexus SUV.

Jack grinned. He and Warren had been teammates at the University of Washington in Seattle. He was sure they'd played in the sun—they must have—but he couldn't remember it. What he remembered was playing in Husky Stadium on days when it seemed as if God himself were pissing on the field. "Elizabeth and Mary used to wear Hefty garbage bags to the games, remember?"

Warren laughed. "What I remember about Mary is her tits and that I never shoulda married her."

They'd been a foursome back then: Jack and Elizabeth–Warren and Mary. They'd been inseparable at the UW; then the draft had sent Warren to Denver and Jack to Pittsburgh. After several years and more than a few transfers, he and Warren had been reunited in New York. By that time, Warren had been married to Phyllis, and both he and Jack were superstars in the hectic, crazy world of the NFL. Of them all, only Elizabeth had kept her wits about her in the golden years, when money had flowed through their home like water. She'd saved as much of it as she could, but Jack hadn't made it easy on her. He'd thought fame would last forever.

"How is Birdie?"

"Great. So are the girls. They're both at Georgetown now. Stephanie is still quiet and much too serious. She's dating this whiz-kid who won the Westinghouse Award. Her grades are perfect. She's graduating this June—with a degree in micro something or other."

"Just like her mom, huh? Birdie was the only straight-A student I ever knew."

Jack had forgotten how much his wife loved school. For years after graduation, she'd talked about getting a master's in fine arts, but she'd never done it. Elizabeth was like that; she talked about a lot of things.

"Jamie's like me. If she weren't one of the best swimmers in the country, she'd be fighting like hell to make it through junior college."

"Remember Callaghan's Pub? Throwing back brewskis with the boys."

And picking up girls. At least Warren hadn't said it out loud. Still, silence didn't change the past. Jack had spent a chunk of his youth in that bar, flirting with the endless stream of girls that followed football. Taking them to bed.

And all the while, Elizabeth had been in a ridiculously big house on Long Island, raising their children alone. When he'd finally come home, smelling of booze and smoke and other women's perfume, she'd always pretended not to notice.

How had they made it through those days? And how was it possible that they'd been happier then than they were now?

It was the kind of question that bugged the shit out of him.

"There's the station," Warren said, cocking his head to the left. "We'll meet the head honchos tomorrow for breakfast. Your audition is scheduled for ten-thirty. I'll read with you."

Jack loosened his tie. "Any pointers for your old buddy?"

Warren pulled up in front of the hotel, then turned to Jack. "I saw your interview with that college girl. My only suggestion is to relax a little. You know the camera is like a woman—it can sense fear and desperation—and desperate guys *never* get blow jobs."

Jack laughed. He couldn't remember the last time he'd gotten a blow job. Maybe desperation had been his problem all along.

His door opened. A uniformed man smiled at him. "Welcome to the Carlyle, sir."

Jack got out of the car and handed his bag to the bellman. "Thanks."

Warren leaned across the empty passenger seat. "Do you want to come over for dinner tonight? Beth is a shitty cook, but she makes a dangerous martini."

"I'll pass. I need to get my head on straight for tomorrow."

"You always did go underground before a big game. I'll swing by around eight. We'll have breakfast at the hotel."

"Great. And, Warren—thanks for all of this."

"Don't thank me until they offer you the job. Then I'll take cash." The electric window rolled soundlessly upward.

Jack watched the red Viper roar down the street and skid to a jerking stop at the light. Then he checked into his hotel and went up to his room. The first thing he did was pour himself a drink. It didn't help. He was as jittery as a rookie on game day. All he could think about was how much this chance meant.

Please, God. He glanced down at the phone and knew he should call Birdie, but the thought exhausted him. He'd have to pretend he was in town to see some college athlete—as if—and she'd blather on about sofa fabrics. Neither one of them would really listen to the other.

It had been that way for years. So why was it bothering him so much lately? With a sigh, he picked up the phone and dialed his home number.

On the fourth ring, the answering machine picked up. Birdie's recorded voice said, *Hi, you've reached Jack and Birdie. We're not here but the answering machine is. Leave your message.*

"Hey, honey," he said, "I'm at the Carlyle Hotel, room 501. The number's on the fridge. Call me. I love you."

Those words came automatically, but in the silence that followed, he found himself thinking about what they meant . . . and how long it had been since they were completely true.

He went to his window and stared out at the glittering Manhattan night. A watery, faded reflection of his own face stared back at him. He closed his eyes, and in the sudden darkness, he saw a younger, brighter version of himself. A man still puffed up with the certainty of his own greatness.

That man walked through another time and place, far from here. Seattle.

Dusk, on a cold winter's day . . .

He'd gone to the Delta Delta Gamma sorority house on Forty-fifth Street and been told that Elizabeth Rhodes always spent Sunday evenings in the Arboretum. He'd had no choice but to go looking for her there. Desperation had spurred him; there was nothing more desperate than a college football star with a failing grade.

He'd found her in the marshy trails along the edge of Lake Washington. She'd been painting. At first, all he'd seen was her hair, gilded by the setting sun. She'd had on a blue shetland wool sweater and baggy denim overalls that completely camouflaged her body, a trio of paintbrushes stuck out of her back pocket.

Odd that he remembered that single detail, but there it was. She'd had three brushes.

He still remembered their conversation, almost word for word. . . .

He cleared his throat and said, "Elizabeth Rhodes?"

She spun around so fast, she dropped a paintbrush. "Who are you?"

Her beauty stunned him.

She tented a hand across her face, squinting into the setting sun. He noticed the strand of pearls at her throat, peeking out from beneath a tattered denim collar. "Who are you?"

"Jackson Shore . . . I got your name from Dr. Lindbloom in the English Department. He said you might have room in your tutoring schedule for a new student." He grinned sheepishly. "I'm flunking out of Lit one-oh-one."

A frown pleated her brow. "What year are you?"

"Junior."

"A junior flunking out of a basic English lit class who calls for

help—on a Sunday—in the final week of the quarter." Her ocean-green eyes narrowed. "Let me guess: athlete."

"Football."

The smile she gave him was thin. "Of course. Look—what was your name, Jock?—I'd love to help, but—"

"That's great. Dr. Lindbloom said I could count on you. When can we get together? My final paper is supposed to be a verse in iambic pentameter. Whatever the hell that is. I really need your help."

She sighed and ran a hand through her hair. The movement left streaks of yellow paint across her forehead. "Damn." After a long moment, she said, "I suppose I could meet with you tonight."

"Tonight? Whoa . . . homework on a Sunday night? I don't think so."

He could see that she was trying to remember his name again, and insanely, that turned him on. He was used to women pursuing him, sleeping with him because he was the quarterback, and yet here he was, drawn to this woman who couldn't remember his name. "I'm sorry. You'll have to find someone else." She inclined her head in dismissal and went back to painting.

He took a step toward her. His tennis shoes sank into the wet, marshy grass. "What if I want you?"

She turned around. Staring up at him intently, she tucked a fly-away lock of blond hair behind her ear. That was when he noticed her huge diamond engagement ring. "Look, Jake—"

"Jack." He took another step closer.

She stepped back. "I only take students who really care about their classes."

He closed the last small distance between them. "I need you."

She laughed. "Come on. They don't care if you jocks actually learn anything."

He heard something in her voice that surprised him, a shadow of an accent. Southern, he thought. He liked the rolling, mint-julep sweetness of it. "I care."

She gazed up at him. As the look went on, she started to blush. "Fine. I'll meet you tomorrow morning at Suzzallo. Ten-forty."

"*Aw, not Suzzallo. It's a goddamn morgue in there.*"

"*It's a library.*"

"*How about meeting in the Quad? I could bring coffee?*"

"*It's not a date.*" *She glanced at her watch.* "*Look, I'll be in the room by the water fountain on the second floor of the undergrad library at ten-forty. If you want help, be on time.*"

That had been the beginning.

Jack had fallen in love with Elizabeth fast, and it hadn't taken him long to charm her. In those days, he'd promised her the moon and the stars, vowed to love her forever. He'd meant it, too. Believed in it.

They hadn't done anything wrong, either one of them.

They simply hadn't understood how long forever was.

NINE

ELIZABETH STOOD IN THE MIDDLE OF HER WALK-IN CLOSET, TRY-
ing to decide what to wear. It seemed that everything she owned
was wrong. A row of ornate belts hung from pegs on one wall.

But now, in what she depressingly referred to as the metabolism-
free years, they were useless. Her old belts might wrap around one
thigh. As her weight had blossomed, she'd gone from belts to
scarves. She had dozens of hand-painted silk scarves, designed to
camouflage a bulkier silhouette, but a flowing scarf didn't seem
quite right for the passionless set.

An ankle-length forest-green knit dress caught her eye. Without wasting any more time, she grabbed it and got dressed. At her
bureau drawer, she chose a hand-hammered pewter and abalone
necklace, a relic from her jewelry period.

"There. Done." She didn't look in the mirror again. Instead,
she walked downstairs, got her handbag off the kitchen table, and
left the house.

At the college, she paused momentarily outside the closed classroom door, then went inside.

The faces were familiar this time, and welcoming. Mina, dressed in another floral polyester housedress, stood talking to Fran, who seemed to be listening intently. Cute little Joey, the waitress from the Pig-in-a-Blanket, was talking animatedly to Sarah. Kim stood back at the coffee table, fiddling with a pack of cigarettes.

At Elizabeth's entrance, Joey smiled and made a beeline across the room.

"I didn't think you'd come back," Joey said, taking a bite of bagel, chewing it like a chipmunk.

Elizabeth was surprised that anyone had thought about her at all. "Why not?"

Joey looked pointedly at Elizabeth's left hand. "Big diamond."

Elizabeth glanced down at her wedding ring—a one-and-a-half-carat solitaire on a wide gold band. She didn't know what to say.

"Most of us were dumped. A few, like me, landed on our heads. On concrete floors. From ten stories." Joey grinned. "Fortunately, I bounce."

"All women bounce," Elizabeth answered, surprising herself. "It's either bounce or splat, isn't it? My husband has worked in about eight cities in the past fifteen years. Believe me, I've done my share of bouncing."

"Wow. Military?"

"No." She didn't want to pinpoint his career. The last thing Elizabeth needed was for everyone to know she was married to Jackson Shore. It always sparked a round of how-lucky-you-are conversation, and that definitely wasn't what she needed from these women. But she had to say something. "He has trouble staying focused on one thing."

Joey giggled. "Well, he's got a dick, doesn't he? They're all that way."

At the front of the room, Sarah clapped her hands together. "Good evening, ladies. It's great to see so many familiar faces."

Joey grabbed Elizabeth's arm and led her to side-by-side chairs, where they sat down.

Sarah was in the middle of her opening remarks when Mina popped to her feet. She was smiling so brightly her face was scrunched up like a dried apple. "I drove here!" Her lower lip, made fuller by pink lipstick, trembled. "I can go anywhere now."

The applause was thunderous.

Elizabeth was surprised by how deeply those few words affected her. *I can go anywhere now.*

What a feeling that must be. How was it that she'd never imagined such a thing, though she'd been driving for years? Freedom had always been there for her, available every time she started the car. Available to any woman who dared to look up from the preplanned route and wonder, *Where would that road take me?*

When the applauding died down, the women returned to their seats. This time, because there were no "new" faces, Sarah led the group in a discussion that delved into previously expressed dreams.

Joey was the first to speak. "I took the kids to the dentist yesterday. I just love all that clean space." She sighed. "The dental hygienist just bought a brand-new Volkswagen Bug. Can you believe it? I'd love to drive that car."

"Have you ever thought about becoming a hygienist?" Sarah asked.

"Yeah, right. I barely got through high school. I think my grade point average was a negative number." She tried to smile, then bent down and rifled through the huge diaper bag at her feet. "I did think about *someone's* dreams this week, though. One of my customers left this on the table last week." She pulled out a paintbrush and handed it to Elizabeth. "Is that, like, karma, or what?"

It was a Big K quality paintbrush, probably from a child's

paint-by-number set. A cheap little brush no self-respecting artist would ever use.

So, why did Elizabeth feel like crying?

"Thank you, Joey," she said, taking the brush. When she touched it, her heart did a funny little flop.

"Tell us about your painting," Sarah said.

Elizabeth took a deep breath. "In college, my professors said I had talent. I was accepted into several fine-arts graduate programs."

"Did you go?" Joey asked, her voice hushed with awe.

"No. After the girls were born, there wasn't time. Later, when Jamie started first grade, I tried to go back to my painting, but when I picked up a brush, nothing happened. I just sat there." She looked around at the women's faces. Every one of them understood. Sometimes you missed your chance.

And yet . . . when she looked down at the paintbrush in her hand, something happened. Nothing major, no Voice of God or anything, but *something*.

She remembered suddenly how it had felt to paint. It was like flying . . . soaring.

Suddenly, she couldn't think about anything else.

After the meeting, she parked in her carport and ran for the house. Without bothering to turn on the downstairs lights, she went up to her room. In the back of her closet, she shoved the clothes aside and dropped to her knees.

There it was: a cardboard box filled with old supplies. She pulled it toward her, inhaling the long-forgotten scent of dried paint. On top lay a single sable brush, its fine bristles a glossy chocolate brown. She reached for it, brushed the tender underside of her chin.

Smiling, she got to her feet and walked into the bedroom to the pair of French doors that opened out onto the second-floor balcony. She pressed a finger to the cool glass, staring out at the night-darkened sea.

If there was anywhere she could paint again, it would be here, in the safety of this yard. She closed her eyes, daring for just a moment to imagine a shiny new future.

JACK DROVE SLOWLY down the twisting once-gravel and now-mud road that led to his house. Although Stormwatch Lane ran for almost a half a mile, there were no other dwellings along the way. For most of its distance, the road was bordered on the west by a sheer cliff. Below it lay the windblown Pacific Ocean.

He pulled into the carport and parked, then grabbed his garment bag and headed for the front door.

A single light fixture cast the porch in orangey light. In the corner, an empty Adirondack chair cast a picket-fence shadow on the plank floor.

Inside, the house smelled of the cinnamony candles Elizabeth burned at Christmas. She always said she was going to save them for the holidays, but she never did. She burned them night after night, until the wicks were blobs of charcoal stuck to the bottom of the jar.

"Elizabeth?"

There was no answer.

The front door opened onto a small entry area. To the left was the living room, to the right, the kitchen. Both rooms were empty. He walked down the middle of the house, past the dining room—Had he told her how good the doors looked?—and headed up to their bedroom.

She stood at the French doors, with her back to him. She touched the windowpane with her finger. Light from the bedside lamp made her look almost ethereal. There was a sad wistfulness in her gaze, one he could see even in the pale lamplight.

"A penny for your thoughts," he said.

She spun around. When she saw him, she laughed. "You scared the shit out of me."

"I caught an earlier flight."

She glanced out to sea again. "That was lucky."

Already he'd lost her attention. But his news would get it back. He started to say something, but her voice stopped him.

"It's such a beautiful night. There are so many colors in the darkness. It makes me want to paint again." She turned to look at him, finally. "I went to this meeting tonight, and—"

"I have a surprise." It flashed through his mind that maybe he should do this differently . . . maybe give her the good news after a great dinner at L'Auberge. But he couldn't wait. "Remember Warren Mitchell?"

She sighed softly, then said, "The horniest running back in New York? Of course I remember him. He's what . . . a studio analyst for Fox now?"

"He was. He had a scare with his heart and decided he needed to change his life. When he tried to quit, the guys at Fox offered him a cushy one-hour, once-a-week gig. Sort of a sports talk show."

"God knows we need more men talking about sports."

Jack was taken aback by that. "This will be a whole new kind of show. They've contracted for twenty-six episodes. They'll be filming in the Fox studio in New York, so no more traveling to the games and stuff."

"That's great for Warren."

"And for us."

"Us?"

He grinned. "I'm going to cohost the show."

"What?"

"That's why I really went to New York. To audition."

"You *lied* to me?"

She made it sound worse than it was. "I didn't want to disappoint you again. But this time I got the job. I wowed the network guys, honey. Think of it, we'll start over. It's almost like being young again."

"Young again? What are you talking about?"

"It'll be great, you'll see. Maybe we'll even hook up with some of the old gang. And we'll only be a few hours from D.C. You'll be able to take the train down to see the girls at school."

"A few hours from D.C.? What are you talking about?"

He winced. This was the tricky part. "We have to move to New York."

"*What?*"

Guilt reared its ugly head. "I know I promised this would be the last move, but they offered me so much money you wouldn't believe it. I even got a new agent—a real Jerry Maguire type. Everything can be ours now."

"Everything *you* want, you mean." She was angry; there was no mistaking it. "You don't give two shits about what I want. I've poured my heart and soul into this place."

"It's just a *house*, Birdie. Four goddamned walls with bad plumbing and windows that leak." He moved toward her. "Does this house mean more to you than I do? You know how long I've dreamed about this."

"What do I dream about, Jack?"

"Huh?"

"Good answer. I'm supposed to put your dreams first always. When is it my turn?"

"How in the hell is anybody supposed to know that you even *want* a turn, Birdie? You spend your whole life on the sidelines. You want a turn? Then take a chance like the rest of us, step up to the plate, but don't rain all over me because I have the guts to go after what I want."

The color faded from her cheeks, and he knew he'd gone too far. With Birdie, you could rant and rave and scream; what you couldn't do was get too close to the truth.

She took a step back. "I'll be back. I have to think."

"No, damn it, stay here and talk to me. Don't run away." He knew it wouldn't do any good, though. She always walked out in the middle of a fight and came back later, calmed down. She couldn't stand the intensity of her own emotions.

He touched her chin and forced her to look up at him. "Think about this, Birdie. I've spent two years in the middle of nowhere. I've commuted three hours a day so you could have your dream house. All this time, you've known I was dying here. I did that for *you*." Then he added softly, "I thought you'd be happy for me."

She sighed heavily. "Oh, Jack. Of course you did."

He didn't know what to say to that. In silence, he watched her walk out of their bedroom. He didn't bother following her; he knew there was no point. Instead, he went to the window and waited.

Sure enough, a few moments later, he saw her emerge from the porch. She walked across the darkened yard, toward the prow of their property, where an old, weathered fence ran along the cliff's ragged edge. She stood at the top of the stairs and stared out to sea.

He had no idea what she was thinking. Yet another sign of how far apart they'd drifted.

Finally, she came back into the house. By then, he'd made a fire in the fireplace and put a frozen lasagna into the oven. The house smelled of baking tomatoes and melting cheese.

She hung her down coat on the hall tree in the entry and came into the living room. For an eternity, she stood there, staring at him, her face streaked by dried tears. Very softly, she said, "I suppose we could live in New York again—for a while."

He pulled her into his arms, swinging her around. "I love you, Birdie."

"You'd better."

"It'll be great this time, you'll see. No kids to keep you house-bound, and no job that keeps me out of town." He could see that she was skeptical, but also that she wanted to believe it.

"Okay. But I want to rent out this house, not sell it. This isn't a permanent move. I want that agreed upon, or it's no deal."

"Deal."

"Someday we'll come back here. We'll grow old in this house."

"Agreed."

"And we'll live outside of Manhattan. Maybe Westchester County. I'll start calling realtors on Monday. They should be able to find us a place by summer."

"I start work on Monday."

"What?"

"That was the deal. They want the show to air quickly."

"What in the hell were you thinking?" She pulled away from him. "We can't move by Monday."

"They offered me a contract and I signed it, Birdie. With my past, what was I supposed to do—negotiate?"

"You can't find a decent place to live in New York that quickly. Last time it took us six months."

"We can use their corporate apartment until we find our own place. I'll fly back on Sunday. As soon as you get this place closed up, you can come and pick out your dream house. Money's no object this time." He smiled. "Come on, Birdie, don't look so pissed off. This is an adventure."

"Let me make sure I understand this correctly." She was speaking slowly, as though she thought he'd gone brain-dead. "You have accepted a job without consulting me, accepted use of a corporate apartment I've never seen, arranged for us to move across the country, and, as the cherry on top of this sundae, I get to close up the house by myself."

She made it sound so bad. It hadn't seemed that way to him. Hell, they'd done it this way lots of times. "We'll give it a few years. If we don't like it, we can always come back."

She walked toward the window.

He came up behind her, placed his hands on her tensed shoulders, and kissed the back of her neck. "We were happy in New York, remember?"

"No," she said, "I do not remember being happy in New York."

He shouldn't have said that. Bringing up the past was a bad call. "We'll be happy this time."

"Will we?" There was a wistful quality to her voice that matched his own deep longings. A subtle hope that a new location could return an old emotion.

"It's closer to the girls," he reminded her, knowing it was his best argument. "You could take the train down to see them anytime you wanted."

"That's true."

"Trust me, Birdie, it'll be good for us."

"I'm sure you're right," she said at last, not leaning back against him the way she once would have. She stepped aside. "I guess I'll need to get started. There are a million things to do. We'll have to call the kids. I'll call the movers tomorrow. . . ." Stress made the beautiful southern lilt in her voice more pronounced.

"We'll be happy," he said again. "You'll see."

She sighed heavily. "Of course we will."

FOR THE WHOLE WEEKEND, Elizabeth felt like a death-row inmate with a Monday morning execution date.

Jack, on the other hand, was like a kid at Christmas, so excited that sometimes he broke into laughter for no reason at all. This job represented everything he'd ever wanted.

There was no way Elizabeth could raise her hand, clear her throat, and say, *I don't want to go*.

There was no reason for them not to go. He was right about that. And it *was* an adventure.

It was simply someone else's adventure; Elizabeth was just along for the ride. A companion fare. Buy one get one free.

On this Sunday night, their last together for several weeks, she found herself edging toward depression. Everywhere she looked, she saw something that mattered to her, something she hated to leave behind. This house meant so much to her, more than she could quite express or understand. The thought of leaving it made her sick to her stomach.

After waking up every morning for two years to a picture-postcard view of the Pacific Ocean, how could she waken, go to her window, and see the building across the street? How could she live without seeing the stars at night, or hearing the roar of the sea on a winter's day? How could she live in a place that was never quiet, where millions of people lived stacked to the sky?

Unfortunately, she had no other option. She was Jack's wife.

On their last night together, she set the table with care, using her best dishes and silverware. For dinner, she served *Coquilles Saint-Jacques* on the translucent Haviland china that had belonged to her great-grandmother.

As she and Jack sat across the table from each other, it seemed that miles separated them. They were like some sad scene in a foreign film, a tableau of marital regret, people who had come together in love long ago and become this . . . pale shadows of who they'd once been and paler illustrations of who they wanted to be.

He cocked his head to the left, his fork poised in midair. She knew he was listening to the television in the living room. Howie Long was pitching phones for Radio Shack.

"Maybe someday you'll get to do an idiotic TV commercial, too."

He grinned. "Wouldn't that be great?"

She wanted to smack him. "Yeah, great."

"So, what will you do in New York?"

Nice of you to finally ask. She forced the thought aside and said instead, "I don't know. I would have said gardening, but there isn't a lot of that in the city."

"Maybe you can plant window boxes."

She thought of the garden in her backyard. She'd spent the last eighteen months designing a plan for it. She'd researched exactly what plant went where. Last spring, she'd planted three hundred bulbs. Daffodils, crocuses, hyacinths, lilies. She'd placed each one carefully to maximize seasonal color. "That's a great idea."

After that, they fell silent. When dinner was over, they went into the kitchen and washed the dishes together. Elizabeth rinsed; Jack loaded the dishwasher. It was a routine they'd perfected over the years.

When the counters had been wiped clean, he said, "I'll be right back."

True to his word, he returned momentarily, carrying a big, flat box that was wrapped in iridescent pink paper. He took her hand and led her into the living room. "Come on," he whispered, and she was reminded of the day, all those years ago, when he'd held out his hand and offered her his heart. *There's nothing to be afraid of,* he'd said then; *I'm the one you want.*

He grabbed the remote off the coffee table and muted the television.

She tried not to think about this room, her favorite, as she sat down on the sofa. She'd poured her heart and soul into every square inch. *Don't think about it.*

He knelt in front of her. "I know I threw you a long bomb on this one."

She didn't answer, afraid that if she said much of anything, her anger would show. "Yes," was all she dared.

"I'm sorry."

The apology deflated her, even embarrassed her. She truly wanted to be the kind of woman who welcomed change. At the very least, she wanted to be happy for her husband's success. "I'm sorry, too. I guess I've forgotten how to be adventurous."

"We'll be happier now." The ferocity in his voice surprised her, reminded her that he had been as unhappy lately as she was.

He pushed the package toward her. "I got this for you in New York."

"It's too big to be a diamond," she joked, opening the box. Inside lay a pair of gray sweats and a hooded sweatshirt that read: *Fox Sports.* It was a size medium. Apparently Jack hadn't noticed that she'd paddled into the "large" pond.

"You used to love your college sweats, remember?"

I was nineteen years old. She smiled at him. "Thanks, honey."

He leaned toward her, put his hands on her thighs. "We can do this, Birdie. We can move to New York and start over."

She sat very still, holding in her middle-aged hands the favorite clothes of her teenaged self. He could dream all he wanted. She knew the truth. Things would change for Jack, but not for her. In a few weeks, she'd fly to a new city and settle into her old marriage.

"It'll be great," she said.

"It *will* be." He was grinning now. She could see how relieved he was.

Her anger resurfaced.

He slipped an arm around her and pulled her to her feet. "Let's watch TV in bed. Like the old days."

They climbed into their king-sized sleigh bed and watched *Sex and the City* and *The Practice*.

When the programs were over, Jack turned off the light and rolled onto his side.

"I love you, Birdie," he said, kissing her. His hand moved down her back and pushed up beneath her flannel nightgown, coming to rest on her naked thigh.

She kissed him back. They made love in the quiet, familiar way that had evolved over the last decade. When it was done, he rolled away from her and went to sleep.

Elizabeth inched away from him. She laid her head on her pillow and listened to the ordinary rhythm of his breathing. She couldn't help but remember how wonderful their lovemaking used to be. For years, even as the marriage had begun to go stale, their passion for each other had remained. Now, even that spark had gone out.

Still . . . they'd been married so long. More than half of her life had been spent with Jack. She'd thought they'd grow old together in this house. Foolishly, she'd believed his promise to live here forever.

Even last week, when she'd looked into her own future, she'd seen them on the porch together, white-haired and smiling, sitting on the wrought-iron garden bench, watching their great-grandchildren play.

Now when she looked into their future, she couldn't see anything at all.

TEN

*J*ACK WALKED UP BROADWAY, ELBOWING HIS WAY THROUGH THE crowd. He'd been in New York two weeks, and already he felt like a local.

It had always been one of his favorite cities. As a boy, growing up in the small, depressed logging town of Aberdeen, Washington, watching his parents work themselves into early graves, he'd had two dreams—one was to play football in the NFL, the other was to live in a city full of lights-camera-action. He'd always longed to be a big fish in the biggest pond, and now, after fifteen anonymous, wasteland years, he was BACK.

Fox's corporate apartment was right in the thick of it all: Midtown. It was a killer location, with great restaurants on every block. If you had a craving for a Krispy Kreme doughnut at three o'clock in the morning, by God, there was a way to get one. He loved everything about this city, but mostly, he loved that in only two weeks he'd become *someone* again.

It was only going to get better. The show, *Good Sports*, hadn't aired yet, but the industry talk was already hot, and in television, buzz was the Holy Grail. Fox had been running an endless series of We've-Got-Jumpin'-Jack-Flash-and-Warlord-together-again pro- motions. Their faces were everywhere, on billboards, on bus- boards, on commercials.

It would gather steam, Jack knew. The celebrity thing always did. It was like the old commercial: she told two friends . . . and he told two friends . . . and the next thing you knew they were saving you a corner table at Le Cirque.

He turned onto Fiftieth Street and headed home. Funny how he already thought of it that way. An impersonal one-bedroom apartment with a kitchen smaller than most bathrooms, and it was home.

A doorman let him into the building. He walked through the narrow, marble-floored lobby to the elevator. On the twenty- fourth floor, he got out.

Inside the apartment, everything was exactly as he'd left it. There was a half-empty bottle of beer on the kitchen counter, and the latest *Sports Illustrated* lay open on the coffee table. In his ab- sence, no one had come along and tidied up after him. He could pick up reading right where he'd left off.

He walked past the shadowy minikitchen. In his bedroom, he kicked off his shoes. One hit the wall with a thunk; the other tumbled across the creamy berber carpet and disappeared under the unmade bed.

He sat down on the twisted pile of white sheets and blankets. He hadn't made the bed since he'd moved in. That was only one of the changes Elizabeth would make.

Elizabeth.

He flicked on the bedside lamp and saw the apartment through her eyes. It wouldn't be good, her reaction to these tiny rooms. Birdie, who loved color and texture and art, would label this place boring. She'd immediately begin a frenzied search for "the" place to call home. The thought of it exhausted him.

He loved her, but lately, it was easier to be apart. It made him feel like a real shit, that admission, but there was no reason to lie. Not here, sitting on this bed that was big enough for two but had been damned comfortable for one.

Here he was at last, poised on the ledge of everything he'd ever wanted. The city, the money, the fame.

But his dream wouldn't match hers. Whatever it was that she longed for—the "turn" she whined about (and he had no idea what that was)—she wouldn't find it in a one-bedroom apartment with a bathroom too small for a towel rack. Her window box would have to be the size of a TV dinner, and she'd rather look down on a toxic waste site than a busy street.

She'd want to live in an established suburban neighborhood, maybe in Connecticut or Westchester County, in a traditional house with a yard big enough to hold her precious roses and a living room capable of displaying all her carefully chosen furniture.

But he'd done it her way.

He'd spent two years in that godforsaken soggy rain forest, miles away from anyone who mattered. He'd done it because it was her "turn" to have the house of her dreams, but had she really thought they'd live there forever? Hell, the only place in the United States with worse year-round weather was Barrow, Alaska.

When he'd lost football and kicked the drug habit, he'd tried to settle onto the responsible adult track. He'd lived in respectable houses in good school districts in towns so far from the limelight they were pitch dark by eight o'clock at night. No more.

Now it was his turn.

His stomach grumbled loudly, reminding him that he hadn't eaten since breakfast. Without bothering to check the fridge, he grabbed his coat.

Outside, the streets were busy. He ducked into one of his favorite new haunts, a bar-and-grill that boasted a big-screen television and all-you-could-eat buffalo wings on game nights.

He waved at the bartender and settled into a booth in the back. When the waitress came to his table, he ordered a beer and a cheeseburger. Within minutes, she was back with his beer.

He was reaching for a napkin when a woman scooted into the seat opposite him.

"Can I sit with you a second?"

He was so surprised he couldn't do anything but nod.

She looked incredibly out of place in the bar. She was wearing a flesh-colored floor-length strapless gown that tucked in at her tiny waist. A huge white silk flower was pinned between her breasts. She looked like an extra on *Sex and the City*.

She gave him a tired smile and raised her hand. When the bartender saw her, she yelled out, "Double tequila straight shot with a Budweiser back. Patron tequila, please." She grinned at him. "Thank Jesus there was a bar nearby."

She was beautiful, and young. Maybe late twenties.

"I'm Jack," he said.

She plopped a glittery designer handbag on the table and scouted through it, finally finding her cigarettes. When she lit up, he smelled cloves. "I'm Amanda." She looked at him, exhaled. "I know you. You're the new guy over at Fox Sports, right? They're spending a buttload to promote you and Warren. I work at BBDO, by the way. Sports ads are my life."

"Really?"

"You're better looking in person. I guess you hear that all the time."

He tried not to be pleased, but the compliment poured through him like a restorative.

"You're probably wondering why I'm wearing this ridiculous dress. My sister just got married. I was in the wedding."

The bartender came over and set her drinks on the scarred table between them. He looked at Jack. "You want another one?"

Jack noticed that he'd drained his glass already. When had he done that? "Sure."

"You got it."

Amanda picked up the first shot glass and drank the tequila in one head-thrown-back swallow. Then she drank the second one, slammed her flat palm on the table and giggled. "Yee-*ha*. I needed that." She looked at him, smiling brightly. "I'm not an alcoholic, not even of the Bridget Jones variety, but this wedding has been a nightmare. My sister, who is all of twenty-four, by the way, has snagged herself one of those Ferrari-drivin', TriBeCa-livin' dot.com boys. And I have to show up at the wedding without a date. You'd think with eight months' notice, I could at least find one man worth spending the evening with but *noooo*. I have to show up alone and hear every white-haired lady in the place say, 'So, Amanda, when will we be coming to your wedding?' Christ." She looked at him. "You'd certainly shut the old biddies up."

He had no idea what she was talking about, so he smiled politely and nodded.

She grinned, leaning forward. "Will you do it?"

"Do what?"

"Come to the reception with me. It's at the Marriott. We could have a few free drinks, eat some of the food that's costing my dad more money than a trip to Greece. There's a *great* band."

He leaned back, trying suddenly to put distance between them.

She looked down at the ring on his finger. "It wouldn't be a date. Really. Just a fun night out."

Promise me, Elizabeth had said to him only two weeks ago, *promise me you won't become the man you were before.*

"You'd be saving me. Really." She raised her hand to signal the bartender that she was ready to pay; then she stood up and reached for his hand.

At the last second, he drew back. If he touched her, he might weaken, and it was weakness that had sent him down that forbidden road so many years ago. "I can't do it," he said softly. "I'm sorry."

She stood there a minute, looking down at him. Finally, she smiled. "She's a lucky woman. Well, wish me luck. I'm back into the fray."

After she left, Jack looked down and saw that his hands were trembling. He felt like a man who'd swerved just in time to avoid a head-on collision.

ELIZABETH LOOKED DOWN at her list. After two weeks of working like a dog, she was nearing the end. Only the kitchen remained unpacked.

She stood in the empty living room. Gone were the beautiful striped chairs she'd re-covered herself, and the down-filled blue-and-yellow toile sofa. Gone, too, were the family photographs that used to line every available surface. Most of them had been put in storage; a few, the ones she couldn't live without, had been shipped to Jack in New York.

In place of her many treasures stood cardboard boxes. Dozens of them, each one marked with a title she'd chosen carefully. In two days, the movers she'd hired would come for this final load, truck them over to the storage facility, and it would be time to go.

She released her breath slowly. It was better not to think about that. If she looked too far ahead, she lost strength.

It was just a house, after all. She reminded herself of that at least fifty times a day.

She had spoken to Jack daily since he'd left. He sounded happier than he'd been in years. He adored his new job. Each time she hung up, she found herself praying, *Please, God, let me find that again, too . . . let us find it.*

At four-thirty, the doorbell rang. She'd been expecting it, but still she jumped at the noise.

I'm not ready yet.

Not that she had a choice. She squared her shoulders, smoothed her wrinkled clothes, and went to the door.

Sharon Solin stood on the porch, with her arms pressed close to her sides. She wore a blackwatch plaid skirt and a navy scoop-necked angora sweater. Elizabeth was reminded of *Love Story*— Jenny Cavilleri doing her first walk-through of a potential rental house.

"Mrs. Shore?" she said, extending her hand. "I'm Sharon Solin."

"Call me Elizabeth, please. Come in."

"It's beautiful," Sharon said when she stepped inside.

Elizabeth had no trouble seeing it through Sharon's eyes. The living room was bright, with butter yellow walls and glossy white crown molding. A pair of oversized windows let in a glorious amount of sunlight, even on this dreary winter's day. The oak floors, stripped and refinished by her own hand, seemed to capture all that golden light.

Sharon turned into the kitchen, exclaimed over the beautiful white cabinetry and granite countertops. She loved the old-fashioned stove. In the dining room, she raved over the beautiful view.

Elizabeth managed to keep up a steady stream of inane conversation as they walked through the kitchen, past the guest bathroom, and up the stairs. She tossed out bits and pieces of her life—My husband has been transferred. . . . We've lived in this house for a little over two years. . . . It was a wreck when we moved in. . . . The previous owners had really let it go. . . . I never got around to finishing the bedrooms, but I picked out the colors. . . . I started planting the garden last spring. . . .

It wasn't until the end of the tour that she cracked. She should have seen it coming, but she'd missed the signs. Instead, she blundered into her bedroom and saw that view.

The room's French doors—the very first addition she'd made to the house—were flanked on either side by floor-to-ceiling windows. Pretty pine molding framed the expansive view.

The ocean stretched from one end of the room to the other in a kaleidoscope of blues. Today, the sky looked gray, but Elizabeth knew that if you looked closely, you'd see a dozen other colors. On the balcony beyond, a pair of white Adirondack chairs glistened with rainwater. A huge, intricate spiderweb connected the chairs. Beaded by raindrops, it looked like a Swarovski crystal necklace.

"It's beautiful," Sharon said, walking over to the window. "It must be magical to wake up to that view."

Last year, Elizabeth had injured her shoulder, and that was how she felt now, as if some muscle in her body was tearing away from the bone. She smiled—too brightly perhaps, but Sharon couldn't know that. "Yes, it was. Well, I'll let you alone for a while. I told you all the terms on the phone, and I have your credit application filled out. I'll be downstairs if you have any questions."

"Thanks."

Elizabeth went downstairs. She was in the living room, trying to remember if she'd packed the aspirin, when the doorbell rang. Before she'd even reached the door, it swung open.

Meghann stood there, grinning, holding a pizza box in one hand and a bottle of wine in the other. "I sensed your cry for help and brought the preferred tranquilizer for the suburban housewife set."

Elizabeth had never been so happy to see a friend. "I love you, Meg."

Footsteps pattered down the stairs.

"Potential renter," Elizabeth said, turning just as Sharon came into the room.

Sharon smiled nervously. "I'd like my husband to see it, if that's all right. He really wanted to buy something, but we can't afford much. I'd rather rent a wonderful place like this than own a dump."

"Certainly. I'll be here for two more days. Give me a call and we'll set up a time for him to do a walk-through."

"I wouldn't want to lose it, but I know he'll want to see it for himself."

Elizabeth understood perfectly; it was exactly the kind of thing she would have said. She had a sudden urge to warn Sharon, to let her know how easy it was to get lost in marriage. It started simply, too, in a decision that couldn't be made alone. "Don't worry. I haven't gotten a ton of calls. There aren't a lot of people who want to live this far out of the way."

Sharon moved forward. "It must be difficult to leave this home. You've obviously loved it."

Elizabeth's composure wavered. "Thank you for coming by. I'll look forward to hearing from you." She led Sharon to the door and said good-bye.

"My God," Meg said when she was gone, "she's a *child*. Is that what's happening out there now—children are renting oceanfront houses?"

"Careful—you sound like a senior citizen. Now, open that wine before I scream."

"That's why I'm here, Birdie. So you can scream."

"Open the wine."

Meghann went into the kitchen, grabbed two glasses, and poured the wine. She handed a glass to Elizabeth. "Did you and Jack ever have that talk?"

Elizabeth sat down cross-legged on the hardwood floor in front of the cold fireplace. Scooting backward, she leaned against a packing box. She didn't see the point in talking about this, but that was the problem with confession. Once you shared a problem with a friend, you had to keep talking about it forever. And if your best friend was a lawyer, well, in the immortal words of Tony Soprano, *fuggedaboudit*. She nodded. "In our way."

"He's unhappy, too?"

"Not since he got this job. He's like a parolee with money in his pocket. Supposedly, this job—and New York—will change everything for us."

"Maybe it will."

"Yeah, maybe."

Meg stared at Elizabeth over the rim of her glass. "Did the support group help?"

"They think I should try painting again."

"I've been saying the same thing for years."

Elizabeth sighed. She really didn't want to have this conversation now, with boxes all around them and the move looming overhead. "It's not like riding a bike, Meg. You can't just jump on and ride away. Art needs . . . fire, and I'm cold."

Meghann studied her. "Maybe Jack is right. Maybe New York is a good answer. You're sure as hell stuck in a mud-rut here."

"Let's talk about something fun. Tell me about your life. Who's the new guy?"

"What makes you think there's a new one?"

"Every year you make a New Year's resolution to quit dating children, so for a few months, you date men without hair."

Meghann laughed. "Jesus, that's pathetic. But as it happens, I'm dating a very nice accountant. It can't last, of course. You know I never date a successful man for long. It jeopardizes my professional standing as a loser magnet."

"I hate it when you talk about yourself that way."

"We're a fine pair, aren't we? One has no guts; the other has no hope. No wonder we're best friends." Meghann lifted her glass in a silent toast. "I'm going to miss you, Birdie."

"I guess we'll have to go back to the Thursday night phone call. We did that for a lot of years."

"Yeah."

"It'll be fine. We'll still talk all the time."

But they both knew it wouldn't be the same.

ELEVEN

IN THE LAST WEEK OF JANUARY, THE WEATHER TURNED BITTERLY cold. The sky gave up all trace of blue and hunkered down as if for battle. Trees shivered along the shoreline, waited for the freezing rain to turn to snow.

Elizabeth made her last trip to town. The two-lane coastal highway curled lazily along the rim of the cliff. To her left lay the mighty Pacific, on the right, a wall of old-growth forest whose trees were among the biggest in the world. Locals claimed that herds of mighty elk lived in those woods, and when you looked into all that black and green darkness, it was easy to believe.

The road took its last hairpin curve, then rolled down to the ocean.

WELCOME TO ECHO BEACH, WHERE GOD ANSWERS BACK, read the sign on her left.

Downtown ran for exactly four blocks. There were no stoplights to slow you down, no sprawling resorts or chain restaurants.

The nearest four-star hotel was the Stephanie Inn, miles down the coast.

Old-fashioned streetlamps stood at regular intervals along the cobblestone sidewalks. The storefronts had beautiful leaded windows and arched doorways. Shingles were on every exterior wall, their wooden surfaces aged to the color of ash. The only signs were handwrought, of wood or iron, and they hung discreetly beside the closed doors.

Even the names were different here. The Tee-it-up Sportswear Shop; the Take a Hike Shoe Store; the Hair We Are Beauty Salon. There were countless gift shops and restaurants and ice cream parlors. Brown, leafless vines of sleeping clematis and wisteria climbed along the fence that separated town from the old-fashioned beach promenade.

Elizabeth parked on the street in front of the Beachcomber restaurant (all you can eat on Thursday nights!) and ran her last few errands. She dropped off a box of clothes and paperback novels at the local Helpline House, alerted the post office to her change of address, picked up her airline tickets, and reminded the local sheriff that the house would be empty until renters were found (John Solin had been too busy to schedule a viewing, but Sharon was still hopeful).

Her last stop was the library. She dropped off a box of canned goods for the local food drive, then headed back to her car. She was halfway across the street when the rain stopped.

The clouds parted suddenly; a shaft of pure yellow sunlight spilled over the street. Rainwater glistened on the pavement. The misty fog lifted itself, revealing the ocean.

A breeze fluttered through town, kicking up wet leaves. In it, she smelled the salty tang of the water and the barest hint of beach grass.

She crossed the empty street and came to the promenade. The wide path was paved in pink-colored stone; on either side of it, evergreen boxwood had been trimmed to a perfectly square hedge. Every few feet there was a lovely iron bench. The one beside her had a plaque that read: IN MEMORY OF ESTHER HAYES. Old-fashioned ironwork streetlamps had been carefully placed at regular intervals along the walkway. It was easy to imagine Gatsby and Daisy strolling along this promenade in their white finery while children in oversized bathing suits ran giggling across the sand.

Elizabeth stepped down onto the sand. Seagulls circled overhead, cawing out at her, diving in close every now and then to see if she was a tourist with food to spare.

The beach stretched out in front of her, miles of gray, wind-sculpted sand. Gigantic black rocks rose from the shallow water like leviathan shark fins. Waves tumbled lazily forward, licking playfully along the shore.

She walked along the beach, enjoying the feel of the breeze on her face. In a secluded cove, she sat down on a flat black rock. Behind her, beach grass swayed in the breeze.

Just looking at it soothed her nerves.

She was no one out here; maybe that was the attraction. Not Mrs. Jackson Shore, not Jamie and Stephanie's mother, not Edward Rhodes's little girl.

She drew in a deep breath and released it slowly. The air smelled of sand and kelp and sea. For the first time in weeks, maybe longer, she could breathe.

She hadn't understood until just now, this very moment, that she'd been breathing badly lately. Holding her breath. Sighing heavily. Tension and unhappiness had stolen this simple gift.

But the clock was ticking. Tomorrow morning, she'd have to board a plane and fly east toward a city that had frightened her in the best of times—and these were far from the best of times in New York.

Once there, she'd have to move into an apartment she hadn't chosen and sleep beside a husband she'd forgotten how to love.

HER LAST DAY IN ECHO BEACH dawned surprisingly bright and clear. The ever-present clouds had scraped clean the sky, left it a tender, hesitant blue.

She woke early—she'd hardly gone to sleep, it seemed, when the alarm rang—took a shower and got ready to go. She called the local taxicab and made arrangements to be picked up in an hour, then dragged her luggage out onto the porch.

She slipped off her loafers and put on the gardening clogs that were always by the door, then walked across her yard toward the cliff.

On the beach below, frothy white foam coughed onto the sand, then drew back, leaving its faded impression behind. Nothing—and no one—made a lasting mark on the beach.

She should have remembered that.

Crossing her arms at the cold, she turned and looked back at the house. *Her* house.

Now, with the sunlight hitting the white-shingled sides, it seemed to belong in Middle Earth, an enchanted cottage tucked between a green hillside and the gray ocean.

She tried not to think about the garden, and all the plans she'd had for it. . . .

It felt as if she'd been standing there a minute or two, but suddenly the cab was pulling into her driveway.

She whispered, "Good-bye, house," and went to get her bags.

By the time she reached the airport, she was breathing badly again.

THE TRIP FROM PORTLAND to New York City was like climbing Mount Everest without oxygen. It went on and on, and by the time you reached your destination, there was no sensation left in your extremities. First, there was a flight to Seattle, then on to Detroit, and finally a landing at Kennedy Airport. All that paled in comparison to the cab ride into Midtown.

By the time the taxi pulled over to the curb, Elizabeth's back was screaming in pain.

She paid the cabdriver and hurried into the building, barely nodding to the doorman. There would be time for introductions later, when she wasn't in desperate need of chiropractic care and an Excedrin.

Clutching the key Jack had sent her, she rode the elevator up to the twenty-fourth floor and found his apartment.

"Jack?"

There was no answer.

She glanced down at her watch. "Jack?"

It was only six-fifteen. He should be home in the next thirty minutes.

She set her purse down on the floor and looked around. The apartment was as elegantly impersonal as an expensive hotel room. A narrow hallway led past a tiny kitchen and into a moderate-size living room. There wasn't a personal touch anywhere. The floors were tiled in a creamy, brown-veined marble; the sofa was a sleek contemporary design, covered in taupe damask. Against either arm were glass end tables that held crystal column lamps. The coffee table was so cluttered with magazines and beer cans that she could barely see it. There were no pictures on the wall and no knickknacks on any surface.

In the corner by the window, a big black velour Barcalounger looked incredibly out of place. When she saw it, she remembered Jack's phone call last week: *I got a great piece of furniture last week from Warren. You'll love it.* She'd asked for a description and been told that it was a surprise. *But I'm sitting in it,* he'd added with a laugh.

"Nice choice, Jack," she muttered, walking toward the chair.

It had a drink-holder built into the puffy, quilted arm.

Built in.

She sat down in the chair. A footrest immediately jerked upward and tossed her into a fully reclined position. When she clutched the armrest for support, the upholstered side flipped open to reveal a built-in minifridge. A few beer cans lined the narrow shelves.

She crawled out of the recliner seat and continued her inspection of the apartment.

The small dining room held a nice glass and stone table with four taupe-upholstered chairs. A matching sideboard stood against one wall, unadorned.

There was only one bedroom, of course. This apartment was meant to be transitional; still, it meant there was nowhere for the girls to sleep. What a lovely message to give your children: *Sorry, no room at the inn.* She wondered if Jack had even considered that.

The bed was big and plain, with ash-gray and taupe bedding. No doubt Jack had added the *Fox Sports* purple mohair blanket. She was surprised he hadn't chosen pillowcases with tiny footballs on them.

She went to the kitchen (such as it was). A quick look in the fridge told her that Jack hadn't been cooking for himself. There were three six-packs of Corona beer, an industrial-size tub of mayonnaise, and a bottle of Gatorade. A half-eaten sandwich was disintegrating into a moldy pile. In the weeks he'd been here, Jack obviously hadn't eaten home much.

In the corner of the kitchen, by a small window, stood a big cardboard box. The side of it read: MEMORIES. Elizabeth had written that herself. The things in that box were the mementos she couldn't live without.

He hadn't even bothered to unpack them.

As usual, the details of their life were hers. He got to throw the game-winning passes. She got to take tickets and clean the stadium.

She poured herself a glass of water and opened the cardboard box. The top layer, sheathed in Bubble Wrap, was a collection of beloved family photos. She unwrapped them one by one, and placed them on the windowsills and countertops. Anywhere she could find.

She'd hoped it would give the apartment a homey feel, but when she finished, she stepped back and surveyed the results.

It didn't help. The pictures only reminded Elizabeth of what a home should be.

The phone rang. She answered it. "Hello?"

"Birdie? Welcome to New York. Isn't the place great?"

"Oh, yeah. Great."

"I can't wait to see you." A pause crackled through the lines. "But I've got a meeting in fifteen minutes. I should be home in an hour and a half. Not more than two hours. You'll be okay there, right?"

It took a conscious effort to simply say, "Of course."

"That's my girl. I love you, Birdie."

"Do you?" She hadn't meant to ask it. The question just popped out.

"Of course. Gotta run. See you soon."

"Okay." She hung up. It was a moment before she realized that she hadn't said, "I love you," in return. That was a first. In the past, she'd always been able to find the words, even when the emotion felt faraway. She wondered if he even noticed.

She walked over to the window. Outside, the world was a glittering combination of black sky and neon lights and streaking yellow cabs.

With a sigh, she went back to the cardboard box and unwrapped a photo album.

There they were, she and Jack, standing in front of Frosh Pond at the UW, holding hands.

Each picture was a stepping-stone on the path of their marriage. First at the UW . . . then the house in Pittsburgh when he'd played for the Steelers, then the second house in Pittsburgh, bigger than the first . . . then the house on Long Island . . . in Albuquerque, and so on and so on.

Elizabeth wandered down the photographic hallway of her married life, seeing all the compromises she'd made.

She'd moved and moved and moved.

Every time had been the same: *Another trade, another job, another city? Sure Jack.*

Here she was again, waiting for Jack. It seemed as if she'd passed her whole life that way, a woman set on *pause.*

At eight-thirty, her cell phone rang. It would be Jack, she knew, calling to tell her he'd be a little later than expected. *Only an hour, honey, I promise.* And just like that, this new city would take them on the same old ride.

She fished the phone out of her purse and answered. "Hello?"

"Birdie?" said a thick-as-molasses Southern voice. "Is this you?"

"Anita?" She glanced at her watch. It was too late for a friendly call. Fear sidled up to her, slipped a cold arm around her waist. "What's the matter?"

"Your daddy had a stroke. Y'all better get down here fast."

TWELVE

THE FIRST THING ELIZABETH DID WAS CALL JACK.

Oh, baby, he'd said softly, *I'm so sorry. I can be home in thirty minutes. I've got blah blah blah to do yet. Will you be okay by yourself until I get there?*

Of course she would. Her husband had never handled tragedy well. Even when he showed up, Elizabeth knew she'd really be alone.

Next, she called her daughters. Stephanie was loving and accommodating; she'd probably gone on-line during their phone conversation and ordered plane tickets. Jamie didn't say much. She'd been hit too hard by the unexpected news. She and her grandfather were so close . . .

Elizabeth heard the fear in Jamie's voice when she said: *Maybe he'll be okay. You think he'll be okay, don't you?*

Elizabeth wanted to rush in then, to salve her daughter's pain, but this was no time to make promises.

After that, Elizabeth concentrated on the details. By the time Jack got home, she'd made most of the necessary arrangements and packed his suitcase.

It took them more than two hours to get to the airport, go through security, and find the gate. Once there, they sat side by side in silence.

Finally, the flight was called and they boarded the plane, finding their seats in first class.

When they were in the air, a flight attendant appeared in the aisle in front of them. A loudspeaker reeled off emergency instructions.

Elizabeth didn't hear a word of it. When you were flying across several states to see your father, who might or might not be dying, it was impossible to think about much else.

Thank God for Christmas.

(Don't think that way.)

"Are you okay?" Jack asked again.

Elizabeth squeezed his hand. "No."

Finally, the plane landed in Nashville. She and Jack hailed a cab and headed north.

Forty-five minutes later, the taxi pulled up in front of a sprawling gray hospital.

"This entrance okay?" The driver asked, turning around to face them.

"Fine," Jack answered, handing a wad of bills to the driver.

Elizabeth got out of the cab and crossed her arms, waiting while Jack gathered their bags.

She was close to falling apart, but she wouldn't allow herself that luxury. If there was one thing motherhood taught a woman, it was how to hold herself together in a crisis.

Still, she clung to her husband's hand as they walked through the electric doors and into the sterile, antiseptic-scented lobby.

At the front desk, she said, "We're looking for Edward Rhodes, please."

The receptionist looked up. "The Colonel's in intensive care. Sixth floor west."

Jack squeezed her hand. "The elevators are right there."

She looked up at him, wanting suddenly to be alone with her fear. "Do you mind if I go alone?"

"What if you need me?"

"That's really sweet, but I'd rather be by myself. Besides, you hate hospitals. And they don't let many people into the ICU."

"You'll come and get me when you know something?"

"Of course."

He pulled her into his arms and kissed her hard. Against her lips, he whispered, "He'll be okay."

"I know." She was unsteady by the time she turned away from him. Without a backward glance, she headed toward the elevators.

On the sixth floor, she stepped out.

The ICU was a hive of white-coated activity. Elizabeth went to the main nurses desk and asked for her father. The nurse— an elderly black woman with hair the color of cold ashes— immediately sobered.

"Hello, Miss Elizabeth. I'm Deb Edwards. I reckon you don't remember me. I used to work for Doc Treamor."

"Hello, Deb. It's nice to see you again." She was surprised by how strong her voice sounded. "How is he doing?"

"Not well, I'm sad to say. But you know your daddy. He's stronger than ten ordinary men."

Elizabeth managed a tired smile. "Thank you." Then she walked down the hallway toward his room.

It was walled in glass on three sides. Through it, she saw a bed sitting amid a cluster of cranelike machines. Lights blinked from ugly black boxes; green lines graphed the unsteady beating of his heart.

There was a man in the bed, lying perfectly still and straight, his legs two parallel lines under the white blankets, his hairy, age-spotted arms pressed in close to the hump of his body.

He didn't look like her daddy. Edward Rhodes was a man who was always in motion, a man who took up *space*.

She moved toward him, her footsteps loud on the linoleum floor.

"Daddy?" Her voice cracked. She smoothed the gray-white hair away from his eyes. Her fingers lingered on his wide, creased brow. Even now, unconscious, he seemed to be thinking hard, planning some new adventure that only he could devise.

Her legs gave out on her for a second. She clutched the bedrail for support. The metal made a jangling, jarring noise.

She leaned forward. "Hey, Daddy, it's me, Birdie." At first, she said all the standard things, the familiar soundtrack that is said to all people in all hospital beds every day. Things like, *You're going to be fine . . .* and, *You're strong, you'll make it*.

But he was so still and pale. The skin that had always looked tan, even in the dead of winter, was grayed now, pale as the pillowcase. There was a breathing tube in his nostril and an IV needle in his white, veiny arm.

He looked older than his seventy-six years. Not at all like the man who walked his fields every day because "a man should touch the ground he owns." It seemed impossible that last year he'd trekked to Nepal, or that the year before that he'd run the rapids on the Snake River.

"Hey, Daddy," she whispered, stroking his forehead. She bent low and kissed his temple. Gone was his usual scent of bay rum and pipe smoke. He smelled of stale perspiration and sickness. She closed her eyes, wondering how to reach him.

Gradually, she became aware of the smell of flowers. Gardenias, to be precise.

Slowly, she straightened, knowing she wasn't alone anymore. She turned around.

Anita stood in the doorway, wearing a tight yellow angora sweater and straight-legged black pants with high-heeled black-and-yellow ankle boots. "Birdie," she said in a quiet voice, not her usual tremblin'-with-excitement sound at all, "I'm glad you could get here s' quick." She went to the bed. "Hey, Daddy," she whispered, touching his face.

"How's he doing?"

When Anita looked up, her gray eyes floated beneath a dome of electric-blue eye shadow. "They're hopin' he'll wake up."

Elizabeth steeled herself. "But he might not?"

"The longer he's . . . out, the worse it is. They're pretty sure he's paralyzed on the left side."

"God," Elizabeth whispered.

She pulled up a chair and sat beside him. Anita did the same thing, positioning herself on the opposite side of the bed. Elizabeth supposed there was a simple truth to be found in their choices. Two women who loved the same man. He'd always been between them, loving them both but unable to bring them together. For the first few minutes, they muddled through polite conversation, talking about nothing—the weather, the flight—but after a while, they gave up. They'd been there almost two hours when the door opened.

A short, stocky man in a white coat walked into the room.

"Hey, Phil," Anita said, trying to smile. She stood up. "He's still restin'."

The doctor looked at Elizabeth. "I'm Phillip Close," he said, extending his hand. "Edward's physician. You must be Birdie. He talks about you all the time."

Elizabeth imagined her daddy, sitting on the edge of an examining table, boring this stern-looking doctor with proud-father stories. It wounded her, that image, brought tears to her eyes. She stood up and shook his hand.

Phillip bent over Daddy, checked a few of the machines, then straightened. "It's still a waiting game. I wish I could do better than that."

"He could be fine, right?" Anita said.

"I'd never bet against the Colonel. He could wake up in ten minutes and ask for a shot of Maker's Mark," Phillip answered.

Elizabeth had to know the truth; it was the only way to prepare. "Or he could never wake up, is that what you're saying?"

"Yes," Phillip answered. "There are a range of possibilities
right now. It's really better not to anticipate too much, just to wait
and see. As I told Anita earlier, the longer he's unconscious, the
worse it looks, but he's always been a strong man."

"Anita tells me he might be paralyzed on one side," she said
slowly.

"Yes. And it took the paramedics quite a while to revive him.
He may have suffered some brain injury. But, as I said, we won't
know much until he wakes up. The biggest concern now is his
heart. Frankly, it's pretty weak."

"Thank you, Phillip," Elizabeth said, although it seemed ridiculous to thank someone for giving you more to worry about. Still, it
was good manners. The way things were done.

"I'll give you two some time with him," he said, then left
the room.

Paralyzed.

Brain injuries.

Weak heart.

The words didn't follow him out; they stayed in the room.

Elizabeth stared across the bed at her stepmother. All that
pancake makeup couldn't conceal Anita's pain.

"He'll make it," Elizabeth said. "He's too ornery to die."

Anita looked pathetically grateful for that small bit of comfort. "He *is* ornery, that's for sure."

"I . . . am . . . not."

Elizabeth and Anita gasped. They leaned down at the same
time.

Daddy's eyes were open; one side of his face remained pathetically slack.

"We can hear you, Daddy," she said. "We're both right here."

"I . . . am . . . not . . . ornery."

Anita took his motionless hand, squeezing it hard. Tears bub-
bled along her lashes. "I knew you couldn't leave me."

He reached across his own body and touched Anita's face. "There you are, Mother. I've been looking for you."

"I'm right here, Daddy," Anita said breathlessly, crying softly. "I wouldn't go anywhere."

Elizabeth knew it was childish, but she felt excluded by their love. She always had. There was something special between Anita and Edward, so special that everything around them paled in comparison.

"Our Birdie is here, too. She hopped on a plane the very second she heard," Anita said, smoothing the hair away from his eyes.

Slowly, he turned to look at Elizabeth. In his eyes, she saw something she'd never seen before—defeat—and it scared her. "Hey, Daddy," she whispered. "You've got a hell of a nerve scaring us this way."

"Give me just a moment with m' little girl, won't you, Mother?"

Anita leaned down and kissed his forehead. When she drew back, the bright pink lipstick print of her kiss remained. "I love you," she whispered fiercely, then left the room.

A second later, the door opened again. White-coated nurses bustled into the room. They shoved Elizabeth aside—politely— and busied themselves around their patient, checking machines, taking blood-pressure readings, listening to his heart. Phillip was the last to arrive. He rushed into the room, a little breathless, then saw his patient and smiled. "So, you decided to quit playing possum, huh? You had two beautiful women mighty worked up."

Daddy's smile was sadly lopsided. "Just wanted you to earn some of that hellacious bill you're gonna send me. It'll probably stop my heart right then and there."

Phillip listened to Daddy's heart, frowned briefly, then straightened. As he made a notation in the chart, he said, "I earn every penny putting up with your sorry butt, and you know it. I suppose I'll have to let you win at golf for a while." He turned to Elizabeth. "Make the old coot take it easy. I'll be back in a little while to check on him. We'll want to run another EKG."

Phillip herded the nurses out of the room and closed the door behind him. Through the glass wall, Elizabeth could see that he was talking to Anita.

"Damn doctors," Edward said, breathing hard. "They won't leave a man in peace." He tried to smile.

All the way down here, Elizabeth had been rehearsing what to say to him, and now nothing came to her. She was afraid that if she said a word, she'd start to cry.

"Where's golden . . . boy? And my granddaughters?"

"Jack is in the waiting room. Stephie and Jamie will be here in a little while."

Edward's eyes fluttered closed. He took a few rattling breaths, then came awake with a start and shouted, "Anita!"

"She's just outside, Daddy. You said you wanted to talk to *me*."

"Ah . . . yes." He calmed down. Very slowly, he lifted his hand and touched her hand. "When I saw that movie, *Forrest Gump*, all I could think about was my little sugar beet. We were peas and carrots, weren't we?"

She squeezed her eyes shut, then slowly opened them. "Yes."

"I didn't handle things well. I surely didn't."

Elizabeth didn't know what he was talking about. Before she could ask, he went on:

"Anita. Marguerite. I shoulda done it differently, God knows. But your mama near killed me . . . I swear, I don't know what I should have told you."

"What are you talking about, Daddy?"

"I thought it best you didn't know, that's all. To protect you. Memories . . . they're important sometimes, more important than the truth. But Anita paid the price. We all did."

"Daddy—"

He started coughing hard, gasping.

"*Sshh*, Daddy," she said. "There's plenty of time for talking. You just rest now."

"You're the best part o' me, Birdie. You always were. From the moment your mama put you in my arms, I knew. I fell in love with you so hard I practically cracked my head. I reckon I should have told you more often."

"You told me all the time, Daddy."

He tried to come forward off the pillows, to sit up. It was heartbreaking to see his failure. With a sigh, he sank back down. "I need you to do somethin' for me, Birdie. It won't be easy for you."

"Anything, Daddy. You know that."

"You take care of Anita. You hear me?"

"Don't say that," she said, hearing the sudden desperation in her voice. "You'll be around to take care of her."

"Don't sass me. This is important." His breathing became shallow, labored. "Promise me you'll take care of her."

"Okay." Elizabeth leaned down and kissed his forehead. "I love you, Daddy."

He looked at her, but his eyes were glassy now, unfocused. As if he'd spent all his energy and had nothing left. "That love'll carry me through the Pearly Gates, sugar beet, it surely will. Now, ask Anita to come in here."

"No . . . please."

"It's time, Birdie. Now go get your mama."

Elizabeth stood there a minute, unable to leave him.

"Go on," he said gently.

She forced herself to move. At the door, she gave him a last smile, then left the room. "He wants you," she said to Anita.

Her stepmother made a sound that was half sigh, half sob, and hurried into the room, closing the door behind her.

At the window, Elizabeth stood close to the glass, on the outside of their love, looking in. She prayed hard. *Be strong, Daddy. Be strong.*

An alarm on one of the machines went off.

Anita stumbled back from the bed, screaming, "Help us, help us!"

Elizabeth jerked to open the door, but nurses and doctors rushed past her, filled the tiny room, pushed Anita out of the way.

People clustered around her father. The noise turned into a dull roar in Elizabeth's ears. She pressed the glass, hard. "Don't you die, Daddy. Don't you dare . . ."

Phillip raced into the room, elbowed his way to her father's side. He reached for the heart paddles.

Elizabeth squeezed her eyes shut. She couldn't breathe. Her own heart kept skipping beats, unreliable now that her father's had stopped. *Please, God, please don't take him. Not yet . . .*

When she opened her eyes, the doctors and nurses were standing still; the machines were cold and black. Anita was sitting by Daddy, her cries had dwindled down to soundless gasps and occasional shudders. The makeup on her face had been washed away in streaks.

Anita looked through the glass at Elizabeth. "He's gone," she mouthed helplessly. The words made her start to cry again. This time, her sobbing was a shrunken, heart-wrenching sound.

Slowly, Elizabeth walked into the room, went up to his bed. She pressed a hand to Anita's frail shoulder, clutching hard, though she'd only meant to squeeze reassuringly.

Daddy lay there, his eyes closed, his great barrel chest sunken and still. "Hey, Daddy," she whispered. It was a split second before she realized that she'd expected an answer. But, of course, there wasn't one.

His heart—the one that had loved her so well—had finally given up.

THIRTEEN

ELIZABETH POINTED TO AN EMPTY STALL IN THE AIRPORT'S underground parking lot. Jack turned the car into it and parked.

She drew in a deep breath and let it out slowly. She'd been careful all the way here. No radio (the last thing she needed was to hear a sad song), no runaway thoughts, no memories. She kept her eyes on the road and her mind on the funeral. Arrangements, she could deal with. Emotions, she couldn't.

She got out of the car—

(*Daddy's car, but don't think about that.*)

—and walked briskly toward the terminal.

Jack sauntered along behind her. She'd snapped at him often enough in the last few hours that he was giving her a wide berth. He'd obviously figured out that it was better to say nothing at all.

She saw the girls first. Stephanie was standing at the gate, with her boyfriend, Tim, beside her. As always, Stephanie looked impeccable. Her shoulder-length dark brown hair was drawn back from her face and held in place by two silver clips. She wore a pair of black wool pants and a pretty yellow sweater. Tim, in Dockers and a striped Brooks Brothers' shirt, was holding her hand. Jamie was close to them, yet separate, and dressed in baggy denim overalls. A baseball cap was pulled down low on her forehead.

Elizabeth quickened her step. "Hey, girls . . . Tim," she said softly, pulling her daughters into her arms.

For the first time in hours, Elizabeth drew in a full breath.

When they separated, Jack came up beside them. He slipped an arm around her waist. She wondered if he'd known that she was losing her control, or if it was sheer dumb luck on his part. Either way, his touch steadied her.

Jamie looked up at her dad. She managed a tired smile. "Holy shit. You're gorgeous. Did you have a face-lift or something?"

Elizabeth was startled by that. With all that had happened in the past day, she hadn't bothered to really look at her husband. Now she did, and she saw what Jamie meant.

He shrugged. "They made me color my hair. Just when I'd gotten used to the start of gray, they took it out. I haven't been this blond since eighth grade."

Jamie frowned. "You look like a movie star, no kidding."

Elizabeth took a step backward. She felt old suddenly, flabby and wrinkled. She hadn't had time to color her own hair, and more than a little gray threaded her darker roots. And she'd slept so poorly last night that her skin was the color and consistency of tapioca. And here was her husband of twenty-four years looking like Jeff Bridges in *The Contender*.

Jack looped an arm around Jamie. "They did this treatment that peeled the skin off my face. It hurt like hell and for almost a week I looked like a burn victim. That's why rich people look so good. They spend money on stuff you can't imagine and pain is no reason to say no."

Stephanie put an arm around Elizabeth's sadly thick waist. "You're as pretty as ever, too, Mom," she said.

"Thanks." It was all she could say.

THE MECHANICS OF DEATH in a small town ticked forward like a well-oiled clock. Everyone pitched in. An intricate ballet played out first in the funeral parlor, then at the graveside, and now at the house.

There were pictures of Daddy everywhere, on tables and counters and windowsills. Some were ornately framed; others sat in plastic-wood frames from the nearest Piggly Wiggly. Everyone who'd come to Sweetwater after the funeral had brought a casserole and a photo. Wherever Elizabeth walked in the house, she was sure to hear soft laughter, a few sighs, and her father's name spoken in a whispered voice.

In a town like this, people came together in triumph and in tragedy. Every emotion was shared, but none were openly discussed. No one asked Elizabeth how she felt or offered an expensive grief-therapist's name. That's how it was done in The Big City. Here, they squeezed your shoulder and remarked that you were "holding up well."

Southern women had been hiding emotions behind competence since crinolines were in fashion. It was bred into them, like the ability to make a flawless mint julep or bake a perfect ham. Elizabeth did as was expected of her.

But as hard as she tried to keep the grief away, it stalked her.

When she couldn't take it anymore, she escaped to the back porch.

It was the last place she should have chosen. She'd sat here so often with Daddy, listening to the cicadas and his tall tales. Memories pressed in on her from all directions. She recalled standing down at the pond trying to land one of the trout they'd thrown into the water as fry . . . or walking the fields at harvest time, when the air smelled of sweet white corn and tobacco smoke. . . .

This was where they'd come on the day after Mama's funeral, too. It had been spring then, not nearly so cold as today. Like today, the house had been full of guests speaking quietly and pictures. *You want to sleep in my room tonight, sugar beet?*

"Hold on, Birdie," she said, squeezing her eyes shut, fisting her hands. Fingernails bit into the soft flesh of her palms.

It didn't work. She had to get out of here. In about ten seconds, she was going to lose it. She went back into the house and disappeared in the bathroom, slamming the door shut behind her.

She closed the toilet lid and sat down.

There, on the floor by the toilet was a magazine. *Travel and Leisure*.

When she picked it up, it fell open to a two-page, dog-eared spread on Costa Rica. There was an advertisement for an adventure camp on the Caribbean coast. Someone—Daddy—had drawn a star in red ink on the page.

There's a place in Costa Rica, sugar beet, called Cloud Mountain— or some damned thing—that speaks right to m' heart.

The magazine fell to the floor and hit with a thump. She cried at last, for all the times she'd had been with her father and all the times she hadn't, and for all the times she never would be.

When the tears had worn themselves out and left her dry, she got unsteadily to her feet.

She splashed cool water on her face, then smoothed her hair back and returned to the fray. As she moved through the crowd, she felt stiff and fragile. If anyone noticed how awful she looked, no one commented.

She checked on the food and opened bottles of wine, then headed for the library, where her family was hiding out.

Stephanie and Tim sat together on the sofa. As usual, Stephanie was the picture of decorum. A plain, scoop-necked, long-sleeved black dress clung to her lithe body. There were red streaks on her porcelain cheeks, and her gray eyes showed the residue of tears. Tim was holding her hand. They looked like a couple from central casting—*young love handles grief well.*

Jamie, on the other hand, had taken no great care in dressing. She sat slouched on an ottoman, her white-blond hair a tangled mass that covered half of her face. Her navy blue dress was already wrinkled. Her pale blue eyes were swollen and red.

"I can't listen to any more stories about him," Jamie said softly, her eyes welling up.

Elizabeth understood. It was difficult out there. Everyone had loved him so much and they wanted to share their favorite story, but every word lodged in your heart like a shard of glass.

Jack rose from the leather wing chair and walked toward Elizabeth, never taking his gaze from her face.

He pulled her into his arms. She held herself back, afraid that if she relaxed, she'd break.

"He loved you," Jack whispered against her ear, too softly for the children to hear. "The first time I met him, he told me he'd kill me if I ever hurt you. He reminded me of that promise when I asked for your hand in marriage. His exact words were: *You hurt my sugar beet, Jackson Shore, and I'll whoop you s' hard you'll see the Milky Way.*'"

Elizabeth looked up at Jack. She'd never heard that story before. It brought her daddy back to her for a perfect, heartbreaking moment; she heard his booming, laughing voice, calling her his sugar beet. She opened her mouth to say something—she wasn't sure what—but nothing came out.

Jack touched her face gently. "You don't have to do everything alone, Birdie," he said, "go ahead and cry."

He was trying to help, but somehow that only made her feel more alone. She knew sorrow would hit her later, hit her hard, the sudden, aching realization that her father was Gone, that she'd never pick up the phone and hear his voice again, or go to her mailbox and get a letter written in his bold, sweeping hand. "Oh, Jack . . ."

"Let me help you, Birdie," he said, stroking her hair.

She loved him for trying, but there was no way to help a person through something like this. Grief was the loneliest road in the world.

"It helps just to have you here," she said, and it was true.

She clung to him then, taking strength from the feel of his arms around her, and for a single, magic moment, it felt as if they loved each other again.

FOURTEEN

*J*ACK WAS BACK IN NEW YORK. THANK GOD.

He knew it was a weakness in him, a moral failing, but he hated death's accessories. The sobbing, the gathering, that god-awful, primitive ritual called a viewing.

As expected, he had looked down the church aisle and seen that flower-draped casket, and all he'd been able to think about was his mother's funeral.

There had been no flowers then, no expensive mahogany casket, and saddest of all, no mourners. Just one skinny boy in a borrowed coat, and a slouched-over, broken stalk of a man, only a few years away from his own death.

Jack loved his wife and he adored his children, but two days in that grieving, too-quiet house had been more than he could stand.

Thankfully, Birdie was good in a crisis. Jack hadn't even had to beg to leave—or to make up a feeble excuse—she'd released him, said, *Go on back to New York; there's nothing for you and the girls to do down here.*

He'd made a lackluster effort at argument. *If you need me . . .*
But she hadn't. Birdie was pure steel when it came to hard times.

Now he was free again.

He stepped out of the cab, overtipped the driver (he was becoming a celebrity again), and hurried into the studio. He went
straight to his office, stowed his carry-on bag in the closet, and sat
down at his desk.

The stack of paper was huge, as was the pile of pink phone
messages. He'd forgotten how much the phone rang when you
were *somebody*. They'd promised him a secretary to handle all this
office grunt work—that was a given. He couldn't go around answering his own phone anymore, and when the fan mail started
coming in, he'd need someone to do that for him, too.

He didn't look forward to training another secretary. It took
weeks, sometimes months, to teach someone your likes and dis-
likes, your quirks and demands. Interviewing, reading résumés,
choosing the right candidate.

What he really needed was an assistant. Someone to train his
secretary as well as to help him formulate questions for the athlete
interviews. There was a lot of research involved in looking smart
off-the-cuff.

The writers and producers were doing that, of course, but
Warren had his own assistant producer, and Jack had noticed that
Warren got the lion's share of the good questions.

Jack picked up a pen and began making a list. His assistant
would have to be bright, ambitious, dedicated, intelligent. Someone like . . . Sally.

Why hadn't he thought of it before? She had the experience.
They had worked well together in Portland, and she was a tiger
behind the scenes. She tracked down every nuance of a story.
She'd be a real addition to the show. As it was, all the producers and writers were male. A young woman who loved sports
would shake up the perspective a bit. And she'd make sure Jack
looked good.

She'd do it, too. He had no doubt about that. Sally was a

woman with big dreams and tall ambitions. A chance to be a production assistant for a network show in the Big Apple would
really charge her batteries.

This was business, pure and simple. That he'd been attracted
to her didn't matter. He'd always be tempted by some young
woman; that was hardwired in his DNA, as much a part of him as
blue eyes and blond hair. He'd been tempted plenty of times in
the past fifteen years—and even more recently—but he hadn't
fallen out of the old marriage bed even once. Those days were behind him.

This was strictly business.

UNABLE TO SLEEP, Elizabeth put on one of the thick terry-cloth
robes that Anita had placed in the guest room closet and went
quietly downstairs. The old house creaked and moaned at her
progress. The wind against the windowpanes sounded like a cat
scratching to be let in.

She didn't doubt that the house knew its master had gone on,
but this place had weathered the storms of death for a long, long
time. The first Rhodes had come to this land long before the Civil
War, one of the working-class poor of England who dared to
dream of a better life. He'd crossed the sea as an indentured
servant and been sold at auction to a farmer in nearby Russellville. He'd worked hard, married well, and planted the seeds of a
dynasty.

In the darkened kitchen, she made herself a cup of tea and
stood at the sink, staring out at the backyard. Moonlight tipped
the dead black branches with pearlescent color. Thin clouds scud-
ded across the breezy sky; they created a shifting pattern of light
on the garden.

She tightened the belt on her robe and went outside. The
screen door banged shut behind her. The wind suddenly died
down. An almost preternatural silence fell.

She shivered, though not only from the cold. It felt as if she'd been summoned out here, perhaps by the memory of their night out here at Christmas.

"Daddy?" she whispered, feeling both silly and hopeful.

There was no answer, no Hollywood moaning or ghostly apparition. No tall man dressed in a flannel shirt and twill pants standing beside her.

She stepped down onto the brick path that bisected and outlined the garden. The thin slippers she wore protected her feet from the cold as she walked past the perfectly shaped boxwood hedges. Here and there, shaped camellia bushes stood above the squared hedge, their glossy green leaves a stark contrast to all the brownness.

This had once been her special place, and now she was a stranger to it. So many times in her youth, especially on long summer nights when the heat made sleep impossible, she'd come out here. Alone and searching. In the winter, she'd scoured the leaf-blackened beds for signs of spring. A patch of lime green moss, a seed pod that had sprouted.

What she'd really been looking for, of course, was her mother, and here, amid the flowers she'd tended so carefully, Elizabeth had thought she felt her mama's spirit.

She'd always tried to picture her mama in the garden, maybe thinning the daffodils or trimming the roses, but all she'd ever seen of her mother were black-and-white photographs, and even those had been scarce. Most of the pictures had been portrait shots—wedding, graduations, that sort of thing. They left Elizabeth with a vague, colorless image of a pretty young woman who always looked perfect but never laughed or spoke.

Elizabeth knelt at the edge of the rose bed. Damp black earth ground itself into the plush fabric beneath her knees.

The bare, grayish brown rosebushes cast shadows on the darkened earth. Moonlight gave them an eerie look, like twisted hands from an ancient reptile, each finger thickened by age and studded with huge thorns.

Behind her, she heard the sound of a door creaking open and clicking closed, then the rhythm of footsteps on the brick path.

"Hey, Anita," she said without turning around.

"It's amazin' to think that those roses'll be bloomin' in just a few months."

"I was just thinking the same thing."

When she was little, Elizabeth had often cried when her mama's favorite flowers wilted and died. Now, though, as a woman full grown, she understood the importance of rest. It was the very bleakness of winter that made spring possible. She wished such a thing could be true for housewives who'd lost their way, that instead of wasting a life, you could be hibernating, gathering strength for the coming spring.

A breeze kicked up, sent a few dry, brittle leaves skittering across the path. "I tended those roses by hand all these years. I never let a gardener near 'em."

Elizabeth sat back on her heels and looked up at Anita. "Why?"

Anita smiled sadly. Her platinum hair was a mass of curlers; thick night moisturizer glistened on her cheeks and forehead. A heavy blue-plaid-flannel nightdress covered her from throat to foot. She looked ten years older than her actual sixty-two. "I smelled her perfume once."

Elizabeth felt a shiver. She remembered the pretty little bottle that had sat on her mama's vanity table. "Mama's?" she whispered.

"It was one of those days—when you were in a mood, as your daddy used to say—you disagreed with everything I said. So I stopped talkin' at all. I came out here, ready to attack your mama's garden. I wanted to fight somethin' I could see. But when I sat out here, all alone, feelin' sorry for myself, I smelled your mama's perfume. Shalimar. It wasn't like she spoke to me or anything weird like that. I just . . . realized I was fightin' with her baby girl, who was broken up inside. After that, whenever you made me crazy, I came out here to the garden."

Elizabeth heard the pain in Anita's voice, and for once, she understood. "No wonder you were out here so often."

"I should have done things differently, I guess. I knew you missed her somethin' awful."

"I started forgetting her. That was the worst part. That's why I always asked Daddy about her. But he wouldn't say a thing, ever. He always said, 'Keep your memories close, Birdie.' He never seemed to understand that my memories of her were like smoke. I couldn't hold on to them."

"I imagine your mama is giving him a piece of her mind about that right now."

"I don't think anyone held as much of Daddy's heart as you did, Anita." Try as she might, a slight bitterness tainted her final words.

"Thank you for that." Anita gazed out over the fallow fields. "Why didn't you fly home with Jack and the girls?"

Elizabeth felt the cold suddenly. She shivered and stood up, crossing her arms. "He had to be at work first thing in the morning. I thought I'd stay and help you clean the house."

"Heloise cleans the house. She has since you were in pigtails." Anita looked down at her. "You *can* tell me to mind my own business, y' know."

"The truth is I don't know why. I just wasn't ready to go back to New York."

Anita took a step forward. Her silly pink slippers sank into the black earth. "Your daddy used to say to me, 'Mother, if that girl don't spread her wings, one day she's plumb gonna forget how to fly.' He was worried that you were missing out on your own life."

"I know." Elizabeth didn't want to be talking about this. It hurt too much, and right now, in her mama's garden, she was fragile. She wiped her eyes—when had she started crying, anyway?— and looked at Anita. "What about you? Will you be okay?"

"I'll get by."

It wasn't really an answer, but it was all there was. They had both known it would come, the day when Anita would be left alone in this white elephant of a house. For a while, the phone would ring almost hourly and friends would show up on the porch with a casserole, but sooner or later, the stream would run dry, and Anita would have to look widowhood in the eye. "I'll call you when I get to New York, just to make sure everything is okay."

"That would be nice."

Silence fell between them again. Wind whispered through the shrubs and played the chimes that hung from the porch roof. A melancholy sound.

Elizabeth wished suddenly that things were different between her and Anita, that they could hold hands and comfort one another. But it was too late now to recraft a relationship whose time had come and gone.

"We've missed our chance, haven't we?" Anita asked softly.

Elizabeth nodded. She didn't know how else to respond.

"It's too bad," Anita said. "But don't you worry about me, honey. I'll be fine. You don't marry a man who is fourteen years older and expect to outlive him. I always knew I'd be alone one day."

Elizabeth had never considered that. To her, the age difference had always fallen on her daddy's side of the equation. She'd seen it from a man's point of view. A younger wife made a man happy. Everyone knew that. Men—shallow as plate glass—had been proving it for years.

Now she saw the other side of that coin. Sure, Anita had gotten a good life and a lot of money. She'd been accepted into the local social scene and married a man who treated her like a piece of the finest French porcelain.

In return, Anita had no children now to comfort her, and no partner with whom to spend the hearing-aid years. She was sixty-two years old and a widow. Alone perhaps for the remainder of her life.

"Why didn't you and Daddy have children?" Elizabeth asked—finally—the question she'd pondered for years.

Anita sighed. "Oh, honey, that's a question for another time, maybe between different women."

"In other words, mind my own business."

"Yes." She smiled, maybe to take the sting out of her answer. "That question cuts to the heart of me, is all. I'm not goin' to answer it as idle chitchat at midnight two days after my husband's death."

Elizabeth understood. They'd missed their chance for intimacy. Now they were simply two grown women, connected by the barest strand of relation, who would go their separate ways. "I'm sorry," she said at last, choosing the sentence she herself had heard a hundred times in the past few days. "You call me if you're feeling too alone."

"There are worse things in life than being alone."

Elizabeth sensed that Anita had chosen those words carefully. She felt transparent suddenly, as if unhappiness ran through her veins, showed in the tiny blue lines that came from her heart.

Anita took a step closer.

Elizabeth stepped backward, needing space between them. "I better get to bed now. Six will come awfully early." She walked away, forcing herself to keep a steady pace. It was difficult.

She went inside the house and slammed the door, then peered cautiously out the window.

Anita was still standing there, shivering, her white hair twined around a dozen pink curlers. Even in the fading moonlight, Elizabeth could make out the glittering tear tracks on her face. Anita was standing alone, crying.

She was looking at the roses.

ELIZABETH PAID THE CABDRIVER and stepped out onto the sidewalk in front of the Nashville airport.

It was cold out today. The air smelled of incipient snow; the skies were gray and bloated.

She wheeled her carry-on bag behind her. It bumped over the threshold as the electronic doors whooshed open. The United Airlines ticket counter was crowded with travelers, so she went instead to the bank of computers along the wall. It took a few minutes to find the departures terminal. She scanned through the flight numbers.

She found hers—989, Nashville to Detroit to Kennedy. While she was reading the gate number, the information changed.

The flight was delayed by two hours.

Groaning, she got in line, inched her way forward amid a chattering crowd. Finally, she reached the counter. The agent checked her ticket and confirmed that the flight was delayed; then she gave Elizabeth a meal voucher.

As if you could eat lunch in an airport for five dollars.

Thanking the agent, she left the counter. She dragged her suitcase behind her as she wandered up and down the aisles. In the bookstore, she bought a copy of the newest novel by Anne Rivers Siddons and the latest *House and Garden* magazine.

Finally, she'd seen everything there was to see, so she went into one of the restaurants, found a table by the window, and sat down. She stared out across the runway, watching the planes take off and land.

There's a place in Costa Rica, sugar beet, called Cloud Mountain— or some damned thing—that speaks right to m' heart.

When was the last time you traveled someplace exotic? Or scared yourself silly? Or took up some crazy thing, like hang gliding or skydiving?

She'd been working to keep the memories at bay, but now they flooded her. She couldn't forget . . .

You're missin' out on your own life. It's passin' you by.

Just 'cause my glasses are thick as Coke bottles doesn't mean I can't still see my little girl's heart. I hear the way you talk to Jack . . . and the way you don't talk to him. I know an unhappy marriage when I see one.

If only she could do something to change it. Maybe get on a

plane and go wherever it took her. Land in a strange country and be someone else.

But where would she go? Machu Picchu, Paris, Nepal? She didn't even have a passport.

She wasn't that kind of woman. Unlike her father, she didn't dream of scaling Mount Everest or hang gliding down cliffs. There was only one place on earth she longed to go.

Home.

Her place by the sea. She remembered the night she'd gone down to the beach at midnight and seen the whales swim past. Their haunting, elegiac cry had seemed drawn out of her, pulled from that sad, hidden place in her heart where she stored the dreams she'd set aside.

She'd done so much of that in her life, put her dreams aside.

. . . your own life . . . it's passin' you by.

It was true. Still, it hurt to realize that her father had known it, too. That he'd looked into his grown daughter's eyes and seen unhappiness.

What would it be like, she wondered, to look in the mirror and see a whole and happy woman staring back at her?

And now, in less than an hour, she would board one of these planes, find her seat, and fly to New York. There, she would move into that trendy, impersonal apartment and once again trim her life to fit Jack's.

"I don't want to go." She whispered the words aloud, looking up. A sad, tired-looking woman mouthed the words back to her. She stared at her reflection, wondering when exactly she'd lost her looks. Had they gone the way of her dreams? And how had she gotten here, to this place so entrenched in the ordinary?

It hadn't been until she'd lost her youth and finished raising her children that she'd bothered to wonder what came next. More important, when it was her turn.

Now she was consumed by the question. It was a brushfire,

burning out of control, and she was terrified that it would char her beyond recognition.

Every little decision had been a brick that had built a wall between the woman she was becoming and the one she imagined she could be.

If that girl don't spread her wings, one day she's plumb gonna forget how to fly.

That was the crux of it. Somewhere along the way of all those ordinary years, she'd forgotten how to fly. Wife-and-motherhood had kept her too close to the ground.

No, that wasn't fair. It wasn't the job she'd done that clipped her wings; it was the way she'd chosen to do it. All across this country women who were good wives and good mothers remembered to become their best selves as well. Elizabeth simply hadn't been one of them.

Maybe it was a weakness in her, a fear of failure that made safety seem more important than fulfillment. Or maybe it was simpler than that. Maybe she'd just . . . gone on, done what needed to be done for the day and been too tired by nightfall to reach for something else. There had been days—years even—when she hadn't been able to find ten spare minutes in a day. In those days, when Jack had been playing ball and the kids had been busy all the time, her biggest dream had been a quiet bath in the evening.

She glanced down at her watch.

Her flight would be boarding soon. Nashville to Detroit to New York.

And she decided.

No more waiting and praying for change to occur like some chemical reaction.

She got up, paid for her lunch, and walked back down the busy aisle toward the newsstand. There, she purchased a box of stationery—the only one they had. At the top of each sheet was a line drawing of Graceland and the words: ELVIS WELCOMES YOU TO WILD AND WONDERFUL TENNESSEE.

She went back to the restaurant and reclaimed her seat. Without thinking—or worrying—she began to write.

*D*ear Jack:

I love you. It seems important to start this letter with those words. We say them to each other all the time, and I know we mean them. I also know it's not enough anymore, is it? Not for either of us.

For twenty-four years, I've been your wife. When we began, I never wanted to be anything else. I guess it became a self-fulfilling prophesy. Now I can't remember the dreams I once had, but I miss them, Jack. I miss me.

I hope you'll be able to understand.

No more cheerleader years for me. I need to get in the game. I'm afraid if I don't do it now, I never will, and I can't be this shadow-woman anymore. I can't.

So—and here's the punch line—I'm not following you to New York. Not this time.

I should have had the guts to tell you this in person. I wish I had that kind of strength. It's funny, I could lift a bus to save your life, but I can't find the courage to say out loud that I've forgotten how it feels to love you. My voice is one of the things I hope to find.

In all our years together, there has only been one place that was mine, and I don't want to leave it. I don't want to follow you again.

I'm going home. I need some time alone. I need to find out who I am and who I can become.

I pray you'll understand. I love you, Jack.

E.

She didn't even reread the letter. She folded it up, put it in an envelope, stamped and mailed it.

Then she went looking for a flight to Portland.

FIFTEEN

AFTER ONLY A FEW DAYS AT THE BEACH, ELIZABETH FELT REJU-
venated. she slept late, until almost eight-thirty, when the cawing
of the shorebirds invariably wakened her; then she made herself a
cup of decaf tea, had a bowl of granola, and went outside.

The days had been gloriously sunny, the kind of crisp, winter
days that invariably drew tourists to the Oregon coast. She'd spent
hours walking up and down the beach, just plain breathing. That
simple gift had been granted her again from the moment she first
saw the sea.

She spent the barest minimum time on chores and errands.
She'd reinstated mail service and arranged for the furniture to be
redelivered, and she'd purchased enough heat-and-eat dinners to
last a week. That was it. No contacting friends, no checking on
the multitude of volunteer activities that used to munch through
so much of her time, no cleaning or cooking. Definitely no To Do
lists. She'd even put off scheduling the telephone reinstallation
and kept her cell phone turned off.

Instead, she walked on the beach. Her beach. It had been there for the two years she and Jack had lived here, just twenty-six steps below her patch of land, and yet, except for that one night with the orcas, she'd never gone down there. The stairs had frightened her, as had the tides. On the first day they'd visited the property, Jack had cautioned her against using the stairs—*too rickety*, he'd said—and the tides. *I grew up near the beach, remember? A big wave can come up out of nowhere and pull a full-grown man out to sea.*

But it was fear that had swept Elizabeth out to sea and left her drowning. No more. Now she tramped up and down the steps like a local and kept a portable tide chart in her back pocket. In her walks, she'd come to know every inch of Echo Beach. She'd found "her" rock, a flat, gray stone, rubbed to velvet softness by the tides. Sometimes, she'd sit there for an hour or more, just staring out to sea.

She'd begun to dream again. Not ethereal visions that came and went with sleep, but real hopes and aspirations. Although she hadn't found the courage to try painting, she'd dug through her belongings and found an old sketchbook and a worn-down bit of charcoal. She'd discovered that her fingers worked better in the sea air; the stiffness that had plagued her for years had gone. Drawing, came—not easily yet, not like it once had, but it came. After all the sagging middle years, simply picking up a piece of charcoal felt like a triumph.

This new life of hers held a freedom she'd never known before. She went to bed when she felt like it, got up when she wanted, and spent the entire day doing whatever popped into her head.

Yesterday she'd gone to town early and walked from store to store. She hadn't even brought a purse with her. Shopping wasn't the point. *Seeing* was the point. She couldn't remember the last time she'd done that, simply experienced town. After a while she'd felt almost like an alien, noticing people's faces . . . their mannerisms . . . the easy way a child smiled when the ice cream shop opened its doors for business. The tourist shops were full of beautiful art and crafts; she hadn't known that. As a local, she'd bypassed the trendy shops and blown through the others in a rush, clutching a To Do list. She'd missed so much.

And yet, throughout it all, Jack was never far from her thoughts.

By her calculations, he'd received her letter yesterday. That was why she hadn't reconnected the phone; she didn't want to talk to him yet. He'd always had an ability to erode any position she'd taken until it—and she—crumpled beneath the weight of what he wanted.

She looked down at her sketch pad, wondering what to draw this morning. Inspiration was everywhere.

She saw a blue jay perched on a broken, leafless branch. The deep jeweltones of its wings were a stark, beautiful contrast to the weather-grayed bark.

The colors jumped out at her; it felt suddenly as if a veil had been lifted, one she didn't even remember donning, and now she saw the world in all its vibrancy, instead of the pale, shadowed version she'd come to expect. The gray-white sky . . . the concrete-colored sand . . . the evergreens . . . the ocher cliffs . . . the white-tipped curl of the waves.

For the first time in years, she *needed* to paint.

The first raindrop hit her forehead. It landed with a cold splat and squiggled down her cheek.

She opened her eyes and saw that clouds had rolled in. The sky was charcoal gray now, underscored in strands of ominous black.

She flipped up her hood, shoved all her supplies into the canvas bag at her feet, and ran for home.

By the time she reached the stairs, it wasn't just raining. It was *raging*. Wind swept up the jagged cliff and slapped her backside.

She raced across the squishy carpet of lawn. Gigantic shrubs shivered in the wind and clattered against one another. Leaves, black and dead, swirled in the violent air, smacking wetly against her shins.

Wiping her eyes, she ran the last few steps to the house and ducked under the eaves. Her hands were freezing cold as she opened the door, went inside, and slammed the door shut behind her. Wind rattled the windowpanes and clattered across the shake roof.

She flicked the switch by the door, and the light came on.

Just then lightning flashed in the window. Somewhere close by a tree cracked open and crashed to the ground.

The lights went out.

For a split second, she panicked. Jack always took care of the house during a storm. He found the flashlights and lit the candles and started the fire. Elizabeth didn't even know if there were any candles handy, or if they were all in boxes somewhere. . . .

What if she went looking for them and fell through that rotten place in the floorboards by the guest bathroom?

Woman found stuck in broken floorboards; dead for days before body discovered.

She took a deep breath. "Okay. First things first. You need to start a fire and find some candles."

She focused on those two tasks, feeling her way through the house, slowly. Without the furniture, there was nothing to hang on to. Just outside the back door, she found a stack of firewood. *Thank God Jack took care of things like this.*

Clutching the wood, she inched back into the kitchen, where she found yesterday's newspaper. At the fireplace, she arranged everything in the hearth. Then she felt up the stones for the tin matchbox holder, found it, and struck a match.

Within a few moments, she had a great fire crackling in the hearth. A red glow spilled across the center of the room, and just that easily, her fear dissipated.

She waited awhile, with her hands outstretched before the heat. When she was sure it was a good, solid fire, she went in search of supplies. In the pantry, way in the back, beneath a stack of area phonebooks, she found a box full of emergency candles and out-of-date calendars. She placed the candles along the mantel and on every windowsill. When she was done, the house was bathed in a beautiful golden glow.

She felt like Tom Hanks in *Cast Away*.

I . . . have made . . . fire.

She grabbed the sleeping bag she'd recently purchased, unzipped it, and wrapped it around her, shawl-like. Then she went out onto the porch to watch the storm.

She'd never done anything like that. Always, she'd been afraid of nature's furies. It was another trait she wanted to shed. In the past days, she'd come to understand the importance of upheaval. The tallest mountains were created by violence and chaos; like them, a woman's independence was born of fire.

Out to sea, thick gray clouds rolled ominously across the sky; their passing was reflected in a kaleidoscope of shadow on the water's turbulent surface. Wind whistled through the tree limbs, scattering dead leaves and pine cones.

It was all so loud: crashing waves, howling wind, rattling glass, hammering rain. Now and then a limb would crack away from its tree and fall to the ground with a *thwack*.

She loved every moment of it. Watching it from here on the porch, instead of burrowed in the safety of her house, made her feel changed, somehow. Stronger.

After a while—she'd lost all track of time—a strange sound came into the storm. At first Elizabeth couldn't place the noise, it was so out of place and her musings had gone so deep. Then she looked up and saw two headlights in the darkness and recognized the roar of a car's engine.

She stood up, wrapping the sleeping bag more tightly around her as she stepped into a corner full of shadows.

The driver was probably lost . . . would turn around in the driveway and disappear.

The car stopped. The headlights snapped off, and the yard was plunged into darkness again. The porch was a small oasis of orange light.

The car door opened. Someone got out.

Elizabeth realized sharply, suddenly, how vulnerable she was out here. All alone. No phone. No one to come looking for her . . .

The stranger crossed the yard and stepped into the light.

Jack.

Rain flattened his hair and dripped down the sides of his face. He tried to smile, but it was tired and didn't reach his equally tired eyes. "Hey, Birdie."

She felt smaller somehow, just standing in front of him. She wished she were surprised to see him, but she thought maybe she'd been expecting him.

Still, she felt an odd reluctance to let Jack in. It was theirs, this house, but in the past few days it had become hers, and she'd become surprisingly possessive of her new solitude. "Come in before you drown."

He followed her into the house. Inside, she saw him look down for the rag rug that belonged in front of the door. It wasn't there.

Rain sluiced down his pant legs and formed a puddle.

"You better get out of those wet clothes. You'll catch a cold," she said matter-of-factly. It had always been her pattern—*take care of him*. "I'll get you a robe." She turned away from him and went upstairs.

She opened the closet door and pulled the robe off its hanger. Then she spun around and slammed into Jack.

At the contact, he stumbled backward. "Sorry. I thought you knew I was behind you."

They were like a couple of fourteen-year-olds on a first date. Nothing but nerves and emotions hanging out of their suddenly too-small sleeves and collars. "I'll make you some tea."

"What I'd really like is a Scotch on the rocks."

"Sorry."

He took the robe and went into the bathroom to change, closing the door behind him.

She stared at that door, seeing it as proof of everything that stood between them.

While he was dressing, she went back down to the living room and tossed another log onto the fire.

When she turned back around, he was there. The worn pink terry-cloth robe looked ridiculous on his big, powerful body. The fabric strained across his chest; the hemline hit him at midthigh.

He looked around at the candles. "There's a huge tree down on Sycamore Street. The power'll be out for hours."

"Did you fly all the way here to talk about electricity?" She sat down on the hearth, looking up at him.

"No."

"I guess you got my letter?"

"Yes." She could barely hear him, he'd said it so softly.

"Then perhaps we should talk about that."

The air seemed to seep out of him, leaving him smaller. He sat down beside her. "I don't know what you want me to say. I'm sorry for taking the job without talking to you?"

"Let me ask you a question."

He drew back; infinitesimal though the movement was, she saw it. An instinctive flinching away. "Okay."

"When you read my letter . . ." She looked him square in the eyes. "Tell me you weren't relieved."

The color faded from his cheeks. She knew he wanted to lie, to say *of course, I wasn't relieved,* but instead he said, "You know how long I've dreamed of a job like this one. And now, when I finally get my shot, you leave me."

"Come on, Jack. We aren't happy. We haven't been happy in a long time."

"But I love you."

It hurt, hearing those words again. "Do you? Then move back home. Let's try our new start here."

"You want me to give up my job? Is that what this is about?"

She'd known what his choice would be, but still it wounded her. "Too hard, huh, Jack?"

"I've waited years for this job. I've *dreamed* about it."

"Our whole marriage has been about your dreams, Jack. I followed you from town to town to town for two decades. Two decades. I've been the best wife and mother I know how to be, but now I'm . . . empty. I wake up in the middle of the night and I can't breathe, did you know that? You're the one who said I need to step up to the plate. Well, this is the plate, Jack. I need time to figure out what *my* dreams are." Despite her best intentions, her voice broke.

He ran a hand through his hair and let out a ragged sigh. "Jesus Christ, Birdie. You really mean it. I thought you were just trying to get my attention, so I'd move out to Connecticut or Westchester County." He sagged forward, resting his arms across his knees. Then he looked at her. "People who want time alone get divorced. Is that what you want?"

Her mouth fell open. "I didn't ask for a divorce."

"What did you think, Birdie? That we'd split up and stay married? That nothing would change? Fuck. What about the girls? What are we supposed to say to them when they ask why we're living apart?"

The girls.

Elizabeth made a small, panicked sound. The enormity of what she'd just done settled into place. When she'd asked for a separation, all she'd thought was: *I need time.* Just that. Now he was asking about what they'd tell their children.

She fought the urge to say, *Wait, Jack, let's talk it through again.*

He went upstairs and slammed the door shut behind him. A few moments later, he walked back into the living room. He was wearing his dripping wet clothes and holding an envelope. "Are you up for a little irony?"

"No," she answered quickly. "I don't think I am."

He offered her the envelope. Her fingers were trembling as

she took it, opened it. Inside was an official-looking document. The word *lease* jumped out at her. It was unsigned, but still. "Oh, Jack . . ."

He barely looked at her. "Read it."

She closed her eyes briefly, summoning the courage she'd so recently lost. It returned in quarter measure, almost useless to her. She unfolded a color flyer of a beautiful Federal-style house in East Hampton.

"There's a view of the water from the master bedroom. The realtor is holding it for me. I was going to surprise you for Valentine's Day. I guess this is your present to me."

She looked up at him through a blur of tears. She knew he wanted her to take it back, to be his wife again, but she couldn't do it. It took every ounce of strength she possessed to remain silent. But she knew if she backed down now, she'd be lost. Maybe forever this time.

"I love you, Birdie." His voice broke, and for a second, she saw how deeply she'd hurt him.

She wondered how long she'd carry this moment in her heart, how long she'd live with this sad and terrible ache. "I love you, too."

"Is that supposed to *help*?" He stared at her for a minute, then walked out of the house and slammed the door behind him.

SIXTEEN

WHAT IN THE HELL HAD MADE HIM SAY DIVORCE?

Jack slammed on the brakes. His rental car fishtailed on the muddy road and skidded to a stop. His headlights pointed out toward the rippling, black ocean.

He hadn't been this shaken since his mother's death, more than thirty years ago. Then, as now, his emotions had been a tangled mass with no clear beginning and no end.

If asked a week ago, he would have sworn that he and Birdie were in one of those rough patches that sometimes befell a long-term marriage. He would have said that it would pass, that nothing fundamental would change between them.

He'd thought—when he'd read her letter—that it was her way of getting his attention. The proverbial two-by-four between the ass's eyes. It had worked. He'd talked to that snooty East Hampton rental agent, then called in sick to work and driven to the airport.

It had never occurred to him that she meant it.

Not his Birdie, who couldn't make a decision to save her soul. How could she suddenly have found the guts to leave him? Her father's death must have really shaken her. He'd known she was unhappy, of course, but *this* . . . this he hadn't expected.

He'd spent more time thinking about his wife in the past twenty-four hours than in the past twenty-four years. He'd relied on his knowledge of her in planning what to say. He'd distilled it down to a script, which he'd practiced on the flight across the country.

But the woman he'd just spoken to wasn't his Birdie.

We aren't happy. We haven't been happy in a long time.

Those two sentences had ruined all of his plans. He'd been scared by them, terrified, even. That was when he'd known she was serious. Fear had immediately put him on the defensive, made him say what he'd never intended to say, never even thought about.

He slumped over the steering wheel, listening to the rain. Always the rain in this godforsaken place.

He almost turned the car around. The urge to go to her, to take her in his arms and beg for forgiveness was so strong he felt choked by it. Desperate.

But what then?

She was right. That was the utter hell of it. He might have reacted impulsively—*saying divorce, for God's sake, what an idiot*—but that didn't change the truth.

If he turned around now, she'd take him back (he couldn't imagine that she wouldn't), and they'd slide back into that boring, half-love rut they'd developed.

Here, alone in the car, he could admit that she was right. They both deserved better.

After all these years, she'd taken the decision out of his hands.

He closed his eyes, then slowly opened them. Rain patterned the windshield, thumped hard on the roof of the car.

"I loved you, Birdie," he whispered aloud.

It didn't escape his notice that even when he spoke to himself, in this cheap little car where no one could hear, he used the past tense.

THE NEXT DAY, the movers showed up with the furniture. Elizabeth stumbled out of bed to greet them. As soon as they left, she went back to bed. She stayed there for three days.

And still, she didn't want to get up.

She pulled the quilt up to her chin and lay there. Rain thumped on the roof, tapped on the window, a constant drip-drip-drip.

She understood now why couples broke up and got back together even if the love had turned stale. There was a safety in the known.

The irony was, *this* was what she'd dreamed of. All those years, as time and responsibility and daily life had slowly—so slowly— eroded her marriage and her personality, she'd dreamed of being On Her Own.

She'd always imagined that as an end in itself. A goal. A pie-in-the-sky dream that would bring with it little bluebirds of happiness.

She knew she'd made the right decision, but still, late at night when the house was dark and rain pummeled the roof, she worried that she would always be alone, that no one would ever kiss her again, or sit with her after dinner and talk about nothing. Worse yet, that no one would look at her slowly aging face and say, "You're beautiful, Birdie," or whisper, "I love you," just before the lights went out.

She flung the quilt aside and sat up.

It was time to start this new life of hers.

(This was a vow she'd made at least twice a day since Jack left.)

This time she meant it.

She swung her legs over the edge of the bed and planted her

bare feet on the cold floor. Like the Bride of Frankenstein, she lumbered to a stand.

"I could paint," she said aloud, just as she'd said every other time she'd managed to crawl out of bed, but even as she uttered the words, she felt defeated.

Slowly, her breath leaked out. She hardly made a sound at all as she sank back onto the bed.

If she didn't do *something*, she'd sink into a pit of depression.

When a woman was in this kind of trouble, there was only one thing to do. Unfortunately, the phone wouldn't be connected until "Sometime between noon and four o'clock."

She reached over to the bedside table for a paper and pen. Before she could talk herself out of it, she started to write.

Dear Meghann:

I'm in trouble. After years of whining, I have finally done something about my unhappiness. Jack and I are separated. It's funny that one little word, only a few syllables, can so profoundly rip the shit out of your life.

And here's the punch line (though it's a joke you've heard before): I'm even more unhappy. I want to kick up my heels and party till the sun goes down, but I can't seem to get my industrial-size ass out of bed.

You were right, it seems, about all of it.

I could use a laugh right about now. (So tell me about your newest boyfriend.)

XXOO

Elizabeth

She immediately felt better.

Reaching out to someone was better than sitting here, wondering what she was going to do with the rest of her life. What would it be like to be a woman alone?

Suddenly she thought about her stepmother, who was also alone.

You take care of Anita, you hear me?

It was the last thing Daddy had asked of her.

She'd made a deathbed promise . . . and then done nothing to keep it.

She reached for another piece of stationery.

*D*ear Anita:

I am at the beach house by myself.

It's quiet here, so quiet that I am beginning to realize how noisy my life was before. It is the way of women, I think, to follow the loudest voice, to constantly do for others.

I am trying now to find my own lost voice. Perhaps you are, too. An empty house can be a lonely, frightening world for women like us, used to listening to others.

My thoughts often drift southward these days, and I pray that you are okay. If there's anything I can do to help you, please don't be afraid to call. I know we've always been distant with each other, Anita, but in the words of Bob Dylan, "the times they are a changin'." Maybe we can find a new way.

My best,

Elizabeth

She got out of bed, dressed in a pair of ragged sweats, green plastic gardening clogs, and a fishing cap, like Kate Hepburn wore in *On Golden Pond*; then she walked up to the mailbox.

By the time she got home, she was breathing hard and soaked with sweat. She *definitely* needed more exercise.

She was in the bedroom, peeling off her wet sweats, when something occurred to her.

The Passionless Women.

She was one of them now.

•   •   •

IN THE DAYS FOLLOWING THE BREAKUP of his marriage, Jack made
sure he was never alone. Each morning, he woke at four A.M. and
was at the office by five, long before any of his colleagues. After
hours, he found someone—anyone—and hung out at the sports
bar on Fiftieth.

He didn't know how else to handle the separation. He'd never
been good at being alone.

Tonight, he stayed at the bar until it closed, downing drinks
with Warren. When he finally stumbled home, he was well past
drunk.

He walked into the apartment and called out Birdie's name.

The silence caught him off guard.

That was when it really hit him. They were separated. Without thinking it through, he picked up the phone and dialed her
number. It rang at least eight times before she answered.

"Hello?" She sounded tired.

He glanced at his watch. It was three in the morning here;
midnight in Oregon. "Heya, Birdie," he said, wincing.

"Oh. Hi."

He imagined her sitting up in bed, turning on the light. "It's
weird being without you," he admitted softly, sitting down on his
unmade bed.

"I know."

"I shouldn't have said 'divorce.' " Even now, the word made
his stomach tighten. "I was angry."

She didn't respond right away. He hated her silence; it made
him feel as if this were all his fault. Finally, she said, "Maybe I
should have done things differently, too."

"What now?" he asked. It was what he really wanted to know.
For twenty-four years, he'd lived with her, slept with her, cared for
her. Any other way was long forgotten.

"I don't know." She sounded faraway. "I need some time
alone."

"But what about us?"

"We go on, I guess. See where the road takes us."

"Well. Yeah." He tried to think of something else to say. "There's plenty of money in the bank account. You can have your bills sent to me if you want."

"Thanks, but I've got a checkbook. I'll be fine."

"Oh. Right." He fell silent again, confused. It felt as if they'd become strangers already. "Well, good night, Birdie."

"Good night, Jack."

He hung up the phone and flopped back onto the bed, staring up at the ceiling.

We go on.

What else was there? At this point, there were only two choices available to them. Go forward or back.

Like her, he wasn't ready to go back.

SEVENTEEN

WITH EACH PASSING DAY, ELIZABETH FELT A LITTLE MORE CONfident. She could sleep alone now; that didn't sound like much. Certainly millions of women did it every night, but to her, a woman who'd slept with the same man for all of her adult life, it was something.

She was no longer afraid to eat out alone. Yesterday, she'd had breakfast at the Wild Rose, all by herself. She even tried tofu.

Today, she was determined to try painting again.

She grabbed her down coat off the hook by the front door and reached for the black canvas bag that held her painting supplies. She kept it filled with charcoal and paper, paint and brushes, and hope.

Outside, the air was crisp and cold. She crossed the porch and paused at the top of the stairs. The ocean was a smear of pastel gray and lavender. The grass in her yard looked like a patch of Christmas felt, tacked down here and there by the snow-white mushrooms that had sprouted overnight. A pair of cormorants flew overhead, circling lazily.

She flipped her hood up and walked across the squishy carpet of lawn, trying to avoid the pretty mushrooms. At the top of the beach stairs, she stopped and looked down.

It was high tide.

Disappointed, she sat down on the damp top step. White breakers bashed themselves against the rocky outcropping at the base of the cliff, spraying foam. Every now and again, she felt a sprinkle of spindrift on her face.

It reminded her of a time, years ago, when Daddy had taken her boating in the Florida Keys. Mr. Potter had offered Daddy the use of a speedboat to pay off a debt, and Daddy had thought, why not? how hard could it be to drive on water?—and off they'd gone.

It had been a disaster, of course. Every time they came into port, Elizabeth had had to lie on the bow and push them away from other boats. Bumper boating, he'd called it.

Elizabeth smiled at the memory.

"Birdie?"

Elizabeth twisted around.

Meghann was standing beside her mud-coated black Porsche Boxster. Her designer jeans and black cashmere sweater were streaked by rain, and her hair was so frizzy it looked as if she'd had shock treatments. "Are you *aware* that it's raining?"

"Meg!" Elizabeth stood up, grabbed her bag, and ran. When Meg pulled her into a bear hug, it was almost impossible to let go.

"Don't you dare start crying. Now, get me under a roof somewhere, preferably with a drink in my hand."

Elizabeth clutched Meg's hand and led her through the gray yard.

"On the way here, I think I saw a fish swimming across the road."

Laughing, Elizabeth led her into the house, then built a fire and got out her only alcohol. A box of wine.

Meghann looked at the box. "This is worse than I thought. You have clearly confused me with a local. Wait here." She marched out of the house and returned a minute later with a suitcase, which she flopped onto the coffee table and opened. "Shoes come in boxes; wine comes in bottles." She burrowed through her clothes and pulled out a bottle of tequila. "After that poor-me letter you sent, I figured we might need this."

"You're the best friend a girl could have."

They each drank two straight shots before another word was spoken. Finally, Meghann scooted back and leaned against the sofa. "So, kiddo, how the hell are you?"

Elizabeth sighed. "It's pathetic, Meg. For years, I dreamed of starting my life over, but now I'm *too* alone. I'm scared to death. What if I've done the wrong thing? What if—"

"Everything you're going through is normal, believe me. It'll get better."

"Tell me you can do better than fortune-cookie scribblings."

"You don't normally want my advice. I'm too harsh."

"I know, but I'm desperate now. What would you tell me if I were a client?"

"Get out your checkbook."

"Very funny. Come on, help me."

Meghann leaned toward her. "I'd tell you that sometimes decisions are made too quickly. You've loved Jack for a long time."

"You mean go back to him." Elizabeth had thought that herself, mostly at night when loneliness and fear crept into bed with her. She knew it would be easier to go back. But she was tired of taking the easy road. "It was like living in quicksand, Meg. I was getting pulled under; more and more of me was disappearing. I can't go back to that."

"Tell me what happened."

"In Tennessee I wrote him a letter. It just said I didn't want to move to New York, that I was going back to Oregon."

"Just?"

Elizabeth ignored that. "When he got here, I told him I needed some time alone. That's actually as far as I thought it through."

"I take it Jack saw the big picture."

"He used the word 'divorce.' I hadn't even *thought* it."

"Jesus, Birdie, what did you expect? He's a man, for God's sake. You abandoned him, refused to follow him. It's like ripping their balls off."

"Unfortunately, I was unaware that his balls were the issue. I thought we were talking about our hearts."

"With men, it's always a dick thing. If I had a daughter, that's the real-world advice I would give her."

"Reason enough to keep you taking your birth control pills." She smiled, then sighed. "I guess I should have been prepared for his anger—he's always had a healthy ego—but I know he was unhappy, too. I figured he would welcome a little time apart."

"He probably didn't think you meant it—the letter, I mean. And then, when he found out you were serious, he blew a gasket. Just because he said 'divorce' doesn't mean he really wants one."

"I know. So, give me some advice here, Meghann. I feel as if I'm treading water in the deep end of the pool. I need your three-hundred-dollar-an-hour plan."

Meghann took a sip of tequila, then said slowly, "Well, for a woman like you, I usually—"

"Like me?"

Meghann winced. "Great mother, decent income, no real work experience."

"Oh, a woman like me. Go on." Elizabeth decided on another shot.

"Anyway, usually I recommend finding a job. It's good for the self-esteem, not to mention the bank account. However, I drove through Echo Beach."

Elizabeth tossed back the drink. "Yeah. Maybe the fish market needs someone to wipe up salmon guts. God knows I have enough cleaning experience."

"I think you should cast your net a little farther. No pun intended."

"Like Cannon Beach?"

Meghann scooted closer. "I thought about this on the drive down here. You always wanted to get your master's degree in fine arts, remember? This would be a great time to do it."

"That was a long time ago."

"Your excuses are wearing thin, Birdie. You could have gone to graduate school twenty years ago; you chose not to. Do you really want to leave Jack and fall into the same old patterns?"

It was true. She could have gotten her master's before the kids were born. Why hadn't she?

Because it would have made life difficult. What if Jack's dinner had been late? Or she'd had a midterm on a game night?

What if she hadn't been talented enough?

"I guess I didn't want it enough." That much was true, at least. She'd never been good at taking big risks unless it benefitted her children. And so she was here, a woman "like her," with nothing to fall back on and nothing to reach for.

"Be bold, Birdie. *Apply.* Take the road you turned away from. Isn't that what this is all about?"

"Come on, Meg. I'm forty-five years old and I haven't painted in twenty years. Sometimes, you really don't get a second chance." She didn't want to talk about this anymore. "I can't imagine applying for grad school on my credentials."

Meghann was clearly disappointed. "What about painting class, then?"

Elizabeth shuddered at the thought. Sitting in a room with a bunch of strangers, pretending she'd refound a lost talent? Hardly.

Meghann looked at her. "Okay, okay. Your eye is twitching. I'll change the subject."

"Thank you."

"How about this: *I* need *your* help. I'm trying to change my slutty ways. The problem is, I need to figure out how to get turned on by a man my own age."

Elizabeth laughed. "Start slowly. Quit dating men who say things like *awesome, dude,* and *that's tight.*"

"And make conversation? I think not. Let me tell you, Birdie. The dating pool is damned shallow out there. You'll see. My last date wiped his nose on the tablecloth at Canlis, which actually placed him on a higher evolutionary rung than the guy who blew his nose out the car window because the Kleenex box was empty. Just wait, Birdie. In about six months, the fish-gut guy will start looking hot. When you finally realize what men our age are like, give me a call. I'll talk you down from the ledge. Wait! Better yet, move up to Seattle. You could have my second bedroom."

"I love it here, you know that."

"Here? It's another damned planet—and an uninhabited one at that. And let me tell you, that is not an ordinary rain. I'm a Seattleite; we know rain."

Laughing, Elizabeth slipped an arm around her friend's shoulders and drew her close. "The beach is beautiful."

"When you can see it. On the way down here, I saw a group of Japanese tourists lashed together for a beach walk. They'll probably never be found."

"When the sun shines—"

"Twice a year."

"It's the prettiest place on earth. You can breathe here."

"I can breathe in Beirut. It doesn't mean I want to live there."

The alarm on the oven beeped. Elizabeth stood up, realizing abruptly how drunk she was. Her legs felt rubbery and she couldn't feel the tips of her fingers at all. It made her giggle. "Come with me."

Meghann crawled to her feet. "Where are we going? Dancing? I love dan—" She frowned. "What was I talking about?"

They clutched each other like eighth-grade girls, their heads cocked together, giggling. Elizabeth led Meghann through the kitchen.

At the front door, Meghann stumbled to a halt. "Outside? It's raining hard enough to put your eye out."

"A little water won't hurt you."

"I'd rather not."

"We're going down to the beach. I go every night at this time. It's become a new ritual for me. Sort of a fear antivenin."

"That's because you have no life. For the next two days, *I'm* here for entertainment."

Elizabeth dragged her forward. "Hurry up or we'll miss them. My whales are very punctual."

Meghann stopped dead. "Whales? You're kidding, right?"

Elizabeth laughed. Damn, it felt good. "Come on, Counselor. For once, you're going to follow instead of lead."

Elizabeth stepped into the darkened yard. Meghann stumbled along beside her, grasped her hand tightly. Rain fell hard and fast, turned the yard into a giant mud puddle.

"Be careful, it's slippery," Elizabeth said.

They were halfway across the yard when the first call sounded. "Hurry up," she said. "They're here."

"You need help," Meghann said, spitting rain. "Serious, long-term, probably medicated help."

JACK ARRIVED AT THE STUDIO a little later than usual. He'd been out late last night, tossing back brewskis with Warren at Hogs 'n Heifers. He barely remembered getting home.

He'd had good reason to celebrate: *Good Sports* had premiered last week and become an instant hit. Ratings had gone through the roof.

Jack was hot again.

In the conference room, he went straight to the coffeemaker and poured himself a cup.

"Good God," Warren said, laughing, "you look like hell. Just can't party like the old days, eh, Jacko?"

Smiling, Jack eased into the leather chair. "You're looking a little the worse for wear yourself, Butterfingers. Maybe you shouldn't have had that last plate of nachos."

Before Warren could answer, the door opened. The show's executive producer, Tom Jinaro, walked briskly into the room. His assistant, Hans, trailed along behind, his violin-bow arms loaded up with yellow notebooks and reams of paper.

Tom took his usual seat at the head of the table. A moment later, Warren's assistant came into the room and sat beside him.

Jack sat alone on his side of the table.

Tom looked down at his notes, then up at the faces around him. "Hans thinks we should do something on ephedrine in supplements. Sort of the secret-deadly-killer kind of thing. What do you think, Warren?"

Warren shrugged. "If someone dropped dead, there's probably a story there."

"Jack? What's your opinion?"

"Truthfully, Tom, I think it's dull as mud. The kind of story that *60 Minutes* or *Dateline* might do because they're on-air so much. We should be pushing the envelope a little more, making people think. I read this article the other day—I think it was in *The Christian Science Monitor*, but it might have been the *Times*—anyway, it was about the 'troubles' in Northern Ireland. Comparing it to the U.S. after September eleventh. The Irish know about living in dangerous, uncertain times. There's got to be a way to tie it to sports."

Tom tapped his pen on the table. After a long minute, he said, "Jack's right. I don't know shit from Shinola about Ireland, but it's a better hook than some drug no one can pronounce." He turned to Hans. "You know anything about Ireland?"

Hans frowned, pushed the glasses higher on his Ichabod Crane nose. "There's a sports camp in the Mideast where they bring Jewish and Palestinian kids together. Maybe there's something like that in Ireland. You know, Catholics and Protestants coming together on the soccer field or some damned thing."

Tom smiled. "That's why you're my guy, Hans. Check it out. Give me a report by tomorrow A.M." Then he thumped his hand on the desk. "Okay, sports fans, let's go through today's script."

They spent the next two hours reading through and editing the script. Then Jack and Warren went into the studio, where their guest—an Olympic long jumper who'd recently been diagnosed with MS—was waiting.

After the show, Jack hung around the studio for a while, talking to the various staffers who'd also stayed late. An hour or so later, when the building was nearly empty, he returned to his office.

He sat down at his desk and picked up the phone, dialing a number from memory.

She answered on the third ring. "Hello?"

"Hey, Sally," he said, leaning back in his chair.

"Jack! It's great to hear from you. How're things in New York? I hear your show is popping some killer numbers."

He couldn't remember the last time someone had sounded so genuinely happy to hear from him. "Things are great. Fox thinks I'm a god."

"We all think that, Jack. It sure isn't as much fun around here without you."

"Then maybe you wouldn't mind moving to New York. I need an assistant."

It was a moment before she asked, "Are you kidding me?"

"No. This is a genuine offer, okayed by my boss. We can't offer a hell of a lot of money, but I'm sure it's more than you're making now."

"I can be there in ten days." She laughed. "I'll live in the YWCA if I have to. Thanks, Jack. You don't know what this means to me."

"You deserve it, Sally."

"Thank you."

After Jack hung up, he sat there a minute. He was just about to leave for home when the phone rang again.

It was Warren. "Hey, Jacko, Beth has her yoga class tonight. How about dinner at Sparks?"

"Count me in."

"Seven-thirty okay?"

"Meet you there."

It took Jack longer than he'd expected to get home, change into Levi's and a black T-shirt, and catch a cab. He pulled up to the restaurant at seven-forty-five.

Outside, he caught a glimpse of his reflection in the darkened window. He paused just long enough to run a hand through his now quite blond hair.

The hostess, a pretty young woman in a skintight black dress, smiled up at him. Her cheeks were as pink as cotton candy. "Welcome back to Sparks, Mr. Shore."

He gave her his showbiz smile. "Well, thanks. It's nice to be here. I'm meeting Warren Mitchell."

"He's already here. Follow me." She turned and walked away from him. Her small, beautiful ass swung gently this way and that. He followed her to a table in the back corner of the restaurant.

There, she touched his arm, smiled sweetly up at him. "I'm here until closing. If there's *anything*"—her voice italicized the word—"you need, just let me know."

God it felt good, being wanted again.

"I'll think about that, darlin'," he said, sliding into the seat. He watched her walk away.

Warren laughed. "I ordered you a Dewar's on the rocks." He raised his own glass in a salute. "It's awesome what a little TV exposure does for a guy's sex appeal, isn't it? Even old guys like us."

Jack reached for his drink. "It feels good to be *somebody* again, I can tell you that."

Warren took a sip of his drink. "It couldn't have been easy, going from the NFL to local sportscaster in Sioux Falls."

"I was never in Sioux Falls, but the point remains. It *was* hell."

"I wasn't there for you back then. When your knee gave out."

"There wasn't anything you could have done."

"Bullshit." Warren took another drink. "It scared the shit out of me, you know? One minute you were on top of the world; the next minute you were down for the count."

"I always knew I had glass knees. It was only a matter of time."

"How'd you get through it?"

Jack leaned back against the tufted seat. That was something he hadn't thought about in years, the *how* of losing everything. After the surgeries, he'd slept a lot; he remembered that. He'd stayed for days, maybe weeks, in his bedroom, holed up in the dark, pretending the pain was worse than it was, popping pills as if they were Sweetarts.

One day, Elizabeth had whipped open the curtains. *That's all the time you get, Jackson Shore. Now, get up, get dressed, and meet me in the living room. We have the rest of your life to plan. In ten minutes, I'm going to dump ice water on you, so don't lollygag.*

True to her word, she'd dumped water on his head. Then a few minutes—hours—later, she'd dared to use the prohibited words: *drug addiction.*

"Elizabeth got me through it."

"That doesn't surprise me. You got lucky with Birdie. If I'd married a girl like her instead of—"

"We broke up." It was the first time he'd said the words aloud. He was surprised by how it felt, both depressing and uplifting at the same time. He'd seen Warren looking at him last night while they were out drinking; more than once his friend had asked when Birdie was getting back to town. "It took me a while to say it out loud, that's all."

"Jesus, you two have been married forever. You're the only hope the rest of us have."

He'd heard that for years, from all of his friends who'd married and divorced and then married again. "Then there's no hope."

"Are you okay?"

The answer to that question had layers and layers. The truth was, he didn't want to look too deep. When he did—mostly late at night when he was lonely—he remembered the good times instead of the bad, and he ached for what they'd lost. It was better to swim on the surface of that pool, to feel good about his new life. "Yeah. It had gotten pretty stale around our house."

"I know how that is. The silence'll kill you. How is she taking it?"

Warlord assumed it had been Jack's decision to separate. Of course. No one would credit Birdie with the guts to end their marriage.

"She's okay. Now can we please talk about something else?"

"Sure, Jack," Warren said slowly. "Anything you want."

EIGHTEEN

THE BEACH HAD BECOME ELIZABETH'S SANCTUARY. IN PLAINEST terms, it had saved her. In the past week, she'd spent hours sitting on "her" rock, rain or shine. The weather didn't bother her one way or the other. Day by day, hour by hour, she became stronger.

Until today, finally, she was ready to step back into her ordinary world.

According to her planner, tonight—Thursday—was the yearly library auction and dinner dance. It was amazing that she'd forgotten, given the countless hours she'd spent organizing the event.

She picked up the phone and called her cochair, Allison Birch. "Hey, Ali," she said when her friend answered. "It's me, Elizabeth."

"Oh, hi. I thought you'd moved to New York already."

"I came back."

She was trying to tack an explanation onto that when Ali said, "Is Jack back on the air? I haven't seen him."

"Just me. *I* came back. Jack and I are . . ."

There was a long pause. "Did you two split up?"

"We're taking a break from each other, that's all."

"Jeez. I never thought he'd leave you. I mean . . . I know you guys were having problems, but I thought it was . . . you know. The way we're all unhappy now and then."

Elizabeth didn't know which part to answer. Of course Allison assumed that the separation was Jack's idea. Women like Elizabeth didn't leave men like Jack.

"So, what are you going to do?" Allison asked.

"I thought I'd look for a job."

"In Echo Beach?" Allison laughed. "Doing what?"

"I don't know yet. Anyway, I'm still here and I wanted you to know that. Maybe we can have lunch together next Wednesday, after the site committee meeting?"

"Sure."

"And tonight is the library auction. I guess I'll see you there."

This time, when Allison paused, Elizabeth tensed up.

"It's a dance," Allison said. "Who will you bring?"

Elizabeth had forgotten how paired up the world was. "I didn't think about that."

"You'd have to sit by yourself at our table. Wouldn't that be weird?"

"I guess I have to learn how to go places alone," Elizabeth said, hearing the little catch in her voice.

"Yeah," Allison said on a sigh. "I guess you do. Should Chuck and I pick you up?"

"No," she said quietly, knowing that she wouldn't go now. Couldn't go. She stumbled through a few more moments of awkward small talk, then pleaded a headache and hung up. She slumped down onto the sofa.

This damned separation was a never-ending series of late hits.

She was single now. A woman alone, one who'd blundered daringly into some unfamiliar country without a map or compass.

She started to get that sorry-for-herself feeling and refused to give in to it. She'd been hiding out long enough.

It was time to merge back into the traffic of her old life. So what that there would be no car-pool lane this time. Such was life. What mattered was conquering fear.

She got up and went into the kitchen for a glass of water. It was there, by the fridge, that she noticed the calendar. Today had two things listed.

Library auction: 6:30
Passionless: 7:00

She'd forgotten all about the meeting, which was odd, since she'd actually intended to go.

But tonight, she was going to the auction.

She went upstairs, showered, dyed her hair, and then poured her more-than-healthy body into the elegant DKNY red knit dress she'd bought last month. She put on her makeup with exquisite care, trying to look her very best. At last, she added a single piece of jewelry, an intricate butterfly necklace, handcrafted of sterling silver and onyx.

When she stood back and looked in the full-length mirror, she saw a slightly overweight woman in a clingingly sexy dress. Not a "new" Elizabeth at all.

She paused, debating the whole question again, then reached in her closet for a black pashmina shawl, and left the house.

She drove past several small seaside towns. At Manzanita, she turned off the main highway and followed the twisting, treelined road down to the beach. Here and there, houses glowed against the falling darkness. Finally, the road spit her out in the parking lot of one of the coast's few glittering four-star hotels. As she neared her destination, nerves fluttered in her stomach.

What was she doing? She couldn't go in there alone—

"Yes, you can."

She parked the car and sat there.

It was twenty-five minutes after six. The auction would be starting any minute. If she waited too long, everyone would notice her entrance. Better to slip in quietly.

She took a deep breath. "Okay. I'm getting out of the car now."

She wrapped the cashmere-blend shawl around her body and headed toward the hotel.

In the lobby, she saw several people she knew. Smiling, nodding, she kept moving, but she was certain she heard, *Where's Jack?* whispered behind her.

She was imagining it, surely.

She hurried up the carpeted stairs toward the ballroom. At the open door, she paused.

Dozens of beautifully dressed people sat at white-clothed tables, chatting with one another.

She knew what they were saying: the same things a group like this always talked about, regardless of what city or town they were in. Men talked about jobs and sports. For women, it was school, kids, and diets.

In the corner, a jazz trio pumped out an uneasy rendition of an old Ella Fitzgerald song.

She didn't need to check her ticket to find her table. There it was, front and center. One of the perks of being Echo Beach's premier volunteer was prime table placement. Of course, it didn't hurt that she was—*had been*—married to one of the town's very few celebrities.

Allison and Chuck were already seated. Even from this distance, Elizabeth could see that Allison was wearing her usual choice: a black St. John knit. Three other couples were already at the table, talking quietly among themselves and sipping champagne. They were all people Elizabeth knew, some well, some only in passing. In a town this size, everyone knew everyone a little.

There were two empty chairs at the table.

Elizabeth could have done it; she knew that suddenly, certainly. She could have tilted her chin up and walked through the whispering crowd and taken her single place at that double opening.

But why?

This wasn't her life. It was the one she'd taken on by default. The by-product of Jack's life. That was why she had so many acquaintances in this room and so few friends.

Long ago, when the girls had been small and money was tight and they'd moved to a new town every two years, she'd discovered that the quickest way to make friends was to volunteer for everything. Town by town, her pattern had stayed the same. Move in, start volunteering, make fragile friendships, move on.

In Echo Beach, she'd automatically shoehorned her life into Jack's footprint without bothering to question her choices.

Now she did just that.

She didn't want to be the woman she'd been before. Wasn't that the whole point of what she'd done? She didn't want to melt into this crowd, talk about the usual things, and become good-old-Elizabeth, the one to turn to in a pinch. Jack's wife.

She backed away from who she'd been and turned around. Like Cinderella, she ran down the stairs with her shawl fluttering out behind her and got into her car.

A quick glance at the dashboard clock told her it was six-forty.

The Passionless women meeting started in twenty minutes.

She started the car and hit the gas. It was seven-fifteen when she reached the community college.

Wrapping the shawl tightly around her, she walked briskly through the empty corridors and stepped into the classroom.

"Elizabeth!" Sarah Taylor said when she walked into the room. "We were afraid you weren't going to make it this week."

Amazingly, Elizabeth laughed. The welcome was what she'd needed. "I got lost."

Mina chuckled. "We're all lost, sweetie. Come on in."

Elizabeth wound through the circle of women and sat in an empty chair beside Kim.

Kim didn't smile. "You should have stayed away. This group'll just drag you down."

Elizabeth looked at the faces of these women who knew exactly how she felt right now. "I've been dragging myself down lately."

"Really? You look happier," Kim said.

Before Elizabeth could answer, Sarah started the meeting. "Who would like to begin tonight?"

To her own amazement, Elizabeth raised her hand. She felt a flash of fear when everyone looked at her. "My husband and I separated."

"And how do you feel about that?" Sarah asked gently.

Once Elizabeth started talking, she found that she couldn't stop. The whole story came tumbling out. She ended with, "Tonight I tried to go back to my old life, but that's not right, either. I need a new life, but I don't quite know how to start. So I came here."

Mina leaned forward. "I was thinking about you this week. Maybe I'm psychic." She gave Elizabeth a sad smile. "Anyhoo, yesterday, I was reading the college catalog, looking for classes I could take now that I can drive, and I noticed that a painting class is starting soon."

Elizabeth felt a little spark of something. Hope, maybe. "Really?"

Mina reached into her leather-patchwork handbag and pulled out a floppy catalog. "I saved it for you." She walked through the middle of the circle and handed the catalog to Elizabeth.

"Thanks," Elizabeth said, surprised to realize that she meant it.

After that, the discussion moved around the circle, dipping time and again into the kind of intimacy that was marked by sudden emotion—tears or laughter.

The only one who didn't speak was Kim. Throughout the

whole meeting, she sat stiffly beside Elizabeth, fiddling with a half-empty cigarette pack, snorting derisively every now and then.

Finally, the meeting broke up. Elizabeth stood around for a few minutes, talking to the women; then she went back to her car.

She was almost to the parking lot when she noticed Kim, standing off by herself, smoking a cigarette.

Elizabeth hesitated for a moment. In her previous life, she would never have ventured into another person's pain. She would have kept her distance, been respectful.

Across the darkness, in the blue-white glare of a streetlamp, she looked at Kim. Their gazes met.

Elizabeth went to her. When she was closer, she saw tear tracks on Kim's pale face. "You want a cigarette?"

"No, thanks."

They stood there, silent, each one staring out toward the parking lot. Smoke scented the cool air.

"You ever go to the sand castle competition on Cannon Beach?" Kim asked, exhaling smoke.

"Sure." She knew the competition well; every local did. People came from miles around to build exquisite, intricate sculptures. Everything from castles to mermaids. Each entry looked beautiful and permanent, but by morning, the sea had taken them all back.

She understood. Kim had thought, as Elizabeth once had, that marriage was solid ground. But it was all sand. Here one minute, shaped into magical forms, and gone the next.

Kim looked at her. "Sarah thinks I'm scared. That I'm afraid to hope."

"We're all afraid."

"I guess." Kim tossed her cigarette down and stomped it out with her boot heel. "Well. See you next week."

"I'll be here."

Kim walked away, got in a pretty blue Miata, and drove away.

Elizabeth followed her. Out on the highway, their paths diverged.

Elizabeth drove down the highway. On Stormwatch Lane, she stopped, pulled her mail out of the box, and then continued down the road for home.

By the time she parked, it was raining again.

Inside the house, she tossed her shawl on the kitchen table and flipped through the mail. There was a big manila envelope from Meghann.

She ripped it open. College catalogs fell out onto the table. Columbia. NYU. SUNY. Three of the graduate programs that had accepted Elizabeth all those years ago.

A Post-it note read: YOU CAN'T SAY YOU DON'T HAVE TIME NOW.

ELIZABETH AVOIDED TALKING to her daughters. She carefully called during school hours or when swim practice was going on, and left cheerful messages that sounded as if everything were unfolding as it always had. Dad was doing great in New York, lighting up the airwaves; Mom was working hard to get the place ready for renters. Lies that stacked like a house of cards.

She glanced at the mantel clock. It was one-forty-five.

Four-forty-five in Washington, D.C.

They'd be in swim practice right now. Saturday was the big meet against UVa.

Coward, Elizabeth thought as she punched in the number. She was so busy devising her pert, upbeat message that it took her a moment to realize Stephanie had answered.

"Hello?"

Elizabeth laughed nervously. "Hey, honey, it's good to hear your voice. I've been thinking about you guys a lot lately."

"Hey, Mom." Stephanie sounded tired. "Your uterine-radar must be working. I'm sick."

"What's wrong?"

A pause slid through the line, and in that split second, Elizabeth imagined the worst. Motherhood was like that; it pushed you out on a ledge and then said, *Be careful. Don't look down.*

"Don't call nine-one-one or anything. I just have the stomach flu. Everything that goes down comes right back up."

"Is Jamie taking care of you?"

"Oh, yeah, that's her specialty. This morning she said, 'If you think you're going to puke, aim away from my new shoes.' "

Elizabeth laughed. It was so Jamie. "I'm sure you'll be back on your feet in no time."

"I hope so. Hey, Mom, I'm glad you called. I need to talk to you about something. Tim's parents invited Jamie and me to go skiing over spring break. They have a place in Vermont. It's the second week in March."

Thank God.

Elizabeth had been worrying about how she and Jack would handle the separation with the girls at home. It was one thing to avoid the truth by phone. It was quite another to lie to your children in person. "That sounds great."

"It's kind of expensive. Lift tickets—"

"Your dad can afford it." Elizabeth winced. She should have said *We can afford it.*

"It'd be the first spring break we haven't come home. Are you okay with that?"

Sweet Stephie, always worried about hurting people's feelings. Elizabeth had a sudden urge to say, *Break a few eggs, honey, be courageous,* but instead she said, "I'll miss you, of course, but you should go. Have fun."

"Thanks, Mom. So, how's it going with the house? You must be going crazy. Every time I call Dad, he sounds so amped about Manhattan. You must really miss him."

"I do," Elizabeth said, flinching at her word choice.

"How much longer will you be in Oregon?"

"I don't know. Nobody seems to want to live this far out, and we can't leave the house empty." She glanced down at her left hand, curled in her lap. The diamond ring was still there. Everything about it, her wearing of it, was both a lie and the deepest truth. Looking at it now, all she saw was the lie.

"So, how're classes going?" she said to change the subject.

It worked. Stephanie told several funny "Jamie stories" about how her sister had gotten into and out of trouble. "As usual," Steph said, "Jamie caused the social equivalent of a ten-car pileup and didn't even notice. Tim says she needs a rearview mirror to see her own life."

Elizabeth laughed. "She gets that from my dad. He never once looked before he leaped. He said it ruined the surprise." Her voice snagged on the thought: *He's gone.*

"Are you okay, Mom?"

"I miss him."

"I know. Jamie's having a hard time with it. She and Grandad were so close. I think it's affecting her swimming. And she's not sleeping well."

Elizabeth sighed. Her poor little girl. Jamie might be all hard shell on the outside, but inside, she had a soft candy center. "Keep your eye on her for me. I'll call her tomorrow after her physical anthro class."

"I tried getting her to see a counselor on campus, but you know Jamie. She told me to butt out."

"You're a good girl, Steph," Elizabeth said. "Do I tell you that often enough?"

"Yes, Mom."

Elizabeth chose her next words carefully. "Just don't forget how to put Stephanie first. Sometimes, you have to be selfish or life can slip through your fingers."

"Are you okay, Mom?"

"Sure. I'm just a little tired, that's all."

Stephanie was quiet for a moment. In the background, a television was playing. There was a swell of applause. "Is there something you wish you'd done, you know, like besides having kids and getting married?"

It was the kind of question a woman usually came to too late in life, after she'd chosen one road and realized it was a dead end. "What makes you ask that?"

"I'm watching this program about a woman who killed her kids. It seems she always wanted to be a policewoman. Like *that* would have been a good choice. Anyway, the shrink is blabbing about how women sublimate their own needs. He compares it to loading a weapon. Someday: bang."

Bang, indeed.

It would have been easy to deflect, but she didn't want to take the easy way. There were things she should have told her daughters, advice she should have given them. Unfortunately, some truths she'd learned too late. "Not *instead of*; then I wouldn't have had you and Jamie. But *in addition to*, maybe. I used to love painting. It got lost somewhere along the way."

"I didn't know that."

That was, perhaps, the worst of all her failings. She'd been so afraid of her own lost dream that she'd pretended it had never existed. How could a woman who'd clipped her own wings teach her babies to fly? "I don't know why I didn't talk about it. I used to be something special, though."

"You still are, Mom."

"I'm thinking of taking a painting class at the local college." There, she'd said it. Molded a dream into words and given it the strength of voice.

"That'd be awesome. I'm sure you'll blow the shit out of the curve."

Elizabeth laughed at that. She hadn't even thought about grades. "You just remember, Stephie, these are your glory years. No husband, no babies, no one to tell you what you can't do. This is your time to dream big and soar." Elizabeth heard the fierce edge of regret in her voice. It was so easy to see the world in retrospect. She started to say something else, then heard a sound that brought her up short. "Baby? Are you crying?"

"You're not *that* inspirational, Mom. I just feel lousy. Now I'm getting a headache. I think I'm gonna crash. I'll have Jamie call when she gets back from swim practice."

"Okay, honey. Drink lots of fluids. And tell Tim hi for me. For us," she amended. How quickly she'd begun to think in the singular.

"Tell Dad I love him."

"I will."

"And tell him to call me tonight. I want to hear how his big interview with Jay went."

(*Jay who?*)

"Okay," she said. "I love you."

"Love you guys, too. Bye."

FOR THE LAST FEW DAYS, Jack's life had been a full-speed running game. Drew Grayland's arraignment had been broadcast on Court TV. The young man had admitted nothing and pled not guilty, but that didn't matter. The whole sordid, sorry story had come front and center. All across America, students and parents were protesting the lack of athlete accountability. Female students from dozens of universities had filed rape charges against football and basketball players.

At the heart of the story stood Jack Shore. By luck and chance—and a ton of Fox advertising money—he'd become the national poster boy for change. Everyone knew who he was again.

Now he was on the edge of his seat. Literally.

Sally sat beside him, her foot tapping unevenly on the floor as she pawed through the fruit basket on the coffee table. "You're going to be *great*," she said for at least the fifteenth time in as many minutes.

To be honest, he needed her to say it, again and again. That was a big part of why he'd hired her. She was great for his ego—and, of course, she was a damned fine assistant. She'd organized every nuance of this opportunity, hadn't she?

There was a knock at the door. In walked Avery Kormane, the woman who'd shown him to the small, windowless waiting room and conducted his pre-interview. "How're you doing?"

"Has anyone ever puked on the *Tonight Show*, or will I be the first?"

"A bird caller from Kentucky took one look at the audience and fell face-first onto the floor." She smiled. "Everyone's nervous in this room. I've seen your tapes. You'll do fine once you're in front of the camera. Just focus on Jay if you get nervous. He's a nice guy. He'll catch you if you fall."

Sally had chosen Leno for that very reason. When the offers started pouring in last week, Jack had instinctively gravitated toward Letterman. It was Sally who'd reminded him that Leno was a hell of lot easier.

Avery consulted her clipboard. "As I told you earlier, your seat is the one closest to Jay. The others should be empty. George Clooney has to catch a flight to D.C. for the next leg of his press junket."

Jack glanced up at the television monitor on the wall. On screen, Thea Cartwright was laughing with Jay. She was the most beautiful woman in Hollywood, bar none. "What about Thea?"

Avery looked up sharply. Behind the world's ugliest black frame glasses, her eyes narrowed. "Do you know her? I don't have that in my notes."

Sally was frowning at him.

"No, no. I just think she's great. That's all." He felt like a complete idiot.

Avery's nose crimped up. "Oh, that. Well, she'll be long gone. She has an opening tonight. You just shake Jay's hand, wave to the audience, and take your seat." She glanced at her watch. "Follow me."

Jack did as he was told. Sally stuck to his side like glue. They walked through the industrial maze of backstage hallways, passing several closed doors that had red *on air* signs above them. Finally, they came to the edge of the stage.

A narrow vertical sign lit up the word *Hollywood* beside him. The lights buzzed softly.

Jack's palms were sweating like geysers. He was wetter than the goddamn *Man from Atlantis*.

"You'll be great," Sally said again.

He wished Elizabeth were here. It only took a look from her, a feather touch, to calm him. He'd wanted this—national exposure—for years, but now that it was here, he was as jumpy as a rookie on the starting line.

This wasn't like reading the news from a teleprompter. He was supposed to be relaxed and witty. Avery had mentioned *funny personal anecdotes* as a good thing.

Had anything even remotely funny ever happened to him?

My wife dumped me last month . . . ba dump ba. Funny enough?

Applause thundered, shook the soundstage. On the wall, a red light flashed.

Avery tapped his shoulder. "You're on, Jack. Break a leg."

He mumbled something—he had no idea what—and stumbled around the corner. The lights were Broadway bright and aimed at his face. He could barely make out the stacked rows of people. He blinked suddenly, realized the lights weren't aimed at him; he was staring right into one.

Idiot.

His smile felt awkward, as if he'd borrowed it from a bigger man.

Jay was coming toward him, hand outstretched.

"Jumpin' Jack Flash," he said, smiling.

And just that easy, Jack's nerves dissipated. He'd forgotten that: he was The Flash. "Hey, Jay." He waved at the crowd, who applauded wildly.

He followed Jay across the brightly lit stage. He was at the big wooden desk when he saw her. At the same time, he heard Jay's voice.

". . . Thea wanted to stay. She says football is her second favorite sport."

There was a whoop of approval from the audience.

Thea got up from her seat and walked toward him. Her thin,

leggy body was barely covered by a strapless black top and a hot pink miniskirt. She wore almost no makeup; her wheat-blond hair looked as it if had been hacked with a Weed Eater. It was sexy as hell. In heels, she was as tall as he.

For a split second, he was sixteen years old again, a kid pinning Farrah Fawcett posters to his wall.

Thea grinned at the crowd. "Now, *this* is a good-looking man, am I wrong, ladies?"

He almost passed out, honest to God. The lights overhead felt interrogation-hot all of a sudden. He smelled her perfume, musky and sweet at the same time. He nodded and forced himself to turn away, afraid he'd look at her too long.

He took his seat.

"So," Jay said, sitting behind his desk, "you've been stirring up the sports world a bit."

"I was in the right place at the right time when the story broke." He'd had to practice humility in the mirror. It didn't come naturally.

Jay grinned. "I'll bet it's good to be back in the limelight."

"It is."

"What were the nonfootball years like?"

Every celebrity asked him that. Nothing scared a famous person more than the thought of a sudden plunge into obscurity. "Like trading in a Ferrari for a used Volvo."

"Ouch," Jay said, and the audience laughed. "What made you do it? A lot of athletes are plenty pissed off."

"I'm a father," he said simply. "It could have been one of my daughters in that room with Drew Grayland. We need to go back to the days when good sportsmanship mattered, on and off the field."

The audience erupted into applause again. A few "boos" rose above the noise.

The interview lasted another few minutes. Jay was a genius at pulling a funny remark out of serious statement, while not making light of the subject.

Then, suddenly, it was over. The music started, the lights came up, and Jay stood. He clapped Jack on the back. "You were great."

Jack felt like he'd just led his team to a Super Bowl victory.

Thea walked over to Jay and kissed his cheek. "Thanks." She lowered her voice, said something else. Jay laughed, then waved at Jack and left the stage.

Still smiling, Thea walked over to Jack. A slow smile curved her full, puffy lips. She was certain of her effect on men; took it for granted, he'd say. "You were good," she purred, leaning closer.

"Thanks."

"Would you like—"

Sally came up beside him. "You were *great*," she said breathlessly. To Thea, she said, "I'm Sally. Jack's assistant. It's an honor to meet you."

Thea looked at Sally's hand, placed possessively on Jack's forearm. "How lucky for you. I'd better run. I've got a premiere tonight." When she smiled at Jack, he felt a rush of pure heat. "It was nice to meet you. I hope to see you again."

"Uh, yeah. Me, too."

When she was gone, he looked down at Sally, who was staring up at him as if he were a god.

NINETEEN

ON FRIDAY, MEGHANN CALLED EXACTLY ON TIME.

Elizabeth considered not answering, but knew it would be pointless. Meghann would just call back every five minutes until she got through.

With a sigh, she answered the phone. "Heya, Meg."

"I would have let it ring forever, you know."

Elizabeth sat down at the kitchen table. "The thought occurred to me."

"Tonight's the big night. The painting class you told me about. God, I wish I could be there."

"You mean you wish you were driving me to class."

"And walking you to the door."

Elizabeth smiled a little. "I did consider not going."

"Of course you did. But if you don't do it now . . ." Meg let the sentence trail off, unfinished. An uncoalesced threat, worse somehow for having no form.

"I know. And I'm going. I *am*."

"Good. Will you call me when you get home? I have a date, so I should be home by nine o'clock at the latest."

"Is that his curfew?"

"Very funny. He happens to be twenty-eight, a most respectable age. I just don't waste time anymore. If a date isn't going well in the first thirty minutes, believe me, it's not going to pick up."

"Maybe he'll surprise you."

"Birdie, they all surprise me. Last week, I hugged my date at the door and felt a bra strap. Well, I gotta go. Keep your chin up and remember how talented you are."

Were.

"I'll remember," she said.

"Keep moving. Don't stop or slow down until your ass is in the chair."

"Okay."

For the next hour, Elizabeth followed her best friend's advice. She didn't allow herself to pause or sigh or slow down or think.

Pack the supply bag.

Take a shower.

Dry your hair.

Get dressed.

Drive.

She managed to get to the community college in less than thirty minutes. She parked right in front and went inside.

Outside classroom 108, a sign was posted. It read: BEGINNING PAINTING/ 5:00.

Cautiously, she opened the door. Inside the small classroom, there were six or seven people—all women—seated in a semicircle. In front of them, a long table was draped in white fabric. A brown wooden bowl sat in the middle; it was piled high with bright red apples.

She tried her best to move invisibly as she sidled around a

pressboard bookcase and toward a vacant seat. She held her can-vas bag against her chest as if it were a bulletproof vest.

Behind her, the door opened, then closed softly. A male voice said, "Welcome to Beginning Painting. If you've brought macramé supplies, you're in the wrong room."

He walked between the chairs in that easy, loose-hipped way one associated with cowboys or dancers. He wore a black T-shirt that pulled taut across his shoulder blades, and a pair of faded Levi's. When he reached the chalkboard and turned around, Elizabeth drew in a sharp breath. She didn't think she was the only woman who reacted that way.

He was young—no more than twenty-nine or thirty—but my God, he was good-looking. Brad Pitt in Thelma and Louise good-looking.

"I'm Daniel Boudreaux," he said, flashing a white smile. "I'm your instructor for the next six weeks. My job is to introduce you to painting." His blue-eyed gaze moved from face to face; it paused for a moment on Elizabeth, or had she imagined that? "Hopefully, this'll be the start of a love affair that will last the rest of your lives. For those of you who care about such things—and you shouldn't, this is art, after all—I studied at RISD and Yale. I have an overload of knowledge and an appalling lack of talent. How-ever, that doesn't stop me. I fish in Alaska all summer and paint all winter." He moved away from the chalkboard and stood by the table with the fruit.

"Let's talk a little about composition . . ."

Elizabeth's heart was pounding hard. Soon, she thought, soon he'd say, "Okay, class, let's begin."

". . . The truest expression of art can't be found on the tip of a brush. It's in the artist's eye. . . ."

Elizabeth had been a fool to think she could do this. She'd for-gotten how to think like an artist, how to let her emotions flow into a paintbrush.

". . . Like anything else, painting requires some preparation.

None of that mixing your own oils yet. We'll start with acrylics and make a working palette. Do you see the foil-covered oval I've placed by your chair?"

Elizabeth unpacked her supplies in slow motion. The lethargy made sense; she was using muscles that had atrophied.

". . . We'll begin on paper, and work our way toward canvas. So pin your paper up . . ."

Elizabeth clipped a long, rough sheet of paper onto the easel in front of her chair. She started to reach into her bag, then realized that no one else had moved. She put her hands back in her lap.

". . . Now look at the fruit, really look at it. Study the way the lines curl and slice, the way light reflects on the flat surfaces and disappears in the hollows. Painting is about *seeing*. Look at the bowl, feel its texture in your mind, discern the colors that combine within it. When you're ready, begin. Later on, we'll start with sketches and ideas, but for now, I want you to dive right in. Imagine yourself as a child with a set of paints. Freedom in its purest form."

Elizabeth heard the sound of paintbrushes being smashed into paint—too hard—the *thwop* of overwet bristles hitting the paper.

She cleared her mind of everything except the fruit. Just that. Light and shadow; color, lines, and composition . . .

She realized with a start that she wasn't alone. He was beside her, Daniel, and he was bending down.

"Is something wrong?" he asked.

She felt herself flush. "I'm sorry. What did you say?" She turned to look up at him so fast they almost conked heads.

He stepped back and laughed. "What's your name?"

"Elizabeth."

"Okay, Elizabeth, what's wrong? You haven't started."

"I can't see it yet."

"The apples? You could move closer."

"No . . . the painting."

"Ah. Now, that's an interesting answer. Close your eyes."

She followed his direction and immediately wished she hadn't. In the darkness, he felt nearer somehow; she could smell the tangy scent of his aftershave.

"Describe the fruit."

"It's in a wooden bowl, hand-carved I think by someone who wasn't very good. It's from a solid piece of wood. The table is one of those metal lunchroom tables, probably with a wood-grain top, that you've covered with an inexpensive white cotton cloth. The apples are McIntosh, red with strands of green and black, almost heart-shaped. Light hits them on the right side. There's a feather at the edge of the table, maybe a blue jay's."

He was quiet for a moment. She could feel the beating of her heart. It was so loud she wondered if he could hear it. *Woman drops dead in art class because hunk tells her to describe apples. Story at eleven.* "You don't like the look of them," he said at last. "Something's wrong. I've set them out badly. How should I have done it?"

"The tablecloth should be yellow. There should be one apple; no, an orange. No bowl. Everything else is clutter."

He leaned closer. She felt the separation of air as he moved, the sound of his breathing. Then he touched her hand. She flinched, tried to pull away. He wouldn't let her. The next thing she knew, she was holding a paintbrush.

She opened her eyes. He was looking right at her.

"Show me what you can do, Elizabeth."

He was so near she couldn't think straight, couldn't draw an even breath. She tilted the paintbrush in her hand, let it settle into its place.

Suddenly all she could see was the painting—her painting. A single, plump Sunkist orange. Everything around it was bright sunlight and yellow cloth. The shadow it cast was the palest lavender. A tiny green blemish marred the orange's puckered peel. She dipped the sable tip into the paint—Naples yellow—and began.

She couldn't stop. Her blood was on fire, her hands were a whir of motion. Her heart was pounding in her chest and in her temples. It felt like the start of a migraine, but she didn't care. It was better than sex—better than any sex she'd had in years, anyway.

When she finished, her breath expelled in a rush, and she realized only then that she'd been holding it.

She was shaking, sweating. She felt sick to her stomach and exhilarated. Slowly, she looked around.

The room was empty.

She glanced up at the clock. It was eight o'clock. An hour after the end of class. "Oh, my God." She laughed, feeling great.

"Where did you study?"

She turned and saw Daniel leaning against the bookcases in the back of the room. He was staring at her with an intensity that was unnerving. She felt a flutter in the pit of her stomach, a kind of restlessness that set her on edge. "The University of Washington. About a thousand years ago."

He moved toward her. "Was Waldgrin there?"

That surprised her. "Yeah, he was. Did you know Leo?"

"Are you kidding? I hitchhiked cross-country to study with him."

"He's a wonderful teacher."

Daniel came up beside her. For a long moment, he looked at her painting—a childish explosion of color, she saw now; no precision, no sophistication—then he looked at her.

She felt it again, that tightening in her stomach that reminded her of high school. And she knew what it was: attraction. She was attracted to this man who was probably half her age.

Oh, God. Could he read it on her face? What if he asked her out—what would she say? *You're too young. Too handsome. I'm too old. My underwear is the size of a circus tent.*

Had she actually thought that? Fantasized about him asking her out? In Jamie-speak: *As if.*

He smiled slowly. "Why are you in my class?"

"I haven't painted in a long time."

"That's a crime."

Her fingers were trembling as she removed her painting from the easel and put the supplies away. Holding the damp paper gently, she slung her canvas bag over her shoulder and headed out. She was at the door when he said, "You have talent, you know."

Elizabeth didn't dare turn around. Her grin was so big she probably looked like the Joker—and with her wrinkles that'd scare pretty boy to death.

She smiled all the way home. More than once, she laughed out loud.

AT HOME, Elizabeth taped the painting to the refrigerator and stared at it.

She couldn't remember the last time she'd felt this good. She'd accomplished something. And not something easy, like negotiating a good deal for an antique or picking the right fabric for the sofa. This was something that *mattered*.

She poured herself a glass of wine, then grabbed the phone and called Meghann. The answering machine picked up.

"I painted, Meg. *Painted! Yee-ha*. And just for the record, my instructor is a doll. The perfect age for you. Call me when you get home."

Laughing, she put on a Smash Mouth CD. "Hey Now, You're an All Star" blasted through the speakers. She sang along, dancing all by herself in the living room. As she twirled past the fireplace, she caught sight of the photo on the mantel and came to a stop.

It was Jack and the girls. She couldn't quite remember when it had been taken, but there was snow in the background and everyone was dressed for an overnight stay in the Arctic.

Jack wore a sheepskin-lined beige suede jacket; his hair was too long. The first threads of gray shaded the hair above his ears.

Suddenly she wished he were here right now. He would be proud of her. The old love, the feeling that had been such a part of her, came back now, reminding her that life had once been good with Jack. She'd almost forgotten that.

She moved on to the picture beside it. This was an old shot, taken years ago. She was dressed in a plaid skirt and a shetland wool sweater, with a strand of pearls at her throat. He wore Calvin Klein jeans, a letterman's jacket, and a football star's cocky smile. Behind them, the ice cream cone of Mount Rainier floated above Frosh Pond.

The University of Washington.

The sand castle years.

She closed her eyes, swaying to the music, remembering those days . . . the first time he'd kissed her . . .

They'd been studying together, sitting on a flat, grassy place in the Quad. It had been late spring; the cherry trees were just past full bloom, and tiny pink blossoms floated randomly to the ground. All around them, kids in shorts and T-shirts played Frisbee and kicked Hacky Sacks around.

Jack leaned over and slapped her book shut. "You know what they say about studying. If you do it too much, you'll go blind."

Laughing, she flopped back onto the grass and rested her hands behind her head.

He lay down beside her, on his side, with his head supported on one hand. "You're so beautiful. I guess your Harvard fiancé tells you that all the time."

"No." Her voice was barely above a whisper. A pink cherry blossom petal landed on her cheek.

He brushed it away, and at the contact, she shivered. Slowly, he leaned toward her, giving her plenty of time to stop him, to roll away.

She lay very still, breathing too quickly.

It wasn't much of a kiss; no more than a quick, scared brushing of lips. When he drew back, she saw that he was as shaken as she. She started to cry.

"Could you ever love a guy like me?"

"Oh, Jack," she answered, *"why do you think I'm crying?"*

She touched the photograph, let her finger glide across his handsome face. No other man's kiss had ever made her cry.

For the first time in weeks, she wondered if there was still a chance for them.

Now that she'd painted again, anything seemed possible. Color and passion had come back into her world; she was no longer a woman drawn in shades of gray.

The phone rang.

Meghann.

Elizabeth swooped down to answer it. "Did you get laid tonight?"

"Uh . . . Birdie?"

Elizabeth winced. *Damn.* "Hi, Anita, sorry about that."

"I'm sorry to call so late. It's just that . . . you said you'd call."

Elizabeth heard the quiver in her stepmother's voice. It was a sound all women knew, that desperate attempt to appear strong. She curled up on the sofa. "I'm sorry, Anita. Things have been a little crazy here. How are you doing?"

Anita laughed. It was a fluttery, sorrowful sound. "Oh, honey, I try not to think about myself too much."

Elizabeth felt a spark of kinship with her stepmother. "That's what we women do, isn't it? We push our lives underwater and float on the surface. Then one day you realize it's someone else's pool."

"What in the Sam Hill are you talkin' about?"

"Sorry, Anita. The truth is I'm half drunk right now. It makes me philosophical." She mangled that word pretty badly.

"I noticed that in your letter. I figured there was a whole bushel of a story I wasn't gettin'."

"You've got enough on your plate, Anita. You don't need my mess piled on top."

"You just can't do it, can you, Birdie?"

"Do what?"

"Share your life with me. I thought now, with Edward gone, we might change things between us."

"I was trying to protect you," she answered, stung. "Jack and I have separated. But the girls don't know, so don't say anything."

"Oh, my." Anita released a breath; it made a squeaking sound, like a child's toy. "But y'all seemed so happy together. What happened?"

"Nothing. Everything." Elizabeth took a big swallow of wine. How could she explain her own formless dissatisfaction to a woman who'd wanted so little from her own life? Anita might understand the high and low tides of a long-term marriage, but she couldn't understand how the ebb tides could erode a woman's soul. And she sure couldn't understand the yawning emptiness of a nest that had lost its chicks. "It's just a bump in the road, Anita. I'm sure we'll be fine." And tonight—three glasses of wine later— she could almost believe that.

"Someday I'll quit expectin' you to grow up, Birdie. They'll probably bury me the next day." She laughed, but it was a bitter sound, not her laugh at all. "Well, I'm sorry y'all are havin' problems. That's what you want me to say, isn't it?"

Elizabeth decided to move onto easy ground. This was getting too personal; it was ruining her good mood. "Enough about me. How've you been? I've been thinking about you." That much was true, at least.

"This big ole house has a lot of ghosts," Anita answered. "Sometimes it's so quiet I think I'll go crazy. Then I remember that I was crazy to start with."

"You know what's helped me? Sitting on the beach. Maybe a change of scenery would do you some good."

"You think?"

This was definitely better. The scenery was a safe topic. "There's something magical about sitting on a beach all by your-self. It's funny, I was scared of the beach for years. Now I can't be away from it too long." Her voice snagged on a suddenly exposed shoal. "I always wanted you and Daddy to see it."

"I know, honey. We thought we had time."

Time. It was the rack everything hung on: life, loss, hope, love. So often, it seemed to slip through your fingers like silk. But sometimes, you could reach back into what was and take hold. "I took a painting class tonight," she said softly.

"Oh, Birdie, that's wonderful. I hated it when you gave up on your talent."

Elizabeth was surprised by that. "You thought I had talent? You never told me that."

Anita sighed, then said, "Ah, honey, I told you. Well. You take care now, y'hear?"

"You, too, Anita. And think about sitting on a beach."

"I'll do that, honey. I surely will. I could use a change of scenery."

TWENTY

IF THERE WAS A STILL A SUN OUT THERE, TETHERING THE EARTH in its orbit, you'd never have known it. The midday sky was as thick and heavy as granite.

On a day like this, neither stormy nor clear, there was nothing to do except build a fire, curl up on the sofa with a cup of tea, and call your best friend. So, that was exactly what Elizabeth did.

"Who's dead?" Meghann answered gruffly.

Elizabeth glanced at the clock. It was nine-forty-five on a Saturday morning. "I'm guessing that my slutty best friend got lucky last night."

"*Lucky* is a relative term. I got laid." Meghann paused. "You know it's not gonna be a long-term relationship when foreplay lasts just under ten minutes and that's twice as long as the sex itself. Hang on. I'm getting coffee." The phone clunked down on a tabletop. A minute later, Meghann picked it up again. "So, how was the class?"

"I did it. I painted."

"I knew you could do it. How was it? Are you still great? Oh, and did you get the college catalogs I sent you?"

"Slow down, Counselor. One step at a time. I painted again. That's enough for now."

"I'm proud of you, Birdie."

"I take it you didn't listen to your messages last night. My instructor is a hunk."

"No shit? A hunk in nowheresville? That's just my luck. They're probably leaving the cities in droves. How old is he?"

"Perfect for you. He'd have no idea what a Pet Rock is."

"Well?"

"Well what?"

Meghann sighed dramatically. "You're forty-five, not ninety-five. Did you feel a little twinge?"

Elizabeth didn't know why she was surprised by that question. For years, Meghann had interrogated her about her so-called fantasy life. Meg had been unable to believe that Elizabeth wasn't attracted to other men.

I'm not saying you'd do anything about it, Meghann used to say, *but you can't tell me you haven't fantasized.*

The conversation had always left Elizabeth feeling vaguely abnormal, but the truth was she hadn't been attracted to other men. Oh, every now and then she'd see a man on television and think, *There's a good-looking guy.* But she'd never brought mental images to the bedroom. God knew, she'd never considered being unfaithful. She still couldn't imagine it. Truthfully, sex with Jack had always been more than good enough. It had been only recently that they'd begun to lose their passion. "Yes, actually," she answered, surprising herself. "Then I remembered what size my underwear is."

"You're pathetic, you know that? If you hadn't had an eating disorder for half of your life, you'd realize that you look good."

"I never had an eating disorder."

"Exactly what Flockhart and Boyle say. The point is, you've put on a few pounds—only a few. You're still beautiful. Brad would be lucky to get a shot with you."

This discussion had turned south faster than a prison escapee. "Yeah, right. I think—Oh, just a second, my other line is beeping." She checked her Caller ID. "Meg? This is the girls. I need to take it. I'll call you later, okay?"

"Okay. I'm proud of you, Birdie. I hope you're proud of yourself."

"I am. Thanks." Elizabeth hung up one call and answered the other. "Hello?"

"Mom?"

It was Jamie. "Hey, Sunshine," Elizabeth said, "it's good to hear your voice. How did the meet go?"

Jamie burst into tears.

"Honey, what's the matter?"

"I h-hate swimming. I'm wet all the time."

"That can't come as much of a surprise. You've been swimming since grade school." Elizabeth honestly tried not to smile, but it was difficult. Her drama queen younger daughter's crises were as dependable as a tropical rainstorm and lasted about as long. She must have lost her races at Saturday's meet.

"I know, but I'm sick of it. And I'm about thirty seconds away from flunking out."

Now, *that* was new. Elizabeth sat up straighter, pulled her knees toward her chest. "What about that tutor we hired for you?"

There was a short pause; then Jamie said, "I'm dating him. Michael. He is *soooo* cute. He plays the saxophone in the college's jazz quartet. How sexy is that? He's the first guy I've ever dated who doesn't talk about ball handling and go gaga over Dad."

It was so Jamie-like to fall in love with her tutor. There was no point asking the serious questions until new love had been discussed. "Okay, tell me about him."

As usual, Jamie had no lack of stories to tell about her new beau. It had, apparently, been impossible to study with Michael because of his eyes—*so brown, Mom, they're like, amazing*—and his voice had presented a problem as well—*He kind of whispers, like some old jazz guy. It's totally sexy.*

Finally, when she'd run down the battery on new love, she came back around to the point. "Anyway, I don't need a tutor anymore. I need time to study. That's why I want to quit swimming. Dad's making buttloads of money now—he told me that—so you guys can afford my tuition, right?"

"One point at a time, kiddo. Don't even try to smoke me about study time. Do you want to quit so you can spend more time with Michael?"

"Get real, Mom. I've been balancing boys and sports since Little League."

"So, what's really going on here? Why do you want to quit?"

"Bottom line?" There was a pause, then, "I'm not good enough."

Elizabeth's heart ached at those softly spoken words. She wanted to argue the point, to tell Jamie that of course she was good enough . . . that being good enough wasn't the point anyway, trying was. But that was the easy road. A childhood answer to an adult question. "Go on."

"These girls have talent, Mom. Hannah Tournilae is Olympic material. To be honest, I might have quit a long time ago, except Dad came to every swim meet, and when I won, he acted like I'd cured cancer. But he's not on the sidelines anymore. He doesn't even call and ask how I did."

"Your dad loves you. You know he does. Neither one of us cares if you swim. We just want you to be happy."

"So, you'll tell him I quit?"

Elizabeth laughed. "No way. You'll have to talk to Dad about this yourself, but I'll tell you this, honey, it's dangerous to quit something because you think you're not good enough. That can be an ugly pattern that repeats itself throughout your life. Believe me, I know."

"You want me to finish out the season." Jamie came to the conclusion so quickly Elizabeth knew the answer had been there all along.

"I'm sure your coach would appreciate it."

"I hate it when you do that."

"Do what?"

"Pretend to agree with me and then lob some grenade of common sense."

Elizabeth smiled. It was a perfect description of motherhood. "I'll support whatever decision you make."

"All right. I'm quitting at the end of the season." Jamie tried to sound strong and self-assured, but hesitation caused a little vibrato in her voice. "I don't suppose you'd tell Dad that for me?"

"Nope."

"Fine."

She knew her daughter was angry with her, just as she knew that the anger wouldn't last. Jamie was like her grandfather, a volatile, larger-than-life personality. She could hate you one minute and adore you the next.

"Jamie?" Elizabeth said, waiting for the waspish, "Yeah, what?"

She knew what she wanted to say, but not how to say it. With Jamie, a serious conversation was like driving on the Los Angeles freeway. You had to change lanes with extreme caution. "Do you think you want to quit swimming because you're depressed about Grandad?"

It took Jamie a moment to answer, and when she did, her voice was soft, trembling. "I miss him all the time."

"Me, too. I still talk to him, though. It helps a little."

"You live by yourself right now. I'm surrounded by thousands of students—tons of whom are probably psych majors. They'd lock me up if I went around talking to my dead grandfather."

"You've never cared what other people think. Don't start now. But if you're embarrassed, talk to him at home. Stephie won't laugh."

"Stephie who?" she said bitterly.

So, that was part of the problem, too. Stephanie was busy getting ready to graduate; Jamie hated to admit that she'd miss her big sister. "She's too busy to spend much time with you, I take it?"

"Tim the wonder boy practically lives here. And he brings her flowers when she aces a test. *Flowers.* Hell, she's aced every test since they asked her to recite the alphabet in kindergarten. Our apartment looks like the flower store in *Little Shop of Horrors.* It makes me sick."

"You mean jealous," Elizabeth said gently.

A pause. "Yeah. Now they want me to tag after them on spring break. Barbie, Ken . . . and Skipper. *Yee-ha.* The only thing worse would be to stay in the apartment by myself and watch her stupid flowers die."

"Why don't you come home, hang with me?" Elizabeth said automatically. Then she realized what she'd done.

I'm getting the house ready for renters. Could she say it out loud, face to face?

"Home? And where's that, with you or Dad? And speaking of that, when are you moving to New York? Dad sounded lonely the last time I called him."

These were dangerous waters, especially with Jamie swimming alongside. "As soon as we find suitable renters."

"Who are you waiting for, the British Royal Family? Just rent the sucker to some poor schmuck who likes mushrooms that grow overnight and rain that hits you in the head like a hammerblow."

"You don't like it here?"

Jamie laughed. "Actually, I do. But it's just a house; we've lived in tons of them."

Elizabeth sighed. That was one of the by-products of her life with Jack. They hadn't given their children a sense of roots, of home. "You're right," she answered.

"So, what would we do? If I remember, March is a particularly sucky month. We probably wouldn't see the sun once."

Elizabeth couldn't help smiling at that. "We could rent movies and play board games."

" 'Be still, my heart.' Board games with my mother over spring break." She laughed. "I'll think about it, Mom. Truly. But I gotta run now. Michael is picking me up in an hour."

"Is your sister home?"

"Sorry. This is her day for curing Alzheimer's. I'll have her call you tomorrow. Love you."

"Love you, too. Bye."

After Elizabeth hung up, she stared down at the phone. Her first thought was: *Call Jack.*

He needed to know what was going on with Jamie. A heads up would make the *I-want-to-quit-swimming* conversation run a lot smoother.

Elizabeth had always greased the wheels of Jack's relationship with his daughters. He . . . missed things sometimes, overlooked the important moments. It had been her job—or one she'd taken on, at least—to facilitate a good father-daughter bond.

Without her guidance, she was afraid he'd inadvertently hurt his daughter's feelings.

She dialed his number.

JACK WAS IN A MEETING with Sally. "He actually threw a punch *after* the match was over—and broke the guy's jaw?"

She nodded. "Every second was caught on tape. The question is this: Is it assault and battery because the match had ended? Or does assumption of the risk cover everything that happens in the ring?"

"That's always been a question with far-reaching implications. Late hits in football, and forget about hockey. With this new interest in—"

The phone rang. He waited for his secretary to answer, then remembered that she'd gone to lunch. "Just a second." He picked up the phone and answered, "Jackson Shore."

"I almost hung up." Elizabeth's laughter sounded forced, nervous.

"Hey, Birdie," he said after a stunned pause.

Sally's smile faded. She glanced at the door.

"Am I catching you at a bad time?" Elizabeth asked.

Her voice sounded different, uncertain, though it didn't surprise him. In a few short weeks, they'd become strangers. He wouldn't have thought it possible, after twenty-four years of living together, but it was true.

The silence between them stretched out, grew uncomfortable. It was all so unexpected; she'd always been his compass, his true north; or so he'd thought. He'd imagined that without her, he'd be lost. But that hadn't happened. Quite the opposite, in fact. He was now afraid that he'd be lost *with* her.

"Jack?"

"I'm here." He didn't know exactly what she expected him to say. Worse, he didn't know what he wanted to say. Maybe nothing at all. He was afraid suddenly that she'd called to reconcile; now *he* was the one who wanted time.

Sally stood up. "I'll leave you alone for a minute," she whispered.

He nodded, mouthed, "Thanks."

"Who's that?" Birdie asked.

He felt guilty suddenly, though there was no need. He and Sally hadn't done anything unprofessional. "It's just my assistant. We were in a meeting."

"Maybe I should call back . . ."

He wanted to say, *Yes, do that,* and then avoid her future call. But such a maneuver would be pointless. With a heavy sigh and a heavier heart, he watched Sally leave the room, then said, "So, Birdie, what's going on?"

"How's your job?"

He didn't know what he'd expected her to say (maybe, *Oh, Jack, I love you, I can't live without you*) but certainly not a question about his job. "Honestly, Birdie, I love it. I feel twenty years younger." He heard the defensiveness in his voice and tried to soften it. "I'd forgotten how it felt."

"To be a star, you mean?"

She knew him so well. "Yes."

"I'm proud of you, Jack. I knew you'd be good at it. That was never the issue."

He smiled. Her opinion of him had always mattered more than anyone else's, more even than his own. He'd never owned success completely until Elizabeth kissed him and said, *You did it, baby.*

What he hadn't known until now—this second—was that even with all that had gone wrong between them, he still needed that from her. "Thanks. How about you, how are you doing?"

"I'm taking a painting class."

To his amazement, he felt a spark of jealousy. He'd tried for years to get her to paint again.

Or had he only meant to encourage her? Now he couldn't separate the intention from the act. Still, when he said, "That's great, Birdie," he meant it.

"I talked—"

"Do you—"

They spoke at once, then both laughed. Jack said, "You first."

"I just talked to Jamie. She's having a hard time. You know . . . school, swimming, Dad's death, Stephie's graduation. It's a lot for her to deal with by herself."

"And she's always had you before."

"That's probably part of it. Anyway, she'll be calling you for advice. Be gentle with her, okay? Listen before you talk."

Whatever the hell that meant. He was a great listener with his girls. "Okay."

"Good." Then, "I'm . . . having a hard time lying to them. Are you?"

"Lying? What do you mean?"

"You know . . . telling them I'm getting the house ready for renters. Jamie won't accept that forever. Pretty soon, I think we'll have to tell them the truth."

Jack felt as if he'd been sucker punched. As much as he loved his new single life, he wasn't ready to contemplate the end of their family.

Their *family*.

In the time it took to draw a breath and push it out, he remembered the whole of their life together, the good times and the bad.

The one thing he'd always counted on, the bedrock of his life, was that Elizabeth loved him. Her plea for a short-term separation hadn't actually altered that belief. But now, he wondered.

All bullshit and adolescent dreams aside, could he live without her love?

"There's a chance for us, isn't there?" he asked.

It took her a moment to answer. When she did, her voice was barely above a whisper. "I hope so."

He smiled, relieved. "I hope so, too, baby."

Another silence fell.

At last, Elizabeth said, "Don't forget about Jamie. She's fragile right now. Be gentle."

She'd said that twice now. "I'm always gentle with her."

Elizabeth sighed . . . or was that a muffled laugh? He couldn't be sure. Either way, it was vaguely irritating. "I can't keep you and your daughters on track anymore, Jack. Your relationship with Jamie is up to you."

He had no idea what she meant by that. "Okay."

"Well, I'd better let you get back to work."

"Yeah. It was good talking to you," he said, and they were strangers again.

"Good talking to you, too."

He realized he was waiting for her to say, *I love you*, when he heard the dial tone.

ELIZABETH FELT A SUDDEN URGE to call him back and say, *We can't be this far apart.*

But they were distant now, emotionally as well as physically. That was what she'd wanted. It was why he'd sounded so confident and happy when he answered the phone—and so guarded and awkward when he realized who'd called.

After twenty-four years of sharing every moment of life, they'd drifted to separate coasts and picked up separate lives. Their conversations came in a kind of Morse code; hurried sentences punctuated by elongated pauses.

She tried to cull through the rubble of her emotions to find the truest one. Only a few days ago, she'd seen an old photograph of them and thought, *There's still a chance for us.* But every day took them farther away from the love that had once bound them together.

She was at a crossroads suddenly; one she hadn't even seen approaching. And yet, here she was, standing at the corner of what she'd dreamed of and what she'd left behind.

If she picked up the phone and called Jack, she would turn back into who she'd been.

Someday (and, yes, she knew she still held that hope close) she would feel strong enough, sure enough of herself, to call Jack and say, *I love you; let's try again.*

But not today.

TWENTY-ONE

Dear Birdie:

That conversation we had the other day has stayed with me. As usual, you're holding your troubles close to your chest, thinking I can't understand. Me being the wicked stepmother and all.

For years, I've let you run the show on who we are. I'm tired of that. Maybe it's because I'm old and you don't scare me like you used to. Or maybe it's because I'm alone now, and life looks different to me.

Believe me, honey, I know what it's like to be unhappy in your marriage. One disappointment feeds on another until one day you leave him. You become the trapped wolf who eats her own foot to be free.

But if you're like me, you discover that the world is a big, dark place. And love—even if it isn't what you'd thought it would be—is the only light for miles.

So, Birdie, darlin', I understand.

I don't have any advice for you. If there's one thing I've discovered in this life it's that deep truths are uncovered alone.

My prayers are with you and Jack and those beautiful girls.
XXOO
Anita

P.S. Don't bother writing back. I'm taking your advice and heading to the beach!

Elizabeth read the letter three times, then carefully folded it up, slipped it back into its violet-scented envelope.

She walked over to the French doors and stared out at the ocean. In those few words, Anita had managed to shake Elizabeth up, to cause a subtle shift in perception.

For years, she had monitored the progress of women—friends, strangers, celebrities—who'd left their marriages. Often, she'd watched with envy as these women picked up stakes and started over. She imagined them living shiny new lives, as different from her own as a quarter from a bottle cap. And she'd thought to herself, *If only I could start over.*

She'd never paid much attention to the women who stayed in their marriages, who hacked through the jungle of ordinary life and found a different kind of treasure.

At some point, Anita had left Edward. She'd packed a bag and moved away from Sweetwater. What had she been looking for . . . and what had brought her back? Had it really been as simple, and as infinitely complex, as true love?

Elizabeth felt a spark of kinship with her stepmother. She wished they could sit down and talk about their disparate and now oddly parallel lives.

She picked up the phone and dialed Anita's number. The phone rang and rang. Finally, an answering machine clicked on.

Her father's slow, drawling voice started. "Ya'll've reached Sweetwater. We aren't here right now, but leave a message and we'll return your call." There was a muffled sound on the tape— Anita's voice—then Daddy went on: "Oh . . . yeah . . . wait for the beep. Thanks."

Elizabeth was so rattled by the sound of her father's voice that she hung up without leaving a message.

Tears stung her eyes. She didn't bother trying to hold them back. It was a thing she'd learned in the last weeks. Grief would have its way. If she gave in to it, wallowed around in the loss for a while, she could go on.

She sat down on the edge of her bed. On the bureau, she saw a framed photograph of a little girl in a frilly pink dress, white tights, and black patent Mary Janes.

Her seventh birthday party. Later that night, Daddy had taken her to see the musical *South Pacific* in Nashville.

After the show, when he'd tucked her into bed, he'd said, *Sugar beet, you were the prettiest girl in the theater tonight. I was danged proud to have you on my arm.* Then he'd pulled her into his big strong arms and made her feel safe.

She needed that—needed him—now.

She sat there a long time, talking to her daddy as if he were sitting right beside her.

THE WEEK FLEW BY.

After years of trudging through a gray, wintry landscape of other people's choices, Elizabeth had finally emerged onto a sunny blue day of her own.

Each morning she woke with a sense of expectation that made her smile, hum even, as she went about her daily chores. Then, at noon, no matter what else pressed at her to be done, no matter what was on her mental To Do list, she ignored everything and painted.

At first, she'd tried to fix her class project. She'd added brush-strokes and dabs of color, layer upon layer, trying to add a complexity to the image that she couldn't quite achieve.

Unfortunately, the old saying was true. You couldn't make a silk purse out of a sow's ear.

The problem with the orange was that it wasn't *hers*. The best in art revealed something of the artist's soul, and Elizabeth's soul had never cared much for fruit.

When she trolled around for something else to paint, she saw possibilities everywhere—and only one true choice.

The ocean.

She started slowly, methodically stretching the canvas in the way she'd been taught more than two dozen years ago. It came so easily, this beginning of it all, that she wondered if, for all these years, she'd been painting in her sleep, dreaming of primed and stretched canvases, of mixing medium and pigment, of colors slurried on a well-used palette.

The sun had been bright and shining on that day she began to put her love of the sea on canvas. She took her new easel and primed canvas and her paints and brushes out to the edge of the yard. There, she laid out an eight-by-ten sheet of thick blue plastic and set up the easel on it.

The sleeping blue ocean stretched out as far as the eye could see. Today, she saw it in tiny increments, in slashes of hue and texture, in light and shadow. She saw each component that comprised the whole; and just that, seeing it as she'd once been able to, made her feel young again—hope-filled, as opposed to the lesser, more common, hopeful.

She held a brush in her now steady hand and stared out to sea, noticing the blurry shapes that came forward and those that remained background. She studied the various tints of light that coalesced into sand and water, rock and sky, then, very slowly, she looked down at her palette and chose a base color.

Cobalt blue.

The color of Jack's eyes.

The thought came out of nowhere and surprised her.

She dipped her paintbrush into the color and began.

Day after day, she returned to this very spot, dragging her easel with her, setting up her work. Each day she added a new layer of color, one atop another, until it was impossible to tell that she'd

started with the cobalt. Gradually, she'd felt it return, her own po-
tent magic. The painting—her painting—revealed everything
that she loved about this view, and everything that she longed to
be. Dangerous, rough-edged, vibrant.

Tonight, at last, she would take her work to class. She couldn't
wait to show it to Daniel.

She had worked her ass off—though all that hard work had
produced not a pound of weight loss (there was something cos-
mically wrong with that)—to get a piece ready for tonight. It
had been the homework assignment. Begin a work of your own.
Any work.

At four o'clock, though it wasn't yet done, she checked that
the paint had dried—it had—then wrapped the canvas in cheese-
cloth and carefully placed it in the backseat of her car. She took a
shower, brushed her hair until it shone, and dressed in a black jer-
sey tunic and straight-legged pantsuit that she'd bought from
Coldwater Creek's last catalog. A chunky turquoise-and-silver
necklace was her only accessory.

All in all, she looked good.

She got to the classroom and found it empty. When she
looked down at her watch, she saw that she was almost twenty
minutes early.

"Idiot," she said aloud. Now she was trapped. If she walked
away, she might meet up with someone from class, or worse, Daniel,
and then have to explain why she was leaving. If she stayed, however, Daniel might come to class early and wonder how long
she'd been standing there by the door like a bridesmaid waiting
for her turn.

"Did you say something?"

And suddenly he was there, standing in front of her, filling the
open doorway. His smile seemed too big for his face; it crinkled his
blue eyes and carved leathery quotation marks on his cheeks.

"I came early," she stammered.

"A great quality in a woman, coming early." His smile broadened, showcased a row of white, even teeth. "Do you have something to show me?"

Elizabeth couldn't tell if he'd meant that "coming" comment as a sexual innuendo or not. She might have asked him, but when she looked up into his handsome face, her mind went blank. "Huh?"

Idiot.

"I asked you if you brought me something."

He knows, she realized. He knew she was trembling and sweating like a teenager trapped beside the best-looking boy in school.

No wonder he was smiling. What young man wouldn't be amused by a middle-aged woman's runaway lust?

"The painting," she said quickly. "You told us to paint something that moved us. I chose the view from my house."

"Let me see."

She waited for him to turn and go inside, but he just stood there, arms crossed, smiling down at her.

Finally, she turned sideways and sidled past him, hoping her ass didn't skim his hips. She went to the blackboard, where an empty easel waited.

Her fingers shook as she set her canvas on the easel.

Daniel came up beside her, moving so quietly she didn't hear his footsteps. Suddenly, he was just there.

"It's Tamarack Cove," he said, not smiling anymore. "I used to kayak down there with my grandfather. There a great tide pool, over—"

"By the black rocks, yes." When she realized that she'd finished his sentence, she wanted to smack her own face. "I didn't know that was the name of my cove. I *should* have known, I guess, since I live there, but I don't spend a lot of time reading maps. Although I'm interested in tide charts."

Shut up, Birdie.

She clamped her teeth together. They hit with an audible click.

"You really don't know how talented you are, do you?" His voice was soft as beach sand.

The compliment filled her up inside, made her feel about twenty years old. "You're nice to say that," she said, praying her cheeks didn't turn red.

He took a step toward her, came so close she could see a thin scimitar-shaped scar on his temple. She had a sudden, stupid urge to reach up and touch it, to ask him when he'd been hurt.

That's it, no more romance novels.

"Come have coffee with me after class," he said.

She stepped back so fast her butt slammed into a desk. "I'm married." She lifted her left hand, wiggled her fingers. "I mean, I *am*. We're separated right now, but that's not a divorce. Though he said 'divorce,' I don't think he meant it. So, yes, I'm married." She tried to shut up, but couldn't. The silence would be horrible, awkward. "I have two daughters. With my luck, they're your age. Oh, God, maybe you know them. Stephanie is—"

His touch stopped her.

"Oh," she sighed.

"It's just coffee," he said.

If possible—and frankly, she doubted it—she felt *more* idiotic. "Yes. Coffee. It's a beverage, that's all. You don't care if I'm married."

"Not for coffee."

Her cheeks were on fire; she was certain of it.

"I don't know what got into me. I'm sorry."

"Don't be sorry. Just meet me after class. There's something I'd like to discuss with you."

She nodded. He undoubtably thought she was a moron. Mrs. Robinson after a head trauma. "Sure. Coffee would be great."

JACK HAD RECEIVED one of the coveted tickets for the opening night premiere of Disney's newest blockbuster movie. He'd dressed carefully, chosen a black Armani mock turtleneck sweater and charcoal gray wool slacks. According to Sally, dark colors set off his newly blond hair and tanned skin to perfection, made his eyes look "Paul Newman blue."

He was just about to grab his coat when the phone rang. It was probably the car service, letting him know that the car had arrived. He answered quickly. "Hello?"

"Dad?"

Jamie. He'd been missing her calls all week. "Hey, baby, how're you doing?"

"You didn't return my last call."

"I know. I'm sorry, too. I've been so busy lately. How about you, how're things going? I meant to call after last Saturday's swim meet, but you know me. I can't remember why I left the house half the time."

"Yeah, Dad. I know."

He glanced at the clock. It was 6:37. The car service would be here any second. *Damn.* "Look, honey, I've got—" His second line beeped. "Just a minute, I have to put you on hold." He depressed the button and answered. "Hello?"

"Mr. Shore? Your car is here."

"Thanks, Billy. I'll be right down," he said, going back to Jamie. "My car is here, honey. I've got to run."

"But I need to talk to you."

He looked around for his coat. Where had he left it? "What is it?" he asked, checking under the bed. It wasn't there. He kept looking. For a small apartment, he seemed to lose an awful lot of stuff in it.

"I'm quitting the swim team."

Ah, there it was. He grabbed the black lambskin blazer off the kitchen table. Then it hit him. He stopped. "You're what?"

She sighed again; her favorite form of communication lately. "I'm quitting the swim team."

He glanced at the clock again: 6:43. The movie would start in seventeen minutes. If he left right now, he'd be on time. Any later . . . "You're just having a rough time, honey. You've had them before, but you know how much you love the sport. Back when I was playing for the—"

"Not another football anecdote, please. And I don't like swimming. I never did."

It was 6:46.

He sat down on the end of the bed. "You're exaggerating, as usual. Believe me, it's hard to be the best. I know. And sometimes the—"

"—training rips your guts out. I know, Dad. I've heard it all before. But you're not listening. I'M QUITTING! At the end of this season, I'm done. Over, finished, wet no more. If I never see another nose plug, it'll be too soon. I would have discussed it with you last week, but you never called me back. I'm going to tell coach tomorrow."

"Don't do that." He didn't know what to say and he didn't have time to think about it now. "Look, honey, I have to run. Honest. I've got important business tonight. People are counting on me. I'll call you back tomorrow, and we'll talk about this. I promise."

"You do that." She paused. "And, Dad?"

"Yeah?"

"Strangers aren't the only people who count on you. How come they're the only ones that matter?" Before he could respond, she hung up.

What in the hell did she mean by *that*?

Then he remembered what Elizabeth had said to him on the phone. Something like, *I can't keep you and your daughters on track anymore. Your relationship with Jamie is up to you.*

They both acted like he'd been distant, unaware of what was going on in his own family. But that was ridiculous. He'd known what was important—to give his girls all the opportunities he'd never had. He'd worked sixty to seventy hours a week to make a good living, and then he'd coached every sports team Jamie had joined.

He slammed the phone onto its cradle and left the apartment. By the time he reached the lobby, he was pissed off. He slid into the town car's backseat and shut the door.

Strangers aren't the only people who count on you.

He flipped open his cell phone and punched in his daughters' number.

Stephanie answered. "Hello?"

"Hi, honey, is Jamie there?" He realized a second too late that he'd been abrupt. Stephanie wore her fragile emotions on her sleeve; her feelings needed Woolite care. Unfortunately, he always seemed to remember that a split second too late. "I'm sorry, babe. Your sister just called. She threw me a real curve ball. I didn't mean to be rude."

"I understand. No one can make you crazier than Jamie."

"Is the princess at home?"

"She just left with her boyfriend."

"Keith?"

"Keith is so yesterday, Dad. You'll have to call more often if you want to keep up with Jamie's love life."

The driver glanced in the rearview mirror. "Here we are, Mr. Shore."

"Thanks. Hang on a minute, Steph." He signed the voucher and got out of the car. Marquee lights tossed yellow streaks across the rain-slicked pavement. A throng of celebrity watchers and paparazzi milled in front of the theater. They stood cordoned behind a red velvet rope. Jules Asner was interviewing some man in a tuxedo.

As Jack emerged from the town car, camera lights flashed in his face. He smiled, waved, and kept walking.

In the lobby, he found a quiet corner. "Stephanie?"

"I'm here, Dad. What's all that noise?"

"It's a film premiere. There's a real crowd."

"Cool. Any movie stars?"

"George Clooney is supposed to show up, and Danny DeVito. And one of those teenybopper girls; I can't remember her name."

"That sounds awesome. Have fun."

"We'll talk tomorrow, okay, honey? You can tell me every-thing that's going on with—" *genetics . . . microbiology . . . physics.* He knew she'd changed majors, but he couldn't remember which it was now. *Shit.* "—your life."

"You promise?"

"You bet. And tell Jamie I'll talk to her, too."

"Okay. We'll be home tomorrow morning until eleven. Will that work?"

"It's a date. Love you, Steph." He snapped the phone shut and put it back in his pocket.

Inside the theater, he found a seat on the aisle.

The theater filled up quickly. Finally, a young man walked onto the stage; his ponytail was at least six inches long and thin-ner than a pencil. He wore a wide-ribbed red turtleneck sweater with sleeves that hung past his fingertips, and a pair of wrinkled brown corduroy slacks. His shoes were clogs. Clogs.

A hush fell over the crowd.

"I'm Simon Aronosky. I directed the film you're about to see. *True Love* is the tragic, yet ultimately uplifting story of a woman in a coma. The deepness of her sleep is a metaphor for life itself. The film explores the hard choices a husband must make to keep his family together. After the show, I'll be available to an-swer a few questions. Oh, and be sure to fill out the comment cards on your way out. The mice at Disney want to know what you thought."

The theater lights dimmed. The credits started.

A Northwest Diversified Entertainment production . . . A Simon Aronosky film . . .

George Clooney.

Thea Cartwright.

The film, shot in black and white, opened on a close-up of Thea's face. She was sitting at a kitchen table, making out a gro-cery list. She was illuminated by a single candle. Her blond hair, long and a mass of curls, seemed to be woven of a dozen shades of gray and white. But it was her eyes that held the camera. Big, smoky-dark eyes that seemed to promise the world.

God, she was beautiful.

Jack tried to concentrate on the film, but he'd never liked black and white much, and it was definitely one of those chick tearjerkers that no one really liked but made a shitload of money.

He was awakened by the sound of applause.

The lights came up.

Simon walked, slump-shouldered, back onstage. He was smiling and laughing. "Thanks. I'll answer any questions you have, but first I'd like to introduce you to our star. Ladies and gentlemen, Thea Cartwright."

Jack straightened.

Thea walked onto the stage, and even from this distance, she was radiant. Flashbulbs erupted, cameras clicked and whirred, people applauded wildly.

She wore a skimpy black top that plunged almost to her nipples, and a pair of skintight, flare-bottomed low-rise jeans. Her belt buckle was a rhinestone-studded *T*. Her black sandals had knife-sharp stiletto heels.

She waved to the crowd, then ran a hand through her chopped blond hair. "Hey, New York," she said, grinning, "how'd you like my movie?"

The audience went wild.

"Who wanted to try kissing my character to wake her up?"

More applause. For the next thirty minutes, Jack watched her seduce a room full of strangers. By the end, they were eating out of her hand. There was something in her luminous black eyes that made every man—including Jack—think she'd singled him out, that her smile meant something.

"Well, guys," she said, lowering her voice to a sexy, disappointed purr, "I've got to run now. They've scheduled me for a few more things tonight. Ciao."

And she was gone.

The director came back onstage. Jack couldn't hold back a groan. The last thing he wanted to do was listen to Mr. Generation-X wax poetic about art in a chick flick. He left the theater. There was an after-premiere party scheduled at a nearby restaurant. He'd go, have a drink, then head home.

He was the first one to arrive at the restaurant. A guard at the door asked for his invitation, looked it over, then nodded. "Go on in."

Jack walked past an open-air, stainless-steel kitchen where chefs in white hats were working their magic. The tables were empty now; waiters in tuxedos stood around, waiting for the party to start.

He walked up to the bar, ordered a Dewar's on the rocks.

Someone came up beside him. "Hey, Jack. I see you got my invitation."

He turned, and there was Thea, smiling at him. "You put me on the guest list?"

"I needed *something* to look forward to at this grinfest. So, where's your handler?"

"Sally?" He laughed. "She's running down facts for an upcoming show. She wanted to see your movie, too. It was . . . good, by the way."

She smiled, a little too brightly to be real. "I hope so. My last one bombed so fast I saw it on the airplane on the way to the premiere. I need a hit." As if she realized what she'd just revealed, she laughed easily and took a sip of her cosmopolitan.

In the other room, a band started to play. Soft, romantic mood music that no one would be able to hear when the crowd hit.

"Dance with me," she said, putting her glass down on the bar.

"Thea . . ." His mouth was so dry he couldn't manage more. He understood suddenly why a man lost at sea would finally drink the ocean water.

She snuggled closer, slipped her arms around his neck.

They stood eye to eye. She moved slowly, seductively. He couldn't help himself; his arms curled around her. He frowned, noticing how thin she was. Bony, even.

It was the first time in more than a dozen years that he'd held another woman, and it reminded him of his old life. Images of other women tumbled through his mind, memories of long, hot, wet nights spent in hotel beds.

And of the night it had come to an end.

He'd been at Tavern on the Green with a woman he couldn't now remember. Another pretty blonde. It had been one of those flawless late spring days in New York; the smog and humidity of summer hadn't yet arrived.

They'd been outside, dancing cheek-to-cheek beneath the light of a hundred Chinese silk lanterns. The band had been playing "My Romance." That, he wouldn't forget.

Jack had heard a sound, something out of place. He'd turned, and there was Birdie, standing on the edge of the grass with her handbag clutched to her chest and tears streaming down her cheeks.

Before he could get through the crowd, she was gone. When he'd gotten home that night the house was empty. She'd taken the children to a hotel.

There was no note. Instead, on their big king-size bed, Birdie had left an open suitcase beside a framed picture of their family.

Her point had been obvious: Choose.

He'd stared at the open suitcase forever.

Then he'd closed it and put it away.

Thea drew back. "Is something wrong?"

He was saved by a sudden noise. People streamed into the restaurant in a buzzing, chattering throng.

"Damn." She eased away from him, smoothed her hair. "I'm staying at the St. Regis, Presidential suite. I'm listed as Scarlett O'Hara. Come see me after the party."

He wanted to say yes.

We're separated, for God's sake. And at Birdie's insistence. That gives you carte blanche, Jacko, said his bad side, the part of him that had been quiet for years.

But he knew.

He knew. Some boundaries remained.

"I don't think so, Thea."

"What do you mean, you 'don't think so'?" She sounded harsh, as if she hadn't been denied something in a long time.

"I can't."

"There she is!" someone cried out as the crowd pushed toward them.

As Thea went to greet her fans, Jack got the hell out of there.

Because if he stayed, he'd finish that Scotch, and then drink another and another, and sooner or later, he'd forget the reasons not to go to Thea's suite.

TWENTY-TWO

THE NEWEST ART GALLERY IN ECHO BEACH WAS ON THE CORNER of First and Main. A scrolled ironwork sign above the door read: ECLECTICA.

Only a few weeks ago, the Flying High Kite Shop had inhabited this space, but the new owners had obviously gone all out in refurbishing the site. Espresso-colored shingles covered the exterior; freshly planted flower boxes graced the area beneath the front window.

That window was blank now, covered from end to end by a sheet of black paper. A small sign was tacked to the glass. It read: NO PEEKING. WE'RE DOING THE WINDOW DISPLAY AND YOU'RE GOING TO LOVE IT.

Elizabeth glanced down at the piece of paper Daniel had given her. This was the place.

Just go see her, he'd said over coffee; *she's new in town and could use a little help.*

Elizabeth had wanted to decline, but when Daniel looked at her with those incredibly blue eyes, she'd automatically nodded.

Now, she wished she'd been firmer. Most of the so-called art galleries in Echo Beach carried knickknacks—coasters made out of polished driftwood . . . Christmas ornaments made of that ugly Mount St. Helens ash that looked like a jumbled swirl of chocolate and vanilla ice cream . . . crocheted doilies . . . dried sand dollars in brown mesh netting, that sort of thing. She stayed away from most of them.

Still, a promise was a promise.

She opened the door and went inside. At her entrance, a bell tinkled overhead and a bird squawked loudly.

"Hello?"

There was no answer. She looked around.

To her left was a table filled with stunning wood sculptures. Most of them were women—nudes—from neck to hips. The wood was unbelievably rich and beautiful, the color of well-aged red wine, polished to silken perfection. She couldn't help touching one of the statues; her finger glided down a delicately curved shoulder.

On the next table was an exhibit of black-and-white photography. Each print was extravagantly matted in black suede and framed in gold. The photographer had masterfully captured the spirit of the coast in a series of strikingly original shots: a beach at low tide on a windy day . . . a misty, ethereal image of the lighthouse called Terrible Tilly . . . a haunting, nighttime picture of Haystack Rock, rising out of the surf like some ancient monolith.

On the back wall were several paintings. Enough, but not too many. There was a watercolor collage of open umbrellas. A multimedia abstract work that suggested a spinnaker puffed out with wind. The largest piece was a spectacular oil painting of Orca Point.

"Amazing," Elizabeth said softly to herself.

"It is, isn't it?"

Elizabeth spun around. With the suddenness of the movement, her hip hit a table; beach glass necklaces clinked together.

A woman stepped out from behind a hanging tapestry. She was at least six feet tall, and nearly as wide as she was tall. Her hair was a bird's nest of brown frizz that hung to her waist. She had on a dress that could have doubled as a sackcloth and fell to her feet, which were bare except for the silver butterfly ring on her left big toe. A plunging neckline revealed breasts that quivered when she walked. A huge white bird was perched on her right shoulder.

She stepped closer, smiling. "I'm Large Marge." She grinned. "I picked up the nickname at a commune in the Bay Area. I never could figure out how a petite, retiring gal like me got saddled with a nickname like that, but there you have it." She frowned dramatically. "Saddled was a poor word choice. I forbid you to run with it."

"I'll rein myself in."

Large Marge laughed heartily. The movement almost tossed her breasts into midair.

Elizabeth offered her hand. "I'm Elizabeth Shore. Daniel Boudreaux asked me to stop by and see you."

Marge grabbed Elizabeth's hand and pumped it hard. "He told me about you. I'm glad you stopped by. I wanted to talk to you about the Stormy Weather Arts Festival."

"It's a big deal around here."

"That's what Danny tells me, though it's hard to imagine an arts walk in this weather. I've never seen so much rain."

"We locals barely notice it, and the tourists find out too late. I'd be happy to help you organize your gallery's event, if that's what you're interested in. I know who's who around here."

"Organization skills I got. Local artists are scarce as hen's teeth. It seems that all the good ones are already taken." She studied Elizabeth. "Danny boy tells me your work might be worth exhibiting."

Elizabeth laughed. "Yeah, right."

Marge said softly, "He told me you'd be scared."

Elizabeth's smile faded. She took a step back. She didn't mean to, and when she realized what she'd done, she stopped. "I just started painting again, after years away from it."

Marge's gaze moved pointedly to Elizabeth's wedding ring. "Raisin' kids, huh?"

"Yes." She smiled, though it felt grim, that smile, almost a grimace.

"Are you any good?"

"I was." It was as confident as she could be.

Marge made a clicking sound, then snorted and slammed her hands on her fleshy hips. "Danny's take is good enough for me. I'd like to show your work for the festival."

"No."

"Why not?"

Elizabeth didn't know what the right answer was. "What if it's no good?"

"Then it won't sell. Or maybe it'll sell anyway. Hell, honey, it's art. Anything can happen. You want a guarantee, get a bank job. What's the point of painting if no one ever sees it?"

"I suppose I could think about it."

Marge glanced at the wall clock. "I'll give you three minutes."

"Come on . . ."

Marge took a step closer. "I know you, Elizabeth. Hell, I've *been* you. I spent ten years trying to fit my full-sized personality into a compact marriage. If you don't give me an answer right now, I'll never hear from you again."

Elizabeth felt exposed by that observation. And empowered. She didn't need psychic abilities to hear Meghann's voice in her head: *Damn it, Birdie, don't you dare hesitate.* "How many pieces would you need?"

"Five. Is that possible?"

Elizabeth had no idea, but she knew she had to try. For once. "They won't sell, you know."

"I'm sure we've both survived worse than that. Come on, Elizabeth, say you'll do it."

"I'll try."

Marge grinned. "I love confidence in a woman." She smacked Elizabeth on the back so hard she stumbled sideways. "Are you still here? You ought to be home painting. Now, git."

IN THE PAST FIVE DAYS, Jack had been in six cities, and every moment in each of those cities had been a blitz. He'd interviewed Alex Rodriguez, Ken Griffey Jr., Randy Johnson, Shawn Kemp, and Brian Bosworth.

When the interviews were finished, he spent another three days in the editing room, working the narration and music into the one-hour special he'd titled: *Breakable Gods*.

He'd loved every minute of it.

"You and Sally did a hell of a job," Tom Jinaro said, leaning back in his chair. "You were right to hire her. She's a pistol."

"Thanks." Jack had been confident coming into this meeting. He knew his special was a virtuoso blend of news and entertainment. He'd dared to expose himself emotionally on camera, just enough to humanize the story. He'd admitted how difficult it had been to be forgotten by a city that had once adored him. Alex and Ken had been honest, too, admitting how much it had hurt to be vilified by their former fans. Brian talked convincingly about being forgotten.

Tom leaned forward again. "I've been in this business a long time. I've seen people come and go—mostly go. But you're the real deal. I've never seen anyone shoot up the ladder quicker. I had Mark produce your special because he's the best we have. Honestly, I didn't think you were ready for this sort of thing, but he tells me you were as good as anyone he's ever worked with."

"Thanks," Jack said again.

"So, what do you want?"

"Excuse me?"

"It's a simple question. What do you want? The *Fox NFL Sunday* show? Your own interview hour? A book deal? What?"

"You know what I was doing three months ago, Tom? Begging for a job on a low-rent regional sports show—and I didn't get it." He let that image sink in. "You hired me when I was in the gutter, professionally. You took a chance on me; believe me, I won't forget that."

Tom smiled tiredly. "You'll mean to remember it, but after a while, you'll start racking up offers, and then you'll think about your age, and your agent will tell you to make hay while the sun shines. It's how the game is played." He leaned forward. "What I'm going to tell you now can't leave this room. If it does, I'll know it was you."

"What is it?"

"One of the guys is quitting *NFL Sunday*. One of the big four. I can't tell you which one. But we're looking at you to fill that slot for next year."

The only show bigger was *Monday Night Football*.

Jack drew in a sharp breath, savoring the moment.

"Thanks." It was all he could say. Any more and he might start laughing.

"It's not for sure." Tom grinned. "But it's damn close to that. So, let me give you some advice, man to man. You had a bad-boy image in the NFL and it doesn't look to me like you've changed. I hear you practically live at Kel's pub."

Jack started to disagree, but Tom stopped him with a laugh.

"Save the denials for your curiously absent wife. I don't care what you do offscreen as long as it doesn't hurt our ratings. But you know what it's like when the tabloids turn on you. Opportunities can vanish in an instant. Stay away from drugs and DUIs and underage women."

"Don't worry. Nothing is going to derail me this time. I'm older and wiser."

"Glad to hear it. Now, get going. Talk to Steve in post-production. I want you and Mark to redub the music. The opening score sounds like the music they played at my aunt Rose's funeral. And there's a bad cut on the Randy Johnson segment."

"Thanks. When do you think we can air it?"

"Sweeps week. I'll set up with Marion to run a series of promo spots. We'll want to shoot them ASAP."

Jack left the office and went straight to the editing room, where he and Mark Lackoft spent the next ten hours examining and refining every split second of footage. By the time he was finished, *Breakable Gods* was worthy of a damned award.

Although he was exhausted and starving, he couldn't remember when he'd felt so good. He left the office and walked home, strutting like Tony Manero. He could practically *hear* "Stayin' Alive" playing in his head.

"Hey, Billy!" he called out to the doorman as he strode through the lobby and rode the elevator to his floor.

He opened his door and walked into the apartment. He almost yelled, *Birdie, I'm home,* but stopped himself just in time.

The apartment was as quiet as a tomb. No candle scented the air, no music had been turned on, no aromatic dinner pulled him toward the kitchen.

Disappointment poked a hole in his good mood. He hadn't realized how lonely success could be if you had no one to share it with.

He made himself a drink, then put a CD into the stereo—an old Queen album. "We Are the Champions" blared through the tiny black speakers.

Sipping his drink, he went to the window and stared out.

Tonight, the view didn't help. All he saw when he looked down was a crowd of strangers. For the first time in this city of millions, Jack felt alone.

He picked up the phone and dialed Birdie's number, then hung up before she answered. He didn't know what to say to her anymore. "I love you" was no longer enough, but what else was there? All he knew was that tonight's victory was hollow without her.

He finished his drink and poured another. By now, the apartment was starting to soften; hard wall edges were blurring. Queen moved on to "Another One Bites the Dust."

He slid down to the floor and sat there, leaned back against his Barcalounger. He flipped open the drink holder hidden in the tufted velour arm. He tried twice to put his glass in the hole, then gave up and downed the rest of the Scotch.

Maybe he should go out, have a few drinks at Kel's.

But he didn't feel like moving.

What he *felt* like was talking to his wife. He wanted to show her the tape, and watch her smile at him afterward. In the old days, she would have teared up; no doubt about it. She would have said, "Oh, baby, that was *amazing*. I always knew you had it in you."

He needed that now.

It was funny how profoundly you could need something that for years you hadn't even noticed was missing.

He got to his feet. The apartment swayed for a second, then righted itself.

He was drunker than he thought. "So wha?"

Why should he stay sober anyway? He'd rather be drunk right now; he had a lot of things he wanted to forget. Like the softness of her touch . . . or the way her green eyes sparkled with pride at his accomplishments.

He stumbled into the kitchen, where he made himself another drink. He'd left the jigger somewhere—God knew where—but it didn't matter.

The doorbell rang. His heart lurched. Against all common sense, he thought, *Birdie.*

He hurried to the door and opened it.

Sally leaned against the doorframe, a bottle of Dom Pérignon dangling from one hand. Her hair was loose and flowing around her shoulders. She wore a pretty, scoop-necked dress that tucked in at her tiny waist and ended just above her knees. "I sneaked past the doorman. I hope that's okay."

"Uh. Sure."

"I saw the final edit," she said, smiling.

The magic words. "Iss good, isn't it?"

"You're a genius, Jack. A *god*. I was practically crying when Alex Rodriguez talked about leaving Seattle."

Her words were a precious water that irrigated his dry heart.

He stepped back to let her inside. He smacked into the wall and stumbled sideways. "Oops. Sorry."

She grabbed his arm to steady him. With one foot, she kicked the door shut. "I guess you don't need champagne."

"I'm a little drunk," he said. He thought maybe he'd whispered the confession.

She moved in close to him.

He felt her small, lithe body pressing against his, and he groaned, realizing suddenly how lonely he'd been in the last few weeks.

"Sally . . ." He didn't know what to say, what to ask for. All he knew was that his head was swimming and his dick was rock-hard. He could feel the blood draining out of his brain.

But he tried. Excuses and reasons staggered through his quickly shrinking brain. He had stumbled onto *Wait, Sally* when she kissed him.

That was the end of even pseudo-rational thought. When her lips touched his, he was lost. Time seemed to slow down and speed up at the same time.

He gave in; it was that simple. In some distant, hazy part of his mind, he knew he was doing a swan dive out of a high-rise building, but he couldn't make himself care. For months—years, really—he'd been holding himself in check, keeping steady to the vows he'd made to Elizabeth.

But now she was living in Oregon and she'd made it very

clear that she didn't want him. Nothing had ever hurt like admitting that.

Sally gazed up at him, her eyes dark with the same runaway passion that was making his dick ache. "Well?"

His mouth was dry—it only made him think of places that were wet. "You know I'm still married," he said, feeling that sentence was a personal triumph of self-control.

"Of course I know. I don't want your ring." Smiling slowly, she reached down into his pants. "I'll take this instead."

Jack couldn't help himself. He moved into her hand. He felt the top button on his pants pop free, felt the warm pressure of her fingers against his flesh.

He started to speak—although what he would say he couldn't imagine—

"Take me to bed," she whispered.

Four little words that were his undoing.

Twenty-three

*E*LIZABETH FINISHED THE DAY ON AUTOPILOT. AS SHE'D DE-
frosted the chicken and started the casserole, she'd thought, *Exhibit. My work.*

She'd already browned the chicken and chopped the onions
when she realized she was cooking for her old life. It was a chicken
casserole that would easily feed eight people.

Once the meal was in the oven, she went into the pantry and
pulled out the seascape. She would finish by tomorrow morning,
and then start something else.

Maybe she'd try a watercolor next. In the old days, she'd loved
oils, but she was older now. The smeary softness of watercolor ap-
pealed to her. And more important, she had a limited amount of
time. She'd be more likely to make her five-works-by-the-festival
deadline if she didn't work in oil.

She thought she heard a car drive up. Then a door slam.

Maybe Meghann had cleared her schedule and headed south
for a girls' weekend.

Elizabeth hurried to the door and flung it open.

Anita stood there, wearing a flowing white dress and pink ballet slippers. A floppy purple hat covered much of her face. Beside her was a huge suitcase and a long, narrow cardboard box. A lime green taxi drove away. "Hey, Birdie," she said, smiling uncertainly, "this is the beach I picked."

Elizabeth didn't quite know how to react. First, there was Anita's appearance: she looked like something out of a Grimm's fairy tale, nothing like the Texas golddigger that was her usual style. Gone were the bright, garish colors and peroxided, high-rise hair. Now a simple white braid hung over one shoulder. There was something almost otherworldly about her, a fragility that bespoke great sadness.

And—even more disconcerting—was the fact that she was *here*, invading the solitude that had cost Elizabeth so dearly.

She remembered their last phone conversation. Elizabeth had been triumphant after painting class—and yes, tipsy. Had she *invited* Anita here?

No.

No invitation had been issued, drunken or otherwise. But she'd written that despairing *we're family* letter right after the break up. All of this flashed through her mind in an instant.

"I hope you don't mind me just showin' up. My mama would be spinnin' in her grave at such a breach of etiquette, but I was lookin' through travel magazines for a place to go, and I saw an ad for Oregon beaches. And I thought, hell's bells it must be a sign."

"You look . . . different," Elizabeth said clumsily. An understatement on par with *It rains in Oregon*.

Anita laughed. "Oh, that. All those clothes were for Edward. This is my natural hair color."

For *Daddy*?

Her regal, aristocratic father had wanted his wife to dress like Dolly Parton?

Elizabeth couldn't process that. She didn't want to step aside, not for Anita-the-Hun, but what choice did she have?

You take care of her, you hear?

"Come on in." Elizabeth grabbed the huge suitcase (What did Anita need with that much stuff? How long did she intend to stay???) and dragged it over the threshold.

Anita stepped inside, looked around. She was wringing her hands together. "So, this is the famous beach house. Your daddy always wanted to see it."

That sentence brought them together for a moment. "I begged him to come up for the Fourth of July."

"Yes," Anita answered softly.

"Come on, I'll show you to the guest bedroom. It's upstairs." Elizabeth turned and walked through the house, dragging the rolling suitcase behind her. When she reached the foot of the stairs, she looked back.

Anita stood in front of the fireplace. A pretty red-gold sheen made her dress appear translucent. She reached out for one of the framed photographs on the mantel.

It was the one taken at Christmas, where the whole family stood clustered around the brightly decorated tree. They were laughing so hard their faces were scrunched up. All except Daddy; he looked grim and irritated.

And no wonder. He'd bought Elizabeth a 35 mm camera for Christmas. It had taken him twenty minutes—and at least that many tries—to get the automatic timer to work.

I don't care if your damned lips are ready to fall off, he'd boomed, frustrated by their laughter, *just smile, damn it. This is fun.*

It was the last picture she had of him.

Anita turned. There were tears in her eyes. "Could I get a copy of this?"

"Of course."

Anita looked at the picture for a second longer, then headed for the stairs. Gone was the Bette Midler mince-step; in its place, a flowing gracefulness that suggested at least a few years of dance training. She stopped in front of Elizabeth.

"I didn't know where else to go, Birdie," she said quietly. "I couldn't stay there another night."

Elizabeth could understand that. Her father had generated a lot of heat. Without him, it would be a cold world. She looked down at her stepmother. Amazingly, she couldn't see the woman she'd fought with for most of her life. This new Anita was frail and fragile, a lost soul. "Of course it's okay, Anita. We're family."

For better or for worse, it was true.

JACK CAME AWAKE SLOWLY, groaning. He felt as if he'd been hit in the head with a crowbar. He rolled over in bed; his outflung arm cracked onto the nightstand, sent the lamp clattering to the floor. He opened one eye. The clock read: 8:07.

There must have been a power outage last night. He never slept past five o'clock.

Then he noticed something on the floor. Red. Small.

Smacking his dry lips, he stared at it, trying to focus.

It was a condom wrapper, ripped in half.

He bolted upright. At the movement, his headache lurched into a run.

Oh, shit. He glanced to the left.

The bed was empty.

Sagging forward, he closed his eyes for a long moment; then slowly, he pushed the covers aside again and got out of bed. He stumbled into the bathroom—where he saw that Sally had written a note on the mirror. In lipstick.

Great sex
XXOO
Sally

The *a* in her name had a little halo above it.

The headache kicked him in the skull, pounding.

It never would have happened if Birdie had moved to New York. If she hadn't left him.

(Yeah, try that one on for size.)

The message on the mirror stared back at him.

Great sex.

It had been pretty damned good; that was true. Not jump-up-hit-your-head-against-the-ceiling great, but damned good. It had rejuvenated him, made him feel young again.

Wanted.

It had always been a weakness in him, that desperate, aching need to be wanted. In rehab, one of the shrinks had told him that his neediness was a by-product of having alcoholic parents who died too young. He didn't know about that, or care particularly. What he did know was that it had almost ruined him once, that desperate need.

And it could ruin him again.

Let me give you some advice, man to man, Tom Jinaro had said on the day he'd dangled the *NFL Sunday* carrot. *Stay away from drugs and DUIs and underage women. Opportunities can vanish in an instant.*

If it got out that he'd had sex with his assistant . . .

The words SEXUAL HARASSMENT came at him hard. If Sally decided to, she could ruin him.

He'd set himself up as Mr. Morality, too.

"Jesus Christ," he whispered, staring into the mirror. Sally's cherry-red love note cut across his reflection.

"Never again," he said out loud. "It was a onetime thing. A mistake."

Elizabeth didn't have to know. Ever.

"A onetime thing," he said again, meaning it.

By the time he'd showered, shaved, dressed, and walked to the office, he felt better. Stronger and more sure of himself. He'd made a mistake—a whopper of one, to be sure—but it would stand alone. A high-rise of stupidity in the vast prairie of the rest of his life.

At his desk, he sat down and immediately started to go through the notes he'd made yesterday afternoon. He was working on a story about a horse camp in Poulsbo, Washington, called Blue Heron Farms, where disabled children learned to ride.

Suddenly the door opened.

Sally stood in the opening, dressed this morning in a slim black suit with an emerald-green silk blouse. Her smile was depressingly cheery.

She managed to make him feel old and young at the same time.

She closed the door behind her. "I'm sorry I left while you were still sleeping. I needed to be at work early," she said.

"Don't mention it." He felt sick to his stomach. Nervous, ashamed, and excited all at once. *Really,* he thought, *don't mention it.*

Smiling, she clasped her hands behind her back and strolled toward him. The clicking of her high heels sounded appallingly loud in the room. The only thing louder was the beating of his heart.

Onetime thing, he reminded himself.

"About last night . . ."

She placed her hands on his desk and leaned forward. From this angle, he could see the lacy beige edge of her bra. Pale, firm breasts swelled beside it.

He tried not to recall how sweet she'd tasted, how pink her nipples were—

Stop it.

"You'll never guess who called for you this morning," she said.

"Who?" He kept his gaze pinned to her face. Nothing below the collar. Or the top button at the very lowest.

"Your publicist. He asked me to pass along an offer . . . from *People* magazine."

"*People?*" He rose out of his chair. "What did they want?"

She hitched one hip onto the edge of his desk. "They want to feature you in the 'Fifty Most Beautiful People' issue."

"You're kidding?"

"This is the big time, Jack," she said. "You're a star again."

He didn't mean to do it, but he reached out, pulled her into his arms.

"Take me on the shoot with you," she said, tracing his lips with one finger. "It's going to be at the Peninsula."

He gazed down at her heart-shaped face and felt a sharp tug of desire. God help him, he wanted her again already.

ELIZABETH TOSSED AND TURNED ALL NIGHT, unable to sleep. She hadn't realized how accustomed she'd become to privacy until Anita showed up.

At dawn, she got dressed and tiptoed across the hall, then eased the door of the guest bedroom open. Anita was still sleeping.

She wrote a quick gone-to-the-beach note, then went outside.

Hugging her canvas supply bag, she climbed down the steps to the beach. The ocean was energetic today, surging forward and back. Thousands of shorebirds circled the distant rocks, cawing loudly.

She left the bag by her rock and kept walking, faster and faster, until it seemed completely natural to break into an easy jog. She took energy from the surf; it made her feel powerful and free. Off in the distance, she could see a pair of box kites sparring with each other in the wind. An osprey flapped down onto its nest in a dead conifer tree.

For a few glorious minutes, she forgot that Anita had shown up last night, dragging a suitcase big enough for a two-month stay.

Finally, she turned around and came back to her spot. Collapsing, breathing hard, she sat down on her flat rock and tucked up her knees, stared out at the endless blue sea. A few diaphanous silver clouds floated across the sky.

It felt good to push herself. After years of ignoring her body, she had finally figured out what really mattered. Who cared if she was a size four or a six or a fourteen? She just wanted to be able to run down the beach and climb up the stairs and ride her bike. Size wasn't the point; health was.

It didn't sound like much, but to a woman who'd spent almost thirty years counting calories and wearing control-top panty hose, it was freedom, pure and simple.

"Birdie, honey? Is that you?"

Elizabeth turned. Anita was standing a few feet away, wearing a long floral skirt and a heavy cable-knit white sweater.

Elizabeth reluctantly scooted sideways on the flat rock. "Here. There's plenty of room."

Anita sat down beside Elizabeth. "Whew! Those stairs are a killer. No wonder you've lost weight."

Elizabeth turned. "I *have?*"

"At least ten pounds, honey. Your clothes hang on you." Her mouth tightened in disapproval. " 'Course the baggy sweats you've been wearing would hang on Mama Cass."

There it was again, the familiar sniping and criticism that had stained their relationship for years. *Just smile and go on,* she thought, *or it'll be a long visit.* "I guess exercising was the key all along."

"I do yoga myself."

Elizabeth hadn't known that. Come to think of it, she didn't know much about Anita's life apart from Edward. She jumped on that; it gave them something to talk about. "What else do you do? At home, I mean."

"Regular things, I guess. I belong to a book club that meets once a month. Last month we read *The Hours.* I play bridge with the girls every Thursday morning. I volunteer at the women's shelter on Tuesdays. I knit enough afghans to cover a small country. 'Course your daddy took up most o' my time." She stopped, fell silent for a long time. Then, softly, she said, "I don't dream about him. Every night I go t' bed, waitin' to see him . . . but he doesn't come."

Elizabeth knew that feeling. "I've waited my whole life to dream about Mama. It's never happened."

"It's like losin' him a second time," Anita said. After another long pause, she added, "I always knew I'd outlive him. I thought I was prepared for it. What a fool I was. You can't prepare for losin' someone you love."

Elizabeth knew there was nothing for her to say. Grief was like the ocean in front of them; waves kept rolling toward you, and sometimes, the tide swelled high enough to pull you under. Usually, it had to be handled alone, in the dark, when you were most afraid. But maybe Anita had come to Echo Beach because the dark was *too* quiet. Maybe she needed to talk about Daddy. "How did you and Daddy meet?" Elizabeth asked.

Anita gave her a grateful smile. "I was working in the beauty salon. Lordy, I still remember the first time I saw him. He looked like a Saturday-matinee hero, with his shaggy black hair and dark eyes. He had a mustache in those days, and his eyes were dark as night. I turned to my friend, Mabel, and said, 'Oh, baby, will you look at that.' " She sighed. "I reckon I fell in love with him right then. 'Course, he barely noticed me at all."

Elizabeth frowned. Daddy had shaved off that mustache the year after Mama died. He'd never worn one since. "When was that?"

Anita didn't look at her. "It doesn't matter."

"You knew my mother," Elizabeth said suddenly, straightening.

Anita started to speak—to deny it, Elizabeth was certain. But when their eyes met, Anita sighed heavily and slumped forward. "Not really. She was with him that day, though. Mabel cut her hair."

"Did you talk to her?"

"Me? Naw. I was just out of beauty school. No one paid me much mind."

"Tell me about her."

"I don't know much, really. I heard stories, o' course. The second wife always hears stories about the first. By all accounts, your mama was the most beautiful, most adventurous woman in Springdale."

"I've heard that line for years. It's starting to sound rehearsed. Tell me something real. Why wouldn't Daddy ever talk about her?" She gazed at Anita. "Please."

"Before you were born, your mama ran away for a spell."

"She left Daddy?"

"In the middle of the night, from what I heard. It took him a while to find her. She was way to North Carolina by then, but he tracked her down and brought her home. After that, folks said, she was different. Sad and quiet. Jenny Pilger saw her break into tears one day at the Piggly Wiggly."

"Depression." Elizabeth had never imagined such a thing. Her mama, the woman everyone said was so bold and adventurous, *depressed*. She didn't quite know how to process this new information.

"She loved you. Old Anna Deaver said that Marguerite never let you out of her sight. She even slept with you most nights. Wouldn't let anyone watch you, ever. But the rumor was that she never did shake that sadness. Some said she clung to you so tightly they thought your little eyes'd pop out. She stopped smilin'. That's what I heard most of all. That she'd left her smile in North Carolina, and she couldn't even come up with one for you."

"I used to beg him for stories about her. He never would say anything beyond, 'You hold your memories close, sugar beet.' But I didn't have any memories. Not enough, anyway." She'd never been able to make him understand the howling emptiness she'd felt as a child.

"Maybe he didn't have any stories to give you. Sometimes unhappiness can settle over a thing and bury it until there's nothin' else left."

Nothing else left. Just unhappiness.

Elizabeth knew how that felt now. "That's how it got between Jack and me."

"It's easy, sometimes, to forget why you fell in love with someone." Anita stared out at the ocean. "I left him once, you know."

"No, I didn't know. Not then, anyway."

"How would you, I guess, livin' so far away, and your own life on top of it? Edward wasn't the kind of man who'd tell his only child that his marriage had gone missin'."

"You could have told me."

"On one of our long, soul-searchin' mother-daughter talks? Honey, you barely said hello to me when you called."

"Where did you go?"

"That doesn't matter. It didn't even matter then. Away, that's all." She sighed, and Elizabeth wondered if that memory hurt more now that he was gone.

"Maybe we shouldn't talk about this."

Anita was quiet for a moment. The ocean whooshed toward them, tumbled lazily across the sand and slunk away again. "He overwhelmed me sometimes. He was so hungry for everything, so needy, and I was young when we got married. I didn't know what I wanted. So I lived his life. For a long time, that was okay."

Elizabeth knew that feeling. Jack and her father had that in common. Both men were like the sun; everything ultimately orbited around them. In the beginning, that was okay, but as you grew older, things changed. You started to see the roads you hadn't taken, and you wondered, *What if . . . ?*

Anita brought her knees up and curled her arms around her ankles. She started to turn toward Elizabeth, then looked down at her wedding ring instead. "I wanted to have a child."

Elizabeth remembered that night in the garden, when she'd blithely asked Anita why she hadn't had kids.

"Oh, honey, that's a question for another time, maybe between different women."

"In other words, mind my own business."

"Yes. That question cuts to the heart of me, is all. I'm not goin' to answer it as idle chitchat at midnight two days after my husband's death."

It must have wounded Anita deeply to hear that question asked aloud.

"I knew I'd be alone one day," Anita went on, fiddling with her wedding ring. "I thought a baby would help. So, after Edward and I got back together, we tried. I had three miscarriages. All boys. Each one took a bigger piece of me, until . . ." She shrugged. "Three was enough, I guess. I figured God knew what he was doing."

Elizabeth felt herself softening toward Anita, glimpsing a woman she'd never imagined before. It felt strangely like coming home. "I had a miscarriage once," she said softly, surprising herself by the admission. "I never told anyone except Jack. It about broke my heart." She touched her stepmother's ankle, squeezing it gently. It was the first time she'd ever done such a thing.

Anita made a sound, a tiny gasp, then turned to her. "I have something for you. I brought it all the way from Tennessee. And it wasn't easy."

None of this was easy, Elizabeth thought but didn't say. Instead, she helped her stepmother to her feet. They climbed up the rickety wood steps and emerged onto the soggy grass.

When they reached the porch, Elizabeth noticed the big cardboard box leaning against the house. "I wondered what was in that thing."

Anita rushed into the house and came back out, holding a knife. "Open it."

Elizabeth took the knife and split the box down the seam.

"You ought to put it down," Anita advised.

Elizabeth slid the box onto the slatted porch floor. It hit with a loud metallic clang. She knelt down and opened the box.

Inside, she saw shiny green poles . . . white knotted rope.

"It's Daddy's hammock."

"Y'all used to snuggle together in that thing for hours, rockin' back and forth. I remember hearin' your giggles from the kitchen while I was cookin' dinner."

Suddenly Daddy was there, beside her. *Heya, sugah beet, hand your old daddy one o' them sweet lemonades, won'tcha?*

"We used to watch the fireflies together," Elizabeth whispered, remembering it in vivid detail. "They flew all around us when we were in this hammock."

"He'd want you to have it," Anita said. "It'd be perfect over there by the stairs, so you can sleep in it on a sunny day and listen to the ocean below . . . and remember how much he loved you."

Elizabeth finally looked up at Anita, her eyes stinging. She couldn't say anything, not even thank you.

Anita smiled. "You're welcome."

MARCH HOWLED INTO NEW YORK on an arctic blast. In the middle of a night so cold that even Times Square was deserted, it began to snow. At first it was just a flake here and there, drifting across the city, but by dawn, God had finished screwing around. Snow fell so hard and fast Jack could barely see the buildings across the street.

He stood at his window, sipping a latte. On the street below, cars were few and far between. City buses rumbled slowly forward, angling toward the stops. Neon signs looked faded and worn against the pewter sky, like collectible postage stamps from a forgotten era. Cottony clouds hung low in the sky, severing the highrises in half.

He was just about to head into the shower when the phone rang.

"Hello, Mr. Shore. This is the Bite Me insurance agency and we need authorization to distribute your assets, since you have Fallen Off The Face Of The Planet."

He couldn't help laughing. "Mea culpa," he said. It was always better to take responsibility with Jamie. Otherwise, she'd chew you up and spit you out.

"No shit, mea culpa. That's not even a question. I suppose you've been so busy big-manning it that you didn't have time to call me back about the swim team."

"We only talked about that two days ago. I knew you wouldn't do anything right away."

"Hel-*lo*, Dad, I think you need to cut back on the peroxide. That conversation was more than a week ago."

He frowned. "A week? No way."

"Oh, yes, way."

"God, I'm sorry, baby. I meant to get back to you. Things have been crazy around here. *People* mag—"

She snorted at the familiar *meant to.* "Yeah, right. It's always other people's fault."

He made a mental note to pay closer attention to the calendar. "I'm working fifteen hours a day."

"That must be why you were out when I called you last night . . . at two o'clock in the morning. Working."

Thank God he wasn't talking to her face-to-face. He felt himself flush. "I took a sleeping pill last night. I've been having trouble sleeping lately . . . you know, without your mom." That was actually true.

And false, of course.

"I didn't even know you missed her. You never mention her."

"I do . . . miss her. She'll be out here any day." Suddenly he knew what Elizabeth meant when she said it was tough to lie to the kids.

"You've been saying that for too long. Stephie and I have come up with a plan. You're invited to make it all happen."

He immediately relaxed. So that was it: Jamie had a plan, and verbally roughing him up was her way of assuring his guilt-ridden participation. "And what exactly am I looking forward to this time, sending you girls to Europe this summer? Or, maybe scuba diving in Aruba for spring break?"

"Stephanie and I are gonna fly into Kennedy Friday morning. You'll meet us at the airport; then we'll all fly to Oregon together for the weekend."

"Huh?"

"It's Mom's birthday. You didn't forget, did you?"

Shit. "No, no. Of course not. I was going to fly out to be with her for the weekend, but then this thing at work—"

"Don't even finish that sentence. Honest to God, Dad, you're coming with us. I mean it. You're a television personality, not a cardiac surgeon. No one is gonna die if you take Friday off."

What a mess. "You're right," he said dully.

"You can meet us at the airport, right? So we can all fly together. We'll buy the tickets on-line and put them on your Visa."

"Sure. Why not?"

"And, Dad, it's a surprise. So don't tell her, okay?"

Jack closed his eyes and sighed. "Oh, it'll be a surprise, all right."

TWENTY-FOUR

LAST NIGHT, ELIZABETH AND ANITA HAD STAYED UP LATE INTO the night, talking. They didn't venture again into intimate territory. They simply talked, two women who'd known each other all their lives and yet had never really known each other at all. To their mutual surprise, they'd found a lot of common ground.

In the morning, after a breakfast of poached eggs and toast, they walked along the beach, talking some more. It was a glorious spring day, bursting with sunlight.

Later, while Anita napped, Elizabeth went to town and stocked up on groceries. It was late afternoon by the time she returned home. She picked up her mail, then turned onto Stormwatch Lane.

Out to sea, the first pink and lavender lights of evening were beginning to tint the sky. She parked in the gravel.

Anita was on the porch, staring out at the ocean. She wore a long, flowing white dress and a beautifully knit coral sweater. Her white hair was twisted into a single braid that fell down the middle of her back.

The light was stunning. Perfect. It drizzled over the house like sweet melted butter, softening all the edges. Anita's face was full of light and shadow right now: sad eyes, smiling mouth, furrowed brow. Her dress seemed to be spun from crushed pearls.

Elizabeth felt a flash of inspiration. "Could I paint you?"

Anita pressed a pale, veiny hand to her chest. "You want to paint my picture?"

"I don't promise that it'll be any good. I've only just started again. But if you'd be willing—"

"I could sit on that log over there by the cliff."

Elizabeth turned. Sure enough, there was a perfect log slanted along the edge of the property. In the newly setting sun, it shone with silvery light. Behind it, the gilded ocean stretched to the horizon. It was the exact place she would have chosen, although it might have taken her an hour to make up her mind. And Anita had chosen it in five seconds.

She looked at Anita. "Are you an artist?"

Anita laughed. "No, but I read that book, *Girl With a Pearl Earring*. The one everyone was talkin' about."

"Stay here. I'll be right back." Elizabeth raced into the house, seasoned a whole chicken and popped it into the oven alongside a few potatoes and carrots, then put the groceries away and got her painting supplies. She was outside again in less than fifteen minutes.

She set up the easel and got everything ready, then looked around for Anita.

Her stepmother was standing by the log instead of sitting on it. Her back was to Elizabeth. Her arms were crossed—that female self-protective stance Elizabeth knew so well.

The twilight sky was pure magic. Pink, purple, gold, and orange lay in layers above the sparkling silver ocean. In the distance, the gnarled trees were already black.

Anita seemed to be fading before Elizabeth's eyes, as if the colors in the sky were drawing their strength from her. She was becoming paler and paler; her hair and dress looked almost opalescent.

"Don't move!"

Elizabeth let pure instinct overtake her. She'd never moved with such speed, such purpose. Mixing colors, slashing lines, trying desperately to capture the lonely beauty of the scene in front of her. Layer upon layer of color, everything taking on a hue that was completely unique.

She painted furiously, desperately, wordlessly, until the last bits of light seeped into the waterline at the edge of the world and disappeared.

It was almost completely dark when she said, "That's it, Anita. No more for tonight."

Anita's body seemed to melt downward and become smaller. Suddenly Elizabeth realized how much she'd asked of the woman. "I'm sorry. Did it hurt to stand so still for so long?"

"I loved every moment of it."

"You must be starving. I know I am. Come on inside."

Anita glanced eagerly at the easel. "Can I see it?"

"No." Elizabeth heard the hard edge to her voice and was instantly contrite. "Sorry. I mean not yet. Is that okay?"

Anita waved her hand in the air. "Of course, honey."

Elizabeth carried the painting into the house and put it in the walk-in pantry to dry. "Dinner'll be ready in a while," she said to Anita; "go on upstairs. Take a hot bath."

"Darlin', you read my mind."

Elizabeth set the table and made the salad, then called for Anita. When there was no answer, she went upstairs and found her stepmother sitting on the end of the bed, holding a small lace-trimmed pillow. Her head was bowed forward. She was so still that for a moment Elizabeth thought she'd nodded off.

"Anita?"

Anita looked up. Her face was pale; in the dull light, her cheekbones created dark hollows in her cheeks. There were tears in her eyes.

Elizabeth sat down on the edge of the bed. "You okay?"

"I guess."

Elizabeth didn't know what to say. Grief was like that: One minute you were tripping the light fantastic; the next minute, an old blue pillow made you cry.

Anita smoothed her hand across the pillow. "Your daddy always tried to get me to take up needlepoint, but I never could master it. Such a feminine thing."

Elizabeth glanced down at the pillow. It was one of the few mementos she had of her mother. She had often tried to imagine her mother in a rocking chair, working with all that beautiful silk thread, but all she could draw up was a black-and-white image of a young woman looking into the camera.

"Your mama made this pillow," Anita said. "I can tell by her dainty stitches. That time she came into the beauty salon? She stitched the whole time Mabel cut her hair."

"I try to picture her sometimes."

Anita set the pillow down and stood up, then placed her thin hands on Elizabeth's shoulders and guided her toward the mirror that hung above the bureau.

Elizabeth stared at her own puffy reflection. Her hair was a mess, her face looked pale without makeup.

"When I first saw your mama, I thought she was the loveliest woman I'd ever seen. She and Edward looked like a pair of movie stars together." Anita pulled the hair back from Elizabeth's face. "You're the spittin' image of her."

As a girl, Elizabeth had spent hours searching through family photographs for pictures of her mother, but she'd never found more than a few.

She'd been looking in the wrong place for years, and no one had ever told her. All she'd needed to see Mama was a mirror. Now, as she looked into her own green eyes, she saw a hint of the woman she'd spent all her life missing. "Thank you, Anita," she said in a shaky voice.

"You're welcome, honey."

•   •   •

Jack barely slept that night.

Bleary-eyed and hungover, he padded into the bathroom and turned on the shower.

Unfortunately, the hot water couldn't wash away his regret. He'd slept with Sally again last night.

He wished he could believe it wouldn't matter; he and Birdie were separated, after all. But he knew better. This separation wasn't a license to screw around. It was a hiatus, a resting period in the midst of a long marriage. If he found out that Birdie had been unfaithful, he would kill the guy.

She'd forgiven him once, but that had been years ago, when they were different people. Back then, she'd been willing to sacrifice a huge amount of herself for their family. Though he'd hurt her, she'd been willing to believe in him again. In them.

But those days were gone. The new Birdie was a woman he couldn't predict.

She might learn about this mistake and file for divorce.

Or maybe she wouldn't care anymore. Maybe she'd drifted so far away that fidelity didn't matter.

He wiped steam off the bathroom mirror and stared at his hazy reflection. After a night of partying, the wrinkles around his eyes were more pronounced, and his skin had a sick gray tinge. It was easy to imagine himself as an old man, stooped by time and bad choices, tottering forward with a cane to steady his walk.

He'd always believed that Birdie would be beside him in those twilight years, still loving him when he had nothing to offer but a shaking hand and his heart. It had never occurred to him—not even in the past weeks—that they wouldn't always be together.

Now, suddenly, he was afraid. What if he'd finally ruined it?

He had just started shaving when the phone rang. Naked, he walked into the bedroom to answer it. "Hello?"

"Hel-*lo*, Dad." Jamie sighed disgustedly. "I told you he was still at home. He forgot us."

Shit. Today was the day they were going to Oregon. "I was just walking out the door."

Lame, Jack. Lame.

"Often, people leave for the airport *before* the plane lands," Jamie said.

"I meant to."

"He *meant* to," Jamie said, clearly talking to her sister. "How long until you'll be here? Maybe we should get a room and wait until it's convenient for you to pick us up."

He glanced at the clock. It was eight-forty-eight. "An hour, max. I don't know what traffic is like. Our plane doesn't leave until . . ."

"Eleven-forty-nine."

"Right. I'll meet you at the gate by ten."

Jamie sighed. "We'll be there, Dad."

"I'm sorry," he said. "Really."

"We know. See you in a few."

Jack hung up the phone, took two aspirin, and rushed to get dressed.

What if Birdie could tell he'd been unfaithful just by looking at him?

Damn. One screwup at a time. For now, he had to deal with the fact that he'd forgotten to meet his children at the airport.

In ten minutes, he was out the door and in a cab, heading toward Kennedy.

That gave him plenty of time to figure out what to say beyond, *I'm sorry.*

Maybe Stephanie would buy it, would smile prettily and say, *That's okay, Dad,* but not Jamie. She'd stare daggers at him and ignore him for as long as she damned well felt like it.

Once again, he needed Birdie. She'd always been the glue that held their family together. She'd guided him, gently and not so gently, toward an easy relationship with his daughters. She'd made sure that he'd apologized when he needed to and listened when it was imperative. Without her, he was on his own, and he had no idea what to say.

•   •   •

"You can quit being strong, you know," Anita said as they sat at the kitchen table, eating an early lunch. A few presents sat on the counter.

"What do you mean?"

"A happy birthday from your stepmother and a little gift doesn't quite cut it. Admit it, you miss your family. You've looked at the phone about fifty times today."

"I'm fine. And you said you were going to teach me how to play cribbage tonight. That's something to look forward to."

She eyed Elizabeth. "What did you normally do on your birthday?"

"You mean besides warn everyone for a week that it was coming?"

Anita nodded.

"Let's see. I usually took the day off from all volunteering projects and slept in. By the time I woke up, the house was empty. Jack and the girls always left birthday messages on the table. Once they tied balloons to the chairbacks." Elizabeth's heart did a little flip. She'd forgotten that . . . "Jack always made dinner for me that night. His one meal—chicken piccata. It took him two hours and two drinks to make it, and you couldn't talk to him while he was cooking. He cursed a blue streak the whole time. After dinner, he gave me a body massage and then we made love. Oh, and I got to kiss and hug the girls as much as I wanted—they weren't allowed to protest."

"It sounds wonderful."

"It was."

"You're good at it, you know."

"What?"

"Denial. I mean, if I didn't know you, I might think everything was just peachy for you."

"I made a choice. I wanted to be alone." Elizabeth's voice softened; hurt feelings flooded through the barriers she'd built.

Suddenly she was drowning in sorrow; a minute ago she'd been happy. She'd buried herself in denial because she knew how much a birthday without her family would hurt. No one had even called her today.

That was the realization she'd been running from all morning. No one had called.

Elizabeth forced a smile. "I'm going to go paint now. I need to finish four more pieces before the festival."

Anita stood up from the table and unwrapped her apron. "Do you mind if I tag along? I could knit while you paint."

"I'd appreciate the company," Elizabeth answered truthfully. "I'll go change my clothes and grab my stuff."

Upstairs, she changed into a pair of baggy Levi's and a well-worn blue denim shirt. She was almost to the door when she realized that she needed a belt.

She went back to the bureau and dug through her clothes, finally finding an old leather belt with a big silver buckle. She threaded it through the loops and cinched it tight, then went back downstairs.

Anita grinned at her. "You look like one of those country-and-western singers from home."

"Daddy bought me this belt at Opryland, remember? I haven't been able to wear it in years." Smiling at that, Elizabeth gathered her supplies. It wasn't ten minutes later that she and Anita were climbing down the steps.

"I can't believe you can carry all that stuff down these horrible old stairs. I keep thinkin' I'm gonna twist my ankle and plant my wrinkled face in the sand."

Elizabeth laughed. She felt good again. The girls would call tonight. Most definitely. "The tide's out," she observed. "We can spend hours down here."

Anita picked up the knitting bag she'd dropped down from the top of the stairs. Flipping her blanket out on the sand, she sat down and started knitting. A pile of fuzzy white yarn settled in her lap like an angora bird's nest.

Elizabeth set up her easel, tacked the paper in place, and looked around for a subject. It was easy to find things to paint, but difficult to settle on just one. Her practiced eye saw a dozen opportunities: Terrible Tilly, the lighthouse in the distance, lonely and stark against the aqua-blue expanse of sea and sky . . . Dagger Rock, the black stone monolith that rose from the ocean in a cuff of foamy surf . . . a Brandt's cormorant circling the land's edge.

She settled on the ocean itself; it was definitely a watercolor day. No oils or acrylics. She needed to complete four paintings in time for the festival; there was no way she could make the deadline if she worked in oil.

Happy with that decision, she started work.

It wasn't as easy as she remembered. She started and stopped three times, unable to find the flow she needed in watercolor. Everything was so damned wet; the colors kept bleeding into one another. She wasn't controlling the paint.

"Damn it." She ripped the latest attempt off the easel and tossed it to the ground.

"It's never easy to start a thing," Anita said, barely looking up. "I guess that's what separates the dreamers from the doers."

Elizabeth sighed, unaware until that moment that she was breathing badly again. "I used to know how to do this."

"In high school, I spoke Spanish."

Elizabeth got the point. Skills came and went in life. If you wanted one back, sometimes you had to dig deep to find it. She walked out to the water and stood there, staring out. She let the colors seduce her, reveal themselves in their own way and time.

She was doing it incorrectly. Trying to impose her will on the paper. That was a level of skill she had lost. Now what she needed to do was *feel*. Be childlike with wonder again.

She released another breath and went back to the easel. She set everything up again. And waited.

Sea air caressed her cheeks, filled her nostrils with the scents of drying kelp and baking sand. The steady, even whooshing of the waves became music. She swayed along with it. This time, when she lifted her brush and dipped it in paint, she felt the old magic.

For the next few hours, she worked at a furious, breathless pace. Finally, she drew back and looked critically at her work.

In a palette of pale blue and rose and lavender, she'd captured the dramatic, sloping coastline and the glistening curve of sand. The distant peak of Dagger Rock was barely discernable, a dark shadow amidst a misty blue-white sky. A few strokes of red and gray formed a couple, far off in the distance, walking along the sand. But something was wrong . . .

"Why, Birdie, that's beautiful."

Elizabeth practically jumped out of her skin. She'd been so intent on her subject that she hadn't even heard Anita walk up. "I can't seem to get the trees right."

"You're missin' the angle. See how they lean backwards? As if the wind's been pushin' 'em for a thousand years and they've given up."

Given up.

In the face of great pressure, they'd quit trying to grow straight. Not unlike what Elizabeth had done in her marriage. She dabbed her brush in the paint and went back to work.

It felt as if only a few minutes had passed when Anita said, "Oh, lordy, it's past two o'clock. We need to get to the house. Hurry up!" She stuffed her knitting back in her bag and started toward the stairs.

Elizabeth watched her stepmother go. Anita was really huffing and puffing up those stairs. You'd think there was a prize to the winner.

She picked up her supplies, carefully held her painting with two fingers and climbed the steps behind Anita. Elizabeth was almost to the top when she smelled smoke. "Anita? Do you smell that?"

And there were voices, as if a radio were turned on high.

Elizabeth came to the top of the stairs and paused, looking around.

Balloons poked through the open windows of her house and

drifted upward. Suddenly the front door banged open. Marge, Anita, and Meghann—*Meghann!*—crowded onto the porch, singing, "Happy Birthday."

Elizabeth almost dropped her stuff. No one had ever thrown her a surprise party before.

Meghann rushed toward her, arms outstretched. She wrapped Elizabeth in a fierce hug, whispering, "You didn't think I'd miss it, did you? Happy birthday."

Then all three of them were there, laughing and talking at once.

Elizabeth couldn't remember the last time she'd felt so special. She'd always been the one who organized everyone else's birthday parties and cooked the food and bought the presents. Even on her own birthday, she'd written detailed gift lists and made her own cake.

She saw Anita, standing over by a brand-new red barbecue.

Marge took the still-damp watercolor from her. "Oh, Birdie, this is exquisite. Is it for me?"

The compliment warmed her. "Of course."

After Marge walked away, Meghann moved closer. "Anita planned all this, you know. Even sent me a plane ticket." She smiled. "Like I couldn't afford it." She sobered. "It's not what I would have expected of her. You know, after all the Anita-the-Hun stories."

Elizabeth flinched. She'd come up with that nickname in eighth grade history class; it had sunk into Anita like a fishhook. In the past few days, it had haunted Elizabeth, shamed her. "She's not who I thought she was," Elizabeth said. "I'll be right back."

She walked across the yard.

Anita had pulled an intricately knitted lavender cardigan over her linen dress. Her hair was drawn back into a thick white coil. She was bent over, busily moving oysters from a tin bucket onto the grill. At Elizabeth's approach, she straightened. "Surprise."

"This is all your doing," Elizabeth said.

"It was nothing." Anita smiled. "Meghann and Marge are the

kind of friends who'll drop anything to party. Besides, I always wanted to throw you a surprise party."

Elizabeth knew how much she'd hurt her stepmother over the years, and yet, Anita had still organized this party. It was the kind of thing Elizabeth would do for her daughters. "Thank you," she said, knowing it wasn't enough.

Anita gently smoothed the flyaway hair from Elizabeth's eyes. "You're welcome, Birdie."

Elizabeth grasped her stepmother's hand, held it. "I want us to start over."

Anita's eyes rounded. "Oh, my . . ."

Meghann came up beside them. She looped one arm around Elizabeth and hip-bumped her. In one hand, she held a white plastic pitcher. "Can I interest you ladies in a margarita? Don't worry, Anita, I can make you a virgin."

Anita laughed shakily, wiped her eyes. "Honey, there ain't nothin' you can do that'll make me a virgin again, but I'll sure-as-tootin' take a margarita."

After that, the party kicked into high gear. Marge set a portable stereo out on the porch and hooked it up, pointing the speakers toward the yard. Meghann brought out a huge CD holder and started playing music Elizabeth had never heard before—stuff from Foo Fighters and Pearl Jam. It was raucous and loud and fun.

They barbecued oysters on the grill and cooked clams in a coffee can filled with butter, wine, and spices. A half salmon, drenched in lemon and onion slices and butter, lay on an alder plank on the barbecue. Dungeness crabs sat in a bucket of shaved ice.

Elizabeth and Meghann carried the kitchen table out into the yard. Within minutes, they'd covered it with food—a bowl of pasta salad, ears of corn wrapped in tinfoil, and a loaf of home-made garlic bread.

Elizabeth couldn't remember when she'd had so much fun. They all danced and talked and laughed. It was like being twenty again, only better.

While the salmon was cooking, Marge turned Sister Sledge's "We Are Family" up to the edge of pain.

Laughing, Elizabeth stood at the table, arranging the silverware. She had just put the knives in a plastic glass when she heard the car drive up.

JACK TURNED ONTO STORMWATCH LANE. "This road is still terrible." He heard the testiness in his voice and wished he'd tempered it. It wasn't enough that they were getting close to Birdie. *Nooo*. The girls had to choose today to give him the near silent treatment. On the flight across the country, Jamie had hardly spoken to him.

His daughters had talked—plenty—in fact. Enough so that his hangover had graduated into full-scale brain warfare. But they talked to each other. Jack's feeble and obviously uncool remarks fell down an empty well.

They were mad at him for forgetting to meet them. He could understand that. What bothered him was the nagging sense that there was more to it. That this was . . . normal and he hadn't realized the truth of their relationship until now.

Whenever the family had been together—mealtimes, holidays, vacations—Birdie had been there, stitching their disparate conversations together.

Hey, Jack, did you tell Jamie about . . .

Stephanie, does Daddy know . . .

Jack had always cared deeply about the big picture of his daughters' lives. He'd wanted to know what they believed in and what they wanted to be when they grew up, and what kind of women they were becoming. But he'd never really concerned himself with the minutiae of their daily lives. That had been Elizabeth's province. But it was that minutiae that fueled conversation.

Now, without Elizabeth, there was a distance between Jack and his girls. He didn't remember enough about their ordinary lives to really communicate, and he was afraid of saying the wrong thing, showing his ignorance. Today would not be a good day to screw up on something like a boyfriend's name or a major that had changed a year ago.

Such an error would make Jamie roll her eyes and say, *Hel-lo, Dad. Like, get a clue*.

He wasn't strong enough to be mentally body slammed by a teenager. Not today.

So he confined himself to safe topics. "We got lucky. It's a beautiful day."

"Totally," Jamie said from the backseat. "I can't believe it's not raining."

The view was breathtaking. For the two years Jack had lived here, all he'd noticed was the falling rain and gray skies. All he'd cared about was earning his way *out* of here, but now, he saw the grandeur and wildness of the coastline. Jagged, cliff-faced rocks, stunted trees, endless gray beach. Today's sunlight turned the sea into glittering silver.

No wonder Elizabeth loved it here. It was spectacularly wild. How was it that he'd never noticed the beauty before?

He rounded the last bend in the road and slowed down. There were a few cars parked along the side of the driveway. When he got out of the car, he noticed the music. It was some old disco song—maybe a Gloria Gaynor.

He pulled in behind a pale blue Toyota Camry and parked. "We'd better grab the stuff and hike in from here."

"You make it sound like we're at the base of Mount Rainier, Dad."

It was Jamie, of course. He was barely listening. His heart was a jackhammer trying to crack through his rib cage.

He should have called. Warned her.

The girls could have been a surprise, but he should have told her he was coming.

The girls ran on ahead. Jack followed, but couldn't work up much speed.

When they reached the yard, the first thing he noticed was the women. They were standing around a table. He barely had time to register that Anita and Meghann were here before Elizabeth turned around.

The girls ran toward her, screaming.

Jack couldn't move. He knew suddenly how it felt to return from war and see the face of the woman you loved for the first time. It hurt like hell to look at her, to be here, on the outside, looking at a life that had once been his. The thought of what he'd done last night with Sally made him physically ill.

Elizabeth was blonder, he saw, and thinner. She had a streak of yellow paint across her cheek and that tiny detail tossed him back to their first meeting.

"Dad, get over here!" Stephanie yelled, waving her hand.

Elizabeth looked up, saw him for the first time. He walked toward her, then clumsily took her in his arms. "Happy birthday, Birdie."

"Hey, Jack," she said. "It's good to see you."

There was something about the way she said his name, a softness that wounded him. When she drew back, he had trouble letting her go.

THE PARTY WENT ON long into the night. At dusk, Marge pulled out a brown paper bag full of fireworks, and they all went down to the beach to light them.

Elizabeth stood apart from the crowd, watching her daughters and friends in the flickering red-and-gold glow of the falling sparks.

Jack was off by himself; he'd stayed that way all day. Oh, he'd mingled, been friendly, but he'd kept his distance. She had just started to go to him, when Stephanie came up beside her. "You haven't lit a single firework. And it's your day."

Elizabeth laughed. "Honestly, honey, I've never lit a firecracker." Her father had set the hook on that fear early. *Girls don't play with fireworks*, he'd said every Fourth of July; *you'll blow your little fingers off. You let the boys handle this.*

Stephanie pulled her forward, then bent down, rummaged through the sack. She withdrew a small, striped thing that was shaped like a rocket. "Just stick it in the sand and light it; then step back."

Elizabeth lit the fuse, then stumbled back so fast she tripped over a piece of driftwood and fell down. The canister rocketed into the dark sky and exploded. White sparkles rained down.

It was beautiful, as perhaps all dangerous things were.

"That's the end of the show, kids," Marge said when the sparks finally faded away.

Within a few minutes, they'd cleaned up the beach and gone up the stairs. One by one, the women got into their cars and drove away, including Anita and Meghann who'd decided to spend the night at the Inn Between in Echo Beach.

Elizabeth hugged everyone good-bye and watched them leave. Finally, she was in her darkened yard with only her family around her.

"I'm exhausted," Stephanie said. "We're on East Coast time, don't forget." She looped an arm around Elizabeth's shoulder. Together, the four of them went into the house.

She led the girls to the guest bedroom. It smelled like Anita, of talcum powder and lavender sachets.

Jamie plopped down on the bed. Stephanie lay down beside her.

"The party meant the world to me," Elizabeth said. "Thanks."

"We missed you," Jamie said simply, kicking off her shoes. She pulled off her jeans and crawled into bed.

Stephanie went down the hall. When she came back, she was wearing a baggy flannel nightgown and her face was pink and shiny. She kissed Elizabeth on her way past, then crawled into bed beside her sister.

Elizabeth wasn't ready to leave yet, to face Jack. "I want to hear about your new boyfriend, Jamie."

"That's it," Stephanie said, giggling. "If she's going to start blabbing about jazz-man with the oh-so-cool eyes, I'm going to sleep. G'night, Mom." She rolled onto her side.

Elizabeth sat down on the floor, leaning against the wall. "Tell me," she said.

Jamie pushed the covers aside and slid down to the floor beside her. "How did you know Dad was the one?"

Elizabeth tilted her head back. She stared up at the white, peaked ceiling where a lonely, rarely used fan collected dust. "The first kiss pretty much cinched the deal." She remembered how it had felt to be swept away, out of control. She would have given up everything to be with him.

In so many ways, she had.

"When your dad kissed me the first time, I cried."

"Why?"

"I guess that's what you do when you're falling and there's no way to land safely. Love's dangerous territory."

Jamie rested her head on Elizabeth's shoulder. "I think I'm in love with Michael. It scares me."

"Then you're growing up, kiddo."

"I think I'm afraid because of Grandad. I never knew that one minute you could be drinking eggnog and opening presents, and the next minute be in some horribly decorated room, picking out a box, and pretending that wood grain and brass accents matter."

Elizabeth put an arm around Jamie and pulled her close. For a long time, she said nothing, just stroked her daughter's hair the way she used to. "Your grandad wouldn't want you to be afraid. He never was."

"That's what I tell myself all the time. But there's a hole in me now."

"I know, honey. But it'll get easier. I promise. You'll always miss him, but after a while, the missing will be more of an ache, not so sharp a wound."

"He wanted me to swim in the Olympics. That's all he talked about at Christmas. And I can't even beat some girl from UVa."

"He didn't care about the Olympics. All he cared about was you, Jaybird. He wanted you to be happy. It'd break his heart if he thought you quit swimming because of him."

Jamie looked at her. "Can I tell you a secret?"

"Always."

"I don't really want to quit swimming. I just wanted Dad's attention. Not that I got it."

"He's a little crazy right now. Be patient with him. It's a big deal to have a dream come true in the middle of your life."

"I know. I just want things to be easier, I guess."

"Life isn't supposed to be easy, Jamie. Who cares if you discover that you'll never swim the three hundred as fast as Hannah Tournilae? What matters is knowing you tried."

"So you'd still be proud of me if I stayed on the swim team but never won a race?"

"You're fishing for compliments now."

"What if I flunked out?"

"Are you close to flunking out?"

Jamie grinned. "Actually, no. Michael's really helped me out. I just wanted to check the parameters of your goodwill while you're all gooey."

Quicksilver Jamie. Her moods were like the coast's weather; if you didn't like it, stick around for ten seconds. "You're a good egg, Jamie. Now, get to bed."

Jamie gave her a kiss on the cheek, then climbed up into bed, snuggling up beside her sister. "G'night, Mom. I love you."

"I love you, too."

Elizabeth stood up and flicked off the light, then went back downstairs.

Jack had built a fire. It crackled loudly and sent spiraling, dancing gold light across the rug. He looked acutely uncomfortable, like a big man trying to negotiate his way through a tea party.

She sat down on the sofa, close but not too close.

For a long time, neither spoke. Finally she said, "I used to remind you guys endlessly about my birthday."

"We know." He laughed, then seemed to relax, as if he'd been afraid of what she'd say.

"I always thought you'd forget, and I was so afraid of how I'd feel if that happened. Why did I do that, Jack? Why did I assume I was so unimportant?"

He faced her. There was a sadness in his eyes that she hadn't often seen. "Because I would have forgotten. Not every year, not even most years, but at some point, it would have happened. Not because I didn't care, but because I never had to think for myself. You always did it for me. You were my backbone; you kept me standing." He sighed. "And I took you for granted."

Elizabeth knew he wouldn't have thought that—let alone said it—a few months ago. "I guess we're both learning a few things about ourselves lately."

"I'm not the father I thought I was." He looked surprised by the admission, as if he hadn't meant to voice it. "Without you, the girls and I have nothing to talk about. They think I'm an idiot."

This was a new side to Jack, vulnerable. It changed him somehow, shifted the balance of power between them. She felt as if they were friends, talking about their kids. "They're nineteen and twenty, Jack; they think anyone who remembers Kennedy should be in a nursing home. I used to treat Anita the same way."

"Jamie rolls her eyes at you, too?"

"Of course. Usually right before she says, 'Hel-*lo* Mom, could you please get real?' And Stephanie gives me that wounded deer-eye blink and shuts up until she gets her way. They've been perfecting the act since sixth grade. They could take it on the road."

"How do you handle it?"

"On a good day, I ignore them. On a bad day, I get my feelings hurt. Fortunately, there are more good days than bad." She saw his frown and asked, "What is it, Jack?"

Minutes ticked past before he answered. "We're going to have to tell them, aren't we?"

She almost touched him then, but something held her back. Fear, maybe. If she touched him now, when her heart was swollen and tender, it might begin again, and she wasn't ready for that. This journey of hers wasn't finished yet. "Yes."

"They'll blame me, you know."

"I'll tell them it was my choice."

"It won't matter."

"They're practically grown-up, Jack. They'll understand. And we won't mention divorce, just separation."

He smiled, but it was bleak and bitter. "We can call it anything we want. Hell, call it a vacation, but they're not stupid. I'll lose them."

Suddenly she was afraid, too. "Maybe we won't have to tell them. Maybe they won't have noticed that anything's wrong between us."

"Birdie," he said, smiling sadly at her. "My dreamer."

She wasn't quite sure why, but the way he said it made her want to cry. "We haven't made a decision about the future, Jack. We're just taking a break. That's all. There's still a chance for us," she said fiercely.

He touched her face gently, as if she were spun from glass that he'd broken long ago. "I want to believe that."

"Me, too."

TWENTY-FIVE

IT WAS LATE SATURDAY AFTERNOON WHEN THE SHIT HIT THE fan.

Jamie was sitting cross-legged on the floor by the fire. Her small, pointed chin was jutted out in the bulldog expression Jack knew meant trouble. "Okay, you guys, spill it."

Stephanie, in the rocking chair in the corner of the room, paled visibly.

"You want me to ask it another way?" Jamie said, her voice rising. "Steph and I aren't idiots. We know something is going on between you two."

"Leave me out of it," Stephanie said.

Elizabeth, who was sitting on the sofa, tucked her legs up underneath her. She didn't answer.

Obviously, she was leaving it up to Jack. That had always been their pattern. Elizabeth decided what the girls could and couldn't do, and Jack was the bad guy who laid down the law, the one who gave them a "talking to" when Elizabeth was unhappy with their grades.

"So?" Jamie demanded again.

The girls looked at Jack. They knew: All bad news came from Dad.

He gazed at his beloved daughters. Jamie's tight, ready-to-be-pissed expression was ruined by eyes that were already sad. And Stephanie never looked up from the hands coiled in her lap. She was like a buck private, hunkered down behind a building, waiting for the shrapnel to start flying.

The thought of telling them, of actually speaking the toxic words aloud, made him almost sick to his stomach. They would always remember that it was his voice that had torn their family apart.

He couldn't do it.

He was so deer-in-the-headlights frozen that he didn't notice when Elizabeth got up, walked around the sofa.

She was behind him now. She squeezed his shoulder, and there was a gentleness to her touch that hurt more than any punch.

"I know you guys sense that something is not normal with Dad and me," she said. Her voice was surprisingly calm.

He couldn't believe she was going to do it. *Birdie.* The woman who ran from conflict and couldn't make a decision to save her life . . . the woman who'd stand in front of a train to spare her children's lives.

"That's an understatement," Jamie said mulishly. "We know Dad slept on the sofa last night."

"People who love each other have fights, Jamie." Stephanie looked up. "That's all it is, right?"

Elizabeth's hold on Jack's shoulders tightened. It occurred to him to reach up, to lay his hand on hers, but he was paralyzed by what was unfolding. He could barely breathe. "It's a little more than a fight," Elizabeth said evenly. "The truth is, your dad and I have separated."

Stephanie's mouth dropped open. The color faded from her cheeks. "Oh, my *God*."

"I know this is difficult to hear," Elizabeth said quickly. "And we're going to have to work together to get through it, but we'll be okay. We'll always be a family, no matter what."

"Oh, this is fucking great. We'll *always* be a family. What a crock of shit." Jamie shot to her feet. She was breathing hard, and Jack could see that she was close to tears. "That's right up there with a guy asking to be just friends. It means he already has another girlfriend."

Elizabeth's grip became painful. "Honey, let us explain."

"No way. I've heard all I can take."

"Listen to us, please. Your dad and I were so young when we got married," Elizabeth said.

Stephanie's head shot up. "That's your reason? Because you got married too young? I thought . . . I mean you always . . . Oh, shit." She burst into tears.

This was ripping Jack's heart out. Nothing had ever hurt this much. Nothing. Ever. "Honey . . ." He didn't know what to say. He glanced helplessly up at Birdie. She gazed down at him; her mouth trembled. And then her beautiful face crumpled.

Jack didn't think. He leaned sideways and pulled her into his arms. "We'll get through this," he whispered against her wet cheek.

He had never loved her more than he did right then. She'd been stronger in this than he could have been, and now he saw the cost of that strength. She was tearing like old cloth, coming apart in his arms.

He looked at his daughters and knew he'd never forget this moment.

This was the price for every bad choice he'd ever made. And of all his poor choices, none had been worse than not loving Birdie enough to fight for their marriage. "This is hard on all of us," he said. His words came slowly; he was a blind man feeling his way down a dark and twisting hallway. "But we love you." He glanced at Birdie, did his damnedest not to cry. "And we love each other. For now, that's all we know. You guys can either help us through this, or you can be angry and shut us out. You're adults. We can't control you anymore." His voice almost broke. "But we need you now—both of us do. Maybe more than we ever have. We need to be a family."

That took the wind out of Jamie's sail. The anger seeped out of her; without it, she crumpled to her knees, whispering something Jack couldn't hear.

Elizabeth slid to the floor beside her. "My girls," she whispered.

Jamie and Stephanie launched themselves at her. The three of them clung together, crying.

Jack stared down at them longingly. He wanted to join them, to for once be part of that inner circle, but he couldn't move. They'd always been a trio first, a family second.

It was Jamie who looked up at him first. Jamie, his warrior princess, whose face was ravaged now by pain. "Daddy," was all she said, reaching out.

She hadn't called him that in years.

Elizabeth reached behind her, felt around for Jack's hand. When she found it, she squeezed hard.

He slid off the sofa to his knees and took them all in his arms.

ELIZABETH FELT as if she'd just gone two rounds with Evander Holyfield. She sat in the porch swing, gliding back and forth. A full moon hung above the midnight-blue ocean, its light a silver beacon across the waves.

The last four hours had been the worst time of her life.

They'd all sat together, alternately weeping and shouting. Jamie had vacillated between fury and despair; Stephanie had been stubbornly silent, refusing to accept that her parents might not get back together.

Now, finally, the girls had gone to sleep.

She heard the screen door open and bang shut.

Jack stepped onto the porch. With a sigh, he slumped down onto the swing beside her. The chains groaned at his weight.

Elizabeth wrapped the woolen blanket more tightly around her shoulders. "We should have lied to them."

"I don't know how you had the guts to tell them," he answered. "When they started crying . . . shit, it was awful."

"It's my fault," she said. "I refused to go to New York. I wrote that letter. I had to be the one to tell them."

"We both know better than that, Birdie. This is a thing we did together."

It meant so much to her, those few and precious words. He'd shouldered part of her guilt. "I still love you," she said, realizing suddenly that it was true. That it had always been true. She turned to him. "Until tonight, I'd forgotten that."

He looked at her steadily. "For years, I asked you what was wrong. You never really answered, did you?"

"You don't know what it's like to disappear, Jack. How could you? You've always been so confident, so sure of yourself."

"Are you kidding, Birdie? I went from all-star in the NFL to nobody. Nobody."

"That's different. I'm talking about who you are inside. Not what your job is."

"You never understood," he said. "For a man, what you do is who you are. When I lost football, I lost myself."

"You never told me that."

"How could I? I was ashamed, and I knew what it had been like for you as a player's wife."

He was right. She'd grown to hate his football years; the better he did in the sport, the farther he moved from the family.

So she hadn't been there for him in his time of need. Instead of his safe harbor, she'd been another port to avoid. "I'm sorry, Jack."

"Don't say that. We've wasted too many years on that."

"Not wasted," she said softly. "We did okay, Jack. We buoyed each other up for twenty-four years. We built a house and home that was a safe and happy place. We created two beautiful, loving young women." She managed a smile. "Not too bad for a couple of kids who ran off to get married in the last semester of college. There were a lot of years when I thought we had everything."

He stood up and offered her his hand. She took it greedily, held on so tightly his strong bones shifted within her grasp. "You're something special, you know that?"

He'd never said that to her before. The simple compliment meant more to her than she'd thought possible. "You, too."

"Well. Good night, Birdie."

"Good night."

She went to her bedroom alone.

JACK PULLED INTO the airport's underground parking lot. When he turned off the rental car's engine, the silence was deafening.

Jamie and Stephanie sat in the backseat, huddled together. There had been no clamoring to sit up with Dad. Not this time.

He glanced in the rearview mirror. "We'd better get going. You don't want to miss your flight."

"That's for sure," Jamie said, reaching for the door handle. "We want to get the hell out of this state."

Stephanie threw Jack a sympathetic look, then followed her sister out of the car. They didn't wait for Jack. Instead, they bolted for the terminal, walking so fast it looked as if they were fleeing a crime scene. Through the endless security checks, neither girl looked at him.

With a sigh, Jack followed them.

At the gate, they were forced to stop. Jamie finally turned to him. For a single second, their gazes met and her armor weakened. In her blue eyes, he saw a pain so raw and deep it rocked him back. She was hurting so damned much . . .

And he and Birdie had caused it. An ache spread through his heart, a combination of guilt and shame and regret. Regret most of all.

"Jamie," he said, moving toward her, hands outstretched.

"You do *not* want to touch me right now," she said loudly, stepping away from him.

He knew then the truth of a broken heart; it wasn't some poetic metaphor. It was muscle and sinew tearing away from bone. It hurt more than any blown knee ever could. "I'm sorry, Jamie. *We're* sorry."

Jamie's face crumpled. She appeared unsteady on her feet. "Bite me." She turned and stomped away from him. Even after she'd reached the Jetway door and stopped, she didn't look back.

"You know Jamie," Stephanie said, "when she gets scared, she gets pissed off."

Jack wanted to say, *I'm scared, too,* but he didn't know how to be that honest with his daughters. It was his job to be the family's strength. "I guess we're all scared."

Stephanie was doing her best not to cry. It was a terrible thing for a father to watch. His Stephie, always so strong, looking as if she were held together by old Scotch tape. "It's like discovering one day that you're schizophrenic. Everything you've believed in is suddenly suspect. I don't know how to live in a world where our family is broken up."

"Keep believing in all of us, Steph. Someday you'll understand. Mom and I have been together since we were your age. That's a long time. Things . . . pile up between people. But we're not even talking about divorce."

Stephanie gave him a pathetically hopeful look. "We thought you were lying about that."

"No. We're just taking a little breathing room; that's all for now."

"Oh."

In the background, a voice came over the loudspeaker, announced the boarding of flight 967.

Jack glanced over at Jamie. Her back was to him. Even from this distance, he could see how stiff she was.

Poor Jamie. Always so terrified of bending. She was probably tearing apart inside, but she wouldn't show it. "Take care of your sister. She acts tough . . ." He couldn't go on. He remembered the day Jamie had broken her arm. All the way to the doctor's office, she'd sat stoically silent. It hadn't been until late that night, in her dark bedroom with its Big Bird nightlight that she'd finally cried. She'd curled into Jack's arms and whispered, *It hurts, Daddy*.

Back then, all he'd had to do was stroke her hair and tell her a bedtime story.

"She's really pissed off at you and Mom. Did you see her at the house? She wouldn't even let Mom ride to the airport with us. I've never seen her so mad."

"I wonder how long she can avoid talking to us."

"Jamie? How long until the polar ice cap melts?"

"Take care of her. And of yourself. I love you, Stephie."

Stephanie looked up at him. "Be honest with us, Daddy, okay? If it's time for us to stop hoping, tell us."

"I promise." He saw by the look on her face that he'd said the wrong thing. Of course. In the past, his promises hadn't meant much. It was another change he'd have to make in the future.

They called the flight again.

"Come on, Stephanie!" Jamie yelled, waving her sister over.

"Bye, Dad." Stephanie shouldered her carry-on bag and hurried toward Jamie. They both boarded the plane without a backward glance.

Jack went to the window and stared out. A hazy reflection of his own face stared back at him. Beyond it, the plane pulled away from the Jetway. Slowly, Jack headed for his own gate.

THE MAKE-BELIEVE SPRING lasted until the end of March. Then the rains returned with a vengeance. Each day, Elizabeth walked to the mailbox in her Eddie Bauer raincoat and knee-high boots, with high hopes. Time and again, she returned empty-handed. Twice in the past weeks, Stephanie had written. Short, pointed letters; each one contained a burning, unanswerable question.

Who stopped loving whom?

Were you lying to us all those years?

Do you want a divorce?

The questions were youthful demands for certainty in uncertain times. Elizabeth knew that her answers were too vague to be of much help. How could it be otherwise? Some issues were simply obscured by the fog of too many lost years.

Jamie hadn't written at all. Nor had she returned any of the phone messages Elizabeth left on their machine.

Elizabeth had always been so close with her daughters. This new distance—and their hurt and anger—was almost unbearable. The old Birdie would have crumpled beneath its weight, but the newer, stronger version of herself knew better. Sometimes a woman had to stand up for what she needed, even against her own children. This was one of those times. And yet, the silence ate at her, ruined her ability to sleep well.

"It would have been better to lie to them . . . or to go back to Jack," Elizabeth said to Anita for at least the hundredth time since the birthday party weekend. "I could have moved to New York and restarted my old life. Everyone would be happier." She stepped back from her painting, frowned, then added the barest streak of Thalo purple to the sunset. It was the painting she'd begun the first night Anita arrived. She'd finished four of the pieces for the Stormy Weather Arts Festival, but the rains had forced her back inside. So, she'd turned her attention back to the portrait.

At the kitchen table, Anita sat knitting. She barely looked up. "I don't suppose everyone would be happier."

"Everyone *else* then," Elizabeth said, standing back from her work again. It was lovely. Perhaps the best work she'd ever done. "Okay. That's it. I'm done."

"Can I finally see it?"

Elizabeth nodded, suddenly nervous. It was one thing to be happy with your art. It was quite another to show it off. She stepped aside and let her stepmother stand directly in front of the easel.

Anita stood there forever, saying nothing.

"You don't like it. I know the colors of the sunset are a little crazy; I wanted to emphasize your softness by exaggerating the world around you. You see how it seems that the sky is drawing the color out of you, leaving you a little paler?"

Elizabeth studied the work for flaws. In it, Anita looked frail and ethereal, yet somehow powerful, like an aged queen from King Arthur's court. There was the barest sadness in her gray eyes, though a hint of a smile curved her lips. "Maybe you think I gave you too many wrinkles. I thought—"

Anita touched her arm, but still said nothing.

"Say something. Please."

"I was never this beautiful," Anita said in a throaty voice.

"Yes, you are."

"Lordy, I wish your daddy could see this. He'd put it up on the wall and make sure everyone saw it. 'Come on in,' he'd say to our guests; 'see what my little girl did.' " Anita finally turned to her. "I guess now it'll be me sayin' that."

ON THE FIRST THURSDAY IN APRIL, Elizabeth drove to the community college. She found a spot close to the entrance and parked. Light from a nearby streetlamp poured into the car, gave everything a weird, blue-white glow.

From the passenger seat, Anita shot her a nervous look. "I don't know about going to this meeting, Birdie," she said, wringing her hands together. "I've never been one to air my troubles in public."

"It'll help, Anita. Honest. I used to call these women passionless, but they're not. They're just like us."

Anita didn't look convinced. "Okay."

They got out of the car and walked down the long, shadowy concrete pathway, then pushed through the orange metal double doors. A wide, linoleum-floored hallway stretched out before them, dotted here and there with blue doors.

Anita paused.

Elizabeth took her stepmother's hand and squeezed it gently. She remembered the feeling with perfect clarity; it had been only a few months ago that she herself had been afraid to walk down this corridor. Now she did it easily, eagerly. "Come on."

At the closed door, she looked at Anita. "Ready?"

"Do I *look* ready? No, I do not"—Anita tried to smile—"but my stepdaughter doesn't care about that." She puffed up her ample chest and tilted her chin up.

Elizabeth recognized the gesture. She'd done the same thing herself that first time, tried—like a frightened bird—to make herself seem larger. She opened the door and went inside, pulling Anita along beside her.

The first thing she noticed was the balloons. Pretty, helium-filled "good luck" balloons hung in the air, tethered to chairbacks. A few rebels had freed themselves and now bumped aimlessly along the ceiling.

"She's here!" someone cried out, and all at once, the women in the room came together in a crowd. They were clapping.

Elizabeth looked down at Anita. "I guess they like it when you rope in a new member."

Sarah Taylor pushed through the group, smiling broadly. In a bright yellow dress, she looked like a ray of sunshine against the drab gray walls. "You tried to keep it a secret, Elizabeth. Quite naughty."

Elizabeth had no idea what Sarah was talking about.

Joey pushed forward. "I saw it in the newspaper. I couldn't believe it. You never told us."

Mina was next. "Joey called me right away. I drove down to buy myself a paper and there it was. I called Sarah immediately."

Fran smiled. "When I saw it . . ." Her face twitched, as if she were about to cry. ". . . I went right out and joined that choir. My first concert is next Sunday."

The only one who had nothing to say was Kim. She hung in the back of the room, by the coffeemaker, wearing her usual mortician's garb, fiddling with a pack of cigarettes. Every once in a while she looked up, then quickly glanced back to the table.

"What in the world are you all talking about?" Elizabeth asked when there was a break in the conversation.

"The art show," Joey said, her voice reverent.

A hush fell over the room.

Elizabeth's cheeks heated up. "Oh. That."

Anita squeezed her hand, steadied her.

"We're so proud of you," Mina said. "It took real guts to sign up for that."

"Balls of steel," Fran agreed.

Joey smiled up at her. "You gave me hope, Elizabeth. I signed up for a dental hygienist class. I thought, if you can do it, so can I."

"But I'm scared to death," Elizabeth said.

"Don't you see?" Fran said. "That's what makes us so proud of you."

Elizabeth's emotions suddenly felt too big for her body. "Well . . . thank you."

"Who's your friend?" Sarah asked.

Elizabeth turned to Anita. "This is my stepmother, Anita."

"Welcome to the group, Anita," Sarah said.

"I lost my husband recently," Anita blurted out, as if she'd been scared of her "turn" and wanted it out of the way. She laughed nervously. " 'Course I didn't actually *lose* him. He's . . . dead."

Mina stepped forward and slipped her arm through Anita's. "Come sit by me. I'll tell you about my Bill and how I'm learning to find a life of my own."

Elizabeth talked to the women for a moment longer, then went back to the food table. Kim stood by the coffeemaker.

"Hi," Elizabeth said.

Kim stared at her through narrowed, heavily made-up eyes. "How will it feel to fail?"

It was the question Elizabeth had chewed on at every meal.

For weeks, she'd worried about it. Every time she dabbed on a bit of paint, she second-guessed her choice and her talent. "I expect to fail," she said at last.

"And you're doing it anyway?"

Elizabeth shrugged. "For years, I failed by omission. I don't think anything can be worse than that."

Kim hitched her purse strap over her shoulder. "I don't know, Elizabeth. Every time I think life can't get worse, my husband sends me a new set of papers. But good luck. I suppose good things have to happen to someone."

Elizabeth was still trying to fish out a response to that when Kim walked past her and left the meeting.

SPRING

The lure of the distant and difficult is deceptive.
The great opportunity is where you are.

—JOHN BURROUGHS

TWENTY-SIX

ELIZABETH WAS A WRECK.

She hadn't slept more than two hours last night. She'd tossed and turned and sweated. She'd even cried, although whether out of fear or frustration, she didn't know. What she did know was that the Stormy Weather Arts Festival officially started in less than an hour, and she—fool that she was—had agreed to show her paintings to the world.

"Was I drunk?" she muttered, changing her clothes for the third time.

The decision of what to wear was simply too big.

She slumped onto the cold wooden floor in front of the sofa. She couldn't remember when she'd been this scared. She would fall face-first today. And then what? She'd fought so hard for this new life of hers. She'd walked out of her marriage and forged her own path. She'd picked up her old paintbrushes and done the unthinkable: she'd dreamed.

"Get a grip, Birdie."

She went up to her bedroom and changed into an ankle-length black knit dress with a boldly patterned leather belt. She left her hair down (in case she needed to hide behind it) and peered into the mirror.

Her face was the size of a volleyball. *Hello, Wilson.*

She stifled the urge to groan aloud and focused on one thing at a time. Foundation first. She put on more than usual, then added blush and mascara. By the time she was finished, she looked nearly human again.

The phone rang—as expected, at eight-forty-five. Elizabeth briefly considered not answering it, but knew such an evasion would be pointless. Meghann would probably send the National Guard down to check on her.

"Hello?" she answered, hoping she didn't sound as brittle as she felt.

"I was afraid you wouldn't answer," Meg said. "Are you okay?"

"I'd rather pull out my own toenails than go to the gallery today. I can't believe I agreed to do this."

"God, I wish I could be there. I'm so sorry."

"Actually, I'm glad you're busy. I'll call you when it's over."

"Birdie?"

"Yes?"

"You're my hero. You remember that. I'm so proud of you. Today is going to change your life."

Unfortunately, that wasn't easy to believe right now. "Thanks, Meg."

They talked for a few more moments; then Elizabeth said goodbye and hung up the phone. She scouted through the bureau drawers for the right necklace. Finally, she found what she wanted: an ornate turquoise squash blossom that Jack had bought her when he got the job in Albuquerque. *This means good luck, baby,* he'd said.

After she put it on, she took one last look in the mirror. Then she went downstairs.

Anita was already there, standing by the front door. She was dressed in a pretty lavender rayon pantsuit. Her snow-white hair was coiled into a huge bun at the base of her neck. "How are you doing?" she asked.

"Shitty. Maybe I won't go. Art should sell itself, right? There's nothing more pathetic than a middle-aged woman crying in public. Oh, God, what if I throw up?"

Anita came forward, grabbed her by the shoulders. "Breathe."

Elizabeth did as she was told.

"In and out, in and out."

Elizabeth relaxed a little. "Thanks," she said, still shaky.

Anita reached down into her pocket, then held out her hand. In her palm lay a small gray stone, polished to a mirror sheen, striated with rust and black and green. "This was your daddy's worry stone. It was always in his pocket. He used to joke that when you were born, it was the size of a bowling ball and he wore it down to the nub."

Elizabeth couldn't imagine her father afraid of anything, let alone carrying a worry stone around in his pocket.

"We're all afraid," Anita said. "It's the going on that matters."

Elizabeth took the stone. It settled in her palm like a kiss. She could almost hear her daddy's booming voice: *Fly, Birdie. You can do it.* It calmed her down, reminded her of what mattered. "Thanks," she said, pulling her stepmother into a hug.

When she drew back, Anita said, "We'd better get going. We don't want to be late."

All the way to town, Elizabeth concentrated on her breathing. The roads were closed off in a lot of places, but she found a parking place in front of the Hair We Are Beauty Salon.

Echo Beach was dressed for a party. Banners and balloons were everywhere. The weather was surprisingly good; steel-gray clouds and cold breezes, but no rain. Every storefront was decorated in bright colors. A few hardy tourists, dressed in down parkas and knee-high boots, walked along the narrow main street. The beach was littered with people flying kites, dogs chasing Frisbees, and kids building sand castles.

Elizabeth stood on the sidewalk across from Eclectica. A white sign filled the window. It read: MEET LOCAL ARTIST ELIZABETH SHORE.

"I think I'm going to be sick."

"You most certainly are not," Anita said. "You're Edward Rhodes's daughter. There will be no vomiting in public. Now, get movin'."

"Elizabeth!" Marge was standing by the gallery, waving her arms. She wore a drop-waisted raisin-colored corduroy dress with open-toed sandals. Her hair had been tamed into a pair of thick braids. A stunningly beautiful cloisonné necklace hung between her breasts. "Hurry up," she yelled, then disappeared inside.

Elizabeth walked across the street. At the gallery, she stopped. Her feet refused to move forward.

Anita said, "Good luck, honey," and shoved her into the gallery.

Inside, the Women's Passion Support Group was waiting. At her entrance, they burst into applause.

Elizabeth stumbled to a halt. "Hey, you guys," she said, hating the tremor in her voice. "It was nice of you to come."

Mina giggled. "You're our new hero. We're putting you on the passionless stamp."

Joey grinned. "I was gonna buy one of your pictures, but *sheesh*, my tips aren't that good. I think I'll have you sign a napkin instead."

Then everyone began talking at once.

"Your work is incredible!"

"Amazing! When did you start painting?"

"So cool! Where did you learn to do this?"

Elizabeth couldn't answer any single question, but it didn't matter. Their enthusiasm was exactly the balm she needed to calm her ragged nerves. For the first time in hours, she relaxed enough to be hopeful.

She even allowed herself to dream of success: *A wonderful review in the* Echo Location . . . *a sellout of her work . . . a call from a bigger gallery in Portland or San Francisco . . .*

"Elizabeth," Marge said impatiently, as if she'd said it more than once.

"What? Huh?"

Marge came forward, holding a bouquet of roses. "These are for you."

"Oh, you didn't have to do that."

Marge gave her a crooked grin. "I didn't." She handed her the flowers.

The card read: *We're mad, but we still love you. Good luck. Jamie and Stephanie. P.S. We're proud of you.*

Proud of you. The words blurred before her eyes.

Anita moved closer. "I told them. I hope you don't mind."

Elizabeth wanted to pull Anita into her arms, but she couldn't seem to move. It took every ounce of willpower she possessed not to cry. "I don't mind," she whispered harshly. "Thank you, Anita."

Her stepmother touched her arm, squeezed gently. "Everything is going to be fine."

Amazingly, with the flowers in her arms and her stepmother beside her, Elizabeth could almost believe it.

Marge began setting out the hors d'oeuvres. Tiny hot dogs wrapped in Kraft cheese strips. Then she plugged in the Crock-Pot. Within minutes, the small gallery smelled like teriyaki.

By ten o'clock, the streets were packed with tourists and locals. A band played oldies in the parking lot of the Windermere Realty office, and every store was crowded with shoppers. A barely-there rain had started to fall.

Out-of-towners bought ice cream cones and kites, sweatshirts and place mats and Christmas ornaments made of driftwood and dried seaweed. They bought wind chimes made of old spoons and photographs of Haystack Rock, and watercolor paintings of the shore.

What they didn't buy was Elizabeth's work.

It became more and more obvious as the day dragged on, as painful as a toothache. Marge stood at the cash register, *ka-chinging* up sales. The walls around Elizabeth's work cleared out.

Joey was the first to leave. She said she needed to get to work—*a big night at the Pig-in-a-Blanket*—but Elizabeth had seen the pity in her new friend's eyes. Joey couldn't stand to watch the slow bloodletting.

Around two o'clock, Fran mentioned something about picking up her kids, and then she was gone. An hour later, Mina went to the market in search of more baby hot dogs, although there were plenty left. The only one who made no excuses was Anita; she sat on a stool in the corner, ostensibly knitting, but Elizabeth knew that her stepmother was really watching her, waiting for signs of meltdown.

Elizabeth stood against the wall, hugging herself so tightly she could barely breathe, standing so stiffly her joints ached. But her smile never faltered.

She'd been stupid to expect anything different. She admitted that tiny disappointment, then tucked it away. This wasn't a mistake she'd make again, and there was no point gnawing over it. What was done was done.

And if she felt as fragile as a damp tissue, that too would pass. As long as she didn't make any sudden moves, she'd get through the rest of this day. Then she'd make it through the night, and the next day, and so on. That was the way of things. Tonight she'd go home, box up her paintings, and try to forget she'd ever bothered.

The bell above the door tinkled. That had been a constant noise all day. She steeled herself to smile at someone else who wouldn't want her work.

Daniel stood there, filling the doorway. Sunlight gilded his blond hair.

"How's it going?" he asked, coming toward her.

"Not good. Actually, that's an overstatement."

He walked past her, stood in front of her work. It was difficult to miss; every other wall was bare. Finally, he turned to look at her. "These are beautiful. You really have a remarkable talent."

"Oh, yeah. I know." She was an eyelash away from losing it. Before he could see how weakened she was, she rushed out of the store.

Outside, she could breathe.

He followed her out. "How about a latte?"

"Great."

They strolled down the busy street together. At the ice cream shop, he bought two cones and two lattes. Then they went onto the Promenade and sat down on a cement bench. Out on the beach, a man was teaching a little boy to fly a kite.

Elizabeth stared at her cone as if the answer to world peace could be found in a scoop of chocolate chip mint.

"You have nothing to be ashamed of," he said finally.

"I know." Her agreement sounded hollow, even to her own ears. She couldn't help it. All her energies were bound up in *maintaining*. There was nothing left over for pretense. "It's more of a free-form depression."

"Did you think it would be easy?"

"I thought *something* would sell."

He touched her cheek, gently forced her to look at him. "Does that matter so much?"

"No, but, aw, *shit*." The tears she'd been swallowing all day burst out.

Daniel took her in his arms. He stroked her hair and let her cry. Finally, she drew back, hiccuping, feeling like a fool. "I'm sorry. It's just been an awful day."

"Don't give up, Birdie. You have talent. I knew that the first time I saw you paint. I think maybe you've given up too easily before."

She realized suddenly that she was in his arms, that he was holding her tightly. She felt his breathing against her forehead. Slowly, she looked up.

He took her face in his hands, wiped the tears with his

thumbs. "It took guts to show your work today. I know. There's nothing worse than standing naked in public and saying, *Here I am.*"

She stared at his mouth. All she heard was, "Naked?"

"You should be proud of yourself, Elizabeth. Anything else would be a crime." He leaned toward her.

She saw the kiss coming and braced for it. Her heart raced. *Oh, God . . .*

His lips pressed against hers, his tongue pushed gently inside her mouth. He tasted of coffee and mint. She slid her arms up around his neck and pulled him closer.

And . . . nothing. No Fourth of July, no fireworks.

When the kiss was over and he drew back, he was frowning. "No good, huh?" He tried to smile.

Elizabeth was surprised. "I guess I'm more married than I thought."

"Too bad." He stood up and pulled her to her feet beside him. Then he held on to her hand and led her across the street.

They cut through the crowd, threaded their way toward the shop.

Elizabeth realized a second too late where he was taking her. She gripped his hand tightly and tried to stop.

He pulled her forward, not stopping until they reached the open door.

"Come on, Daniel. It's a death-by-hanging in there."

"Then put your neck in the noose; it's what artists do." He smiled down at her. "I expect big things of you, Elizabeth Shore. Now, get in there where you belong."

She squared her shoulders and went back inside.

Marge smiled at her entrance, obviously relieved to see her. "I'm glad you came back."

"I didn't want to." She forced the admission out. When she glanced at the door, she saw that Daniel was gone. "Chicken," she muttered.

"It's always difficult on the artist. I should have warned you."

"Difficult?" Elizabeth said. "Difficult is making hollandaise sauce. This is a near-death experience."

Marge laughed, then immediately sobered. "I'm sorry. I know it's not funny."

Elizabeth actually smiled. "I'm glad my humiliation is amusing. Maybe I'll get hit by a bus later and you can really crack up."

"You'll be okay, Elizabeth. Don't you worry."

The bell above the door jangled.

"Oh, good," Elizabeth muttered. She forced a fake smile.

Kim walked into the gallery. She looked pale and skittery; her gaze darted nervously from side to side. She was dressed in black lambskin pants and a black cashmere turtleneck sweater. Surprisingly, a scarlet pashmina shawl hung draped over one shoulder.

"Welcome to Eclectica," Marge said.

Kim waved a hand dismissively and headed for the back wall. In front of Elizabeth's work, she stopped.

"The artist is right there," Marge said loudly.

Elizabeth came out from the corner. "Hello, Kim. You missed the group."

Kim snapped open her purse, digging through it. "And I so wanted to spend more time with them." She cocked her head toward the wall. "Are these your paintings?"

"Yes."

Kim looked at them. For a split second, her gaze softened, and Elizabeth saw the longing in her eyes.

She knew how it felt, that longing. For years, she'd been locked inside herself, unable to imagine a way out. That was where Kim stood right now.

"I'll take that one," Kim said, pointing to the seascape.

"Sorry, the store has a policy against mercy purchases."

"What do you mean?"

"Well, as you and I knew would happen, I bombed today. The only thing less in demand than my paintings was the tofu-flavored ice cream. And Marge's hors d'oeuvres."

"But what's a mercy purchase?"

"That's when a friend feels sorry for the artist and buys a piece. No thanks. But I really appreciate the gesture."

Kim looked at her. "You think we're friends?"

"Of course we are," Elizabeth said quietly.

Kim smiled suddenly, and the change in her demeanor was remarkable. "Take that painting down and wrap it up. And don't you dare call it a mercy purchase. I want to hang it in my living room. Every time I look at it, I'll remember that it's possible to start over. You'd sell that hope to a friend, wouldn't you?"

It was a lovely gesture; there was no way for Kim to know that it only made her feel worse.

Elizabeth took the painting down from the wall and carried it to the register.

To Marge, she said, "The price on this was wrong. It's—"

"No way," Kim said, barreling up beside her. "Shitheel left me loaded. Let me do this my way."

Elizabeth longed to feel good about this sale, but she couldn't quite make it over the hump. The painting hadn't sold because of its beauty. "Okay."

When Kim was finished paying for the piece, she turned to Elizabeth. "Will you be at the meeting this week?"

"Of course."

"Maybe we could meet for dinner afterward? If you have plans, I completely understand. I know it's short notice."

"I'd love to."

Kim actually smiled again. "Great. I'll see you there."

Elizabeth hung around for a while longer, watching tourists mill through the store. Finally, she couldn't take it anymore.

The last thing she saw as she left the gallery was the wall filled with her work.

JACK STOOD AT HIS OFFICE WINDOW, staring out at the beautiful spring day.

This ought to be the best day of his life. Twenty-four hours ago, they'd offered him the best job in broadcasting: *NFL Sunday*.

He'd been dreaming of a moment like this for years, maybe his whole life, and yet, now that it was here, he felt curiously numb.

The door to his office cracked open. "There you are," Warren said. "I just heard the news about your photo shoot. *People* magazine, huh? Pretty hot stuff."

"I'll probably be the oldest guy in the issue."

Warren frowned. "That's it. There's something wrong with you. Let's go."

Jack grabbed his coat and followed Warren out of the building. By tacit consent, they went straight to the pub on the corner and headed for the back booth.

"Double bourbon on the rocks," Warren said when the barmaid appeared.

She looked at Jack.

"Club soda with lime."

"Now I *know* something's wrong," Warren said. "A club soda?"

"I've been drinking pretty hard lately. It blurs the lines."

"Isn't that the point?"

"I used to think so. Now I'm not so sure." He paused, then said, "Fox just offered me *NFL Sunday*."

Warren sat back. "Jesus, Jack. Most guys would give their left nut for that job, and here you are, slurping club soda and practically crying. What gives?"

Jack glanced to the left. It wasn't his way to talk about shit like this, but these silences—and the new loneliness—were killing him. And if there was anyone who ought to understand marital problems, it was the thrice-married Warren. "We told the kids about the separation."

"Ouch. That's the reason I've never had kids. How'd they take it?"

"Badly. They cried and screamed and stomped around. Then they went back to school. I've been getting the silent treatment ever since."

"It'll pass. They'll come to accept their new family after a while. Trust me."

There it was, the source of his sleepless nights. *New family.* "What if I can't accept it, either?"

"What do you mean?"

"I miss Birdie." There, he'd said it.

"You made a bad trade, Jacko, but you're not the first guy to do it. You thought the heat of all this was real, but at the end of the day, all that matters is finding a woman who loves the real you." He looked at Jack. "One who'll be there for you in the bad times. And that, my friend, was Birdie. You never should have let her go."

"She left me."

"Birdie left you?"

"The marriage went to shit slowly. I'm not even sure when. I think it started with me, though, when I lost football. All I could think about was what I'd lost. I'd gotten married so young; I never got to be the young hot shot of my imaginations. You know, the superstar who slept with a different woman every night. I wanted that." He sighed. "For years, I dreamed about going back in time and making a different choice. I guess, after a while, all that dreaming of somewhere else became a goal; it ruined our marriage. Maybe a part of me even blamed her for tying me down. I don't know. All I know is that I was desperate to be *someone* again. Then this job came along, and I got it all back." He smiled bitterly. "For the first time in my whole adult life, I'm free, rich, and famous. I can do anything I want. Hell, I'm sleeping with a beautiful woman half my age, and she doesn't care that I don't love her. It's what I always dreamed of. And I hate it. I miss Birdie all the time."

"Have you told her?"

He looked up. "I'm afraid it's too late."

Warren took a sip of his drink. "I've never met a woman who'd stay with me for twenty-four years. Who'd get me off dope and forgive my screwups. If I found a woman like that, Jacko, I'd never let her go."

"What if she tells me it's too late?" He paused. "What if she doesn't love me anymore?"

Warren looked at him. "Then you aren't gonna have a movie ending, my friend. Sometimes, a bad choice can haunt you forever."

TWENTY-SEVEN

THE DRIVE HOME FROM THE GALLERY SEEMED TO TAKE FOREVER. Elizabeth had failed.

The realization was like a canker sore; no matter how much it hurt, you couldn't leave it alone.

She felt Anita looking at her from the passenger seat, staring worriedly every now and then, but fortunately, her stepmother kept her opinions to herself. This was not the time for one of those pumped-up pep talks. Elizabeth had listened to plenty of those in the last few months, from Meghann and Anita and Daniel. She'd listened to her friends and let herself believe.

And here she was. Forty-six years old and a failure.

She turned onto Stormwatch Lane and drove home. When she'd parked the car, she turned to Anita and forced a tired smile. "Thanks for everything today. It meant a lot to me that you were there."

Anita looked stricken. "Birdie, I don't know what to say."

"Don't say anything. Please. It was bad enough to live through. I can't talk about it, too."

Anita nodded. If there was one thing bred into southern women, it was the ability to politely ignore unpleasantness. "I'll go cook us a nice dinner."

"I'm not very hungry. I think I'll go soak in a hot bath." She almost sat there a second too long, looking at her stepmother. She felt the first hairline crack in her composure. If she wasn't careful, she'd break like old porcelain, and that wouldn't help anyone. She reached for the car door and shoved it open, then hurried toward her beloved house.

It welcomed her with soft lights and sweet scents and safety.

She drew in a deep breath and slowly released it. When she heard Anita come up behind her, she bolted upstairs and shut the bedroom door behind her. She went to the window, trying to draw comfort from her view, but night came early this time of year, and there was nothing but darkness beyond the glass.

She ran a bath and poured a capful of almond-scented oil into the water. She let the tub fill past the point of caution, knowing water would spill over when she climbed in. So, she would clean up the mess. That, at least, was something she did well.

She undressed and lowered herself into the nearly scalding water. Sure enough, it splashed onto the tile floor. Heat enveloped her; steamed up toward her face. The sweet, cloying scent of almonds filled the tiny bathroom.

She leaned her head back and closed her eyes.

Images of the endless day tumbled through her mind. Customers buying sculptures and lithographs and photographs and other artists' paintings . . . walking past her work.

She wished she could cry, but it wasn't that kind of hurt. She felt numb. A prisoner who'd dared to believe in parole and then been sent back to her cell, unforgiven.

The worst of it was she'd *believed* in herself. She'd known better, and yet still she'd stumbled into that quicksand and been caught. She'd believed, she'd dared, she'd dreamed.

And she'd failed.

Her work wasn't good enough. That much was clear.

What now? She'd walked away from every good thing she'd ever built so that she could find herself.

Well, she'd found a woman whose greatest gift lay in helping others, in loving people and supporting their dreams. As she sat in the hot water, she asked herself why that hadn't been enough.

She was no artist. She must have known that twenty-five years ago. That was why she hadn't pushed harder to attend grad school. She'd known the truth, or suspected it. Turning away from that road had saved her from this terrible moment.

She stayed in the bath until the water turned cold and her skin pruned. Then, reluctantly, she climbed out. Wrapped in a towel, she flopped on her bed.

She saw the phone, and she thought, *Call Jack.*

She wasn't sure why exactly, except that he had always been her safe place. She scooted toward the nightstand, picked up the phone, and punched in his number. Bits of conversation flitted through her mind as it rang. She searched for the perfect first sentence.

I love you. Nice and direct.

I miss you. Certainly true.

I need you. The God's honest truth.

The answering machine clicked on, told her that Jack and Birdie weren't home right now.

Jack and Birdie.

He hadn't changed the message. That gave her courage. "Hey, Jack," she said, rolling onto her back, staring up at the peaked ceiling. "I thought maybe it was time we talked about the future." She paused, trying to think of what to say next, but nothing came to her. She was afraid that if she spoke, she'd start to cry.

She hung up, then dialed her daughters' number.

Another answering machine. She left a forcibly upbeat message, sneaked in a short apology and a thank-you for the flowers, then hung up.

She lay there a long time, staring up at her ceiling, watching a spider spin a web in the rafters. He was always there, that same little black spider, returning to his spot no matter how many times she dusted his web away. There was a life lesson in that.

There was a knock at her door. "Birdie, honey?"

Elizabeth closed her eyes. She really wanted to be left alone in her misery a while longer. "I'm okay, Anita."

"Dinner's ready."

"I can't eat. Sorry. But thanks for cooking. I'll see you in the morning." She heard footsteps walking away . . . then coming back.

The door opened. Anita stood there, clutching a flat black metal strongbox. "Come on, Birdie. It's time for you to see this." She patted the box in her arms. "This belonged to your mama. If you want to see what's inside, you'd better come downstairs." Then she turned and walked away.

Elizabeth didn't want to follow, but Anita had dangled the biggest carrot of all: Mama.

With a sigh, she rolled out of bed and got dressed.

Downstairs, she sat down on the sofa beside Anita. That metal box was on the coffee table now, waiting.

Elizabeth stared at it. For a blessed few seconds, she forgot about the debacle at the gallery.

She imagined a letter to a daughter, or better yet, a journal of precious memories. Photographs. Mementos. She turned to Anita.

Anita looked pale in the lamplight. Fragile. She'd chewed on her lower lip until it was raw. "I brought this with me. I knew I'd know if the time was right to open it." She tried to smile, but the transparent falsity of it only underscored her nervousness. "Your daddy loved you. More than anything on this earth."

"I know that."

"He was a man of his time and place, and he believed that men protected their women from anything . . . unpleasant."

"Come on. I know that."

Anita reached for the box, flipped the latch, and opened it. Elizabeth noticed that her stepmother's fingers were shaking as she handed the box over.

Elizabeth took it onto her lap.

Inside, a rubber-banded pile of scallop-edged photographs were piled in one corner. A long cardboard tube lay diagonally from end to end.

She withdrew the pictures first. There, on the top of the heap, was Mama. She was sitting on the porch swing, wearing pink pants and a flowery chiffon blouse with small cap sleeves and a Peter Pan collar. Her legs were tucked up underneath her; only a bit of bare feet stuck out. Her toenails were polished.

She was laughing.

Not smiling, not posing. Laughing.

A cigarette dangled from her right hand and a half-finished cocktail was at her feet. She looked marvelously, wonderfully alive.

For the first time, she saw her mother as a real woman. Someone who laughed, who smoked cigarettes and wore pedal pushers, who polished her toenails.

"She's beautiful," Elizabeth said.

"Yes."

The next picture was of a different woman. Someone with intense, flashing eyes and curly black hair that hung in a tangled curtain to her heavy hips. She looked like an Italian peasant, earthy and hot-tempered. In every way the opposite of her delicate, aristocratic mother.

All of the remaining pictures were of the other woman. At the beach . . . on a white-painted porch . . . at a county fair . . . flying kites.

Elizabeth frowned in disappointment.

At last, she picked up the cardboard tube, uncapped it. Inside was a rolled-up canvas. She eased it out, spread it on the coffee table.

It was a painting of the dark-haired woman, done in vibrant acrylics. She was reclined on a mound of red pillows, with her black hair artlessly arranged around her. Except for a pale pink shawl that was draped across her ample hips, she was nude. Her breasts were full, with half-dollar-sized brown nipples.

The detail was exquisite. It reminded her of an early Modigliani. Elizabeth could almost feel the angora of the shawl and the velvet softness of the woman's tanned skin. There were hundreds of pink and yellow rose petals scattered across the pillows and on the woman's flesh.

There was a sadness to the work. The woman's black eyes were filled with a desperate longing. As if, perhaps, she were looking at a lover who'd already begun to leave her.

Elizabeth glanced at the signature. *Marguerite Rhodes*.

Time seemed to slow down. She could hear the thudding of her own heart. "Mama was an artist?"

"Yes."

There it was, after all these years, the link between them, the thing that had been handed down from mother to daughter, a talent carried in the blood. Elizabeth looked up. "Why didn't Daddy tell me?"

"That's the only painting there is."

"So? He knew I dreamed of being a painter. He had to know what this would have meant to me."

Anita looked terribly sad. For a frightening moment, Elizabeth thought her stepmother was going to draw back now, too afraid of what she'd revealed to go forward. "Remember when I told you that your mother had run away from Edward? That was in 1955."

Elizabeth noticed the date on the painting: *1955*.

Anita sighed heavily. "The world was different then. Not as open and accepting of things . . . as we are now."

Elizabeth looked at the painting again; this time she saw the passion in it. The falling-snow softness of the brushstrokes, the poignant sorrow in the woman's eyes. And she understood the secret that had been withheld from her all these years. "My mother fell in love with this woman," she said softly.

"Her name was Missy Esteban. And, yes, she was your mother's lover."

Elizabeth leaned back in her seat. Dozens of vague childhood memories made sense suddenly. The closed door to Mama's bedroom; the sound of crying coming from within. "That's why she was depressed," Elizabeth said aloud. Her whole life seemed to settle into place, a puzzle with all the pieces finally where they belonged. It felt as if it should matter more, as if she should feel more betrayed. But she'd never really known her mama; that much was painfully clear. "That's why Daddy wouldn't talk about her. He was ashamed."

"You know your daddy; he thought he was better than other men. The whole danged town treated him as if he owned the patent on fresh air. To have his wife run away was one thing. He could handle that because she came back. He could laugh with his friends about how spirited his little filly was, but when he found out that she'd fallen in love out there—and with a woman—well, there was no handlin' that for Edward. So he shut it up tighter than a drum. Pretended it had never happened."

"How did you find out?"

"Twenty-year-old bourbon. Your daddy got liquored up one night and spilled the beans."

Elizabeth sat back. It all made sense. The silences, the lack of photographs, the missing family stories. Mama had inflicted a terrible blow to Daddy's self-esteem. No wonder he clung to Anita so tightly.

"But why don't I have any memories of her? She didn't die until I was six."

"She loved you, Birdie, somethin' fierce, but after she got back, she was broken inside. Lost. She couldn't care for you. She would hold you close one day and then lock herself in her bedroom and ignore you for weeks at a time. It almost killed your daddy. 'Course, she was on serious medications. Back then, a woman who did a thing like that was crazy. Everyone would have thought so—especially her. And she was from a good, church-going family, don't forget. Good girls just didn't have sex with other women."

That sparked a sudden memory. On the day after her fourth birthday, Elizabeth had gotten up early and run into Mama's bedroom. She found her mama sitting on the floor, with her knees drawn up to her chest, crying. Elizabeth couldn't remember exactly what she'd said, but she remembered Mama's answer. *Don't you be like me, little Birdie. Don't you be afraid.*

Anita reached out, touched Elizabeth's hand. "Your mama found what she wanted in life, but she turned away from it. She let family pressures be more important than what was in her heart. She walked away from her love and her talent. And it killed her. I know you, Birdie. You were up in your bedroom, thinking of quitting, telling yourself you were a fool to think you had talent."

Elizabeth felt transparent suddenly. "When did you get to know me so well?"

"Don't you dare give up on Elizabeth Shore. You've come too far and worked too hard to go back to your old life because you're scared. If you give up, you'll be making the same mistake as your mama. It might not kill you, but it'll break you, Birdie."

Elizabeth closed her eyes. She wanted to deny it, but there was no point. She knew.

What had she said to Kim that day? *For years, I failed by omission.* It was true, and each untried thing had left her emptier.

Now, at least, she'd tried and failed. But she'd tried. She could take pride in that.

She managed an uneven smile. "You're something else," she

said softly, remembering so many times Anita had reached out to her and been turned away.

"You, too, Birdie."

"All these years I thought I had no mother," Elizabeth said. "I was wrong, wasn't I? I had two. I love you, Anita. I should have told you that a long time ago."

Anita's mouth trembled. She made a don't-you-worry-about-a-thing gesture with her hand. "Your daddy always told me you'd figure that out someday."

IN THE HOTEL BALLROOM, waiting for his turn to speak, Jack couldn't think about anything except Birdie. It surprised him, actually. Every time he tried to consider his great new job offer or the upcoming *People* magazine shoot, he wanted to pick up the phone and call his wife. None of his triumphs were quite as sweet without her beside him, saying softly, *You did it, baby.*

That was the thing about sobriety. It cleared the mind, scrubbed away all those blurred edges, and left everything standing in a bright, true light.

Since his conversation with Warren, that light had been particularly unflinching. He saw the whole of his life.

Every day had been a search for *more*. Nothing had ever been enough. Not even Birdie. He could admit that now. There was no point in lying to himself anymore.

Because of the man he'd been, he was alone now. A husband estranged from his wife, a father estranged from his daughters. Except for work, he had no responsibilities beyond the ones he chose.

But freedom wasn't what he'd thought.

For years, he'd imagined Starting Over. In his endless fantasies, he'd gotten a second chance at all of it—fame, youth, adoration. And mostly *(be honest, Jack)* what he'd dreamed of were other women. Younger women with firm bodies and skimpy dresses who climbed in bed with a man and wanted nothing more than his hard cock. That had been his dream. A faceless, nameless woman who loved his body and never asked him to put down the toilet seat or to buy tampons on his way home from work.

Now he had that. The affair with Sally was front-burner hot. The sex was great—physically satisfying, anyway—and afterward was perfect. She got up, dressed quietly, and left for her own apartment. No scenes about staying over, no pretense about love.

No sharing, no laughter, no warmth.

Warren had been right; Jack had made a bad trade. True warmth for false heat.

The dream—that *lights, camera, action* life—wasn't full. It was frighteningly empty.

Now, as he sat in the middle of his so-called exciting life, all alone, he realized at last that he, too, was empty.

"Jack?" Sally tapped his elbow.

He came stumbling out of his thoughts. The audience was clapping. A quick look at Sally told Jack he'd missed his introduction.

He got to his feet and threaded his way through the crowded ballroom of the hotel. The place was filled with white-clothed tables.

He stepped up to the microphone and gave the same speech he'd given at least a dozen times in the past few months. A plea for athletic accountability and good sportsmanship. The local chapter of the Boys and Girls Clubs of America applauded wildly when he was done. Then he spent the next hour posing for photographs, answering questions, and signing autographs.

Sally came up beside him. "Thanks for doing this for me. My brother-in-law owes me one now. Everyone thinks he's a god for getting you to speak."

"It's always nice to help out kids." Jack couldn't believe that canned response came out of his mouth, and to Sally, of all people.

A tiny frown pleated her brow. She took his arm and led him out of the ballroom and down to a quiet corner table in the bar. "I'm confused." She kept her voice lowered, pausing only long enough to order a glass of white wine.

"Why are you confused?" He knew, of course.

"You've been avoiding me all week. I didn't put any pressure on you, did I? I know you're married. So, what's wrong? I thought we were on the same page."

In the dim light, she seemed impossibly young. It made him feel even older. "For the last fifteen years—until you—I was completely faithful to my wife. But I counted and remembered every woman I'd denied myself."

"You kept score?"

It was an ugly way to phrase it, but true. "I was so proud of every woman I didn't sleep with. I thought, 'Good for you, Jacko, you're strong as steel.' Every night, I went home and crawled into bed with my wife and I told her I loved her. I meant it, too."

"What does this have to do with me?"

The decision that had been rolling obliquely toward him was suddenly crystal clear. "I don't want to be that guy anymore. I don't want to be sleeping with a woman simply because I can."

"That's a shitty thing to say. I know we aren't head-over-heels in love, but I thought we were friends."

"Come on, Sally. Friends talk. Get to know each other. They don't crawl into bed together and wake up alone."

"You never wanted to wake up with me." Hurt crept into her eyes. "Whenever I offered to spend the night, you changed the subject."

"You're a great woman, Sally."

"Another quick-change remark, Jack. What you're trying to say is I'm not Elizabeth. I know that. But *I* was the one who followed you to New York. She didn't."

"I'm still in love with her," he said gently. "I didn't know how much until I lost her."

Sally looked at him. "Are you saying it's over between us? Just like that, you've changed your mind, and who cares how Sally feels about it?"

"You deserve more than I can give you."

"No, I don't."

"Then you should." He saw how hard she was trying to appear calm, but her lips were trembling. She thought she loved him; that had never occurred to him before. How had he been so blind? He reached out, covered her hand with his. Suddenly he felt every one of the years between them. "I'm not The One, Sally. Believe me." He remembered the first time he kissed Elizabeth, how she'd cried. "When it's right, you know it."

"Fuck." Sally sighed. "You know what the really shitty thing about that confession is? It only makes you more attractive. What about my job?"

"Tom thinks you'd make a great associate producer."

"Great. I've become one of those women who sleep their way up the ladder." She downed the rest of her wine. "I'm outta here. A girl's self-esteem can only take so much honesty. Bye, Jack." She took a few steps, then turned back around. She wasn't smiling. "I'll take the promotion, by the way."

"You earned it."

"I guess I'll always wonder about that, won't I? Good-bye, Jack."

He watched her walk away, afraid of what he'd feel. In the old days, it would have been regret.

It was relief.

He paid for the drinks and went outside. The portico of the hotel was crowded with people—tourists, guests, liveried bellmen. He barely noticed them.

As he reached the street, rain hit him in the face and made him think of Oregon. Of home.

He understood his love for Elizabeth now. It wasn't a skin-deep emotion like so many others. It was in his bones and sinews; it was what had kept him standing straight and tall for all these years.

They'd said the words to each other every day for years, but they hadn't meant it often enough.

He knew where he wanted to be right now, and it wasn't in his empty apartment, surrounded by too many regrets. He'd already lost the ability to see his wife whenever he wanted. He didn't want to make that mistake again. Once, he'd imagined that the opportunities in a man's life were endless; now he saw how easy it was to make a wrong turn and lose everything. There wasn't always time to make amends.

For the first time in years, he prayed: *Please, God, don't let it be too late.*

TWENTY-EIGHT

ELIZABETH SAT ON HER FAVORITE BEACH ROCK, STARING OUT AT the view that owned such a piece of her heart. She was alone out here today. There were no seals lazing on the rocks along the shoreline, no otters zipping back and forth. No birds diving down into the water. Waves washed forward, a foamy white line that pushed her back, back.

All last night she'd tossed and turned in bed, unable to find the sweet relief of sleep. She'd thought of so many things. Her mother and the terrible price she paid for love. Her daddy, her children, her marriage, her art.

Her whole life had been in bed with her, crowding her with memories of times both good and bad, of choices taken and roads not taken. For the first time, perhaps, she saw the big picture. She loved Jack. True, she'd let weakness in, and loss and regret, and those emotions had tainted her view of herself, but her love had run deep and been honest.

Her biggest failure had been an inability to love herself as well as she'd loved her family.

Then she'd finally taken the wheel and changed her course. She'd put her needs first and left Jack and dared to dream her own dream. She'd worked hard for it, painted until her fingers cramped up and her back ached.

But at the first bump in the road, she'd crumpled, pure and simple.

One little setback and she'd folded into the old Birdie. She'd considered quitting. As if the point of art could be found in supply-and-demand economics.

That pissed her off.

She stood up, walked forward. The tide tried to stop her. Water lapped over her rubber gardening clogs; icy water slid inside, dampened the hem of her pants. But nothing could push her back anymore. She'd *never* quit painting again. Even if no one ever liked her work. It would be enough that she did.

She ran forward suddenly, splashed into the freezing cold surf. It wasn't until the very last moment, when the water hit her full in the face, that she realized she wasn't going to turn around.

She dove headfirst into the next wave—something she'd never had the courage to do before. She came up on the other side, where the water was calm.

Life, she realized suddenly, was like this wave. Sometimes you had to dive into trouble to come out on the other side. That was what she'd learned at her failed art show: perspective. She needed to work harder, study more. Nothing in life came easily; it was time she said okay to that.

A big wave scooped her up and sent her tumbling toward the beach. She landed spread-eagled on the shore and burst out laughing.

WHEN ELIZABETH CAME HOME, soaking wet and freezing cold, the house smelled heavenly, of vanilla and cinnamon and freshly brewed coffee. It reminded her of her childhood. Anita had always made wonderful Sunday brunches after church.

She kicked her wet clogs into a corner, where they hit with a splat. "Breakfast smells great," she said, shivering.

Anita was at the stove, cooking. Her face was flushed from the heat. "What happened to you?"

Elizabeth grinned. Water ran in icy squiggles down her forehead. "I started over. Again."

Anita smiled back. "Well, start for the stairs and change your clothes. I'm starving. And don't give me any of your new calorie crap, either. I've been dying for French toast."

"I'll eat anything someone else cooks, you know that."

Elizabeth ran upstairs, dried off, and changed into a pair of fleece sweats, then hurried back downstairs. By the time she got to the kitchen, Anita had already dished up—French toast soaked in Grand Marnier, fresh strawberry slices, and soft-boiled eggs—and was sitting at her place. Half of Anita's toast was missing.

"I waited for you like one pig waits for another."

Elizabeth laughed and sat down. "Daddy used to say that."

"I dreamed about him last night."

Elizabeth looked up. "Really? What was he doing?"

"Sitting in that white wicker rocking chair on the porch—the one he always bitched about bein' too small for a real man's ass. But he wasn't complainin'. He was smokin' one of his cigars and staring out at his fields. I sat down at his feet and he squeezed my neck just like he'd done a million times. 'Mother,' he said, 'it's time.' "

Elizabeth could picture it—picture him—perfectly. "He was probably mad because the corn didn't get planted this year."

Anita set down her fork. "I don't think that's it, actually. I think he was talkin' about me."

Elizabeth took a bite of her French toast. "This is sinful it's so good. So, what did he mean?"

"It's time for me to go home," Anita answered gently, "time

for me to get on with my new life. I've been hiding here long enough. I had a long talk with Mina that night at the meeting. She convinced me that I need to start living again. We talked about going on a cruise together."

Elizabeth set down her fork. She was surprised at how much she wanted Anita to stay. "Are you sure you're ready?"

"I left Sweetwater because I couldn't stand to be so alone. But now I have you."

"Yes," Elizabeth answered slowly, "you do."

"Will you be okay alone?"

"Yes. I guess that's something we both learned. It's okay to be alone. But I'll miss you."

"Do you love Jack?" Anita asked suddenly.

Elizabeth was surprised by the question, but the answer came easily. "Yes."

Anita smiled broadly. "Well, honey, I'm not one o' those women who hand out advice as if it were hard candy, but let me say this: True love is a rare thing. We lean on it for years without botherin' to look at what's holdin' us up. It lasts forever, as the poets say, but life doesn't. One minute you're in bed with your husband, and the next second you're alone. You'd best think about that."

Elizabeth knew her stepmother was right. In her months away from Jack, she'd been waiting for her new life to unfold in a line that was straight and true. No hairpin turns, no sudden drop-offs. She'd wanted *certainty*.

But life wasn't like that.

I love you.

Those were the words that mattered. She'd been six years old when she'd learned that you could wake up one sunny Sunday morning and think that everything was right in your world, and then find out that someone you loved was gone.

She loved Jack. Needed him, though not in the desperate, frightened way of before. She could live without him. She knew that now. Maybe when all was said and done, that was the truth she'd gone in search of.

She could make her way alone in the world, but when she stared out over the rest of her life, she wanted him beside her, holding her hand and whispering to her that she was still beautiful. She wanted to watch his hair turn white and his eyes grow dim and know that none of it mattered, that their love lived in a deeper place. Whatever else she would search for in life, he would always be at the center of it. The place she came home to.

Anita was watching her closely.

"I'll miss you," Elizabeth said again, feeling her throat tighten.

"The planes fly east, too, you know." Anita stabbed a piece of French toast and popped it into her mouth. "Now, what about your painting?"

"What do you mean?"

"You won't give up, will you?"

Elizabeth smiled. "Because of one little old failure? No. I won't give up. That's a promise."

YEARS AGO, when Jack's life had been falling apart the first time, he'd been called on the carpet by his network boss. He'd begged for a second chance, but it hadn't worked.

He'd been young then, still swollen by his own importance. Begging had felt unnatural and vaguely unnecessary; it wasn't surprising that he'd done it poorly.

Now, all these years—and losses—later, he knew better. Some things, once lost, were worth dropping to your knees for. Even if your knees were made of glass and might shatter on impact.

He sat in his rental car, thinking about all the mistakes he'd made in his life. Of this extensive list of wrongs, nothing had been as bad as taking his family for granted.

He got out of the car.

The Washington, D.C., weather was bitingly cold. The promise of spring felt distant today, even though the winter air was thick with tiny pink cherry blossoms.

As he walked up the concrete steps toward the building, he realized that it was the first time he'd been here.

Shameful, Jack.

He pushed through the double glass door and stepped into the chlorine-scented humidity. The familiar scent and heat immediately reminded him of long ago. So many family hours had been spent sitting on wooden bleachers, cheering Jamie on.

At the front desk, a green-haired kid sat in front of a computer screen.

"Are the ECAC Championships here today?" Jack asked.

The kid didn't look up. "They're almost over. Go through the men's locker room. Take the first door on your left."

"Thanks." Jack took off his suede coat and slung it over his shoulder as he walked through the busy locker room. He emerged into the hot, damp world of an indoor pool.

The bleachers were full to capacity. Along the back wall, dozens of women in Speedo bathing suits and bright rubber swim caps stood clustered together, talking to one another.

A sound blared. Instantly, a row of swimmers dove into the pool and raced for the other side.

Jack eased his way up the bleachers and sat down. His narrowed gaze studied the Georgetown team.

There she was. His Jamie.

She stood head and shoulders above her teammates. She had her hands at her mouth; she was yelling encouragements to a woman in the pool.

He felt a bittersweet ache at the sight of her, so tall and grown-up. Only yesterday, she'd been seven years old, a water baby who once dove into the pool when it wasn't even her race.

I just wanted to swim, Daddy.

He'd been so proud of her then. Why hadn't he pulled her into his arms and whispered, *Good for you,* instead of telling her to wait her turn?

Suddenly the race was over. A new group of swimmers was walking toward the edge of the pool.

Jamie stepped into place, stretched, then bent into position.

It was the 200 IM. Never her best event.

The horn blared, and the swimmers dove into the water.

Jack couldn't yell. Slowly, feeling as if he were the one in deep water, he got to his feet.

She was in second place at the first turn.

"Come on, Jamie," he said.

By the second turn, she'd fallen into fourth place. In the old days, he would have gone to the pool's edge, bent down, and encouraged her to try harder.

He'd thought that winning was everything. Now he knew better.

At the final turn, she picked up speed. Her strokes were damned near perfect.

He moved down the bleachers, stepped onto the floor. "Come on, Jamie," he said, still moving.

The finish was close.

She came in third, with a time of 2:33. If it wasn't her personal best, it was damned close. He'd never been so proud of her.

When she got out of the pool, her teammates clustered around her, hugging and congratulating her.

Jack stood there, waiting for her to notice him.

When she finally looked up, her smile faded. In that moment, across the crowded room, everything blurred and fell away. Only the two of them were left.

He was the first to move. He closed the distance between them, mentally preparing for her anger. God knew, it could hit you like a hammerblow. Sometimes, you had to duck fast. "Hey, Jamie. Good race."

She crossed her arms and jutted out her chin, but there was a softness in her eyes that gave him hope. "I came in third."

"You swam your heart out. I was proud of you."

She immediately looked down. "Why are you here? Business in town?"

"I came to watch you swim."

Slowly, she looked up. "It's been a long time." She obviously meant to sound tough, but her voice cracked.

"Too long."

In her eyes, he saw a flash of the girl who'd once followed him everywhere, afraid he'd get lonely without her. "Well. Thanks for coming. I'll tell Stephie you were here. She's finishing a big paper." She turned and walked away.

For a minute, he was so shocked he just stood there. Then he called out, "Wait!"

She stopped, but didn't turn around.

He came up behind her. "Forgive me," he whispered, hearing the desperate harshness in his voice. "I spent too much time looking at my own life."

"Forgive you?"

His voice fell to an intimate whisper, "Remember when you had that bad start at the state meet when you were a junior in high school? I took you aside and told you you'd had your stance wrong. But you knew that, didn't you?"

"Of course."

He stared at her back, wondering if he dared touch her. "I should have hugged you and told you it didn't matter. What you do is nothing compared to who you are. It took me too long to figure that out. I'm sorry, Jamie. I let you down."

Slowly, she turned around. Her eyes were moist.

"Please don't cry."

"I'm not. What about you and Mom?"

"I don't know."

"What *happened?* I don't get it."

"Think about you and your boyfriend, Mark."

"Michael," she said.

Damn. "Sorry. Anyway, imagine marrying him. You live with him for twenty-four years. Day in and day out, you're together. You raise children together and change jobs and move from town to town. Along the years, you bury parents and watch your friends divorce and say good-bye to your daughters. It's easy, in all that time, to forget why you fell in love in the first place." He took a step toward her. "But you know what I found out?"

"What?"

"You can remember if you want to."

"Do you still love her?"

"I'll always love her. Just like I'll always love you and Stephanie. We're a *family*." He said the word gently, with a newfound reverence. "I don't know what's going to happen with me and your mom, but I know this: You're my heart, Jaybird. Always."

She looked at him then, her eyes watery with tears that didn't fall. "I love you, Daddy."

He pulled her into his arms.

BY THE TIME ELIZABETH RETURNED to the house from the airport, it was almost completely dark outside. Night coated the trees; they stood in black relief against the neon pink sunset. When she opened the door and went inside, she opened her mouth to call out for Anita.

I'm home.

But Anita was on an airplane, flying east.

Elizabeth took a deep breath and went up to her bedroom, where the papers Meghann had sent to her were stacked neatly beside her bed. She picked them up, stared down at them. Letterheads blurred before her eyes. Columbia University . . . SUNY . . . NYU. All New York schools. Near Jack.

Pretty subtle, Meg.

She tucked the papers under her arm, then grabbed a yellow legal pad and a pen. Downstairs, she took a seat at the kitchen table and began filling out the forms. When she'd finished that, she picked up the phone and called Meghann.

"Hey, Meg," she said without preamble. "I need you to write a letter of recommendation for me. I'm applying for grad school."

Meghann screamed into the phone. "Oh, my *God*! I'm so

proud of you. I'm hanging up now; I have to draft a letter that makes my best friend sound like da Vinci in a bra and panties."

Elizabeth hung up, then called Daniel, who had pretty much the same reaction. She spoke to him for a few minutes, gave him the schools and addresses, then hung up. A third call to the University of Washington had her dusty transcripts sent out.

There were only two things left to do. Photograph her work so that she'd have slides to put in a portfolio to be included with the application, and write her admission essay. Three hundred words on why they should let a forty-six-year-old woman into graduate school.

She poured herself a glass of wine and returned to the kitchen table.

She opened the yellow pad to a blank page and began to write.

Right off the bat, I should tell you that I'm forty-six years old. Perhaps that's relevant only to me, and then again, perhaps not. I'm sure your school will be inundated with applications from twenty-one-year-old students with perfect grades and stellar talents. Honestly, I don't see how my record can compete with theirs.

Unless dreams matter. I know a dream is a dream is a dream, but to the young, such a thing is simply a goal to reach for, a prize to win. For a woman like me, who has spent half a lifetime facilitating other people's aspirations, it has a whole different meaning.

Once, years ago, I was told that I had talent. It seemed an insubstantial thing then, not unlike hair color or gender. Something that had traveled in my DNA. I didn't see then—as of course I do now—that such a thing is a gift. A starting place upon which whole lives can be built. I let it pass me by, and went on with everyday life. I got married, had children, and put aside thoughts of who I'd once wanted to be.

Life goes by so quickly. One minute you're twenty years old and filled with fire; the next, you're forty-six and tired in the mornings. But if you're very lucky, a single moment can change everything.

That's what happened to me this year. I wakened. Like Sleeping

Beauty, I opened my eyes, yawned, and dared to look around. What I saw was a woman who'd forgotten how it felt to paint.

Now, I remember. I have spent the last few months studying again, pouring my heart and soul onto canvas, and have found—miraculously—that my talent survived. Certainly it is weaker, less formed than it was long ago, but I am stronger. My vision is clearer. This time, I know, I have something to say with my art.

And so, I am here, sitting at my kitchen table, entreating you to give me a chance, to make a place for me in your classrooms next fall. I cannot guarantee that I will become famous or exceptional. I can, however, promise that I will give everything inside me to the pursuit of excellence.

I will not stop trying.

JACK MANEUVERED HIS RENTAL CAR down Stormwatch Lane. It was full-on night now, as dark as pitch as he pulled into the carport.

The house glowed with golden light against the onyx hillside.

He went to the front door and knocked. There was no answer, so he let himself in.

She was in the living room, dancing all by herself, wearing a long white T-shirt and fuzzy pink socks. She held an empty wineglass to her mouth and sang along with the record, "I can see clearly now, the rain is gone." Her butt twitched back and forth.

She turned suddenly and saw him. A bright smile lit up her face, and it was an arrow straight into his heart. Now he knew what the poets meant when they wrote about coming home.

In the old days, when he'd come home after a long absence, she'd run full tilt into his arms. They'd fit together like pieces of a puzzle; another thing he'd taken for granted.

Now they stared at each other, with the whole of the living room stretched between them. There was so much he wanted to say. He'd practiced the words all the way across the country, but how much would she want to hear?

"You won't believe what I did tonight," she said, coming toward him, doing a little dance.

"What?" It threw him off-balance, seeing her so shiny and bright. She looked happier than he could ever remember. Maybe it was because she *liked* being away from him.

"I applied to grad school."

"Grad school?" Whatever he'd expected, it sure as hell wasn't that. He felt a rush of pride that immediately turned cold. "Where?"

"Oh, I thought I'd try . . . New York." She smiled up at him. "That's where my husband lives. I didn't see any reason to go to school somewhere else."

He could breathe again. "I'm proud of you, baby. I always knew you had talent."

"They might not accept me."

"They'll accept you."

"If they don't, I'll try again next year, and the year after that. Maybe I'll go for the *Guinness Book of Records*." She smiled.

"They offered me the *NFL Sunday* show."

"That's great. When do you start?"

"I haven't given them an answer. I told them I needed to talk to my wife."

"You're kidding?"

He dared to reach for her. When he took her hand, she let him lead her to the sofa. He thought about all the words he'd come prepared to offer. *I love you, Birdie.* Those were the ones that mattered most of all; everything else was frosting. Somewhere along the course of two dozen years, they'd let that simple phrase erode into rote. Now he wanted to have it back, all of it. "I don't want to live without you anymore."

"You don't?" Her easy smile faded away. There was a new look in her eyes, something he didn't quite recognize. It frightened him a little, reminded him that she had Changed.

"You're my center, Birdie. I never knew how much I loved you until you were gone."

She leaned forward and kissed him, whispering, "I missed you," against his lips.

The words he'd been waiting for. And just that easily, he was home.

After the kiss, he drew back slightly, just enough to look her in the eyes. "This time it's *our* life, Birdie. I mean it. Nothing matters more than us. Nothing. That's why I didn't agree to take the job yet."

"Oh, Jack." She gently touched his face, and the familiarity of the gesture was almost painful. "I've learned something about dreams. They don't come true every day. And love . . . love might be fragile, but it's also stronger than I ever imagined. Take the job. We'll find a nice loft in Chelsea or TriBeCa. Somewhere I can paint."

They would make it this time, he knew it. After twenty-four years of marriage, and two children, they had finally found their way.

"Show me your work," he said.

Her face lit up. She grabbed his hand and pulled him to his feet. Hand in hand, they walked through the kitchen. She let go of his hand just long enough to dart into the pantry, then came out holding a huge painting.

She set it up against the cupboards and stood back. "You don't have to pretend you like it," she said nervously.

He was too stunned to say anything.

Her painting was a haunting, sorrowful stretch of coastline in winter, painted in grays and purples and blacks. In the distance, a lone figure walked along the beach. It saddened him somehow, made him think about how fast life could pass a person by, how easy it was to walk past what mattered because you were busy looking into the future. "Jesus, Birdie . . . it's amazing." He turned to her, said softly, "You were painting the first time we met, remember? Near the marshes at the edge of Lake Washington. There was a dock in your painting and it looked lonely, too, like this beach . . . abandoned. I remember wanting to tell you that the picture made me feel sad, but I didn't dare."

She tilted her chin up. "I can't believe you remember all that."

"I forgot it for a long time. But nothing felt right without you. My world went from color to black-and-white." He touched her face, felt the warmth of her skin. "You take my breath away, Birdie."

"I love you, Jack. I'll never forget that again."

This time, when Jack leaned down to kiss her, he was the one who cried.

SUMMER

*You are never given a wish
without also being given the power
to make it true.
You may have to work for it, however.*

—RICHARD BACH, *ILLUSIONS*

THE LETTER CAME NEARLY SIX WEEKS LATER.

Dear Ms. Shore:
    We are pleased to welcome you to Columbia University School of
the Arts. . . .

DISTANT SHORES

Kristin Hannah

A Reader's Guide

A Conversation with Kristin Hannah

Random House Reader's Circle: This is somewhat of a departure from your other novels, in that this novel is about a marriage in crisis, and not about the relationships between mothers and daughters or between sisters. What inspired you to tackle this subject?

Kristin Hannah: Actually, I don't feel that this novel is such a departure. For most of my career I have written about ordinary women during extraordinary times in their lives. As a long-time married woman myself, I certainly understand the challenges and joys of keeping love alive during difficult times. We all change over the course of our lives and are faced with the ramifications of those changes. I really see *Distant Shores* as a novel about a woman who has lost a piece of herself; she needs to take the time and have the courage to go in search of who she wants to be in the middle of her life.

RHRC: You've written nineteen books to date. How do you find fresh, new ideas for your books?

KH: Finding ideas is the most difficult part of writing for me. Because it takes me more than a year to write a novel, I have to find an idea—and characters—that really fire my imagination. I have to want to live a story, day in and day out, for a long time. So ideas are tough but the passion I have for writing never dims. Once I begin a project, I fall in love with it.

RHRC: This story is very much about hidden passions. What, aside from writing, is your passion?

KH: I wouldn't say that I have too many hidden passions. I'm a pretty upfront gal. My family and friends are definitely the most important things in my life.

RHRC: Did you always know that Jack and Birdie would reconcile and remain married at the end?

KH: I did. I always saw this as very much a love story. One with a rocky road, perhaps, but there are few things I find more romantic than love that makes it through the hard times.

RHRC: Are you a big football or sports fan?

KH: Hmmm . . . I would have to say that I'm not a huge sports fan. Of course, I loved football in high school and college, but I'm not a big follower of professional sports—unless you count the Olympics, which I adore.

RHRC: The ocean inspires Elizabeth to face her fears, to open up to life, and to begin to find herself again. Does the ocean speak to you in the same way?

KH: Absolutely. I spend half of every year living in Hawaii. There I wake up every morning and go to bed every night listening to the surf. It is one of the most peaceful places in the world for me. Also, I think it helps to sit by the ocean and be reminded that we are small parts of the planet. It helps to put things in perspective.

RHRC: If Birdie's life remained the same—if her father didn't die, if Jack didn't get a job in New York—would she have ever found the courage to change her life?

KH: That's a great question. I saw Birdie as the kind of woman who needed a real push to change her life, so perhaps not. But that wouldn't have been a good thing.

RHRC: What made you decide to write from both Elizabeth's and Jack's points of view? Did you feel empathy for one more than the other?

KH: Initially I planned this novel to be written from only Elizabeth's point of view. I saw it as a woman's journey novel, but as the writing unfurled, I began to understand that Jack had a story to tell as well. Their lives were inextricably intertwined and their marriage was the core of that story. In the end, I wanted the reader to understand Jack's fears and insecurities and challenges as well as Birdie's.

RHRC: Anita seemed like such a sweet, thoughtful stepmother. Why did you decide to have Elizabeth be so distant with her?

KH: I wanted to explore the idea that sometimes we make judgments about people early on and never take the time to revisit those opinions. Especially as children, we can be wrong. Birdie didn't give Anita a chance because she was hurt and angry. It wasn't until she was older, and had more life experience, that she was able to see the truth of Anita's character. I always love the idea that we can fall in love with people after years of knowing them.

RHRC: A small but important part of this novel concerns Birdie's relationship with her best friend, Meghann Dontess, who clearly doesn't believe in marriage. Why did you give Birdie a best friend who would challenge her so much?

KH: Female friendship is an extremely important part of my own life. We all know that once you have a best friend, you're always going to hear the hard truth from her—even when you don't want to. Birdie needed that. Additionally, it was important to me to show that Birdie had a support system. When I was writing Meghann's book, *Between Sisters*, it was really fun to check back in on Birdie, and to show Meghann that sometimes love can surprise you when you least expect it.

RHRC: What are you working on now?

KH: My new novel, *Night Road,* is a story that's very close to my heart. Like many of my novels, it explores a time I know intimately: a mother facing an empty nest. I can honestly say that my son's senior year of high school was the best, worst, scariest, most challenging year of my life. We mothers are trying so hard to keep our kids safe, while they're doing their best to break free. So many choices have to be made, and so many difficult moments arise. It's a novel about finding a way to let your children go, even if you aren't ready, and even if you think they aren't ready.

Questions and Topics for Discussion

1. Why do women feel the need to give so much of themselves to their marriages and their children? If we give up too much willingly, whose fault is it that we end up unfulfilled?

2. What do men give up for their marriages and families? Do you think society makes it difficult for men to be good fathers?

3. In previous generations, men were expected primarily to "bring home the bacon." How do you think changing societal expectations on fatherhood have put new pressures on men? Do you think Jack was a good father?

4. Besides love, what else is needed to make a relationship last and be fulfilling for both parties?

5. Jack tells Elizabeth that marriage "shouldn't be this hard." Do you think this sentiment is true? Do couples give up too easily these days?

6. At one point, Elizabeth takes a sledgehammer to break down the walls of her house. Why is this action so significant?

7. Does Elizabeth truly realize her worth by the end? If so, why did it take her so long?

8. Was it selfish of Jack to want to recapture some of the glory of his golden days? Should Elizabeth have seen it coming?

9. Should Birdie forgive Jack for his infidelity with his assistant? If she does forgive him, does that say something about her newfound sense of self? If she doesn't, what does it say about her marriage?

10. Is there a way to balance a marriage or a relationship so that one person does not give more than the other?

11. What does freedom mean to a wife, to a mother?

12. Should this have been a love story, ultimately? Or should Jack and Birdie have gotten a divorce and gone on with separate lives?

13. Why did Kim keep attending the Passionless meetings when she just seemed distant from all the women and what they were trying to accomplish? Do you think people often pretend to try to change?

14. Anita dressed a certain way because Edward liked it. Was she giving up some part of herself by giving him control over her attire? Do you think that Anita found it belittling or felt she was simply doing something nice for her husband? What if she genuinely did not care about what she wore or how her hair was styled?

15. What did Birdie learn from Anita that changed her life?

16. Is it sleeping your way up the ladder if someone genuinely cared about the person they had an affair with, and if career success wasn't their intention?

17. Is it harder for fathers to connect with their daughters than it is for fathers to connect with their sons? Would Jack have

been more in tune with his children and their lives had they been boys instead of girls?

18. How do you think Jack and Birdie's marriage will unfold in the years to come? Do you believe it's possible to fall back in love—and trust—with someone who broke your heart?

19. How does Birdie's newfound sense of self, and her inner strength, contribute to a new kind of marriage for them?

KRISTIN HANNAH is the *New York Times* bestselling author of nineteen novels, including the blockbuster *Firefly Lane*. She lives in the Pacific Northwest and Hawaii with her husband.

For more information, please visit
www.KristinHannah.com

DON'T MISS THESE
CAPTIVATING NOVELS BY

Kristin Hannah

Magic Hour

Comfort & Joy

The Things We Do for Love

Between Sisters

Distant Shores

Summer Island

Angel Falls

On Mystic Lake

Home Again

Waiting for the Moon

When Lightning Strikes

If You Believe

Once in Every Life

THE RANDOM HOUSE PUBLISHING GROUP
Available wherever books are sold • www.RandomHouseReadersCircle.com